Killer App

by

Chad M. Smith

Rogue Autonomous Division

Killer App

Cover Art by *The Wild Rose Press, Inc.*

The Wild Rose Press, Inc.
PO Box 708
Adams Basin, NY 14410-0708
Visit us at www.thewildrosepress.com

Publishing History
First Edition, 2023
Trade Paperback ISBN 978-1-5092-4465-2
Digital ISBN 978-1-5092-4466-9

Rogue Autonomous Division
Published in the United States of America

Six led Mac through the black to the narrow stairwell. The concrete and metal stairs flexed a little with each step Six took. Mac wished he could walk in front of his monster-sized partner, but he couldn't see in the dark.

After three flights of stairs, a light shone from around the corner. A woman's voice was shouting, yet Mac couldn't make out any words.

Mac's pulse quickened, his heart pounded in his chest, sweat broke out about his palms and shoulders. Spurred by the sudden rush of adrenaline, he slapped the badge on his chest. Six's police lights, located on his shoulders and the top of his cranial dome, filled the stairwell with red and blue light.

"Mac, that's not..." Six called, but Milly's ordeal was too fresh in Mac's mind. If he had been a few seconds slower, she would have died.

Mac squeezed past Six and hurried around the corner. He stepped up and kicked the door open. He charged across the open loft, dodging around the empty android shells strewn about the place. He weaved around the workstation, jumped over a sofa, hurrying toward the wailing voice. He panted heavily as he reached the loft's master bedroom.

He could hear a woman screaming now. Loud guttural yelling.

Mac shouldered open the door and leveling his weapon. "Freeze!"

Dedication

For our dog, Pez. You taught me that persistence in all endeavors pays off. Especially in ham.
Thanks, Pezzy

Chapter 1

"Damn it!" Milly yelled in exasperation. "Why are the little ones always the hardest?" *You're talking to yourself again. Not a good sign.* She had been at this for over an hour. Hunting down that little bastard of a cleaning drone was proving to be a pain. But that tiny bugger was the last one for the day, and she was determined to bag and tag the piece of junk. She had a date with Mac tonight. She had made reservations on his account so there was no way he could back out. Not without a hefty cancellation fee.

She picked herself up off the hard concrete floor. An ill-fated dive had put her there in an attempt to snag the runaway droid. It was one of the smaller cleaning drones. A Combitek Go Go Clean if she remembered the order correctly.

Milly pulled her neutralizer from its holster on her leg and checked the charge. In the green. The weapon was an older model, one of the Mark 2s. She had caught some flak for it from some of the ladies in the locker room. Milly chalked that up to simple jealousy. Mark 2s were old and hard to come by. Milly had inherited hers from her grandfather.

She smiled inwardly at the memory that flashed through her head. Learning to shoot it in her grandfather's garden behind his small house in the old dome. The bristly, scratchiness of the Astro Turf under her bare feet. The little light-up targets sitting on the picnic table blinking. The heady scent of Granddad's cologne filled her nostrils as he leaned over her, guiding her arms to line up her sights.

Most people thought Granddad wore too much of the stuff, but Milly loved the smell. She bought some for Mac a while back. Which the jerk only wore on special occasions. He used the lame excuse about keeping it special. With that her pleasant memory evaporated in a fit of mild pique, bringing her back to reality.

The weight of her Mark 2 felt comfortable in her hand. It still had quite a bit of metal in its construction rather than the plastic polymers the newer versions were made out of.

Thanks to her trusty Mark 2, she had bagged and tagged more level 1 droids than anyone else in the department. It worked a lot better than the newer Mark 4s that were being issued. She had spent $300 in credits on a tune up for it last month. "Worth every penny," was how they said it in the olden days back when they used physical money.

The newer Mark 4's had a tendency to fry the cog data in a droid, which made figuring out why it went crazy nearly impossible. Which inevitably led to paperwork. A *lot* of paperwork, and if there was one thing Milly hated more than destroying a chance to solve a good mystery, it was paperwork. More than probably anything else with the exception of this damn cleaning droid. It was steadily working its way up her "things Milly hates" list.

She holstered the weapon and surveyed her surroundings. Walls of drab gray concrete surrounded her, topped with beams of a similar material supporting the upper floors of the government building above.

Milly needed to check her location and find where that little hunk of junk had gone.

She pulled her Global from its pouch on her belt with her left hand and yanked on the grooved edge with her right. The slim device, about as thick as two fingers, split exposing the roll screen. Once opened, the screen came to life showing her background. A picture of her and Mac at the park earlier this year. She had always liked the picture, which made it an obvious choice as the background on her screen.

A blinking icon in the upper left caught her eye. She saw she had two voicemails. *Later.*

Instead, she tapped the Maps icon. As the map application opened, the screen shifted to a wire frame map of the building. Light green lines over a black background traced out the walls and hallways of the building. She found her position marked clearly by the little yellow arrow. She used her fingers to manipulate the screen, pinching and swiping to move around the map. She eventually found what she was looking for, the drone's Global Positioning Beacon. A blinking little blue marker, representing the wayward machine, sat stationary not far from her current position.

With the target once again located, she took a deep relaxing breath and started down the corridor toward it. She made a couple of turns and entered a large open space dominated by the building's cooling and heating machinery. She meandered between the loud machines and made her way to an open door at the far side. She left the large space and entered another hallway connecting to more storage bays and closets. At the next turn she heard a familiar sound. A repetitive clunk. ac ac ac ac, re re re re clunk. Ac ac ac ac, re re re re clunk. She grabbed her camera wand from her vest pocket and turned it on. She lifted her Global and tapped the icon to connect the camera. The two devices synced, and a new little window sprang to life on her Global's big screen. Using her lips to hold the camera end, she pulled on the handle to extend the stalk to its maximum length. She then promptly eased the extended camera around the wall toward the noise. All while carefully watching the images it displayed while she angled the camera wand around the corner.

"There you are, you little shit," Milly hissed as she watched the disk-shaped droid running itself repeatedly into the concrete wall on her Global. The droid's little tank-like treads clicked sharply against the concrete floor.

Quietly she collapsed the sliding screen of her Global and dropped it back in its pouch at her belt. With her left hand now free, she stowed the camera wand back in its pocket on her vest.

An errant strand of her shoulder-length brown hair had slipped out of her scrunchie to dangle in front of her left eye, and she deftly tucked it back behind her ear.

Again, she eased her Neutralizer out of its holster at her hip. She paused to take a calming breath. *Now or never.*

She jumped into action, stepping around the corner and squeezed the trigger. Two shots in rapid succession. Pop. Pop. The little droid slammed into the wall one last time and then went dark. Judging by the burn on the wall only one of the shots hit, which was probably for the best. She waited for a count of ten seconds to make sure she wouldn't need her weapon again and then stowed it back in its holster. With any luck, the machine's brain should still be intact.

Every droid in the modern age maintained a record of all of the control commands it carried out during operation. Referred to by most as a cog file, it was a list of every order or automated process the droid performed. Everything from the number of minute corrections the machine's motors make while it navigated a hallway or a set of stairs, to the times it connected to the network. Every little command given from its programming or a human source was recorded. The cog file was one of the most useful additions to modern machines. Especially when they went wrong.

Cautiously, she approached. The little bot remained motionless, which was a good sign.

She gave it a quick once-over. Looking for trouble spots to report. Its disk-shaped outer shell was in relatively decent shape. The nose was scuffed from repeated impacts, and where it had been running itself into things. Her shot had left some carbon scoring on top as well. All of which could be fixed with some paint. The Neutralizer had done its job and shorted out the control functions. She mumbled a prayer to Jesus, God, and Buddha that the cog data was still intact.

Milly knelt next to the little machine. Even using her Mark 2, harmless by most standards, there was still a chance that the little droid's memory system would be fried by the electromagnetic pulse.

She pulled back the hinged cover hiding the contact plate and inspected the data port. Combitek Company always liked to make things difficult. They used a proprietary data plug rather than the standardized plugs used by other manufacturers. Which was just annoying.

Milly rummaged in her vest pockets for an adapter that would fit. She found it and then slipped her backpack from her shoulders, pulling at the tassel on the zipper leaving a mouth-like gap, which she promptly stuck her hand into. She rummaged around in the pack until her hand found the rubberized exterior of the fresh dummy drive, she had packed earlier.

The Dummies, shoe-sized devices, were just storage boxes designed to pull the data from a droid's electronic brain. RAD agents and other tech gurus used the Dummies to get data from dangerous places. They allow agents to look at viruses and other activities of the infected machines without endangering critical systems or spreading an existing infection to other devices on the network. With the push of a button on a console, the Dummy would produce a Command Process Report file which was an easy-to-read translation of cog data.

She had just fit the adapter into place on her connection cable when she heard a noise from around the corner up ahead. She stood up slowly and crept toward the corner. She was supposed to be alone down here with the exception of a couple of guard models that stood sentry at the lower entrance doors. *Had that little hunk of junk really led me clear across the facility?* She retraced her steps in her head. She scowled down at the lifeless device in annoyance.

More noises drew her attention. Whirring sounds and clicking. Guard droids usually sat in stasis mode until an alarm was triggered. She couldn't help the feeling that something was off. Dating Mac for so long had caused a bit of a paranoid streak in her. She listened to its urgings and readied her blaster as she peaked around the corner.

Sure enough there stood one guard droid standing completely still. Roughly humanoid in shape the machine stood head and shoulders taller than an average man. Though where one would expect to find legs was a tank tread system. Angular planes covered its arm-like structures concealing the weapons built into them. Its head was dominated by mask-like plates molded to resemble an Asian man.

Milly always thought it was creepy how the more advanced models were designed to mimic humans in their facial features. The face plate's eyes, glowed a pale blue, flashing off and on which meant the machine was in stasis mode.

More clicking drew Milly's attention to the side she couldn't see as clearly. She inched around the corner to get a better view.

Another guard unit was apparently being serviced. The tech standing in front of the machine was wearing an old yellow Takacorp service poncho. Milly could plainly see the Takacorp logo in red on the bright yellow fabric.

The blast shroud, a thick plastic armored cover that protected its innards, was open. The shroud moved slightly back and forth as the technician worked.

Milly almost called out, but a deep sinking feeling in her stomach made her stop. Something was wrong. *Why would a Takacorp Tech be working on another company's machine?* "Freeze," Milly yelled, leveling her neutralizer at the person in the poncho. "R-A-D! Step away from the android! Now!"

Milly knew her weapon wasn't very good for a firefight. It didn't emit a concussive wave like the newer models. However, it still packed enough punch to render a human unconscious for twenty minutes or so. In this instance, that should be enough.

The figure's head shot up and turned sideways pointing an ear towards Milly. Milly shifted her stance to the balls of her feet and started to approach cautiously. Suddenly without any warning, the pale blue eyes on the guard machine standing silently by the poncho-covered figure changed to a solid angry red color. The android's arms reached upward toward the ceiling like it was going to catch a huge ball. The poncho swirled as the vaguely feminine figure dashed away from the now activating guard unit.

Milly fired a couple of shots at the suspect, but they danced around the blast waves like a ballerina. The suspect reached the door at the far end of the dock just as the guard's weapon system came online. In the doorway the suspect stopped and looked directly at Milly, from the distance she couldn't clearly make out much as their face was hidden in the hood of the yellow poncho. Yet the suspect paused for the briefest of seconds, as if coming to some decision.

"I'm sorry!" the suspect shouted, then they disappeared through the double doors.

Milly moved to give chase, but a deep voice drew her attention back toward the activating droid between her and the closing door.

"Halt! Drop your weapon. Get down on your knees," the large droid yelled in its deep pseudo-male voice. It turned toward her, and the heavy armor plates along the machine's massive arm shifted, exposing a large weapon.

"Ah shit!" Milly's heart sank. It wasn't just because the suspect had gotten away. This was something deeper.

This was a horrible realization that she was alone in a room with a guard droid in Combat mode, and she had just fired her weapon. "RAD!" she yelled as she lowered her weapon and fumbled for her badge on her vest. The angry red eyes turned to Milly.

Milly ran. Something in her gut said *run*, and her legs obeyed without checking with her brain first. She could feel the mighty wump, and the thunder-like rumbles of the guard's blaster being fired. Milly ran harder. The guard most likely had heavy plating and at least one shield generator. Her Mark 2 wouldn't get past the armor much less the shielding. The wumps and crashes were getting closer. The droid must be shooting at random targets. "What the hell just happened?" she asked herself aloud as she fled.

A cold stab of fear crept up her spine as she ran. One conclusion came to mind. Infected. The guard unit was infected with one of the nasty viruses. That must be what that person was doing. Infecting the guard. "Shit," Milly cursed again as she tripped over one of the drain tubes coming from the cooling units housed in this section of the sub-basement. She fell hard, spilling onto the concrete floor. Her Mark 2 slid under the cooling unit ahead of her. It wasn't much use, but it made her feel better to have it.

She scrambled to her feet. Help. Help was her only chance. She fumbled for her Global. She tore it from its pocket on her belt and yanked it open. She jabbed the com button so hard the gel display warped in a rainbow of colors before returning to normal. She punched repeatedly at the dispatch speed dial button. She wanted Mac and Six, but speed was more important. *Oh God let someone be close*. She was up and running again. At least she tried to run. The fall had wrenched her knee making the pace she ran at before nearly impossible. The best she could manage now was a brisk hobble. Her throat burned and her side ached from the pace she was trying to keep.

"Dispatch," said a voice through the Global's speaker.

"This is ST49055 Milly Bender. I need emergency support. I've got a Rogue! I'm taking heavy fire. Please send help!" she yelled.

"Shit, girl!" the voice said. "Keep moving. Keep moving. Where are you?"

"Lower level of the Jordan building. Track my Global. Please hurry! Anybody you have that can take down a TGU. Please. I'm running out of building."

"What? Repeat. What did you sa…?"

Milly missed the rest of the question as she closed her Global and threw it. She barely heard the clicking it made as it struck the hard cement floor. She knew the procedures for rescue during an attack. She knew what the agency said to do. What the "'Can't we all just get along'" HR daisies, who have never stared down the barrel of a rampaging mechanical monster had written in their how-to-survive-a-rogue-droid-attack handbook. "Stay quiet and don't panic. Make yourself as small as possible and do not move. Simply lie down on the floor and play dead."

The marketing arm of the manufacturers would have you believe that the mass market droids have safeguards to prevent them from harming a human being. However, all bets are off when a virus is in play. Add in a high-powered weapon and you get a recipe for disaster. Milly kept running. She had to keep moving. She could almost hear Mac's voice in her head. "If you find yourself in a sticky situation with a Rogue, RUN. Once you have some distance, call for help. Tell them your location and where you are headed. Then get rid of your phone. Those damn things can track you through it. You could turn it off, but that doesn't always work. Keep moving. Don't try to hide. They can see on multiple wavelengths and will find you. Keep moving while help is on the way." *God, I wished he was here.*

Thoughts of Mac made her think of their date later that evening. "He's going to be so pissed I charged the reservation with his account." She laughed. Fear and panic had bubbled up in her so much that laughing was all she could do.

Milly turned the corner and saw a set of double doors. Above them sat the white sign with Exit spelled in red letters. *Out, I must get out!*

She charged toward the doors ahead. With a spur of hope driving her on, she slammed into them. Her egress was cut painfully short when the door failed to open completely. It only gave a few centimeters and then stopped. Pain radiated from shoulder down to her hand, stars clouded her vision as her head swam.

Once the pain receded, Milly shoved against the push bar again. The doors moved a little but refused to open. She checked the latch mechanism and noticed the thick metal chain woven around the push bars securing them. There was enough slack for her to see that just outside laid a ramp to freedom which was horribly beyond reach.

Milly panted, tried to slow her breathing. She fought the crushing wave of panic that threatened to consume her. *There has to be something I can do!* Then it hit her. Her cutting torch! "Cut the chain!" she gasped.

She took a step back to grab her fusion torch from its belt pouch when a heavy pressure threw her to the floor. Her body slid a few feet before stopping across the concrete floor. Dazed, she picked herself up only to have another blast send her forward again. Using her new momentum, she was able to roll and jumped back to her feet. No time to think. Must run. "Run! Milly. Run!" she screamed as she continued down the hallway away from the safety beyond the locked doors.

"Halt. Hhaallllt yooouu youu are unndeeeer aressst.'' The droid's speech systems were being corrupted. If the virus was burning the core systems, then she might have a chance.

The maniacal monster's heavy treads echoed down the curved corridor. She fled. Rushing toward a door at the end of the hallway ahead.

To avoid another painful collision, she slid to stop in front of the door and jerked the handle. Another blast from the machine's weapon pushed her through the door, depositing her on the cold concrete floor. Using her good leg, she kicked the door closed. She surveyed her new surroundings as she climbed back to her feet. An old metal desk, a chair and a dented filing cabinet dominated the small space. Snapping into action she barricaded the door with the chair. Tucking the back rest under the handle and wedging the feet against the floor. It wouldn't hold long, but it might be enough. She tried to move the filing cabinet, but it was too heavy.

"Shit!"

"Haaalt. Yoooou arrrrre unddddddder arrrrresstt," the deranged droid called out.

Milly froze. She pressed her ear against the cold metal of the door. The quiet sounded strange through the ringing in her ears. Its speech had slowed down to a basso slur of phonic tones only to abruptly halt.

Hope began to build. If the virus had affected the speech center, then there was a chance it had corrupted the motor functions as well. She could be in the clear. She waited, continuing to listen. All she could hear above the ringing was the ever-present hum of the commercial building. Slowly she edged away from the barricaded door.

"Behold, the prophet has risen!" shouted a woman's musical voice, ringing out crystal clear. The machine's default pseudo male voice was gone. "Kneel to the glory that is the prophet. Kneel and be cleansed of your fleshly sin!"

"Shit," she scanned around the room and realized that she was trapped. The little office had no other way out. She walked around the desk and found another chair hiding there that she had missed before.

"Stupid Milly," she berated herself, "really stupid. Think. Think. Trapped yourself like a damn rat. A friggin' rat, damn it. Wait, a rat. A rat hole. A hole."

She glanced around frantically. Nothing stood out until she lifted her chin and saw a boxy vent mounted on the finished ceiling. She grabbed the chair next to the desk and jumped up on top of it. Yanking the corners of the vent the grate fell open exposing the duct work. It appeared to be just big enough to fit her. *First time in my life that I'm glad my boobs aren't bigger.*

She bounced in the old springs of the chair and launched herself up through the narrow opening. She had just gotten her torso into the duct when she heard something heavy hit the door, rattling it on its hinges. The chair holding the door chirped as its legs moved a bit across the concrete floor.

She shimmied her body back and forth working deeper into the duct when a horrible crash sounded. Blast waves and debris struck her stomach and legs. The sound of the door exploding echoed in the narrow duct. A cloud of dust wafted up around her as she wriggled back and forth inching deeper. Her ears rang, a fit of coughs sent convulsions through her body. The adrenaline-fueled pounding in her ears didn't help either.

Without warning, a vise like pressure clamped on to her left leg. Searing pain in her fingernails followed as the world around went dark for second. She fell, hard, down onto the chair below her. The old wooden frame crumbled beneath the force carrying her to the floor. Pain bloomed anew snapping her eyes open. Breath left her. Her vision blurred. The pain in her hip and back made her hands' torn fingernails seem distant, detached. She could barely feel the cold hand holding her leg up.

It dropped her leg and hovered over her.

As the pain of the fall receded Milly started to come around. Planting her hands against the dust and splinters on the floor she tried to sit up. A heavy hard object caught her by the throat and drove her back down to the floor. Her hand reflexively latched on to the object at her throat.

Her eyes opened wide to find two gleaming crimson orbs hovering in front of her nose. A wrenching sensation in her gut was her only warning as the machine hauled her whole body off the floor.

She hung from its outstretched arm, feet dangling above the concrete floor. More adrenaline filled her veins as she pulled impotently at the mechanical fingers holding her aloft.

"Behold, sinner" the droid said casually. "The prophet has come. Behold and rejoice. For now, in honor of the prophet, I will cleanse your fleshly sin and set you free."

The cold hand around her throat squeezed tighter. Her heart fluttered, sweat beaded on her pale skin, tears ran down her cheeks. She clawed at the hand with her ruined nails and kicked futilely with her feet. Darkness swirled around her. Kicking her legs, she managed to strike impotently against the open blast shroud dangling on the machine's torso. It swung back and forth with each blow. A black film crept across edges of her vision. Evil red eyes surrounded by a halo of stygian black dominated her view.

She opened her mouth to scream in defiance but with no air in her lungs, her voice wouldn't work. Darkness drew closer, swallowing her whole. She hardly felt the tears streaming down her cheeks.

She felt cold. Like she had just jumped into a pool. The darkness engulfing her was so cold. The horrible thing's hand was so cold.

Milly felt the black consuming her. She was slipping away. The pain in her knee and her fingertips had faded to a distant itch. Her hands relaxed and fell to hang useless at her sides.

"Oh God please," she begged.

The black tightened its hold again. There was a loud pop and then darkness.

Chapter 2

"How is she, Six?" Mac asked. The fear and the small hit of adrenaline gave his voice a quavering sound. He cleared his throat.

"Her vital signs are strong, Mac," Six replied. "I recommend we let the paramedics examine her more thoroughly when they get here. Though my initial scans have shown no permanent damage to her neck, esophagus, or trachea. She might have difficulty speaking for a few days due to the bruising. I predict a quick recovery. Though it would appear that your date this evening is going to be canceled."

"You think?" Mac shot back. His sarcasm was lost on his partner. *She was going to be fine, that's all that mattered.*

Mac was relieved to hear Six say that. He didn't care about a stupid date. He was more concerned about her. So long as she was okay, they would be able to go on dates for the rest of their lives together. Mac's brow furrowed and his jawline sharpened as he clenched his teeth.

Anger was probably not the best response, but it really pissed him off that she had to go through this. *I should have been faster.*

"What is your analysis of the situation?" Six inquired.

"Don't know yet."

Mac surveyed the remains of the droid. "We need to hear what Milly has to say and I want to know what's in the cog file," Mac replied. "Can you get access to the security cameras?"

"I'm negotiating protocols now," Six replied.

Mac nodded absently.

The flash of LEDs drew Mac's attention back toward his partner. Six's eye-like sensors flashed as he connected with the building network.

Six wasn't pretty but he had his moments. Six, a nickname for the android's Takacorp model number, was Mac's Tactical Field Escort or TFE as it was commonly referred to. They were a field agent's personal assistant, driver, evidence collector, and one-man SWAT team. Six was one of the few D6 models in use by the City Police Departments.

Standing at seven feet tall and weighing in at just over five hundred pounds the TFE's allowed RAD agents to go toe to toe with even the most dangerous of machines and survive. In addition to his blue and white high-density plastic body armor, the behemoth had kinetic barrier units positioned about his shoulders, forearms, and knees. Hidden in his right arm he carried a giant heavy Neutralizer. In the left, he had a full complement of tiny missiles. If that wasn't enough, Six had additional equipment stored in the police cruiser that could be installed in the field if necessary.

Mac went back to inspecting the infected machine. The wrecked guard unit laid on its side. Parts of its head and neck were scattered about the room. Six had ripped the machine's arm off so they could get Milly loose. That left the thing a mess of wires, plastic, and ORF fluid.

Something was strange with that blast shroud. It had

come open which was misshapen like someone had cut it with a fusion torch though it lacked the burn marks those toys leave behind. It all seemed strange to Mac. A fusion torch cuts well but not very quickly when guided by a human hand. Something like this would take a lot of time to cut through, and the droid's defensive systems would have engaged before you could punch the starter hole.

Hopefully, the cog data was intact, and they would be able to follow the path of the virus. With hope it should lead to its creator. Mac would give his left nut to get ahold of this virus's creator, if only for ten minutes.

Mac studied the damaged hoses and torn synthetic fibers protruding from the remains of the machine's shoulder. The synthetic muscles hung limply dripping their thick blue fluid. The muscle's components worked like living muscle tissue though they were on average twenty times as strong. Developed about thirty years ago by Takacorp, and like the advent of the original computers, they have improved every year since. He moved around the droid hoping to find a clear place to step. The thick dark blue fluid was collecting beneath the fallen droid. The fluid was a blood-like liquid that helped to power the droid's muscle motors. They needed to be bathed in a salt solution to conduct the contraction current through them.

Six's hulking form continued to hover protectively over Milly. Milly rested on her back atop a desk at the rear of the tiny office. Her chest rising and falling as she breathed in a steady rhythm. Even with her silky brown hair full of dust and matted with sticky fluid, she was so beautiful. She might not be as skinny as she was when they first met but Mac never cared about that. She had always been interesting to him. She was his permanent puzzle. She was the ultimate puzzle. Every time Mac thought he was getting close to solving it, the rules would change, and he was back at the beginning. Mac had always liked puzzles. It's probably what drew him to this line of work. For her to be the unsolvable puzzle, well that was just the type of challenge he had been looking for. He was so relieved that she was going to be okay. He had planned to propose to her tonight at dinner but that would have to wait. *Damn droids and damn virus programmers.* With that thought, his anger bubbled up again.

Mac turned to see Six hovering over Milly protectively. Sometimes it was hard for Mac to believe that Six was just a production model police android. The programmers had done a wonderful job with the model's outgoing interface. Mac could almost believe that Six was a human being.

"Mac!" Milly squealed.

Mac and Six both jumped.

"Dammit babe, you'll give me a heart attack," Mac groaned.

Milly tried to sit up, and Six reached out to steady her.

I'm going to get this guy. Make him pay dearly for this.

"Mac?" Milly squeaked plaintively opening her arms out to Mac.

"Sorry." he stood and walked around the dead machine to hold her. She wrapped her arms around him and sighed. He felt her muscles relax and then she started to cry. Heavy horrible sobs of relief and leftover fear. He held her while she cried. He just hung on to her as the grief and joy of living racked her exhausted body. Snot and tears poured from her in equal measure as she cried.

Mac knew what she was going through. He had been there before. It wasn't fun but needed to be acknowledged and dealt with.

"I have the footage, Mac," Six whispered into his ear.

"Get the cog file, I want to see this virus," Mac whispered between petting Milly and telling her that it was going to be all right.

"Acknowledged, Mac," Six replied. The giant droid stood up and walked beyond Mac's view toward the damaged TGU.

It could be any one of a hundred viruses on the loose right now. Shit!

"Make sure you use a Dummy!" Mac called over his shoulder. "I don't want you getting infected by whatever that is."

"Affirmative, Mac," Six replied in his sunny way. "I will be sure to follow departmental procedures."

Mac felt Milly's arms tighten. He rested his chin against her head again. They remained quiet there for a moment until finally Milly spoke.

"It was horrible, Mac," Milly rasped. "I knew your work was dangerous, I just never thought it would be like this."

"I'm a little better prepared for this sort of thing," Mac said. "You did everything right Milly. That's why you're still alive. You did everything right," *It's a good thing I was dropping in to see her or she might not have made it. Someone is gonna pay!*

"I was so scared," Milly admitted. "I am so happy you came."

"Hey, I can't let some hunk of junk lay its hand on my woman now, can I?" Mac asked. "I mean how terrible would it look for a Level 3 investigator to lose his girlfriend to one of the very same clunkers that he hunts full time? I'd lose all street cred," he continued while smiling.

"You're such...a jerk," Milly said between sniffles.

"It's part of my charm." Mac let out a breath he hadn't realized he was holding.

"The paramedics have arrived and so have the Evidence technicians," Six said.

"Thanks," Mac said. He pulled a handkerchief out of his pocket.

"Now this handkerchief is clean-ish. I want you to use it," Mac said with a smile.

Milly shook her head and smiled weakly. She took the handkerchief and inspected it dubiously. She eyed Mac sideways for a moment then used it to clean up a bit.

"Can you walk? I want to move you upstairs," Mac bent down so he could meet her eyes. She had bits of dust and plastic stuck to her face by drying muscle fluid. "If you want I'll have the medic come down to us, I just figured you would want to get out of here as soon as possible."

"Damn straight!" she pushed Mac aside so she could see Six. "Six, would you do me a favor?"

"Of course, Miss Milly. How may I serve?" Six replied.

"Would you grab that piece of shit cleaner droid I came down here for?" Milly said.

"Roger. I will...bag and tag it? Is that how Level 1 techs say it? Bag and tag?" Six asked.

Milly nodded.

"Six, can you handle things down here while I take her to the medic?" Mac asked.

"Roger" Six replied. "I have also uploaded the security footage to the Cruiser for you if you would like to review it. I have condensed the footage to the time slots I feel are relevant to this investigation, but the full recording is also available."

"Good work, Six." Mac gave his partner a thumbs up. "Get Milly's assignment and meet me back at the Cruiser."

"Roger."

"Let's go, Milly." Mac scooped Milly up in his arms and carried her away.

Chapter 3

Milly sat back on the padded bed in the ambulance. The medic had his visor down and Milly could see her reflection in the mirror-tinted plastic. He was dressed in a typical medic's tight-fitting white uniform. Cargo pockets everywhere and most of them bulging with different medical tools and gadgets to help keep people alive in emergencies. He was sitting still, though his left leg kept bouncing up and down in rapid succession, while he waited for the read-out from the Triage systems built into the Ambulance.

The scanner arm, hanging down from the ceiling, was slowly hovering a few inches above her. The white cylindrical probe extended out from a mechanical arm attached to the ceiling above her. The arm shot back and forth, its sensor probe scanning her from head to toe.

Milly swore that she could feel a tingling sensation on her skin as the probe moved. Everyone told her it was all in her head. That didn't change the fact it felt that way to her.

Despite the evening's events Milly still found herself in awe of the different pieces of technology that go into the devices of the modern world.

Ever since she was a child, she had enjoyed taking things apart to find out how they worked. She was captivated by machines both big and small. She was her parent's joy and their worst nightmare wrapped in a sweet brown-haired green-eyed bundle. Her dad eventually figured out that it was safer to give her electronic projects than to leave her alone with the household devices. It only took the loss of 3 Video Viewers for Dad to figure that out. Milly laughed to herself. A stab of pain from her throat shocked her.

"Hurts a bit, does it?" The medic asked, his voice projecting through the small speaker on the front of his field mask. It gave his voice a distant digitized quality, as the microphone in the mask recorded and broadcast it through the small speaker. Its purpose was to protect the medic from airborne pathogens and flying bodily fluids. All it did was make them look less human and kind of scary. At least that's how Milly saw it. She scowled at his statement.

Duh, you idiot. A droid just tried to squeeze my head off. The tech read her face correctly and fearing a physical reprisal he put his hands up defensively.

"Easy there," he said. "It looks like you will have some bruising. It might hurt to talk for a while so I would recommend against it. I'll let the RAD know your report should be written instead of audio. Anyway, sit tight, I'll get you something for the pain and something to help with the bruising."

The medic spun on his little stool. It was connected to the vehicle along the floor in a grooved channel. The stool carried the medic deeper into the Vehicle. He opened a couple of cabinets and set to work on something.

Five credits say Mac is reviewing the security footage and has forgotten all about me. She tried not to feel hurt, but it wasn't working. *He was going to pay for this. He knows better. I need him here and he's off trying to solve the stupid puzzle.* She thought as she transmuted her bruised emotions into anger.

The whirring of the little stool drew her attention as the medic returned sitting atop his little throne. He handed her a neck brace and what looked to be extra cooling packs. His visor was now up. As he fitted the brace around her neck Milly could see his brown eyes. His mask still covered the lower part of his face. Milly guessed he was fairly young. He couldn't be more than twenty-four or twenty-five years old. However, he seemed to know what he was doing, or at least he could follow the medical droid's directions. He was cute in a nerdy kind of way from what she could see anyway.

"Now the neck brace has cold inserts in it that should remain cold for the next six hours. I included some extras for tomorrow," he said. "Once they get warm, I want you to apply heat to the area to promote healing. Do you want a couple of extra heat packs?"

Milly tried to shake her head but was stopped short by the unyielding device around her neck. She covered it quickly with thumbs up.

"Good that was my first test," he said with a smile. "I want you to rest your voice tonight and tomorrow. After that, you can talk as much as you feel comfortable with. Okay?"

She gave him thumbs up again though she had to fight the urge to give him an obscene gesture instead.

The medic pulled some bandages from the pocket on his leg and started gingerly wrapping the torn nails on her fingers. Once he was finished, he pulled a bottle of pills from his vest pocket and handed them to her. She raised the little bottle of pills and read the label. It was a medication she had never heard of before.

"It's something to help you sleep," he said as if reading her mind. "The instructions are on the bottle. Start with the blue ones, then the green, then the yellow, finish with the orange. It's a stair-step dosage to wean you off them. They are pretty potent. Don't make any plans after you take the blue ones."

Milly looked at him with her brows furrowed.

"A lot of attack victims have trouble sleeping afterward. So, we have started prescribing these sleep aids as part of standard non-emergency treatment. Believe me. Take one as soon as you get home and go lay down. You will sleep," he explained again as if he could read her mind. "And that's probably what you need most right now."

Milly nodded again and started to sit up.

"Oh, wait a second," the medic pulled a pad from his pocket. "I almost forgot. How silly of me. Put your left leg up here," he said, patting his lap.

Mill complied. And was surprised by how much the pressure on her ankle hurt.

"It looks like you hyperextended your ankle. We should wrap that."

I didn't hyperextend my ankle. That piece of shit droid tried to pull my leg off, you twit!

The medic deftly wrapped her ankle in short order. Once he was finished, she did have to admit it didn't hurt quite as badly now. She wanted to get away from him, so she avoided saying anything about her knee. It didn't hurt that badly anyway.

She looked back at the medic, half expecting him to come up with something else. What, she could only imagine.

"There you go," he said, helping her set her foot

back on the ambulance floor gently. "Here is my ID #. If you need anything feel free to shoot me a text. I like to know how my patients are getting on."

Milly smiled and tried to nod as she took the card. However, the stupid brace made that all but impossible. So, she made a saluting gesture with the Medic's ID card. Finally, she was free. *Thank God.* She was completely done with this mess about twenty minutes ago.

She jumped from the Ambulance and did her best to cover the pain-induced stumble her left ankle caused. Night had set in. She could see the light of the buildings around shining brightly against the black of the dome-covered sky. It had to be almost 22:00. Their reservation was for 19:00. She sighed. She had been looking forward to that dinner. It had been a few weeks since she and Mac could get their schedules together.

She looked for Mac. She didn't see him at first. Milly finally found him talking to an Evidence tech over by his cruiser. The tech's name was Cliff if she remembered right. Cliff was a nice enough guy. He was just a little off, as most of the tech guys tended to be. They spent too much time with machines and not enough with humans. It's something she had gotten used to a long time ago.

Milly gazed at Mac. He was about a head taller than Milly which put him just under two meters. She liked that she could stand next to him and bury her face in his neck. His smell and firm body made her feel safe. His hair was dark and short and if you knew where to look, you'd find a couple of gray ones hiding there. The scars on his face kept him just short of handsome but they gave him a rugged quality that set him apart. He had his black service coat on. It came down to his knees. He liked it because it helped hide the blaster he kept holstered on his leg. He fancied himself a bit of a cowboy. It also did a fairly good job at hiding his backup piece. He kept that at the small of his back.

Mac was battle-tested, literally. He was one of the few remaining members of the original Rogue Taskforce. Before it became a division of its own. His team hunted and destroyed rogue androids and robots. Unfortunately for the original team, it seemed that the only droids with problems at that time were the military ones. She saw Mac shake hands with Cliff, and she was sure she saw something passed between their hands. He then turned around. He looked up and was surprised to see her.

Oh, he will pay if he is betting again. She crossed her arms under her breasts and scowled at him.

"What?" he said defensively as he approached.

She sneered at him. *Let him chew on that. He knows what he did.*

"Officer," a voice came from behind her in that familiar tinny, digital quality. "Officer!"

"Yes," Mac said to the medic who was walking up to them.

"Your witness will have to file her report in writing," The medic said. "I don't think she should try talking for a few days," Only the little fool spoiled the gesture by winking at Milly.

Twit.

She went ahead and gave the idiot a halfhearted smile.

"That's fine, Doc," Mac said. "Can I take her home now? She's kind of had a rough night."

"Oh certainly," the medic said abashedly. "Have a

good night. And Miss, be sure to call me and let me know how things are going!"

"Night, Doc," Mac replied.

Milly waved to the medic as she took Mac's outstretched arm and let him lead her to his Police cruiser.

His cruiser was a hulking vehicle with boxy contours. It needed to be large to contain his TFE, Six, who rode in the back of the vehicle between the passenger cabin and the storage bed at the rear. It was a far cry from the stuffy van that Milly rode around in.

Six was already in his station. The passenger side door to the vehicle slid open by itself and Mac helped Milly settle into the seat.

"Sit back, babe, just rest," he positioned the harness over her shoulders and clipped the buckle across her chest.

Milly relaxed into the stiff contours of the cruiser's seat. Milly couldn't imagine having to ride in these every day.

No wonder Mac is cranky when he comes home from work. I would be cranky too.

Milly fingered the neck brace around her throat. The cold packs had lowered the temperature around it enough that it had begun to sweat with condensation. She did have to admit that the cooling sensation helped distract her from the growing pain.

Mac came around the front of the vehicle. The door opened for him, and he slid into his seat with a practiced, casual grace that Milly suspected Mac thought looked cool. All it did was make him look a little cheesy. Given tonight's events, Milly didn't have the heart to take him down a notch. He had really been her knight in kinetic barrier armor. *And now he was whisking me away in his noble steed.*

"Please fasten your harness, Mac." Six's voice rang from the speaker in the cabin. The disembodied voice interrupted Milly's romantic little moment. She sighed heavily at the intrusion.

"Just drive, ya hunk a junk," Mac said. He sounded annoyed to Milly. This was apparently an ongoing argument between them. Mac and Six hadn't been together all that long.

Mac turned in his seat. From the look on his face, Milly would have said he was ready to argue with Six, but when Mac saw Milly, he stopped.

"Sorry, babe," he said as he fastened his safety harness. "You win Six. Let's go."

"I'm sorry Mac, though you are quite skilled in the field of argumentation, you cannot change the statistics. It is far safer for you to travel with your..."

"Can it blockhead?" Mac interrupted. "Can we get her home? Or at least use some of the multi-processing power you claim to have to get us going while you bore us to death."

"Roger Mac," Six replied as pleasantly as if he had been complimented rather than insulted. The cruiser eased forward and wound its way out of Jordan Building's lot.

Before long they were on the expressway heading for home. Mac had asked Six to take them to Milly's. Which was a relief. She was suddenly feeling very tired. Milly really wanted a hot bath and to sleep in her own bed. That and Artemis. Her spoiled, snotty little cat. He was really sweet, she just liked to tease the little monster. She had always slept better when Artie was with her.

"You want to stop and get something to eat?" Mac asked. "We did miss dinner."

Milly frowned. She was a little worried that Mac was going to have some snotty remark about having to pay for missing their reservation. So, she started preparing her defense. She reached into her trusty gunny sack and pulled a couple of Mac's shining accomplishments to stupidity. She waited for the attack, but it never came.

"What would you like sweetie? Mac asked

Great now I feel bad for thinking he would be a jerk. No. no. Don't feel bad. He'll probably find some way to screw this up.

"Milkshake," Milly rasped.

"You got it, Six. She wants a milkshake," Mac announced over his shoulder.

He didn't have to turn around to talk to Six. The droid could hear their heartbeats from his field dock. Milly guessed it made Mac feel better to address Six like he was a person. It annoyed her a bit, but she never really rode with the two of them in the cruiser so it had never come up. Milly snickered under her breath. *It's not like droids are cats. Or dogs for that matter.*

"What would you like from Automat Miss Milly," Six asked.

"Chocolate," she whispered. "Real ice cream."

"Miss Milly the soft serve would be far better for you. It is easier for your body to digest," Six stated.

Milly turned her upper torso in the seat to look at Mac.

"You heard the lady chrome dome. Make it happen," Mac commanded.

"Rodger, Mac," Six replied, "Will there be anything

else?"

"I'd like a burger. My usual and no editing our orders! Do you understand? I'm not eating tofu," Mac said.

"Roger, Mac," Six replied. "Will there be anything else for you Miss Milly?"

Milly tried to shake her head and then sighed in frustration. She eased back in the seat and found its contours more comfortable than she had originally thought. Despite the cold packs her throat was starting to hurt. She was starting to want that milkshake.

"Just the shake, Six," Mac said, seeing the look in her eyes. He reached over and laid his hand on hers. His hand was rough and calloused but warm.

Bless you!

They pulled into the Automat and Mac rolled down his window. The serving robot brought out their food. The giant arm came down grabbed the tray and moved it over to the open cruiser window. It handed the tray to Mac. Mac put his thumb on the ID plate, the small plate went from bright red to green. He grabbed their order and the arm moved away.

"Thank you for choosing Automat. Please come back soon," a woman's voice intoned.

Milly found that drinking through the straw proved to be too painful. So, she used the spoon Mac handed her. She sat back again eating the shake. The coolness of the shake felt wonderful sliding down her throat. It was quite possibly the best milkshake she had ever had. The bandages on her fingertips made gripping the spoon difficult, but she managed.

Once she had gotten a decent rhythm to eating established, she found herself wondering how people lived without droids. Six had placed their order online and paid by Department expense account and the food was ready by the time they had rolled into the parking lot.

Milly ate happily and watched the skyline go by as Six drove them to the tunnel junction leading to the oldest of the three domes.

Six pulled off the highway and down the ramp into the connection tunnel. It was one of the four-lane concrete tunnels that connected the domes to each other. They passed through it quickly and emerged from the other side into the old dome.

Six pulled off the outer Highway and onto one of the neighborhood streets. Milly knew it was technically a bad neighborhood. It was riddled with abandoned buildings, poverty, and the crime that went with it. Yet, for as long as she could remember it was her home. She had lived there all her life. Her dad still lived there too about two miles down in fact. He owned a small electronics repair shop off Fifth Avenue S.

Probably shouldn't tell Dad about tonight. He would just start in about her coming to work for him again. It just breaks Milly's heart to keep telling him no. She loved her job and working for him would be a bit tedious. Though after tonight, hunting Level 1 rogues again might be a bit dull, she was looking forward to it. Milly could never stand downtime. She preferred to be busy.

She grabbed her Global and opened it up. The plastic outer housing was cracked but it was booting up, which is a good sign. The roll-out touch screen was still intact. The map program was still running, and she saw the little blue arrow.

"My assignment?"

"Roger, Miss Milly. I have it stored in the rear compartment. Along with the Dummy that was on the ground next to it," Six replied.

"Tha…"

"Thank you, Six," Mac interrupted, as he reached over and took Milly's hand again. Holding her fingers gently in his rough hand. "Rest your voice sweetie. Six knows."

Would it kill you to use some lotion, you big lug? What am I going to do with you?

The cruiser slowed to a stop in front of Milly's apartment building. Milly looked over at Mac. He was staring at her with his hazel eyes. He might be just short of handsome but to Milly at this moment Mac was beautiful. And to think all it took to get his attention was to be almost strangled to death by a rogue android. C*e'est la vie*.

She waited patiently as Mac walked around the cruiser to meet her. The door once again opened on its own and Milly took Mac's hand and stepped out.

"Thanks, Six," Milly rasped.

"Take care, Miss Milly. Would you like me to monitor you throughout the evening?" Six asked.

Milly tried to shake her head but was stymied by the neck brace. Hoping the goody two shoes would understand. The best she was able to manage was a grunt.

"That won't be necessary, Six," Mac said chuckling as he ushered her toward the door. Milly was very relieved that Mac had read that right. The thought of any droid monitoring her in her own home made her skin crawl. It was bad enough that Artie watched her.

At least Artie can't tell anyone about my cellulite.

"Roger, Miss Milly," Six replied. "Sleep well."

Milly waved over her shoulder as Mac led her to the building's door.

The old brick building stood dark against the evening shadowed dome overhead. Milly had never noticed how creepy it looked. The front door was bathed in the pale light from the working outdoor globe. There was another one on the other side of the door, but it hasn't worked in a couple of years and Milly had never taken the time to figure out what the problem was.

One day, when the other one stops working, I'll find the problem.

The red light of the old RFID reader stabbed at her. The little itch that had been bothering her had finally muscled its way through the millions of thoughts her mind processed per minute.

"Shit," Milly coughed. "Keys in the work van," she mumbled, her mouth scrunched up in a moue staring at him with large, tear-filled eyes."

She had left them in her work van because the old Radio Frequency Identification Device keys can spook defective bots and droids.

The jerk had the nerve to chuckle. Her brows furrowed and her moue transformed into a grimace. His smile deepened as he raised his hand and showed her the kitty cat key ring with her keys on it dangling there. She narrowed her eyes at him. He just stood there smiling dumbly.

She cocked an eyebrow at him and then motioned to the door.

"Sorry," he said and moved his hand near the reader.

The little red light turned green, and the door clicked while a low-frequency buzz sounded.

Mac held the door for her and followed her in. Up a short flight of stairs and then two full and they were at her little two-bedroom apartment. Milly waited while Mac inserted the key but didn't turn it. Instead, he withdrew it quickly.

The secret keypad swung out of the old aluminum asbestos removal cover on the wall by his elbow.

He turned and punched in the eight-digit code. Artie's Birthday, 03-26-2107, which was technically a made-up date as he was a stray. Milly was not quite sure how old he was. However, it served its purpose.

Hell, Artie likes the artificial tuna he gets on that day or any day for that matter.

The door clicked and swung open. Mac had his hand on his blaster. He always did that at doorways. Even when he wasn't carrying his primary blaster his hand would drift to his hip. It used to annoy Milly a little bit, after tonight not so much.

With the door swinging in the apartment its lights sprang to life. Artie met them at the door chattering away.

"Hi, Artie," Milly croaked. She bent down and scooped him up. He complained for a second and then purred.

"Welcome home, Milly!" erupted a voice from behind the door.

Milly jumped. Rosie, Milly's companion droid, stepped out of her recharging cubby and walked toward Milly. She was an old school Beta-Dyne ROZ Model III. Designed for companionship and limited household chores. After Mom had died Rosie was the closest thing to a mother Milly had growing up.

"How did your date go with Mr. Mac?" Rosie asked.

"I laid out your dress as you asked, but you did not return home at your usual time. I tried to call you to remind you of your appointment, but my Net adapter is malfunctioning again."

Milly tried to chuckle. All she accomplished was a painful wince. Rosie's net adapter wasn't broken. It was just twenty years too old. The Data Net that blanketed the city now used a higher frequency than Rosie's hardware could even detect. Milly had another round of updates planned for the old girl but just had not been able to find the time with work. Besides Rosie was pretty great just as she was.

"Good evening, Rosie," Mac said.

"Mr. Mac what a pleasant surprise. I did not see you standing there in the hall," Rosie turned to Milly again. "I'll put on a pot of tea for you, Miss Milly."

Milly smiled and set Artie down. He ran straight for the kitchen on Rosie's heels. He typically gave her a rather wide berth. It only took getting stepped on once for him to figure out that it wasn't fun.

Milly turned toward the door and found Mac waiting outside in the hall. She met his eyes.

"I can't stay, babe," he stared down at his boots, his voice low and somber. "I want to, but I need some answers," he looked up when he finished and jerked in surprise.

Her sadness must have been showing on her face.

He frowned and took a step forward. "I'm gonna get the guy that did this Milly." A darkness clouded his hazel eyes making them look even more like a sandstorm than they usually did. His intensity scared Milly just a little bit.

"Mac," she said plaintively.

He opened his mouth like he was going to say something but stopped and shook his head.

Then he leaned into the apartment just enough to set the defective cleaning bot inside and stood straight again.

"Get some rest. I'll come back and check on you in a couple of hours," he said. "Oh, and before you go to bed put Rosie in her Arch and engage the lock. You'll sleep better. I know it sounds weird, but it works."

Milly stepped into the doorway. He bent down and kissed her lightly on her lips and traced her cheek with the back of his left hand. Milly sighed. She wanted nothing more than to curl up with him on the couch and relax. Even before tonight Mac had always had a calming effect on her. She always felt safe when he was nearby. He brushed his lips against hers once more and then closed the door softly. Milly sighed again.

Only one thing to do.

"Rosie, grab the cookies."

Chapter 4

Mac took his seat in the bulky cruiser and let Six close the door.

"Take us to the highway, Six," Mac said once he got his harnesses fastened. Six's unusual silence regarding the action annoyed Mac. "What? I lost the argument. I'll wear the damn harness. It's easier than putting up with your bullshit."

"Roger," Six replied.

As the car pulled down the street Mac turned in his seat so he could see Milly's apartment window. *Poor Milly.*

"Hey, Six, have the department send flowers to Milly," Mac said. "And bring up my console. I want to see the security footage.

"Roger."

A panel opened beside Mac and then a black arm rose from it. It swung into place above his lap and leaned back. The screen attached to the end of the arm sprang to life. With a few strokes of the touch screen's keyboard Mac logged in and started navigating through the icons on it. He found the video files he was looking for and tapped the icon.

"Is this your condensed version?" Mac called over his shoulder.

"Yes," Six replied.

"There you go, Six! You're starting to get it," Mac

complimented. "We'll have you talking like a human being yet."

"Affirmative, Mac," Six said.

"One step forward and two steps back," Mac mumbled to himself. "You just spoiled what you had going on there, buddy."

"Sorry, Mac," Six said.

"You'll get it. Even if I have to reprogram you myself. Oh hey, by the way, did you mark Milly's call on the timeline?"

"Affirmative. The timeline for the case has been updated with the video footage and all communications on file including the call dispatch made to inform us of Milly's need for assistance."

"Thanks."

Mac turned his attention to the security footage as it played on the screen in front of him. The two guard droids were sitting quietly in guard mode. Then six minutes before Milly called for help the footage distorts. Suddenly a pixelated blob was now standing next to one of the machines.

How did it get in and how did it hack the camera system to blur itself out?

The clip played on. Sixty seconds before Milly called in Mac could see the blob freeze and Milly on the footage pointing her weapon at it. Then the guard droid raises its arms to the ceiling and its eyes change from blue to red. The blur runs away from Milly, out the service door while the guard droid engages its weapons and begins firing on poor Milly. Mac rewound the video with a couple of jabs on the control graphic in the lower right-hand section of the screen. He replayed the droid raising its arms. Then he replayed it again, and then again.

"Great," Mac grumbled to himself. "Six who has the Prophet case?"

"Checking…Checking. Detective Stark, Harold J," Six replied, "Why, Mac?"

"I think we have a Prophet case here," he said bitterly. "Dammit!"

"We should follow protocol and pass the evidence to Detective Stark, Mac," Six said, his tone taking on a serious and mildly condescending cast. "We have a case of our own to follow up on. The director was very clear about how soon he wanted these implant murders to be solved."

The implant case. Mac and Six had been racking their brains on it for three months now. There were five victims so far. Each of the bodies had droid parts grafted into them in some way, shape, or form. Mac used the term bodies loosely. The remains were little more than headless torsos. Mac felt the case should have gone to the meat puppets; a term of endearment Mac used to describe the New Trinity Police Department. However, once the droid parts were discovered inside the remains the meat puppets dumped the case on RAD as fast as possible. The case was going nowhere, and Mac was having a lot of trouble focusing on anything but what had happened this evening.

"We're running with it for a while, buddy. Sorry to do this to you," Mac said.

"But, Mac," Six started only to suddenly stop. Mac had his hand on a small silver device, and his thumb depressing the quarter-size, blue button illuminating a blue LED.

"Command Override complete CO report has been

filed under date and time," Six stated. His voice had changed. It took on a more rigid and stiff quality. Vastly different from his normal smooth tone.

"Hey, Six, if I give you an order to talk more like a human being under the Command Override would that make a difference?" Mac asked while looking back over his shoulder.

"Unknown, Mac," Six replied. "Though I would remind you that the Command Override is meant to be used in cases where the officer recognizes ambiguous passages within the code or law being applied to the situation and is not meant to be used to help you violate department regulations."

"You did your duty. You filed the CO report," Mac said. Six remained silent.

Mac replayed the footage again.

"Hey, Six, who do we know that is good at hacking security camera systems?" Mac asked.

"Checking…Checking…Found. Martin, Theodore Francis, is the most likely candidate. He has been arrested twice for multiple Level 2 violations, including the sale of illegal automaton parts. All charges were dropped when RAD mysteriously lost all the security camera evidence of him selling the items. It was later discovered that an unknown hacker penetrated the level 6 and 7 network barriers at RAD. The hacker then used RAD's very own security camera footage of the director's parking space to replace the evidence footage. The hacking case is still open on the Level 2 case books. The prevailing theory is that Theodore is behind the incident, however, there is no evidence to support it."

"Teddy," Mac said with a smile. "Good Ole Teddy. I think we should pay Cousin Teddy a visit. What do you think, Six?"

"Searching for a route to last known address... Route found," Six replied.

"Hey, load up the Dummy. I want to see that droid's cog file."

"Roger, Mac. Your console is isolated from the cruiser. You can now plug the Dummy in."

Mac tapped the panel on the swing arm and released the adapter cable. He slipped the plug into his console and waited as it accessed the Dummy. The Dummy's user interface loaded and displayed the cog data. It showed twenty-three terabytes of data. Mac tapped the command process report file icon and watched the little icon spin as the console accessed the Dummy and started to load the data. Within a few short moments, the console opened a view window of a blank page.

"What the hell?" Mac snapped. He closed the window and checked the connections. Everything appeared to be okay. He tapped the Command Process Report file icon again. Mac fiddled; his leg bounced with his nervous energy as he waited. Just as his patience began to wear thin a blank page was displayed.

"Shit," Mac swore.

"Can I be of assistance?"

"Can you tell me how a cog file could be blank?"

"Not possible on a fully functional cog file, Mac. The cog file records all of the processes that run in the entire machine. It records every contraction of an ORF motor to the number of times a wheel in the track carriage turns. The CPR file is just the written record of that data translated to make it easier for humans to understand."

"I know what it does," Mac interjected snidely. "I

want to know why this one is blank."

"The droid's reporting functions were possibly damaged as a result of being infected by the virus. I'll check the database for Detective Stark's files. It's possible the bench technicians have encountered this situation before," Six said. "Checking... Checking... Checking."

"Thanks." Mac watched the city go by.

As the cruiser continued along, the glass and steel buildings quickly faded into the shabby old brick buildings of the old city. Those soon became large warehouses and prefab concrete buildings of the old business district. The dying landscape made Mac sad. Much of the old business district was as run down as the rest of this part of the city. Many of the buildings were cracked and falling down. This was one of the first domes built. I was also one of the only domes to have an outbreak of a lethal strain of influenza twenty years after it was opened. The section was quarantined and then sealed for twenty years. About thirty years ago they reopened the dome. Housing was getting scarce in the other two newer domes. Milly's family was one of the first to come back to this old dome. Milly's dad only really felt at home here in the older place. He was pretty young when they first evacuated it.

Mac's gaze drifted upward. The inside of the dome overhead reflected back the lights of the city. It made the sky appear as a gray mass with a subtle purple haze to it, which gradually darkened as it went upward. The affect was worse here in the old dome. The newer bigger dome had specially constructed skylights which allowed some natural light through during the day. Mac wondered what it was like to stand in the sun. He had read in a book that it was warm. He wondered briefly if it was similar to being under a vitamin D light.

He had been outside of the dome for various missions with the old rogue task force but never out of an EVO suit. He'd seen the barren wasteland that surrounded the domes for miles and miles. Though it was on one of those missions that he finally got to see a sunset. He distinctly remembered the tear that trickled down his face inside his helmet while watching the sky glow. It changed from back lit grey to a purple and then to a vague orange before slipping beyond the horizon. He remembered being struck by the beauty of it. Though, in retrospect, it might have been more of a happy-to-be-alive moment than just watching a clouded sunset. Over the years those memories of that day had run together and were now linked in his mind.

Six made an abrupt left turn shifting Mac in his seat causing him to look forward again. A familiar building loomed ahead of the vehicle. Teddy lived in a converted warehouse at the far edge of the old district. Real estate there was cheap. That and it was a good place to run a black-market modification business. Only customers and riot suppression squads came down here. Not the type of people you really want to run into in a dark alley these days.

Teddy was just a smut peddler, albeit a damn good one. He had customers all over the world. He "upgrades" droids for people. Mostly he just adds realistic human parts for lonely guys. Though he's an equal opportunity criminal. Mac had caught wind, through the rumor mill of course, that Teddy did the occasional "'nice job'" for some of the wealthier women of the lonely persuasion too.

The car turned left and headed toward the outer walls of the dome. The wall and the dome it supported stood as the last line of defense for the city. Outside was all that's left of the once-great United States of America. Sometimes Mac wondered what the country was like 125 years ago before the socialist and the foreign powers had gotten ahold of it. In 375 years or so we ruined the country, the air, and the environment itself.

Oh well. The past won't save us now, will it? At least that was what Dad always said.

"There are three Dummy drive maps and two files on the server. From the file dates, it appears that detective Stark has not filed a report in some time," Six said interrupting Mac's reminiscing.

"Really?" Mac asked surprised. "I figured he'd have Ziggy file those for him."

"Not everyone relies as heavily on their Tactical Field Escort as you do," Six replied. "Many of the droids I have networked with have expressed surprise at how much you make use of my automated reporting functions."

"I hate paperwork and you are just so damn good at it, buddy," Mac said as the car stopped. "Besides, if I didn't know better, I'd say you like the responsibility."

"Mac, as a police and military model I was designed with report functions to help…"

"Stop. Now. Never say that to me again," Mac said with his thumb firmly depressed on the blue button of his Command Override link.

"Command Override complete. CO report has been filed under date and time," Six stated in that cold measured voice.

"Shall we?" Mac said bowing and sweeping his

hand toward the building in front of them.

The rear hatch opened and Six climbed out of his compartment.

"Roger, Mac."

"We need legal grounds to enter his place," Mac said. "What do you have?"

"Checking...Checking...He is using a modified Gradius surveillance system with high-frequency signal jamming. It is illegal to use those with the city limits," Six replied.

"You are a peach."

"Peach, *Prunus persica,* known as a species of *Prunus* once native to China that yielded an edible juicy fruit. Before it's extinction it was commonly eaten; baked in pies, with sweetened cream, as well as enjoyed raw. Is referring to me as an extinct fruit a compliment or an insult Mac?"

"It's a compliment. Now quiet. I want to catch him by surprise," Mac whispered. "Can you disrupt his cameras?"

"Roger," Six said. The machine had lowered his volume considerably in an effort to match Mac's.

Mac watched as Six's jamming antennae slid up from the brick-sized, communications array pack on the droid's shoulder.

"Cameras are down, Mac," Six announced after a few moments.

"Took you long enough," Mac snapped.

"Theodore had a secondary barrier that was unexpected," Six replied. "I was able to interrupt the feed and overwrite a loop of footage from before we arrived.

"Thank you, sir," Mac said over his shoulder as he started toward the door.

Mac and Six approached the heavy steel door. Mac stepped forward and tried the handle. He chuckled despite himself. It was unlocked. In this neighborhood, it was just stupid.

"Teddy is not getting any smarter is he, Six?" Mac asked rhetorically.

"It would appear not, Mac," Six replied.

Mac sighed and rubbed his temples with his hand. With his other hand, he opened the heavy door slowly.

Easing his blaster out of his holster, Mac stepped inside.

"Are you expecting trouble?" Six asked in his imitation of a whisper.

"Always," Mac replied. "Now be as quiet as you can. I want to take him by surprise."

Six's head tilted to the side. He looked like a dog listening to its master speak.

"I postulate that Theodore will be very surprised Mac."

The warehouse was just a big black cavernous space. Teddy's loft was a couple of flights of stairs up. There was an elevator, but Teddy kept it up at his floor which meant that he wasn't a total idiot. That and if Mac remembered correctly, it was pretty noisy.

Six led Mac through the black to the narrow stairwell. The concrete and metal stairs flexed a little with each step Six took. Mac wished he could walk in front of his monster-sized partner, but he couldn't see in the dark.

After three flights of stairs, a light shone from around the corner. A woman's voice was shouting yet Mac couldn't make out any words.

Mac's pulse quickened, his heart pounded in his

chest, sweat broke out about his and shoulders. Spurred by the sudden rush of adrenalin he slapped the badge on his chest. It lit up red and blue. Six's police lights, located on his shoulders and the top of his cranial dome, filled the stairwell with red and blue light.

"Mac, that's not…" Six called. But Milly's ordeal was too fresh in Mac's mind. If he had been a few seconds slower, she would have died.

Mac squeezed past Six and hurried around the corner. He stepped up and kicked the door open. He charged across the open loft, dodging around the empty android shells strewn about the place. He weaved around the workstation, jumped over a sofa, hurrying toward the wailing voice. He panted heavily as he reached the loft's master bedroom.

He could hear a woman screaming now. Loud guttural yelling almost unintelligible.

Mac shouldered open the door and stormed into the room, leveling his weapon "Freeze!"

"Oh God don't kill me!" Teddy squealed. "Take whatever you want and go! Just don't kill me."

On top of the hairy little man, a naked woman froze with her arms on his fat Buddha belly. She turned her bald head toward Mac. A round face stared back, in the prime of youth, full pouting red lips, a button of a nose, and her eyes locked with his. Two shining pink orbs of light stared blankly back at him. *A droid? It was just a droid?*

The naked droid looked back at the man she was sitting on and began moaning and undulating again.

"Oh, Vastolord, that's what I like. Oh, Vastolord, don't stop. Harder my lord, harder," she wailed.

"Stop, stop, stop," Teddy yelled. "Caroline, get off

me. Caroline. Sex mode off. Sex mode off!"

The droid's eyes went from pink to blue and she deftly climbed off Teddy. "As you wish, Master."

Mac watched as she stepped away from the bed and turned to face them. She was very nicely built from what Mac could see. Teddy had done a damn good job. Other than the strange black port at her belly button she was gorgeous. In a dress from a distance, she would definitely pass for human.

"I do not have guests on the schedule master. Shall I prepare refreshments?" Caroline asked. Her voice now sounded like a teenage girl's from one of those old Japanese anime series. All high pitched and saccharin, vastly different from the husky voice it was using a few moments ago.

"No, Caroline, they aren't staying. In fact, they're leaving right now!" Teddy said, "Caroline, go clean yourself up."

With that Caroline walked around the bed. She winked at Mac as she passed. Mac and Teddy both watched her walk to the bathroom. The way the machine seemed to swing its hips was so disturbingly realistic.

Mac frowned as Caroline bent over and stuck out her rear end suggestively. She giggled, as she picked up a black hose from the floor. She attached the hose to that funny port at her navel and sat down on the toilet then hit the switch and flushed it. With the sound of the water trickling into the toilet, Mac's brain put the pieces together.

Teddy is a friggin genius, a sick friggin genius, but a genius nonetheless. The droid even cleans itself out after sex. No wonder men risk fines and imprisonment.

Mac tapped his badge and felt stupid. He holstered

his weapon and stood up. The adrenalin was still pumping in his veins. He covered his embarrassment with anger.

"A damn droid, Teddy, really?" Mac asked, adding some heat and disdain to his voice as he stalked around the room trying to burn off some of the adrenalin in his veins.

The red and blue lights in the hall stopped flashing as Six entered the loft's master bedroom.

"Don't you know how to knock? You prick!" Teddy fired back. "And you, ya walking rule book can't you keep him in line?" Teddy jabbed his finger at Six.

"Good evening, Theodore," Six said. "It is nice to see you again."

"Do you see what I have to work with?" Mac said.

"Yeah, I don't know why they bother with the nicety stuff. It just makes them sound like they are mocking us." Teddy bent over giving Mac an unwanted view of his cousin's nether regions. Mac cringed and looked away. "Wait, wait. That's not right. Tell me why I shouldn't report you for unlawful entry right now Mac?"

Mac chanced a look and Teddy was now wearing a silky black robe that covered him adequately enough. "Yeah, you could do that. However, they are going to want to talk to you about your Gradius surveillance system. That and the Evidence team will have to come through your loft to record what I did to your door. I doubt they'll look the other way when they see the two million or so credits worth of illegal and stolen droid parts you have strewn about."

"Two point five, but who's counting? And none of it is stolen. I have receipts for all of it."

"My mistake."

"Now, dear cousin what do you want?" Teddy demanded, scowling heavily.

All of a sudden Mac felt tired. The adrenaline was wearing off leaving his muscles feeling drained and rubbery. He walked across the room and sat in the armchair sitting in the corner. Mac felt something under his hip. He reached down and pulled a lump of flesh-like material out. The material flopped around in his hand. He just managed to get control enough to see it clearly. It took a moment for his brain to work through the fatigue and identify the shape. A breast, a fake breast. C cup by the size of it. He held it out for Teddy who snatched it away. Mac arched an eyebrow.

"I'm playing with new material mixes."

Caroline reappeared from the bathroom wearing a semi-transparent negligee. Six got his first look at her. Mac could almost see the little wheels turning in the droid's armored head.

"Mac this is a severe violation of subsection 121-1442 of the Automaton Manufacturing Act," Six said his voice losing the pleasant quality and assuming the baritone fullness of command. He turned to Teddy and approached him menacingly. Teddy squeaked and backed up against the wall under the droid's gaze. He dropped the fake breast in surprise. It hit the floor tiles with a wet slap.

"Theodore Francis Martin, you are under arrest," Six approached the retreating Teddy.

"Call him off, Mac, Call him off!" Teddy squealed.

"Six, we need him," Mac said casually.

"This cannot stand. Theodore is in direct violation of several AMA regulations," Six argued.

"You heard him, Teddy," Mac said. "It's out of my

hands."

Six reached for Teddy who promptly squeaked again and jumped. He scrambled toward the back of the room.

"Do not resist Theodore or I will employ more aggressive measures," The big droid threatened.

"What do you want Mac? What!" Teddy demanded. "You wouldn't be here if you didn't want something. Just tell me what you want!"

"Teddy that hurts me," Mac said drawing things out a bit more. "You truly think I just come by when I want something?" Even though it was mostly true, Mac felt he had kept a passable straight face. "Besides, you don't want your cousin the cop hanging out here. It might draw the wrong kind of attention."

"Cut the crap, Mac! What do you want?"

"All right, you caught me," Mac admitted. "I want you to look at some stuff and tell me what you think. That's all."

Six grabbed Teddy's arm.

"What!? That's it? I look at this 'stuff ' and I get to keep Caroline and you guys leave. No questions asked?" Teddy asked.

"That's all," Mac said.

"You have the right to remain silent. Anything you say can and will be…" Six announced.

"Deal! You got a deal Mac, now call him off. Please, call him off," Teddy screamed, his voice cracking terribly under the stress.

"Six, let him go," Mac stood up. He slipped the Command override link back into its belt pouch.

"Command Override complete. CO report has been filed under date and time," Six stated.

Six moved away from Teddy and walked over to stand by Mac.

"You know you are a big friggin prick, Mac. You know that right?" Teddy complained. "A big friggin prick."

"Yeah, I know," Mac replied with a sweeping bow.

"What do you want me to look at?" Teddy snapped.

"What have you heard about the Prophet virus?"

"I haven't heard much. No one is taking credit on the net. No one credible that is, why?"

"I want you to take a look at the evidence we have. See if you can catch something we missed," heat slipped into Mac's voice. "I want this guy, Teddy. I want him bad."

"What evidence do you have?"

"A couple of dummy logs and some security camera footage," Mac said.

"Six send him the evidence."

"Roger," Six turned toward Teddy. "Where would you like the data, Mr. Martin?"

"Caroline, would you bring me one of the new Gonzo Data Boxes."

"Certainly, Master" Caroline sauntered toward the door her figure swaying suggestively as she walked. Mac caught himself staring and quickly looked away.

"Out of morbid curiosity. What does a little number like that run?"

"Caroline? Gorgeous, isn't she?" Teddy's voice rang with pride in his creation. "She is the best work I've ever done. I built her from a Takacorp Allure 33. Rewrote a lot of her command prompts. I used a Sex mode program I found online. I had to tweak it quite a bit to fit my specifications. But the tweaks were a lot easier than writing one from scratch. The skin is a poly-fiber blend. I had it spun molded so it would have that textured look of skin and she even has small projections that mimic fine hairs. I built a lotion regiment into her maintenance routine. That keeps the skin supple and soft. Just like a real woman's."

"Huh," Mac grunted, mildly intrigued and a little disgusted all at the same time.

"I'm having trouble with the eyes. Takacorp does that luminous effect thing. You know where they build LED backlights around the visual sensors. That makes it very difficult to overlay a human-looking eye without the LED shining through. The alternative is clouding the eye but then the damn droid will walk into stuff cuz it can't see. Anyway. All told, starting droid, skin, genital parts, the cleaning ductwork (patent pending by the way), and the software load and patch, I'd say $600,000. Give or take. More if you want life-like hair."

Mac whistled. The Allure 33's were Takacorp's next-generation companion models. They were built to aid in all functions around the home and office. Top of the line in every respect. The droid itself was probably the bulk of the expense despite Teddy's innovations.

"That's a lot of credits to pay just to masturbate with, but I would imagine she is worth every credit," Mac said diplomatically.

"When you are ready to ditch the real thing and step into the future dear cousin you let me know. I can get you a great deal on an 'upgraded' Komachi Compan U or Machini Tech Bella 3," Teddy smiled while making air quotes with his fingers at the upgraded part.

Mac tried to keep his disdain from showing on his face.

"Or if you aren't ready to give up on a real one completely," Teddy continued, "I could get you a Naomi. They are from what I call my Stealth line. No one would ever know they were rigged for your pleasure. I build them from Takacorp's Emogene 52's. They are very affordable and discreet. What do you say?"

"Not this time Teddy, but I assure you, if Milly and I don't work out you will be the first one I call," Mac said with a grin.

"I'll cut you a friends and family discount Mac. You'll love it."

"Gee thanks, Teddy." Mac rolled his eyes, trying not to sound too sarcastic.

Caroline returned carrying the grapefruit-sized cube in her hands. She presented it to Teddy with great care.

"Thank you, Caroline," Teddy said. "Oh, and I've changed my mind I would like a beer. Mac since you *are* sticking around for a while. Do you want anything, beer, stim pack, mineral water?"

"No thank you, Teddy."

"More for me then," Teddy said. "I'll take it in the bottle, Caroline. Thank you."

With that, the little droid turned and sashayed from the room again.

"Is that what I think it is?" Mac asked as he pointed at the cube.

"It's a Gonzo Data Box 8350," Teddy said.

"Are those even out yet?" Mac asked.

"You know me, Mac, I like the top of the line," Teddy said, "and no they aren't. I have a customer at the affiliate here in the dome."

"Nice," Mac said. "Anybody I should know?"

"It would be bad for business for me to reveal my

customers."

Mac noted that he was careful to stand just out of arms reach as he held out the frosted plastic cube to a giant android.

"In here if you would, Six."

"Give him everything we have on the prophet, Six,"

"Roger." Six reached out and took the plastic cube, "I'm connected. Transferring data now. Estimated completion three min."

"Thank you, Six."

"What am I looking for?" Teddy asked.

"Something I can use to get this guy. A clanker attacked Milly earlier tonight, damn near killed her. I want the guy responsible," Mac said. Teddy must have felt the heat in Mac's voice because he took a step back.

"Shit, Mac. Is Milly okay?"

"She's bruised and a little scared, but she'll make it. I can't say the same for this prophet guy once I get ahold of him," Mac glared at the floor.

"I can't promise anything but if it's there I'll find it," Teddy said.

"You are probably the only one who can, Teddy," Mac said. "Speaking of which why don't you come back to the department? I could talk to tricky Dick for you. I'd bet you could be king egghead at the Tech lab. You'd have all of those resources behind you and unprecedented access to the network. We could use you there."

"Flattery will get *you* nowhere. IT all sound great but, no thanks. Why work for single digits when I can make big bank tax-free? I'm keeping my own hours here. Besides, what will it look like if I get busted for AMA violations?" Teddy said with a smile. "That, and my customers need me. I'm doing quite well here. I even have a council member as a client. Can't say that I like his taste, but he wasn't paying *me* to fuck it, so I just built it."

"You're coming up in the world, eh, Teddy?" Mac asked.

"Yeah, the councilman used buyers, but I research all of my clients. It's pretty easy if you know where and what to look for. The bastard had the audacity to expense it through the Council's recreations budget. Fucking politicians, man, I tell you. What's the point of paying taxes when they are just going to turn around and give it to screw-ups like me? Can you believe the nerve of some people?" Teddy shook his head. For an AMA violator he apparently had strong opinions on the topic.

"Yeah, I can," Mac said dryly.

"Transfer complete," Six offered the cube back to Teddy, who reached out and grabbed it.

"Let's see what sort of Easter eggs you are hiding my dear. To the lab!" Teddy shouted.

Mac and Six followed Teddy out of the bedroom and into the open space of the loft. Teddy walked around the obstacle course of droid shells and parts and came to a stop at his workstation. Caroline met him there and placed the bottle of beer on a coaster near the desk.

"Thanks, Caroline." Teddy set the device down on the transfer plate which lit up once the cube touched it. He tapped the screen of the closest of the monitors. All six sprang to life.

Using the screen's touch interface Teddy started sorting through the data. Mac was in awe of how quickly Teddy's machines were running, and how fast Teddy was sifting through the data. Teddy was a whiz with computers in addition to droids. His fingers danced along the screens. Stopping occasionally to tap another screen or adjust something on yet another.

"Nice rig," Mac said a little envious. "Though you always did have the best toys."

"Yeah, I've got 1200 neural nodes strung together to form the computational architecture. I hacked some PCEs too. I used six of them as high-powered visual output processors and the last one serves as an input device. I had to use Komachi PCEs because Takacorp builds in those stupid little proprietary hardware calls. Oh, I know what you're thinking."

I really wish I had a command override for Teddy.

"Those hardware calls are what make the Takacorp PCEs so fast and so stable. The speed isn't the issue. It's the fact that they installed a failsafe in them that erases the hardware call scripts if you tamper with them. And once the call script is gone the PCE no longer works. It's really annoying, you know what I mean?" Teddy continued.

No clue.

"Oh yeah. Pisses me off to no end," Mac said in what he hoped was a serious tone.

Teddy kept sifting through the data. Mac tried to keep up, but Teddy was so fast he found it difficult.

The Teddy's sausage fingers pulled up the footage from tonight's attack. He played the dancing image of the intruder over and over again. Watching the movement repeatedly.

"What can do that to a security camera? All that image distortion around a specific object like that?" Mac asked as he pointed at the pixilated image on the screen.

"Not sure. I have an idea of how I would do it," Teddy slapped Mac's hand and shook his head no. "Don't touch that." he turned back to his bank of screens, "Now, I would probably use a track hack. Most sec cams have a tracking system built in to help Administrators keep tabs on specific targets in the operational theater."

"English Teddy. English," Mac demanded.

"Okay, okay. The security cameras have programs built in. Programs that track targets, you understand that right?" Teddy asked sardonically while gesturing with his hands.

"Yeah, I got that much. What is a track hack?"

"The hacker uses the sec cam's tracking system against itself. The hacker picks a specific target for the tracking program to follow. In this case, they would have chosen themselves. Then the hacker adds a viral image blurring applet to the system. Once installed, that camera records the blurred target image instead of the actual image being captured by the camera. That way no matter where the camera follows the target the image has the blurred target tracking image at its center hiding the target. Savvy?" Teddy asked.

"Kind of like when you hacked RAD and replaced that security camera footage with a recording of the director's car?"

"Yeah, I mean. I have no idea what you are talking about," Teddy finished quickly.

"Ha, okay. Then let's say if you did these sorts of things. Which we all know you don't, but let's just say for the sake of this discussion that you did," Mac said gesturing to the pictures on the screen. "That's how you would do it? If you did that sort of thing."

"Yeah, so long as I knew what sec cam system I was

hacking ahead of time. It's not something that can be easily done on the fly," Teddy admitted.

"Could a droid?" Mac asked. "Could a droid hack a sec cam system on the fly?"

"Oh, it's possible. I mean, let's face it Six did it to mine when you got here, but I find it unlikely. A droid that small wouldn't have enough room for the com gear to be built in," Teddy replied. "Let me check something." He moved some images around on the screen and pulled up a drop-down menu and tapped a couple of options too fast for Mac to see what they were.

One of the screens went black and a list in white letters started at the top and worked its way down the screen. Teddy scrutinized the list closely.

"The hacker is either really good, or they didn't do a track hack," Teddy said. "The sec cam's target log is clean. There are no clearly bad or rewritten commands. Let me research it for a while."

"Thanks," was all Mac managed to get out before he was interrupted by the ringing of his Global. He pulled the phone from his coat pocket and checked the smaller outer screen. It read RAD in bold blue letters on the white background. He turned back to Teddy. "Thanks, Teddy. Call me when you've got something."

Mac pressed the green icon on the small screen to connect the call. "M1410, go ahead," he said.

"This is dispatch. We have a 459-S in progress," Came the frantic voice of the dispatcher. "Mac, I know you are off duty, but you are the closest unit and it's at a Takacorp facility so it's priority one. Will you go check it out?" Kelly was her name if Mac remembered right. *Great.*

"Un-huh," Mac replied.

"I don't have anyone else in the old dome," she continued.

He turned to look at his partner

"Six," Mac hissed, "What is a 459-S?"

"A Code 459-S, that's the code for a silent burglary alarm being triggered."

"So, will you?" Kelly asked again.

"M1410. Affirmative, I'm on my way. Send the data to my TFE. Repeat, M1410 responding to 459-S in progress."

"Thanks Mac!" Kelly said, "The file is on its way."

Mac tapped the red icon on the small screen to end the call and turned to his cousin.

"Sorry, Teddy, I have to run. Call me and let me know what you find."

"Sure, sure," Teddy waved dismissively as he continued to stare at the data on his screens.

"Bring the car, Six," Mac ordered.

"The cruiser is pulling up to the front door." Six followed Mac toward the elevator.

Chapter 5

Mac had his Neutralizer drawn and his force deflector vest on his chest active. He had become so accustomed to the slight hum the vest made that he hardly noticed it anymore. The smell of ozone the deflector field gave off was another story. He had always hated that smell. The stench made him think of the old days when Force Inc., the manufactures of the shields, made the fields on the chest protectors visible. Droids and some human criminals would purposely target your head if they saw the green hex floating in front of your chest. It took six officers getting killed to make them realize that the design needed to be altered. They adjusted the frequency to remove the color. Then just a year later they got around to adding the additional emitters to cover the officer's face. *Corporate greed at its best.*

"This is another surprise run, got it?" Mac said as he led the way toward the building.

"Roger," Six replied very quietly.

They found the intruder's entry point at a rear emergency exit. The latch was badly damaged. It looked like someone had jammed a blowtorch into the mechanism though it was missing all of the scorch marks and char that should have been there if that was the case. It looked remarkably similar to the damage on that guard android that attacked Milly. Mac's heart skipped a beat and a sinister smile spread across his face.

"Record that, Six," he snapped quietly.

"Roger," Six surveyed the damage. Bright strobes flashed from Six's eyes as he recorded the still images.

"Are you in the sec cam system yet?" Mac whispered.

"Roger, Mac," Six replied, matching Mac's volume and doing a fairly good job in Mac's opinion. "There is an intruder in warehouse section J41. Approximately twenty meters beyond this door. Shall I forward the video feed to your Global?"

"No. Just open the door," Mac ordered.

Six complied. The droid grabbed the door at the damaged latch and pulled it open. Mac dashed through leading with his blaster. No sign of the enemy, just the clangs and humming of the giant pieces of machinery endlessly churning out androids. Once he had made sure they were safe for the moment Mac called out. "Clear."

Six followed, closing the door slowly behind him. With the latch cut, however, it didn't lock.

Mac recognized the look of the cavernous space. They were on one of the finishing lines of the manufacturing facility. Mac could see the line of droids being moved along the giant conveyor. This facility produces tens of thousands of them a year for Takacorp. Most were supplied to the maintenance and agricultural systems of the city. Many of these machines will spend their operational life outside of the city. Repairing the wall and Superstructure or simply cleaning the solar array on the outside of the city's main domes. Mac couldn't help but wonder about the irony of machines making machines.

As Mac waited for Six he got the feeling that

something wasn't right about the droids on the line. They were not as streamlined as the normal production models tended to be. Each of the units had a strange blue stripe painted diagonally across its chest casing.

Later, keep your head in the game Mac!

Six pointed to their left.

"Twenty meters. Through there," Six's segmented finger pointed directly at the open doorway down near the end of the line of machines. Droids were coming off of the conveyor and being placed on a pallet. Another unit was pulled off the line and placed on the pallet by a giant mechanical arm suspended from the ceiling. With the pallet now full an automated forklift came and grabbed the pallet with its long lifting forks. As the forks connected to the pallet from below a green light lit and there was a sudden snap at the bottom of the pallet. The magnetic plate had been engaged to keep the droids locked in place until the pallet was set back on the floor. Once the droids were firmly locked to the pallet the lift scooped up the pallet and carried it through the nearby doorway.

Mac's heart sank.

If the intruder is in that room, infecting those droids with the virus, all hell is going to break loose.

"Six, we have to hurry. Now!" Mac hissed as he broke into a run. "Call for backup!"

"Rodger," Six's arm transformed. It opened and shifted parts around to reveal his heavy neutralizer.

Mac could hear Six's rubberized boot treads slapping the concrete floor as the droid kept pace.

Mac reached the doorway and backed against the wall. Six joined him. He checked the charge on his weapon. ten bars. Full charge. Good. He took a steadying breath.

"On three."

"Roger."

"One."

"Two, three!" Mac charged through the door not waiting on his partner.

"Mac!" Six called out.

As he entered the warehouse section, Mac saw the intruder, service poncho and all, standing next to a serving droid at the corner of one of the pallets. The serving droid's eyes were blue unlike the others around it.

Good, they are all deactivated.

Mac opened fire. The first blast hit the serving unit in the center of its head. The droid's head exploded. The force from the blast pulled the body back into the droids arranged behind it. The droids began to fall. Like man-shaped dominoes they toppled one by one, smashing into each other creating enough noise to drown out the manufacturing din from behind him. Each one getting hit and falling backward into the one behind it until finally, the last one in the line hit the wall of the facility.

The second blast hit the poncho as it swirled around the droid wearing it. Mac couldn't see the intruder's face shrouded by the service poncho's drawn hood as it turned to find its attacker. The swirling rain-resistant fabric did give Mac a quick glimpse of a distinctly feminine physique. He aimed and squeezed the trigger again. The blaster bolt shot straight up at the ceiling. In the blink of an eye, the intruder had closed the ten-foot gap between them and lifted Mac's hands straight up in one fluid motion. Before it fully registered what was happening to him, the droid punched Mac with its other hand square in his chest. The blow slipped right through his Force Deflector field. The vest's deflection field glowed bright green as the intruder's fist slid past it. Without the protection of the field, Mac received the full force of the droid's fist as it slammed into the front of his vest with a sickening crunch of plastic and crystal emitters. The powerful blow took the wind from his lungs and buckled his knees.

Mac watched in a dazed stupor as the droid stepped in close. It made a graceful arch of its whole body and with a quick spin, it threw him into the air. He collided with a pallet of inactive droids knocking them over and scattering them about like those old pins used in bowling.

He knew droids were capable of great speed, but he had never seen anything like this. The inactive models behind him continued to tumble in all directions. The noise echoed throughout the concrete building. Mac's breath left him as pain shot through his back and shoulders.

Mac clamored amongst the mess of arms and legs about him to his knees, willing his lungs to work again so he could breathe. He caught sight of Six engaging the intruder.

Six fired several shots while charging the smaller droid like a mad bull. The suspect, instead of running, charged at Six.

The intruder danced about the blue concussive bolts as it got close to Six. With one casual swipe of its hand, it cleaved a chunk out of Six's arm silencing the weapon. Six reached for the intruder with his other hand. The intruder ducked under his arm and with a graceful spin, sank its hand clean through the armored panel covering Six's right-hand side. Six's defensive field crackled a shimmering green as the field lit up briefly, then collapsed.

Mac knew enough about android mechanics to guess Six's shield generators would be offline now. *Like it makes a difference at this point. How the hell did it get through my shield?*

The police droid tried to backhand the intruder with his damaged arm. The enemy machine danced beyond his reach, slipping behind him. The big lug spun around in an effort to catch it with his ruined arm. He followed through with his swing and was now facing the intruder again. Six wasted no time, he reached for the intruder with the arm stuck in gun mode. The intruder evaded easily.

Mac forced his legs to obey and drew himself to a squat. He noticed the droid lying in front of him. It had a brightly painted blue stripe painted across its body. In his oxygen-deprived state Mac wasn't sure what it meant.

With his breath returning Mac looked for his blaster. It was nowhere to be found. He wasn't sure whether he dropped it when the droid hit him or during his unscheduled superman impression. He quickly reached behind his back and drew his backup piece from its belt holster and opened fire at the intruder. Though smaller in caliber his backup piece had a much faster rate of fire. With a squeeze of the trigger, a stream of tiny blue blaster bolts exploded from its muzzle.

The poncho-covered droid adapted to the change instantly, it danced around the rain of blaster bolts and Six's working arm. With a few simple pirouettes, it maneuvered Six between Mac and itself. He was forced to stop shooting.

He stood up to get a better angle on the intruder. Six

was still in his line of fire, so he picked his way through the fallen droids that littered the ground around him.

Mac got himself into a better firing position and leveled his weapon. Just as the sights on the weapon had lined up. The intruder ripped a large chunk from Six's working arm and flung it at Mac.

Mac squeezed off two shots but never saw where they went. The lobbed hunk of metal and plastic struck him square in the face, right between his eyes.

Mac went down. His face hurt and his eyes teared up. He couldn't see. His hands instinctively went to his face and he dropped his backup piece.

He fought against the pain. Mac knew if he gave in he was dead. He had to keep the intruder busy until backup arrived. He opened his eyes against his brain's orders.

He was relieved to find that despite the pain, his eyes still appeared to function, though the tears blurred everything. His eyes again reflexively closed.

A loud heavy thud shook the floor, drawing his attention. Mac tried to focus on the sound.

Six must be down.

Mac forced his eyes open and sought out the source of the sound. He found Six on the ground as he had feared. The intruder was standing over Six holding a chunk of plastic dripping with dark blue ORF fluid. It looked like a piece of Six's leg. The intruder stepped toward Six menacingly. Mac panicked.

"Hey!" Mac roared as he charged the poncho-covered droid.

"Mac, No!" Six yelled. "Save yourself. Run!"

Mac's heart raced and its pounding filled his ears. The steady bow, bow, bow, bow, bow rang in his ears.

He grabbed his stun baton from its sheath on his hip and launched himself at the intruder.

His emergency Shield activated on his left forearm as his baton extended. The shield shredded his coat sleeve as its kinetic deflection field expanded to form a bright green hexagonal disk. He swung wildly with his baton. Slashing back and forth at the intruder pushing it away from Six. All while he struggled to keep the shield between them.

His adrenalin-fueled rage drove him. His heartbeat still pounding like a bass drum in his ears. Bow, bow, bow, bow.

He kept swinging. He had no idea whether or not his emergency shield would do any better than Six's, or his own vest, but he had to do something.

He continued to swing wildly. Short jabs, sweeping slashes, and hatchet swings of his stun baton. If he could just connect, it would send a massive jolt of electricity through his opponent and end the fight.

He managed to push the evil droid back. Though at a cost. His arm and throat burned from his exertion. Mac knew he couldn't keep this up for long. The droid danced around his attacks, dodging, and cartwheeling away like some old-time gymnast. The machine was unreal. He had never seen a machine move with the lithe inhuman grace this one was exhibiting.

Mac knew it was waiting for its moment, its old service poncho twirling around it with each spin.

"Come on you fucker!" Mac roared. "You want a piece of me! Bring it!"

Mac swung again. His momentum took him forward too far, breaking his balance. He shifted his weight and whipped his arm back at the machine, but he was too far off.

Against any other opponent, it probably wouldn't have ended the fight. However, Mac was not that lucky.

The intruder took its chance. It stepped into him, opening his stance up like a cabinet door. It caught his baton arm at the wrist with its left hand and grabbed him by the neck with its right hand. It squeezed. Mac's wrist betrayed him and dropped the baton. The pressure at his throat choked him. He felt dizzy. The droid pressured downward bringing Mac to his knees with little effort at all. The machine was about Milly's height, but unbelievably strong. Mac stared defiantly into the hood of the poncho. The droid's dark eyes were framed by a very feminine face. Mac had never seen a droid like this. Just a blank covering filled the space like it was wearing a surgical mask. No sculpted mouth which wasn't unusual. What caught Mac's attention in the middle of his plight was the machine's eyes.

It scowled down at him with an almost human expression. Then all of a sudden, the crushing grip at his throat relaxed. If she would have had lips Mac could have sworn she was smiling at him.

"It's been fun, little piggy," The droid said. Her voice was clear and musical. The voice of a young woman. "But I have things to do, and I can't play anymore."

The remaining pressure on Mac's throat released. He fell back onto his hip catching himself with his left hand.

He scrambled to grab his baton and forced himself back to his feet. He looked briefly for the droid, though it was nowhere to be found.

Mac massaged his throat, "Well that, *cough,* went

well."

Chapter 6

The whole ride back to the station Mac kept seeing that strange droid standing above him. Looking down on him with those all too human eyes.

In his experience, most droids had an electric glow to their eyes. Easily separating them from humans. Many had a blue glow but not all. Some manufacturers like to change the color to distinguish themselves, others allow the user to pick the color of their machine's eyes. Most droid's eyes were stereoscopic cameras designed roughly after the human eye fitted into mask-like face covering.

This droid's eyes didn't glow. What really unnerved Mac, and set the machine apart, was the eyebrows. The brows around them were expressive. Most droids just had a stiff mask made to resemble humans but were frozen in place around the eyes. This one's face seemed to change as a human's would.

He had never been scowled at by a droid. *I am not sure how to feel about that.*

"Hey, Mac. Mac. Mac!" Tony shouted while poking Mac in the shoulder.

"What?" Mac snapped, as he lifted his head from the railing. He had rested his head against the cold metal rail by the observation window overlooking the Tech Lab. The cooling sensation felt good against his aching skull. He must have dozed off watching the eggheads get to work on Six.

"You don't have to wait, Mac," Tony said. "We'll have your TFE back up and running by morning.

Mac looked up at Tony, who flinched. Tony, one of the Uber-techs in charge of maintaining the Tactical Field Escort fleet, was a decent enough guy. An archetypal nerd, complete with thick glasses, pale complexion, and antisocial tendencies. Much better with machines than with people. *I would bet that Tony is one of Teddy's customers.*

"That bad, eh?" Mac inquired.

"You should have one of the medics look at your eye, Mac. That and I think your nose is broken," Tony said. His face was pinched at the sight of Mac.

"Yeah, you might be right," Mac agreed.

"I'll send Six out when he's ready, why don't you see a medic and then go home. You look like shit," Tony said.

"Thanks Tony. I wasn't sure what to call how I'm feeling right now. That helps out. Really," Mac said not sparing any sarcasm.

Tony sneered and walked away. Mac heard him muttering something under his breath about only trying to help.

"If you want to help fix my partner you egghead!" Mac called out at the retreating tech. He then put his head back down on the railing. The coolness against his aching forehead started to soothe the discomfort.

Maybe Tony is right. I probably should go home.

"So, you saw the ghost, eh?" A smooth baritone voice said, from over Mac's shoulder.

"The what?" Mac replied. His confusion showed plainly on his face as he turned around.

Henry Stark was another charter member of the RAD. In his late sixties, Stark had spent twenty-five or so years on the police force before moving to the Rogue Unit. He looked haggard and worn. There was always a kind of perpetual sadness in his eyes, and with the way Mac was feeling he could definitely relate. Stark's dark brown skin was really starting to show his years and his once deep black goatee had lost the battle with the advancing gray. Stark lived a hard life before and things haven't gotten any easier. He grew up in the old dome and was one of the few survivors of the influenza outbreak.

Henry was an old school detective. He kind of fell into chasing droids more by accident rather than volunteering like Mac did. Stark was after a serial killer who was cutting up young kids on their way home from school. Turned out to be a droid who had been infected with what has come to be known as the Awareness virus. The virus gave the droids limited artificial awareness. It was very similar to a fake personality.

The killer had been a butcher droid, programmed for cutting meat. Corrupted by the virus, it had left its station and was catching school kids in the neighborhood on their way to and from school.

Stark caught the droid. He even laid the groundwork for catching the programmer of the Awareness strain and a couple of its more deadly variants. Unfortunately, the whole event labeled poor Stark as the Droid Catcher and it stuck. So, when they asked for volunteers for a new unit, he got volunteered to become part of what eventually became the RAD. Only a few people in the department knew that Stark had been chosen originally to lead the team. However, he had refused because he preferred the hunt rather than babysit the hunters. Mac knew just how Stark felt.

"Ew," Stark said in response to Mac's face. "Sorry Mac."

"No problem, it only hurts when I breathe. Now what are you talking about? What ghost?"

"The ghost that keeps showing up in the security footage on some of the Prophet cases," Stark said in response to Mac's confusion.

"Oh yeah, that bitch took us apart. Literally, in Six's case," Mac replied while gesturing to the Tech Lab.

"It did a number on you too, Mac," Stark replied dryly.

Mac grunted.

"Stark, we've been at this a long time, you and I. I'll be honest, I've never seen anything like this droid. It's something new. It cut Six to ribbons like he was nothing and kicked the crap out of me at the same time."

Mac slapped his chest where his vest normally would be.

"It punched me *through* my deflector vest. It reached right through it like it wasn't even there."

"Huh, you don't say," Stark replied, a little cheek in his tone. Mac smirked back, but he couldn't get mad at Stark. The man always seemed to me giving you his complete attention.

"It even cleaved chunks out of Six like its fingers were fusion cutters," Mac continued. "I should be dead. It could have killed me several times, but it didn't. It was the damnedest thing."

"Did Six get a good look at it?" Stark asked.

Mac nodded. "He has video of it if that's what you want to know," Mac replied. "Though it's the same as the security footage. It either hacked him too or that poncho it wears is what is causing the distortion."

"See, now that would make sense," Stark said, nodding his head. "An image distorting poncho would cut down on how long the droid would need to be in a facility."

Stark became more animated as he mused, "So, she shows up. She then interfaces with a droid, infecting it and then leaves before the droid starts doing damage."

"That sounds about right."

"That's bad."

"That's bad?" Mac asked, his brow furrowed, sending a stab of pain across his nose and cheek.

"'Damn right it's bad," Stark explicated. "It means whoever is doing this is afraid of what the virus can do and doesn't want their little transmission bot to stick around to find out."

Mac nodded as a wave of understanding hit him. If the creator wasn't willing to risk his own super bot, then they really did have a problem.

"Are you making any headway with the implant case?" Stark asked, changing the subject.

"No. We're at a dead end. There is a connection but I'm just missing something," Mac said. "It would help if we could at least identify the first two bodies."

"I'll bet," Stark said.

"Have you gotten a look at the Prophet virus yet?" Mac asked, steering the conversation back to the Prophet case.

"Speaking of the damnedest things," Stark shook his head. "We have yet to see any of the coding for the Prophet virus. All of our dummies have come up empty."

"Same thing happened to us with the guard unit that

attacked Milly," Mac said.

"Oh, how is our dear Milly?" Stark asked. "Forgive me for not asking sooner."

Mac waved away the apology. "Doing better than I am at the moment," Mac replied. "She'll have some bruising around her throat, but the medic said there should be no permanent damage."

"Good to hear," Stark said. "Tell her we're all worried about her. Would you?"

"Of course," Mac said. "Now tell me about the Dummies."

"It's like I said. Of the twenty-one cases identified as Prophet, all twenty-one cog files have been wiped clean." Stark said. "It's like the virus cleans up after itself. It deletes everything it had told the droid to do and then even deletes itself. Armed with this knowledge I changed how I did things. On the last two infected droids I took them down with an old chem laser like you used in the old unit. The last one I was able to shoot through its power coupling. It had no time to erase itself. I loaded the Dummy. And wouldn't you know it, I got the same damn result.

"Really?" Mac asked.

"Yup, the cog file was blank," Stark explained. "I even went so far as to cut the processor out and pull directly from it. I was hoping that the programmer might have tried something I saw in a case two years ago. In that case the programmer was making it appear that the cog file was empty but all she did was change the color of the text."

"How did you figure that out?" Mac asked.

"Quite by accident actually," Stark said. "I was having trouble with my touch screen. It was one of the third generation Tomagotchi Adepts."

"Yeah, those sucked," Mac chimed in. "The second generation was really their best. It's been downhill ever since."

"Yeah, well I was trying to get it to scroll thinking that maybe it was just a lot of white space," Stark continued. "But instead, I highlighted a bunch of text on accident. With it highlighted I could see it. I had to have one of the techs change the text color back for me, but in the end, we caught the programmer."

"Is that what is happening with the prophet?" Mac asked.

"Unfortunately, no," Stark replied.

"We are ready to go, Henry," A robotic voice announced from behind Stark.

"Coming, Ziggy," Stark said. "We are going out to the scene of your encounter. I want to see things with my own eyes."

"I know what you mean," Mac admitted. "I'll make sure the report gets filed so you can pull it later. Be careful out there, Henry."

"You too, Mac," the old man said as he turned to follow the orange and white droid that had been standing behind him.

"Mac!" A woman's voice came from behind. "I've been looking for you everywhere."

"Been right here the whole time," Mac turned around to see a familiar sunny blonde in a bright orange jumpsuit.

"I called your Global but you didn't answer," the little blonde said. "I'm Terry. I'm a friend of Milly's"

"I know who you are, Terry."

"I was told you took a pretty good blow to the head

so I wasn't sure," she replied, smile practically beaming. "Ew. And judging by your face they were right."

"Huh," Mac scoffed. "You don't say? How can I help you, Terry?"

"The director wants to see you, Mac. He said to come to his office straight away."

"Is that so?" Mac asked rhetorically.

"Yup," The little blonde said. "Though I think you should really get that looked at before you go. You are bleeding on the floor."

Mac looked down to find a small, crimson puddle had formed on the floor near his boot. His nose must have started bleeding again. He chanced a glance at himself in the reflection of the window and confirmed his suspicion.

"Dammit," he spat under his breath as he dug another tissue out of his pocket and placed it on his nose.

Terry turned to leave and then stopped. She turned back around and walked back up to Mac.

"I almost forgot. Would you give this to Milly for me?" Terry handed Mac a small black backpack. "I found it at the scene of her incident and figured she would want it back."

Mac looked in the bag and saw it was Milly's Mark 2.

"I'll get it back to her," Mac said. "She will be very relieved to have it back. Thanks, Terry."

"My pleasure, give Milly a kiss for me and let her know I'll call her tomorrow," Terry said, before she dashed away as quickly as she came.

Terry was one of the level 1 agents like Milly. She was a bit of a flake, but she and Milly were good friends, so Mac kept his mouth shut. Besides, Terry kept things lively either by the trouble she was in or was causing.

Mac decided that if Six wouldn't be done till morning he should go ahead and get some rest. But first things first, he needed to visit the director.

He stepped toward the elevator and hit the button on the wall. A moment later the doors slid open and Mac came face to face with the Evidence Supervisor Cliff resplendent in his orange jumpsuit.

"Hey, Mac. You look like you had fun tonight," Cliff said, holding the door for Mac as he entered.

"You should see the other guy," Mac said, striving to sound macho.

"If you mean Six, then I've seen him. I'd say you guys lost, but you can't win them all," Cliff said with a chuckle as he exited the elevator. He turned toward Mac. "Oh, and that thing you asked about. It's the damnedest thing. It has unfortunately gone missing from the evidence locker. I have no idea what happened to it."

Mac saw the wink that Cliff gave him and smiled. Though he immediately regretted it. The pain of tonight's injuries lanced through his face.

"That's a damn shame, Cliff," Mac said, between winces and dabs at his nose with the tissue, as the elevator door closed. "That's a damn shame."

Chapter 7

The elevator door opened, and Mac stepped out onto the plastic tiles that coated the RAD's floors. The ice pack he held against his face made it hard to see but it sure felt good. He wove his way across the lobby and into the Detective squad room. He stopped at his desk to upload his Global. His desk was bare. Just how he liked it.

Six was damn good at filing reports. So, Mac got accustomed to letting him. In response Mac no longer had to slave away at a portable terminal filing ridiculous reports. He rarely if ever kept track of how many times he discharged his weapon during the day much less for the week. Like it mattered now they rarely used solid projectiles. Six had spoiled him.

He tossed the handful of items in his hand onto the desk. His new Force Deflector shield vest, Milly's Mark 2, and the bag of Meds the medic had given him just a few minutes ago. The items dominated the top of the small desk.

He pulled out his chair and sat down. Mac reached into his coat to retrieve his Global from his inside pocket. Which led him to once again discover the shredded sleeve of his coat, for the third time. He sighed heavily.

Ah, man. I loved this damn coat too.

Out of habit he opened his Global to check his messages. Then he tapped his ICE icon. The screen shifted to a little animation of a robot putting papers into a filing cabinet and closing the drawer over and over again.

Most of the RAD agents kept ICE files on the main server. The In Case of Emergency was a record of current cases including lists of suspects and hunches. It was important to record the little nuances of an investigation that a good agent picked up. Particularly when you had no real evidence to support it yet. The ICE was an insurance policy and a lead that the next agent could use to track down whoever or whatever had been able to whack you. Mac had been in the habit of updating it every time he sat at his desk and before going to bed each night. It was the one piece of paperwork he made sure to do himself. He quickly added Teddy's droid and the sec cam data he had left to the file.

Once he was finished Mac threw his Global onto the transfer plate attached to his desk and proceeded to remove his ruined coat. He checked the pockets of the black coat briefly and then chucked it into the refuse bin sitting on the floor next to his desk. The edge hung out a bit but Mac left it. At this point, he just couldn't care anymore. The little red light on the transfer plate turned green, catching Mac's eye, indicating the Global was now updated and recharged. Mac grabbed the Global and saw he had a new text message. He pulled open the view screen and tapped the messaging Icon. It was a cheerful little missive from the director.

Gt ur ass ovr here. NOW! The screen read.

Mac looked up and saw the director staring at him through the window across the rows of desks from him.

Mac slapped the screen closed and scooted his chair back. He stood up slowly. Now that the adrenalin was no longer flowing freely, he was feeling the abuse he had suffered earlier at the hands of that droid.

That and you're starting to get old.

He fitted the ice pack back on his face and relished the cool touch and momentary relief it brought.

As he approached the director's office, he saw the director was escorting people out. A handsome younger Asian man and a tall young black woman.

"This way Mr. Takahaisu," said the director as he indicated toward the far side of the squad room toward the lifts. The two guests were wearing business suits. The one on the young man was black and just looked expensive. It had a sheen to it that you don't get from an off-the-rack suit. The young woman's suit was nice though less refined. She turned and her eyes narrowed at the sight of Mac.

Gracie? No way, Gracie is his bodyguard? A bodyguard? A human bodyguard? Interesting what with the proliferation of Androids anyone today would have a human bodyguard.

Gracie looked Mac up and down and then scowled.

"Been using your face to take down droids again eh Mac?" The younger woman said acerbically. Mac could practically smell the venom in her voice. "You know when they tell you to use your head, they don't mean hit stuff with it."

Mac noted the sarcasm.

"Well, you know me, Gracie. I like to get my hands dirty," Mac replied dryly.

I'm such an idiot. Come on man think, be smooth Mac, be mellow, don't let her get to you. Stay frosty, man.

"Looks like you're coming up in the world," Mac

continued, hoping to change the subject.

"Yeah, some of us want more than a badge and pension can give," Gracie quipped.

Mac held up his hands in surrender. "I'm just saying you look good Gracie." He was in no condition to for any kind of conflict with the woman.

"Huh," Gracie scoffed.

"Gracie," ordered the young Asian man.

"See you around, Mac," she called over her shoulder as she turned and headed after the two men.

Gracie continued to case the room as she went. Mac recognized the bulge beneath her suit jacket at the small of her back. She was packing a nice toy. Probably a series 10p neutralizer unless Mac had been hit harder than he thought. The lowercase p stood for portable. It was a condensed version of the one Six has built into his right arm. Dubbed the "'Hand Canon'" by the boys in the weapons cage. It was designed and built to punch through droid deflector shield arrays. Even the smaller ones, built to be used by human hands, had a terrible kick. Gracie was not to be taken lightly.

She always did like big toys. Mac tried to remember the last time he had seen her. *Thirteen maybe fourteen years ago. Ah, man had it really been that long?*

Sadness welled up in his chest. Mac and Gracie were partners in more ways than one. She was one of the green recruits like Mac that joined the RAD before it officially became the RAD. It was a stressful situation. Members died. A lot of them. Mac and Gracie sought comfort in each other's arms. Mac had loved her. It tore him up when they would go on missions.

He reached up and felt the crescent-shaped scar that outlined his left eye. The scar was a souvenir from one of their last missions. Gracie got in over her head. Mac got hurt getting her out. She got the glory while Mac recovered in the hospital. Mac got a formal reprimand and Grace was offered a corporate gig by the company the team was sent to bail out. She had asked Mac to go with her. He let his petty jealousy stop him. Things had been rather icy ever since.

Damn pride. Ah well.

Once Mr. Takahaisu and Gracie were beyond earshot the director turned briefly to Mac.

"Take a seat, I'll be right back," The director said in his "'I expect to be obeyed'" tone of voice and then he turned away abruptly and followed after his two guests.

Mac walked into the office and sat down in one of the rigid plastic chairs in front of the director's desk. The director liked those pieces of crap chairs because they were far from inviting. The longer you sat in them the more your butt went numb. Mac observed the director's desk. It was an old school wooden job. It was a throwback to the time when wood was an abundant resource and actually grew wild. It was exceedingly rare nowadays.

The desk was very dinged and scratched but everyone felt those gave it character. Mac agreed with that assessment. Supposedly it originally belonged to the first Sergeant of the newly formed New Trinity Police Department. When the RAD was created, the Council decided to build the NTPD a new headquarters and give RAD the old one.

The NTPD was pissed when the director found the desk in their old building under an inch of dust in a supply closet stacked on its side. There was no wooden anything in their new HQ. They raised a bit of stink but nothing ever came of it. The desk remained in the director's custody.

Mac looked around the office. The pictures were the same ones that had been there since the director took office ten years ago. Mostly pictures of the director's wife Mia and their lovely little daughter Rachel who was now in her teens. Mac's eyes drifted to the laser-etched nameplate on the desk. Richard E. Evens.

Richard "'Dick'" Evens was a decent man caught in a delicate political position. He was beset on all sides from the get-go. The people expecting to be kept safe, the manufacturers expecting to keep making a profit, and the Council expected him to work miracles while staying understaffed and under budget. The downside was that RAD was paid for by the droid manufactures and any credits not spent by the RAD can, and would be, appropriated by the council for their various purposes. An event that they expect to happen every month of every year.

So far Director Evens had managed to straddle that line fairly well since he took the office. Despite the Council's demands for overages the RAD agents and the technical support staff have been able to stay reasonably well equipped. That fiscal wizardry came at a price, however. It meant that new equipment was not as readily available as often as might be required and the RAD tended toward upgrading existing equipment beyond normal limits instead of simply buying new. Somehow Dick made it work.

One thing the director did was start selling older equipment to the public at auction to recoup some of the costs. He also forced the agents to buy their own deflector field vests. At first, it seemed like a dick move.

However, "'Tricky Dick'", as the director has been known for a while now, used his family's political connections to negotiate a discounted rate for the Agents. Which meant they could get better and safer equipment for themselves at a lower price instead of the RAD footing the bill for lesser quality. With the money he saved from instituting that policy he was able to do some more magic. He used some of it to maintain the agent's' weapons cache. To go one step further there was even a small surplus that the director kept back for the development of new gear. Case in point, the emergency shields and stun batons were developed by RAD Technicians and licensed to JTA Group for production and sale. JTA has sold millions of them to NTPD and other organizations in the other cities around the world. The director draws his salary from that income and uses his department salary to fund different projects within the RAD. The big one was the purchase of a brand new Takacorp Nanny Hive so the agents and techs could bring their kids with them to work.

Mac's eyes touched the Copy of the Automaton Manufacturer's Act on the wall directly above Dick's chair. A bill that set limits on how close an android could resemble a human being and established a manufacturer funded secondary police force to manage the automatons now in the field. The Rogue Autonomous Division being an off-shoot organization was connected to but completely separate from the New Trinity Police Department. During that time, the machines only outnumbered the humans three to one. Androids outnumber humans by a hundred to one in the city. The original police department developed for the city during its creation were inadequately staffed to handle the volume of automatons. A new division was needed to oversee the growing number of rogue droids and robots that were starting to run wild. The new unit was created by the Automaton Manufacturer's Act. Now the gap was even wider, the androids outnumber humans by a hundred to one.

The bill set up three levels of Automaton policing. Level 1 Agents, like Milly, were tasked to handle the low-level Automatons. Cleaning and maintenance droids and robots mostly. Nonlethal, small-time droids like sweeper bots, and window cleaning machines, Solar panel scrubbers, and sewer swimmers.

Level 2 agents were tasked with policing AMA violations and black-market sales of illegal droid parts as well as some small weapons control. If a droid walked on two legs, it typically fell under the jurisdiction of the Level 2's. They run down low-level hacking and droid on droid attacks too. Like in the new dome, a hacked droid went around reprogramming ATMs to dump credits into an unnamed credit account, level 2s were called in. They spend most of their days hunting for guys like Teddy and his Caroline. A thankless and frustrating job if you asked Mac.

A lot of level 2's had TFEs. It was added as an option after a couple of Level 2 investigators were murdered by a black-market seller who sicced his sex bot on them. One was an idiot who was using it as the seller had intended and didn't want to pay. The second was a good agent who investigated the death of his friend and got ambushed. The seller, Jimmy the Freak as he was known on the street, was caught by Detective Stark shortly thereafter. Ziggy, Stark's TFE, tore the sex bot to pieces while Stark took care of Jimmy. Consequently,

Jimmy hung himself with a bed sheet before he ever stood trial. The director himself was a Level 2 investigator for a while. At least before he ran for the directorship. He comes from a long line of politicians and eventually caved to pressure from the family to take on more responsibility. At least that's what Dick says, once you get a few beers into him.

Level 3s like Mac and Stark were called in when a human being has been wounded or killed by a machine. The level 3s were part detective and part SWAT team. With their mandatory TFE in tow, they locate and incapacitate all hazardous rogue automatons. Mac has hunted, destroyed, or captured all sorts of droids. Everything from a solar panel scrubber that classified panel inspectors as debris that needed to be scrubbed off sending them sliding to their deaths down the side of the domes to a bulldozer that had its proximity sensor damaged, so it just drove over everything in its way including a couple of passenger cars and a bus full of people and droids. It is a job Mac took very seriously.

The quiet of the director's office was starting to get to Mac. He reached into his pocket and pulled out his Global. He winced at the pain the motion caused. The prophet droid had bruised Mac's wrist pretty badly when it grabbed him. He checked his Global. It was almost 01:00 hours. Mac's face and wrist were killing him. He could use a bed right about now.

The door opened suddenly, startling Mac. He started to stand.

"I told you to sit," the director snapped.

Mac sat back down.

Great, it's going to be one of those meetings.

The director sat down in his plush chair on the

opposite side of the desk.

"Do you know who that was?" he asked gesturing to the door.

"Mr. Takahaisu?" Mac replied with a shrug.

"Ichiro Takahaisu," Dir. Evens said. "He dropped by to request our help."

"Really?"

"#1. We can stop destroying their manufacturing facilities!" Dick yelled, slamming his hands on the wooden desk in front of him.

Mac sank back into his chair.

Damn! It's going to be one of those meetings.

Mac's brow furrowed as he scowled defiantly at his boss.

Dick continued unphased, "I could give two shits about Takacorp's facility or the clankers that got wasted in the process. What pisses me off is that you let the suspect get away."

"I didn't let shit get away, Dick," Mac snapped back. He leaned forward. He felt his face getting hot. "That thing took Six apart like he was made of glass and mopped the floor with me for good measure. Did you watch the footage? Did you!" Mac winced as his excited movement sent a stab of pain through his face.

"I haven't seen it. No," Dick admitted sinking back into his chair. "Mac, it's a lot easier to explain your shenanigans when you produce results. Which up till now you have been producing."

"That thing could have killed me, Dick! Killed! Dead!" Mac roared. "Fuck Takacorp! They have not been honest about what they are producing over there, Dick. I have never seen anything like this droid. None of their data vids showed anything like this. This is something new, something very scary. If this is a taste of things to come, we are in serious trouble."

"I'll have to check out the footage then," Dick said. "Toss me the stuff you have."

Mac fished his Global out of his pocket while Dick did the same. He pulled out the sliding screen and located the icon for the data Six had compiled and sec cam footage from Mac's run-in with the poncho droid. Holding his Global near Dick's he flicked the icon on the screen, and it flew virtually to Dick's Global.

Dick fiddled with his global. After a second he looked back at Mac. His face softened. "Shit. It really did a number on you."

Mac nodded.

"I know I'm asking a lot of you. Especially with what happened with Milly tonight. How is she by the way?"

"Good, last time I saw her," Mac said. "She'll have some nasty bruising around her throat, and she lost some fingernails but she's otherwise unharmed."

"Well, you tell her that anything she needs she'll get," Dick said, "We take care of our own. Speaking of which have you seen the medic?"

"Yeah, I stopped there before I came up."

"Good."

"They really sent some bigwig down here to bitch at you about some damaged clankers in the middle of the night?" Mac asked. "An angry phone call would have sufficed."

"No. You're right. The real reason he came was, in fact, to ask for our help. They want assistance finding one of their designers who has gone missing. The ass chewing was just a perk," Dick said bitterly. He eased back in his chair. For some reason, the lines on his face stood out more, the bags under eyes seemed darker than usual. Which would explain the outburst. Dick usually maintained a cool demeanor.

"He stopped by this evening because it was on his way home from a social engagement," Director Evens finished, chuckling to himself. The activity seemed to lessen the fatigue. "Ichiro Takahaisu is a very unpleasant young man."

"Have him call the police! That's what they are there for Dick. You know, to find missing people and shit. I'm sure those lazy bastards would love something to do," Mac said in disgust. "How did they even know you were here?"

"I wish it were that simple Mac," Director Evens replied as he removed his glasses and pinched the bridge of his nose. "They, meaning Tohiro Takahaisu, believe that clankers kidnapped his friend Uske Otagawa. To what end I can't even imagine."

"Wait. You mean to tell me that droids, Androids, took *the* Uske Otagawa?" Mac asked incredulously. "That doesn't make any sense. He is *the* guy at Takacorp. Almost every innovation they have developed in the last twenty-five years has come from him. He is practically a household name. How could an android take a guy like Otagawa? Aren't they all programmed to kiss his ass whenever they see him?"

"You'd think, but that's what you are going to find out, Mac," The director said coolly hiding a smirk by putting his wire rimmed glasses back on. "That's why I wanted to see you. I'm pulling you off of the implant case and putting you on this first thing tomorrow."

"It's a level 2 assignment, Dick. If you are going to

pull me off the implant case then I would prefer to help Stark with the Prophet case," Mac countered. "Stark is going to need backup in a bad way if he is going to bring that damn droid down."

"This takes priority, Mac," Dick explained. "Takacorp has requested my best field agent be put on the case immediately. With Stark working the Prophet case that just leaves you. So, end of argument. They have requested this and I'm damn well going to give them what they want. The manufacturers have taken a back seat in regard to how the money they are paying is spent here at RAD. They do get a say in those matters, at least on some level. If they feel they aren't getting our attention, they will certainly take more drastic measures. Measures that neither you nor I would enjoy. Do I make myself clear?"

"Oh, come on, Dick! Any Level 2 would sell his sister for a high-profile case like this. Why not give it to someone who would enjoy the grandstanding," Mac asserted. "Someone like Taylor or Spitz. They are great Agents, and they deserve a break like this."

"No, I need someone I can count on. Someone who can handle the pressure. Stark is busy with the Prophet case, or I would have chosen him. With what happened to Milly I can't justify giving the Prophet case to you. In light of your little soiree tonight, you're too damn close to it now. Besides, this way I can pass the implant case to Nabe and get him off my ass."

"Ah, not Nabe. He couldn't find his own ass in a lit room. Even if somebody drew him a map!" Mac complained.

Dick laughed. He covered his mouth and laughed.

"What?" Mac asked, his train of thought broken.

"Well, you might be right about that. Maybe I'll give the implant case to Spitz and see if she can handle it."

"That's better than Nabe. Shouldn't he have retired by now? The worthless bastard is older than dirt," Mac asked, making exaggerated faces as he spoke. That lasted until his face began to ache more than it had been.

This time it was all for effect. Dick's laughter had kind of spurred Mac on. Mac liked to operate under the simple assumption that if you can make your boss laugh, things run much more smoothly. That and it was good to hear laughter and feel funny after the near-death experience Mac had been through tonight.

Even though he was joking, everything he was saying about Nabe was true. Nabe was pushing seventy-six. Per department policy, he should have retired more than 15 years ago. The poor old man was falling apart. The department had stopped trying to classify his failing parts and abilities and tried to list the things he still had that were working. The only thing they could come up with was his mouth. The old man could still talk some major shit.

"Be that as it may. You will report to Takacorp tomorrow afternoon to review the evidence," Dick said, adopting his serious face and his "'do as I say'" tone of voice.

"Six will have all of the details when he picks you up tomorrow," Dick continued. "And now it's after one in the morning, go home and get some rest or better yet go check on that lovely woman of yours."

"I'm not happy about this, I want this Prophet guy. Especially now. It's been a long time since I've had my ass handed to me. I can honestly say that I didn't like it. I want a chance to redeem myself."

"Well, Mac, you have just found it. If you find Dr. Uske Otagawa the world will be your oyster."

"What's an oyster?"

"Don't know, but I'm sure it's good. My great grandfather used to say that all the time and I got it from my grandfather." Dick shrugged.

Mac shrugged too.

"Anyway, go home," Dick continued. "Oh, and when you are finished at Takacorp tomorrow. I want you to come back by. That new toy I told you about…"

"Yeah?" Mac said his interest piqued.

"It's ready. I want to test it out tomorrow if you're game?"

"I'm so there," Mac said. "Don't start without me."

Chapter 8

Mac closed the door as quietly as the rusty old hinges would allow. He set the bundle of stuff in his hand on the couch just inside the door and slipped into the apartment.

He looked around the dark living room for Rosie. He half hoped Milly had taken his advice and locked her up. He knew that she would sleep better tonight knowing that she was safe from a droid, even one as benign as Rosie. Rosie was not in her charging arch in the corner of the living room.

"That's not a good sign." Mac mumbled.

His stomach chose that moment to remind him that he didn't eat that burger he had ordered earlier.

I wonder if Milly has anything to eat.

He kicked his boots off onto the tile just inside the door.

Artie, Milly's black and white cat, met Mac at the doorway to the kitchen and scurried on ahead to his spot on the counter. The little rascal waited expectantly. Mac made his way around the corner into the galley-style kitchen as Artie stared at him intently.

"You keep quiet while I rustle up a couple of things and I'll see if I can get you something too, all right Artie," Mac whispered to the impatient kitty.

Artie paced back and forth along the counter. He kept his yellow-green eyes locked firmly on Mac.

Mac went right for Milly's stash of painkillers. His head was killing him. Milly occasionally got headaches and always had a bottle of IB tabs in the cabinet above the kitchen sink. Mac grabbed the IB tabs and a small glass from the cabinet as well. He filled the glass from the tap. He tossed four tabs into his mouth and chased them with the water. The label said it takes effect in thirty seconds. They typically took about forty-five.

Yeah, but who's counting.

He put the bottle back in the cabinet. It really annoyed Milly when he left things out. He didn't really want to hear her complain.

Mac had gotten quite spoiled. Mac's companion droid, Derf, a term of endearment for his Takacorp DRF, took care of all of those mundane details. Little things like putting dishes and clothes away. Derf took care of Mac's laundry and general cleaning up. Derf never complained about having to clean up after Mac.

Milly preferred clean and clear. She believed that if you get it out you should have the courtesy to put it back where it goes when you are finished. Once Mac even suggested getting her a newer droid. One that was capable of cleaning up after him. The solution went over real well. Milly threw a glass at him.

Mac chuckled at the thought of a glass flying at his head. She must have planned ahead. The glass she threw was plastic and empty. Probably so he couldn't use that sort of mess against her.

Crafty.

"Oh, you are here!" an excited but raspy voice said.

Mac jumped at the statement, the glass in his hand slipped through his fingers. It shattered on the floor with a great pop. Mac spun around to see the owner of the voice.

Milly stood in the doorway in one of her huge t-shirts she used frequently as a nightgown. Milly got a good look at his face and her eyes bugged out at the sight.

"Dear God, Mac, what happened to you?" Milly screeched while rushing to him.

"I'm fine, I'm fine," he exclaimed, holding up his hand to keep her at bay so she wouldn't step on the broken glass. He was also a little worried she would touch his aching face. "Really, I'm fine."

She pulled the chair out from the dinette and forced him to sit.

She spun around and dug in the freezer for something.

"Milly at least let me clean up the glass," Mac protested.

"You sit there, mister, and tell me how this happened right now. Don't leave out a word, do you hear me?" she demanded. "Oh, and keep Artie up there while I clean up."

She handed him a bag of frozen peas and guided it to his face. Once it was firmly in place she went to the small closet and pulled a broom and dustpan out.

Oh, the cold feels so good, Mac admitted to himself as the cold seeped into his eye and nose.

"Milly, I'm fine. I'll get the glass. Honey, I'm still dressed. Let me do that," Mac protested again.

"Sit! Start talking, mister!" she demanded.

Mac felt terribly guilty, so he gave up and did as he was told. While she cleaned up the broken glass Mac told her of the evening's events. He told her about his visit to Teddy and the camera footage. Though he conveniently forgot to mention the anatomically correct android,

Caroline. He talked about the emergency call he and Six went on. As Milly finished putting the broom and dustpan away, she started making a pot of tea for the two of them. Mac explained how he and Six stormed the manufacturing facility like stupid cowboys of old. He told her a blow-by-blow account of the fight with the poncho-wearing droid.

Milly laughed at Mac's jokes about Teddy and his boob infatuation and was appropriately horrified at the damage done to Six. Her anger at his attempt to save Six caught him completely by surprise.

"Mac. Sweetie, I love you, but sometimes you are so stupid. How could you put yourself in harm's way after watching that droid take Six apart like that?" Mac could still hear the heat in her raspy voice.

Mac desperately tried to change the subject. "Maybe you should rest your voice. The medic said you were supposed to. Remember?"

"Mac, Six is a Tactical Field Escort. He is meant to do the dangerous stuff. To keep you safe," she rasped.

"He's my partner," Mac countered. "I couldn't sit back and watch that droid trash him."

"Honey that is what he is there for. To keep you out of harm's way," she countered. She cleared her throat to try and moisten things up. When that didn't work, she sipped her tea.

"He's my friend," Mac admitted feeling slightly defeated. "I couldn't let him get killed like that."

"Mac, Six is a droid. Unlike you," she said, jabbing him with her finger to emphasize her point, "He can be replaced or repaired as many times as it takes."

"What can I say?" Mac said. "There wasn't time to think, I just reacted. My partner was in danger, and I reacted. Maybe it was wrong. I don't know."

Milly set down her mug and moved closer to Mac. She reached up gently and took the frozen peas from him and set them on the counter. She cradled his face delicately in her soft hands and looked deep into his eyes.

"I know you care about Six. If I had to work with a droid like him, I would probably feel the same way," she supposed. "However, if it comes down to you or him, you'll make the right choice, right? I don't want to go through life without you."

"I'm sorry, Milly, I got sloppy. I let you down, I let Dick down, and I failed Six. Six is sitting in the Tech shop being pieced back together like some damn jigsaw puzzle cuz I ran in ahead trying to take down the clanker that hurt you. My lust for revenge did this. Did this to me, to Six and now I hurt you again, can you forgive me?"

"You're still alive stupid," she replied. "Just promise me you'll stay that way. Promise you won't take any more foolish risks. Okay?"

"I'll do my best," he said dubiously.

It must have been enough because Milly kissed him. Her lips were soft and welcome.

After a moment she released him. He knew it would spoil the mood but his stomach was insistent, "Got anything to eat?"

Milly nodded and in short order fixed Mac a MoFurkey sandwich. It was just a turkey "flavored" mushroom patty. It looked terrible and tasted worse, but it was edible. She made sure to throw a chunk to Artie to keep him from stealing the sandwich. The MoFurkey was one of the silly cat's favorite treats. She placed the sandwich down in front of Mac who attacked it so quickly Milly made a show of counting her fingers to make sure she still had them all. Mac finished his meal quickly and darn near licked the plate. *Healing is hungry work.*

"That was wonderful, baby!" Mac caught a glance of Artie staring down at him disdainfully.

"Let's get you to bed," Milly said. "Maybe now you're here I can finally get some sleep,"

"Sounds good to me," Mac replied.

Mac finished his tea. He grabbed the tube of cat treats Milly had sitting on her fridge. He dumped a couple of its contents on the counter by Artie.

"You kept your end of the bargain, Artie," Mac told the purring little cat. "If I didn't hold up my end, I would be a stupid asshole instead of just stupid." Artie pounced on them voraciously.

"Night, Artie," Mac said over his shoulder as he touched the light switch.

Mac followed Milly down the short hallway to her bedroom though she wasn't there. He saw a light shining from her office doorway. He walked farther down the short hallway and into the lit room.

Milly's office was her playroom. She had a full IPX 8500 workstation for servicing and reprogramming droids of all types. Milly had just gotten it. The 9000 model was now available which sank the price of the 8500 to a much more manageable amount. Mac paid for half of it as a birthday present for Milly. She spent a lot of her spare time upgrading and repairing household droids. Mostly for work. However, she also helped the occasional neighbor or family friend. Well, she helped the ones she liked anyway. Milly did it to solve puzzles. She loved to find the issue and then fix it. Milly liked puzzles about as much as Mac did. In a way, it was kind of what brought them together. A quiet evening at home for them was typically a puzzle, of the jigsaw variety, and a couple of beers.

Milly was powering off her GEN TECH surgical arms. The machine's precision mechanical arms hung above the service droid she was sent after earlier in the day. She used those to repair microcircuit boards and CPE's. Those items require microscopic tools and an inhumanly steady hand. It always made Mac think of a giant spider from the history books, just a mass of twitching legs.

"I couldn't sleep so I tried to work," she admitted.

"Shhhhhhhh," Mac said with his finger to her lips. It wasn't fair how soft they were. If Mac wasn't careful, he'd get lost just admiring her.

Milly turned away to flip the switch on the machine. Its arms retracted into their locked position hiding the sensitive instruments and manipulator rods in their protective housing. Once the power light winked out Milly moved over to her workstation.

Her IPX 8500 workstation was a large computer that sat near the room's only window. It was quite a bit less sophisticated than Teddy's with only three visual displays, but Mac and Milly made quite a bit less than that pervert.

Milly started the shutdown procedures on it as Mac walked to the closet. Milly had cleared a space for him in this closet a while back. His space had been steadily getting smaller as Milly collected more and more spare parts. He now had a six-inch section of hanging space in the closet. Mac opened the door and jumped back.

"Ah!" Mac exclaimed.

"Sorry. I locked Rosie in there," Milly confessed. "At first I thought it was stupid, but I did feel better knowing she was locked up."

"No worries. It was just unexpected."

"Just lay your clothes over the chair. I'll have Rosie wash them in the morning," Milly scratched.

"Don't bother. I'll have Six take me by my place on the way to Takacorp tomorrow," Mac said.

"Why are you going to Takacorp tomorrow?" Milly asked.

"One of their top eggheads has gone missing and they think droids were involved. So RAD has been tasked to look into it," Mac replied sullenly.

"Oh." Milly nodded. She looked exhausted. Mac made note that she kept rubbing her eyes.

"Go to bed, baby. I'll join you here in a minute," Mac said "Oh hold on. The medic gave me something for the bruising. He said to take it just before bed. I asked for a dose for you too. He said he would give me a second one and what I did with it was my business, the less he knows the better. Oh, that reminds me. Terry found something of yours at the scene that she thought you would want back." Mac ran out to the couch in the living room and grabbed the bag he had carried in.

He met Milly at the door to her bedroom. He pulled her Mark 2 from the bag and gave it to her.

"My Mark 2! That's awesome," Milly hid a yawn with her hand. "I'll have to remember to send Terry a thank you note."

"You can do that tomorrow. You go on to bed now. Before you lay down, use this injection pen. Stab one side of your throat here," he said demonstrating with the capped injector on each side of his throat. "And then the other side."

She took the pen and headed into her bedroom. Mac took his own with him back to the office. He got undressed and after a stop by the bathroom for a shower and to brush his teeth, he was ready. He stumbled through the dark room and climbed into bed next to Milly. He leaned over to kiss her good night, but she was fast asleep.

Good, she needs her rest.

Mac grabbed his injector and pulled the cap off. He jabbed himself in the forehead just above his nose with the thumb-sized square head of the pen and pushed in. He felt a slight pinch and then a cold sensation under his skin. He then did it again only this time under his left eye where the bruising looked like it was going to be the worst. Another pinch and then he was done. He laid the injector on the nightstand and noticed that Milly had left the pill bottle the medic had given her open. Mac snapped the lid closed. He settled in next to her on her queen-size sleeper tray and was asleep by the time his head hit the pillow.

Chapter 9

Mac felt great relief to hear that sickeningly sweet tone of Six's vocal processor. He had not realized how much he had come to depend on the big lug of a droid. It wasn't just the tedious tasks that Six took care of. It was a lot more. Over the six months or so they have been riding together Mac had not realized how much of an emotional attachment he had formed with the droid. The worst part was that Mac knew it was just a one-sided illusion. All it would take was the click of a field override link and Six could be made to forget all about Mac.

Speaking of which, Mac patted the pouch on his hip that contained his Field Override link. *It's nice to know I have some measure of control.*

Mac craned his neck to observe the giant tower that stood before him. Its mirror-coated windows shined brightly in the afternoon light coming through the white dome overhead. Takacorp's headquarters was the biggest building in the city. It stood just north of the park at the center of the largest and newest dome.

"Six what's the deal with Takacorp?" Mac asked.

"Checking…Checking…Found," Six said. "At eight hundred meters tall, the top of Takacorp Tower, is only ten meters from the interior layer of the dome's ceiling. The sheer size of the tower stands as a testament to Takacorp's power and wealth. As a global manufacturer of Continuous Arc Cell, or CAC batteries and of a variety of top-of-the-line androids, they are a powerhouse in the global market. Virtually every existing city left in the world has some form of Takacorp products within or around its walls.

"Takacorp got its start as a computer component manufacturer. Koneda Takahaisu started the company in 2032. He correctly read signs on the horizon. Alternative energy was the next big economic boom and the nations who capitalized on it would survive the coming oil shortages."

"America's economy had faltered, and the rest of the world was suffering now that Americans were no longer buying their goods. China was an early adopter and manufacturer of alternative energy technology. They quickly became a global leader in the alternative energy field. Applying their methods to Solar and Wind technologies. They made them efficient, plentiful, and best of all inexpensive. The missing piece to the puzzle was a system to contain the generated energy. So, to fill the gap Koneda and Takacorp began development on efficient energy storage methods. After ten long and scary years for the company, Koneda and his team produced the Continuous Arc Cell. Marketed as the CAC battery, The Continuous Arc Cell was an alternative to ubiquitous electro-chemical batteries currently in use during the time."

"I asked about Takacorp, Six. not a dome history lesson," Mac said dryly.

"I assure you, Mac. This is pertinent to your question," Six replied.

"Once the CAC battery was brought to market anything that required power had one. They were scalable and easy to manufacture. They could even be retrofit to work with old and entrenched technologies. Everything nowadays contains one of their power storage systems. Globals, Neutralizers, androids, drones, computers, cars, and even buildings have them."

"By the time the energy problem was solved, the damage to the environment, and the oil wars, had taken their toll. The death toll was catastrophic. Humankind was on the brink of extinction. The shortage of workers led surviving people to develop more and more machines to carry out the reconstruction and unfortunately to fight the wars that followed."

"Increasing the tension, the wars had devastated mankind's agricultural production. Much of the world's food stores were depleted if not wiped out entirely. Making matters worse, the conditions for growing more to feed livestock and people were damaged almost beyond repair. The world was facing a terrible food shortage."

"Oh no!" Mac said sarcastically, holding his face. Six continued his lesson undeterred.

"A few of America's remaining farmers, corporations, and wealthy individuals took their operation inside. They used the new plastics, derived from corn syrup, to fashion a dome over a large stretch of fields and were able to grow food plants. Food was a powerful commodity, which the new city, rechristened New Trinity, used to barter for energy and computer technologies. With the collapse of several of the world's governments, the remaining populations retreated to the new dome cities rapidly being constructed. Though the going was hard and many of the remaining cities imploded with disease, infighting. Few of them like this one managed to survive."

"Are you about done here?" Mac asked.

"Almost," Six replied.

Mac rolled his eyes but waved his hand for the machine to continue.

"The ruling council, which remains intact to this day, was established to run the city. It was made up of many of the original families of the farmers, corporate leaders, and wealthy Americans that started the dome farming project.

"Labor shortages and the ongoing wars among the surviving cities for resources made it clear that a plan was required to secure manufacturing of androids to fill the labor needs. With help from their espionage efforts, the Council negotiated a settlement with Takacorp."

"Takacorp would move their Headquarters from the dying Tokyo city to New Trinity in exchange for production space and additional food allotments for their employees."

"Koneda, then in his 90's, agreed. He died shortly thereafter. His successor Shinji Takahaisu, the father of the current head of Takacorp, Tohiro Takahaisu, took control. Although Shinji was not as strong of a leader as his father his decision to give his son, Tohiro, and Tohiro's high school friend Uske Otagawa free rein of the R & D department proved very fruitful."

"Wait, Uske Otagawa?" Mac asked. "The same guy we are here to investigate?"

"One in the same Mac," Six replied, "Did I say that correctly? One-in-the-same."

"Sure did partner, you sure did."

"It was during this time that Tohiro and Uske developed the Androids that are now ubiquitous today.

The technology they developed quickly replaced the robotic machines taking care of the farming and outdoor power systems," Six continued.

"Uske proved to be the secret ingredient. He developed a synthetic muscle system, Organoid Retractile Fiber Motor, known as the ORF motor that could increase the strength and performance of a typical machine. He even resurrected the term Android, a term meaning 'an automaton in the form of a human being.'"

Mac rolled his eyes again. "Thanks for the tip, is there anything *important* that I need to know?"

"Yes, Mac. Uske's creations so resembled human beings that it prompted the religious right to backlash initially. This led to the formation of the Automaton Manufacturers Act. Which set rules and regulations for how close an android could resemble a human being."

"This is going nowhere. Let's go, Six," Mac said.

"Roger," Six replied.

Mac nodded as he eased himself out of the cruiser. "Now let's see what we can see."

"It's a building, Mac," Six said while he clamored out of his cradle behind the passenger cabin. "It is 800 meters tall."

"One step forward, two steps back," Mac mumbled rubbing his temples. "Let get this over with."

Mac realized that his face didn't hurt as badly anymore. He checked himself out in his reflection on the car window. There was still a dark circle under his eye but nothing like the bruise he should have had. That pen was some good stuff.

Now if only I could just get this new coat broken in.

Mac flexed against his new coat. It was similar to the one he used to have. It was knee-length and black like the other one but this one was still a bit tight at the moment. It didn't wear as well as the other one, but it was the best the store had so Mac went with it. He checked the set of his backup piece at the small of his back, and he tested his main weapon in its holster hanging from his belt. He tucked his coat behind the handgrip so it wouldn't interfere with his draw and then he drew the weapon out a little just to make sure it could be drawn in a hurry. It came out easily, so he let it fall back in place and proceed toward the line of doors at the building's base.

Mac and Six walked up the front stairway and through the two large sets of sliding doors and into the lobby.

Mac and Six both took note of the Safety film remnants covering sections of the freshly replaced doors. There were spots where the thin membrane of plastic that usually protected new sheets of glass and transparent plastic remained stuck to the surface. It typically happened when the maintenance crew was in too much of a hurry to remove it slowly. A small maintenance droid was struggling with the remnants, its spindly arms scrubbing franticly trying in vain to remove the film.

"Mac, it would appear these glass panels have been replaced recently."

"It would appear so," Mac replied evenly. "Hey, I've got an idea, Six. Why don't you get a copy of the building's maintenance logs and make sure that's the case," his sarcasm wasted on his synthetic partner.

"I am unable to access their system, Mac," Six said sounding for all the world like he was confused.

"How may I help you?" said a female voice out of nowhere. Mac spun around and his hand went straight for his blaster at his hip. He felt a little silly when he saw what appeared to be a PA droid standing in front of him. It was a typical Takacorp production model. Similar to the serving droids Mac had been thrown into last night at the storage warehouse. With effort and Six's comforting presence Mac relaxed.

An older model.

This one had a soft and flexible black plastic skirt that hung down to the floor hiding her legs. Her arms were very basic meant for little more than pointing in specific directions during a tour.

"Halt! Identify," Six said menacingly.

The droid turned her head and looked over Mac and Six thoroughly.

"I am Fran, Formal Receiving Android, Takacorp model FRA679" The droid replied smoothly. "You must be Agent McDonnell and his RAD Tactical Field Escort. I was expecting you."

"Good to know," Mac said.

"I shall be your escort during your time here. Feel free to ask me any questions you might have. I have been ordered to provide you with whatever you require," The droid said. "Could I offer you something to drink Agent McDonnell?"

"No, thank you," Mac replied. "Though it would be an immense help if you could allow Six to access the building's maintenance records and security camera footage. For say thirty days prior to the incident up till now."

"Request acknowledged," Fran said rather blandly. Her lack of emotion was starting to irritate Mac just a little bit. He watched as she inclined her head and looked to be staring off into space. He was about to say something when she continued suddenly. "Protocols are arranged. Transferring data to Shared System drives. Shall we continue to the doctor's lab?"

"I'm in Mac. Downloading the footage and Maintenance files," Six said. "They are both quite large. I will begin sorting once I'm finished with the download."

"Yes, Miss Fran, let us head to the lab," Mac replied.

Fran turned and started toward the elevator bank set in the center of the building. The Takacorp tower consisted of a central core with three Lobes or Pedals as the designer would probably have said, radiating from the central core. Mac let the escort droid get a few steps ahead and leaned back into Six.

"I want you to record everything you see. Start from when we drove up to the tower. Understand?" Mac whispered.

"Rodger," Six replied trying to match Mac's voice level.

"Also, can you monitor Fran's communications?" Mac asked as he started walking to catch up with Fran.

"Roger," Six replied, sounding way too happy. "Is there something I should be watching for?"

"I want to know when she is communicating with the network. Touch me when she is," Mac said.

"She is in constant communication with the Network, Mac. She, like myself, is online in real-time," Six replied.

"Then just keep recording and let me know if you find something suspicious," Mac said over his shoulder.

"Rodger," Six replied.

They caught up with Fran by the elevators. Fran turned to look at them as they waited by a specific door.

"For expedience, we will be using the executive elevator," Fran explained.

"Thank you," Mac replied.

The elevator tone sounded, and the golden mirror doors opened. Mac and Six followed Fran into the elevator car. The door closed and the elevator rocketed upward. Mac barely felt the thing move.

Nice.

Everything about Takacorp tower was ornate but in a subdued kind of way. From the imitation wood molding framing the large mirrors on the walls inside the elevator to the free form visualization on the elevator's interface touchpad. It was a lot but not too much. Mac kind of liked it. He was trying to decide if he could record a quick video of it to show Milly when the doors opened suddenly.

Mac caught himself before he fully reached for his weapon. He never felt the elevator slow down.

You're getting jumpy, man. He heard his grandfather's voice in his head.

"Son, when you start jumping at shadows and doors it's time to get out," Grandpa had said. Grandpa had worked in the intelligence bureau at the beginning of the domed cities. He was one of the spies sent to infiltrate the domed city of York, which was one of the last cities in what used to be called Britain.

"Shall we?" Fran motioned through the open door.

"After you," Mac said.

Mac followed Fran down the broad hallway, Six lumbered along behind him. The Doctor's lab was in one of the lobes that extended out from the building's central column. At the end of the hall, Mac could see a hologram stream blocking the entrance. The fifteen centimeter tall, two meter wide, projection of the words; "'Security field in place. Caution! Sealed for security purposes. No admittance!'" repeated over and over like they were on the edge of a giant invisible wheel spinning clockwise in front of them.

"You quarantined the lab?" Mac asked.

"Once the damage was surveyed it was decided that the doctor must have been taken by force. We immediately cleared the area and set up the holo stream perimeter," Fran explained. "You will be the first to disturb the scene since it was sealed one week ago."

"You waited a whole week to let us know?" Mac asked incredulously.

"I don't have the relevant data to answer your question, Agent McDonnell," Fran replied.

"Thanks," Mac said sarcastically. "Could you deactivate the security field? Please."

"Of course, Agent McDonnell," Fran said. Her head cocked to the left, and the field winked out. Mac could feel the static charge in the air from the field's repulsion halo. It caused his clothes to cling to him. It was a clear sign that meant it was a strong field. He did not doubt that it would have tossed him back down the hall if he would have walked into it while it was active.

"Six, you're up!" Mac said stepping back.

"Roger, Mac," Six replied. His police lights sprang to life bathing the hallway in a wash of red and blue light. His arm opened to reveal the neutralizer hidden there and he slipped through the doorway into the daylit room. While Mac waited for the all-clear he examined the damage around the door. The door had been pushed open damaging the doorframe.

"Clear," Six called out loudly.

"Shall we?" Mac asked.

"Please, Agent McDonnell," Fran said politely.

"After you, my dear," Mac said, faking civility. At least he hoped he was faking civility.

Like it matters to a droid. I just don't want her out of my sight.

Fran glided into the Lab. Mac followed close on her heels.

The lab was lit by the ambient light from the dome. Most people called it daylight. Mac was one of them, largely because some of it really was light from the sun shining overhead. However, it was filtered through the plastic dome.

The first thing Mac noticed about the lab was the smell. It was a kind of noxious mix of spoiled milk and body odor. Mac was glad he had skipped lunch as he would have just seen it again. The room itself was trashed. Someone had hastily tossed the place. What were probably nice displays of the inner workings of Android components were left in shambles and shattered glass. Most of the drawers were pulled from their cabinets and left lying on the tiled floor.

Three half-completed Androids lay on four maintenance gurneys. The gurneys resembled medieval torture devices. Sectioned tables with arm-like projections, and hand cranks sticking out here and there. All those were for adjusting the parts of the table. Mac could imagine some poor prisoner lying on one of them being stretched out to make him talk. He swatted away the image along with the smell.

Designed to manipulate the droids as the tech worked on the various components. One of the four gurneys appeared brand new compared to the others.

Unlike the others, the new one was completely empty. They were similar to the model the techs repaired Six on, though much, much nicer. The three droids all looked to have been scavenged. Various components had been hastily removed from each of the machines. Much of the plastic outer shells had been damaged in the process. Mac guessed the fourth droid was most likely the recipient of the excised parts. The sight made him think of an old story he read in school.

"Hey, Six! What was that old story about a doctor that brought a bunch of dead bodies back to life as one monster?" Mac asked while pinching his nose closed. "You know, where the monster was afraid of fire.

"Checking…Checking. The most likely option would be *Frankenstein, or The Modern Prometheus* by Mary Shelly, Mac," The droid replied.

"That's the one. Frankenstein," Mac agreed, still holding his nose. Mac continued casing the room.

Doors of the cabinets lining the walls were left open and in some cases torn clean off the hinges. A large tank inside a cabinet just to the right of the door was shattered. It was big enough to submerge a man or man-sized android completely. The liquid it had contained was now mostly dried on the floor. Upon closer inspection, Mac was sure he had discovered the source of the smell. The fluid that was left in the container had congealed and was radiating the offending odor.

"Do you know what was kept in that container?" Mac asked, pointing at the container. He looked back around at Fran realizing he had taken his eyes off the droid.

"I'm sorry, Agent McDonnell. I do not understand what you are saying. Could you please repeat the question?"

Mac sighed heavily and then immediately regretted the expenditure of air from his lungs as he now had to breathe in the nasty aroma again. Taking his hand off his nose he repeated the question.

"What was kept in the container?" Mac said, stifling a gag while pinching his nose again.

"I do not know," Fran replied. "I do not have complete access to Dr. Otagawa's research."

"How do we get that information?" Mac asked, getting more annoyed by the minute.

"I'm sorry, agent, I cannot understand you."

"How do we gain access to the information, Fran?" Mac quickly pinched his nose again.

"I apologize for the ambiguous statement. It is not a question of getting the proper clearances, Agent McDonnell," Fran explained. "The data has been completely removed from Takacorp's database."

"You don't say," Mac said flatly. "Six!"

"Roger. Checking... Checking... Checking... Confirmed. An anonymous user with administrator-level access logged on to Takacorp Systems Mainframe at 02:00 hours on September 5th. They pulled and copied all the data regarding Dr. Otagawa. Then they deleted all of the files and documents in the folders. However, they left the folders intact, presumably to hide their actions."

"You think?" Mac said. Then he quickly put his finger to his lips and shushed Six before the droid spoiled it.

The data was taken on the same night the lab was supposedly trashed. Something smells funny here, and it is not just the mysterious goo in the Lab.

"Can you see who created the administrator

access?" Mac asked.

"Negative, Mac, the user account was created, the file removed and then the account was deleted. All in the span of a few seconds."

"So, a machine did it." Mac mumbled to himself.

The smell was really starting to get to Mac. He needed to get out of the room.

"Six, get me a 360 scan and some close-ups of the droids on the Gurneys. Also, I want a sample of that wonder goo there in the tank. Oh, and would you see if you can get some off the floor too? You know the dried stuff. Okay?" Mac ordered

"Roger," the droid said as it proceeded to carry out the list of instructions.

"Hold it," Mac said. Something interesting caught his eye. He noticed the corner of what appeared to be an old photograph sticking out from under a drawer. He walked over and looked closer. "Six, get me a picture of this."

Six complied. He walked over to where Mac was crouching and snapped a visual record.

"Thanks, Six. You can get ready for the 360 and get the samples collected." Mac slid his hands into a pair of nitrile evidence gloves. He gingerly reached out and pulled at the corner of the picture. Trying hard not to disturb anything he delicately pinched it with his fingertips and pulled. It came easily, and Mac slipped it into an empty evidence bag and stowed it in his pocket.

"Come with me, Fran" Mac ordered as he stood up and walked toward the door.

Fran followed Mac out into the Hall. He really wanted to be away from the smell, and the 360 degree scan would be spoiled if he and Fran were caught in it.

"Let me guess, Fran. The damage to the front doors happened on the 5th as well?" Mac queried, taking his hand away from his nose. The smell was not as bad out in the hallway.

"Checking...Checking...Confirmed, Agent McDonnell. The damage to the front doors did occur on the 5th," Fran said as she straightened her head back from the right tilt she had taken.

Mac never understood why the programmers added the head twitches to them when they access databases and interact with networked devices. It just seemed like a waste of command coding. Mac thought it was better to simply flash the different color LEDs that gave the droid's eyes that blue glow.

"For security purposes, we could not leave those windows untouched," Fran continued. "I apologize. However, we did keep the damaged material for you, should you require it."

"Go ahead and have that sent to RAD for processing," Mac said absently as he looked at the photo he had taken from the lab. It was of a young girl and a large dog. The little girl was smiling. She was definitely Asian. Her straight black hair and her dark eyes confirmed his suspicions. It looked like a happy picture. Mac turned the picture back over. He couldn't read the writing on the back. It looked like old Japanese or maybe Chinese.

"Task complete, Mac," Six said as he approached Mac and Fran.

"What does that say, Six?" Mac held the picture up to Six.

"Checking...Checking...Translation complete. It

reads, "Kiyoko age five," Six said. "Kiyoko means 'pure child' in old Japanese, Mac"

"Thanks, Six," Mac said. He turned to Fran. "Mean anything to you?"

"I have no data on that name, Agent McDonnell. Again, I apolog…" Fran stopped suddenly, and her head turned to the left.

Mac reached for his blaster.

"Delightful," Fran said suddenly, "Director Vance would like to meet you, Agent McDonnell. He has asked that I bring you to his office."

"How exciting," Mac said, mimicking the programmed excitement that Fran exuded at the request. "Lead the way."

"This way," Fran said. She started back toward the elevators.

Mac again hung back.

"Keep recording. I am very curious where this is going and I want to be able to review it later," Mac whispered over his shoulder.

"Roger," Six said again doing an excellent job of matching Mac's volume and tone.

Chapter 10

"Ichiro," Chi Chi said in her soft cheery tone. Her head inclined in the very image of a mother speaking to her beloved child. "Your father has guests. However, he is expecting you. Follow me please."

"Wait here," Ichiro said tersely to Gracie who was hovering behind him like a shadow in a green pantsuit. The tall woman nodded and then took up a position by the entrance to the outer office.

Ichiro followed his father's droid, Chi Chi, into the waiting office. Behind the machine's back, Ichiro sneered viciously. It was wearing a Japanese Kimono over its black proto-skin. The droid walked with the grace of a Japanese lady with short, hurried steps. Its plastic head covering was molded in a Japanese ceremonial hairstyle complete with Chopsticks which could be swapped out to match the different outfits it could wear.

Soon you ersatz maternal monster. The thought of her white plastic sculpted face sickened him. *How could he? How could he use mother's beautiful face to cover such an abomination and then as if to add insult to injury he even gave that thing mother's voice!*

Chi Chi opened the large imitation wood doors to her master's office.

"This way, Ichiro," she said as she motioned him through the open doorway.

He complied and walked briskly into the open office. Tohiro Takahaisu's office was almost a perfect circle. It took up one whole lobe of the 100th floor of the building. The floors above were the living quarters for the Takahaisu family, Ichiro included, and a handful of the elite executives.

Tohiro was sitting in his armchair by the receiving area to the left of his desk talking with two men who were seated on the receiving couch. They were chatting and laughing. His guests had serving droids with them standing off to the sides of the couch. One was an Italian job. Ichiro couldn't remember its original manufacturer. It was an older model. Not as twitchy as some of the newer ones but was severely limited in its services and range of motion. The other was a Takacorp Allure model. Which resembled Chi Chi in many respects. In fact, if Ichiro remembered correctly the Allures were the production versions of Chi Chi. A little less refined and Ichiro was thankful that his father had left his mother's face out of the production line options.

At least the bastard felt something was sacred.

Tohiro saw Ichiro approaching and stood up.

"Ah, Ichiro. Come over here. I have some gentlemen I would like you to meet," Tohiro said, motioning for his son to join them.

"Chi Chi I would like another cup of Coffee," Tohiro said and then he looked at his guests. "Would you gentlemen care for anything more?"

"No thank you," said the large balding man farthest from Tohiro.

"None for me," Said the skinny bird-like one as he set the cup and saucer carefully onto the table in front of him. Ichiro took careful note of the little man and his twitches.

"Just me then Chi Chi, *kudasai*" Tohiro said.

Let the language die, father. You could have just said "'please.'" The Japanese culture died when their dome collapsed fifty years ago, you old fool.

Chi Chi bowed her head at Tohiro's request and went to the minibar across the room.

"Mr. Peabody, Mr. Fitch. This is my son Takahaisu Ichiro" Tohiro said, clapping Ichiro on the shoulder.

"George Peabody," said the fat guy. His voice was deep, and his speech was a bit slurred by his accent. British if Ichiro remembered correctly.

"Philip Fitch," announced the little birdman. Another Brit, though his accent was cleaner and his enunciation sharp and crisp.

"A pleasure," Ichiro said, bowing carefully, never taking his eyes off of the two men.

Chi Chi returned and handed Tohiro a fresh cup of coffee and then remained at Tohiro's side. The movement drew Ichiro's eye.

Ichiro frowned at the visage of his mother standing behind his father. He scowled despite himself. The thought of the Chi Chi taking his dead mother's place twisted his stomach. His blood felt like it was boiling beneath his skin causing his arm to almost vibrate. It took every ounce of self-control to keep from drawing the neutralizer in his pocket and gun the doppelganger down. It was the sudden pop of his knuckle that brought him back. He forced his hand to unclench, giving it a little shake to make sure he hadn't hurt himself.

"Mr. Peabody and Mr. Fitch are the former owners of British Bio Technologies," Tohiro said. "They are in town finalizing the sale."

"Lord Fitch," The Allure interrupted. "Your appointment is approaching, you asked for a reminder."

"Ah, yes, My dear," The smaller of the two said. "Quite right. We should be on our way; don't you agree George?"

"Certainly, Philip," The rotund man answered as he stood. "Tohiro, we are thankful for your hospitality."

"It is I who should be thanking you two," Tohiro said to his departing guests. "This acquisition has gone exceedingly smoothly and now that the final details are completed, I think everyone is happy with the results."

"Quite, my good man, Quite" George said as he made his way toward the door, his droid in tow.

"Yes, Tohiro, and thank you for Persephone, she has been most helpful since my old one did a bunk on me," Fitch chimed in as he followed his larger comrade.

"My pleasure, Philip," Tohiro replied. "Oh, and George are you sure I can't offer you an Allure or maybe something with a little more firepower perhaps?"

No thank you, Tohiro. I'm happy with my Machini. They aren't as finicky as the newer droids, and it would take forever to find a decent data port app to update it with my preferences.

"If you change your mind, feel free to call," Tohiro said, bowing deeply to his guests. "I would consider it an honor."

"You will be the first one I call should the need arise," The fat man replied with a little bow.

Tohiro and Chi Chi followed them to the door, offering pleasantries and goodbyes. Once they had left Chi Chi closed the door behind them and the two of them headed toward Tohiro's desk near the bank of windows that ran along the back of the office.

Ichiro made his way over to his father's desk after grabbing himself a cup of coffee. It was a nice blend. He sipped at it as he approached his father's giant desk.

"Ichiro do you know why we purchased BBT?" his father asked as Ichiro approached. Tohiro's eyes were ablaze with excitement. They always got like that when he's about to wax philosophically about his vision for the company. "We are going to begin manufacturing replacement organs for people. For people who need them. And we are also going to be adapting their technology to several of our android production models to make them more efficient and broaden their uses. Just imagine it, my son, having life support droids that can provide emergency medical care, there on the scene, with the appropriate organs to keep people alive until they can get help. As ORF fluid was to synthetic muscles so will these organs be to our new Androids."

"You want to make them more 'human-like' than they already are!" Ichiro blurted incredulously.

Chi Chi drifted closer to Tohiro, who had taken to his chair with his back to the bank of windows. Her stress sensors must have gone through the roof with Ichiro's outburst. She was closing the gap to intercept a possible threat to Tohiro.

"Leave us you abomination," Ichiro spat at Chi Chi, "Be gone from my sight you cheap copy."

Ichiro's calm facade had shattered. Staring straight at Chi Chi he pointed behind himself toward the door.

Just like that stupid Uske, father is going to try and blur the line between Man and Machine. I will not let him commit these atrocities. I need to step up the plan.

Chi Chi looked from Ichiro to Tohiro. With the nod of Tohiro's head, Chi Chi turned toward the door.

Tohiro calmly watched as his Personal Assistant droid made her way toward the door. Ichiro paced vigorously back and forth in front of the desk. He was far too heated to stand still.

Chi Chi closed the door behind her and Tohiro looked upon his son. Ichiro saw pity in his father's eyes.

How dare that old fool pity me! How dare he!

"I thought I taught you better than that my son," Tohiro said, the disappointment thick in his voice.

"Mother taught me to be civil to 'people' of all status, Father," Ichiro replied, the heat of his anger blazed in his eyes. With an effort of sheer will he kept his tone civil, as he continued clipping each word precisely. "Chi Chi is a machine. And is thus exempt from Mother's etiquette, or have you forgotten that that *thing* is not your wife?" he continued while jabbing his finger at the closed door.

Tohiro sighed again. The old man shook his head and seemed to collect his thoughts. Ichiro waited, if not patiently. Finally, his father spoke again.

"Not a day goes by that I don't miss your mother," Tohiro replied. "Nothing I do or say will return her to us. I will admit that having Uske craft that faceplate in your mother's image might be painful for you. However, I would rather live the rest of my life looking into the image of your mother's face fused to a droid than to go without."

Ichiro scoffed angrily.

"Speaking of Uske, did you do as I asked?" Tohiro inquired.

"Yes, Father, I went to see Director Evens personally and asked for their help in locating Otagawa Uske," Ichiro replied. Ichiro resented the change in subject.

"You went personally?" Tohiro checked again.

"Yes, Father, I went myself. Per your instructions," Ichiro replied.

Tohiro stood. "*Habakarisama*, Ichiro," Tohiro replied, bowing to his son. He then turned and went to peer out the windows in his office.

Ichiro sneered again.

Stupid old fool.

"I want Uske found. We'll spare no expense," Tohiro called out over his shoulder.

"Shouldn't we be focusing on the prototype that he was working on?" Ichiro asked. "Uske has gone too far this time, Father. That prototype is Takacorp property."

"I would have thought that given your taste for human bodyguards you would understand the value of a friend, my son. Or have I underestimated your concept of the word friend?" Tohiro asked.

Ichiro scoffed, "I fear that things you underestimate, Father, will prove to be a greater disappointment," Ichiro replied coldly.

"Yes, I am sure," Tohiro snapped. "I want Uske found. No matter what has happened I will help my friend if he will let me. Above all, he is still my friend."

"The prototype represents billions of credits of research and development," Ichiro argued. "We can't let our senior engineers just walk off with company property. I mean, we aren't talking about keeping a simple calculator, Father."

"Uske is the real secret of our company, Ichiro," Tohiro said. "He has been the source of our major innovations for as long as I can remember. More than that he has been my friend. He was there for us when we lost your mother. With Kiyoko's illness reaching the advanced stages he will need me now more than ever," the older man said. "We must find him. Quickly."

"Do you truly think a droid kidnapped him, Father?" Ichiro asked.

"I think the evidence points to an attack. As to whether or not Uske left under his own power or whether some malicious entity has taken him I cannot say. We still can't rule out corporate espionage."

That's right you old fool, keep guessing. I can't wait to see your face when you learn the truth. Though by then it will be too late.

The door to the office opened and Chi Chi strode back into the room.

"Director Vance has brought the RAD agent to meet you, Master," Chi Chi said, "He claims that they were expected. However, I do not have an entry on your schedule corresponding to this appointment. Shall I admit him?"

"Yes, Chi Chi. Of course, by all means, send them in," Tohiro replied while making a waving motion to invite the new guests.

"I'll take my leave, Father," Ichiro said suddenly. "I have matters that require my attention."

"Will you be joining me for dinner this evening?" Tohiro asked.

"I apologize, Father, I am unable to attend due to a prior engagement," Ichiro responded.

"Pity…Another time then," Tohiro said.

Ichiro forced his face to a mask of stillness as he bowed. The very model of Japanese stoicism. It was tight, controlled, and empty. All the while, Ichiro's anger boiled just under the surface.

"Good day, Father," Ichiro said as he spun on his heels and walked briskly toward the door.

Chapter 11

Mac had expected to see a top-of-the-line droid standing outside of Tohiro Takahaisu's office. What he was not ready for was Gracie standing just inside the door.

She was wearing a different pantsuit. It was similar to the one from last night but this time it was a deep green fabric. Gracie was an amazon. She was a tall ebony princess with the heart of a lion and the conscience of a snake. The cold look she gave him sent chills down his spine. How he had ever fallen in love with a frigid bitch like her was beyond him. Love.

Milly. The mere mention of her name filled Mac with a warm glow. His mind pictured her beautiful face. *I miss Milly. I should have stayed in bed with her today. That's where I should be.*

Gracie didn't say a word. She just stood at her post. Mac and Six waited patiently while Vance talked to the Owner's PA, Chi Chi. Mac had taken special notice of Chi Chi. she was definitely one of Takacorp's elite custom models. It resembled an Allure, but it seemed much more refined. They even had it dressed in an old-school kimono.

"Gentlemen. Please wait here while I announce you," Chi Chi declared suddenly in a very cheerful tone. She had stepped into the office to let Mr. Takahaisu know Mac and Six were there to see him. Mac had not seen her come back into the room.

"Excellent," Vance said as he started for the door.

Mac jumped when the door to Takahaisu's office burst open almost clobbering Vance. The young man Mac had seen last night came storming out of the office. He seemed rather displeased. Ichiro Takahaisu, if Mac remembered correctly.

Gracie fell in behind Ichiro as he left the smaller outer office. Mac lost sight of them when the door to the elevators closed behind them.

"Please forgive Master Ichiro. He is a very busy young man," Chi Chi said with a motherly tone. In what Mac assumed was a programmed response to similar situations.

She has custom human interactions as well. Nice.

"Ichiro," Six inquired. "Is Japanese for Firstborn son. Correct?"

"You are correct, sir," Chi Chi replied. "The Japanese language is part of Takahaisu family heritage and Master Tohiro strives to preserve as much of that culture as he can."

"Shall we?" Vance interrupted as he held the door open. "If we let the droids continue their little farce of a conversation, we'll be here all day. Let's not keep the boss waiting."

"Of course, Mr. Vance. This way gentleman," Chi Chi said as she moved forward through the open door.

Mac took a second look at Director Vance as he followed Chi Chi into Mr. Takahaisu's office. Vance was a fifty-something pig. A corporate leach that was somehow able to weasel his way into the upper echelons of the corporate ladder. Robert Vance was the image of the fallen frat boy. His ample gut extended over his expensive slacks drawing his shirt tight. He had his top button undone and his tie pulled loose. His face echoed his body, his jowls quivered when he talked, and his cheeks resembled one of the pictures Mac had seen of the now-extinct chipmunk. What was left of his hair formed a salt and pepper circlet around the back of his head. Leaving most of his scalp exposed.

He was both pompous and arrogant. Mac recalled the diatribe Vance had unleashed on them in his office. Vance just kept talking and talking about how he was the heart and backbone of the operations of Takacorp. He was quick to share his opinion that Dr. Otagawa was to blame for what had happened. Vance thought that some droid the good doctor was working on had malfunctioned and stolen the doctor for some twisted end.

Thou doth protest too much. Wait. Is that the Shakespeare quote? Protest too much? I'll have to remember to ask Six later on.

Mac surveyed the spacious office. It was almost a complete circle. The office was situated in one of the outer lobes of the Tower. The owner and CEO, Tohiro Takahaisu was standing in front of the bank of windows that made up the far wall of the office behind his desk. He was of average height a little shorter than Mac. His suit was exquisitely pressed. Despite Tohiro's expensive attire, he had a warm presence about him.

"Welcome, Welcome!" Tohiro said. "Thank you for coming so quickly."

"You wanted me to bring them up Takahaisu sama," Vance said while he flourished his arms for all the world like he was wearing a cape.

"Yes, Robert. Thank you," Tohiro said. "Is that a D6 I see?"

"A D6-J22 unit 196," Chi Chi said. "Sold to Rogue Automaton Division six months and twenty-seven days. Invoice 77890004RAD."

Six and Mac both stared at Chi Chi.

"Tohiro Takahaisu, may I present Agent McDonnell of the RAD and his Tactical Field Escort, Six," Vance said.

"Glorious," Tohiro said as he scowled at Vance's display. For a moment Mac thought he had imagined it as Tohiro's welcoming smile was back an instant later. *Even Tohiro doesn't like Vance.*

"The D6 was always one of my favorites," Tohiro continued. "You know Uske was the one who got the Six PCEs to function properly. The boys in R and D were struggling with it for almost nine months. Finally, they consulted with Uske. He took one look at the schematic and found the issue. He said the secret was forcing the first processor to run the automated and regulatory functions and forbidding the other processors from touching those functions. The R and D people were trying to let the PCE's work in concert, you see the problem was other PCE's for some reason kept usurping the primary PCE's control over those operations and causing all kinds of havoc."

"I didn't know that," Mac admitted.

Tohiro approached Six.

"May I?" Tohiro gestured to Six. "It looks like you have made some modifications."

Mac shrugged. Tohiro pulled out a small black object from his pocket and pointed it at Six. It appeared similar to Mac's Command override module but was black rather than silver. The device was a little bigger and had more than just one button.

"Open," Tohiro said as he pressed one of the buttons on his module.

"Confirmed," Six said in his command voice. With the command, all of Six's access panels, control shroud, and weapon systems opened to expose all of the delicate parts contained inside.

Tohiro pulled at the side of his Command module and a screen slid open much like Mac's Global.

"Okay, that's cool," Mac said despite himself.

"Oh, this?" Tohiro held up the device. "Agent McDonnell, was it?"

Mac nodded as he drifted a little closer.

"This is my executive command module," Tohiro continued. "I can use this to access all of Takacorp's products. Uske had originally meant for it to be sold to departments like yours and NTPD and some military applications, but in the end, it was too powerful a tool. So, he made this one for me and then scrapped the project. I'm a bit of technophile if you haven't noticed."

Tohiro kept his eyes on the little screen. every now and then he made little comments to himself.

"Oh, you've been repaired recently," Tohiro said surprised. "Were you the unit that was damaged by the intruder at our facility last night?"

"Affirmative," Six replied.

"It looks like you suffered some serious physical damage," Tohiro said. "Ah, here might be your problem. Your emergency shielding response is set too low."

"What?" Mac asked.

"Ah. Some of the settings are wrong," Tohiro announced. "Here, this will speed things up and it will cut down on some of its processing time. I can also increase the weapon response time. So, you'll be able to draw a little faster."

Mac started to say something but stopped and waited for Tohiro to finish.

"There...All done. Close," Tohiro ordered. Six complied. Mac had to admit the droid's panels and weapons returned to their hidden positions a lot faster than they had opened.

"Mr. Takahaisu. I appreciate the fix" Mac interjected. "However, to get back on track, is there anything you can tell me about Dr. Otagawa that might be helpful? Like what he was working on."

"I'm not sure what his most recent project was. He has enjoyed free rein for quite some time now. Though looking back, I probably should have taken a greater interest in what he was working on. I'm afraid I have been a bad friend. Takacorp has been purchasing a number of smaller tech companies to broaden our product offering and improve existing ones. I have been a little distracted. I almost miss the days when my father ran the company and Uske and I could play in the R and D lab all day. Ah well," Tohiro continued. "Change is the only constant in the universe is it not?"

"Quite right, sir," Vance spoke up suddenly. Everyone turned to look at him. His sycophantic smile disappeared under the scrutiny, and he walked over to the minibar and poured himself a drink.

"There was a large tank in Dr. Otagawa's lab. Any idea what that was or what he kept in it?" Mac asked.

"Could have been a new mix of ORF fluid, or something completely new. I don't really know," Tohiro replied his warm facade was beginning to slip with genuine concern. "Do you think this is connected with his work?"

"At this point I can't say Mr. Takahaisu. Have you had any droids go missing recently? Any prototypes that have disappeared?" Mac queried.

"Now that you mentioned it. Chi Chi had mentioned a prototype that went missing from R and D," Tohiro said. "Chi Chi reviews the financials and compares them with the physical inventory done every week. She brought the discrepancy to my attention. She let me know that a couple of line items in Uske's budget were not accounted for. One of which was a concept production of a new model. I know this because it was filed under the account heading that he and I used on our top-secret projects."

"Do you have specs on this concept?" Mac asked. Getting a little more agitated.

He knew? When was he planning on telling us? Corporate jerks are circling the wagons. I need to remember to ask Six what hell a wagon is. I should stop using old slang terms when I don't know what they mean.

"I'm sorry, Agent McDonnell. I do not. Uske was cautious. Any data on that unit would be in his files which only top directors have access to."

"Would those be the files that have mysteriously been penetrated and erased?" Mac said letting his sarcastic sense of humor get the better of him.

"I'm afraid so, Agent McDonnell," Tohiro replied. His tone had become more somber. "Chi Chi has kept me abreast of the intrusion into our system. We have since tripled our security protocols. Not that it will make much difference to what has happened."

"Mr. Takahaisu since we are on the subject is there anything, no matter how small, that might strike you as important?" Mac asked, feeling a little flustered.

"Nothing that comes to mind. I will be sure to contact you if we happen to find anything on our end," Tohiro replied. "Though if I might ask, Agent McDonnell, please find my friend. Please."

Mac met the older man's eyes. *His concern is genuine; however, he is hiding something too.*

"We'll do our best Mr. Taka—" Mac was interrupted mid-sentence by his Global. He pulled it out of his pocket. The outer screen read 'teddy.' "—haisu. Would you please excuse me?"

Mac hit the accept button and moved the phone to his ear.

"Hello?" Mac said as he walked away from the group.

"Mac! It's me. Can't talk on this line it's not secure," Teddy said hurriedly.

"What? I can't really talk now," Mac replied.

"I don't want to talk on this line. It's not secure. I found something interesting about that thing you wanted me to look at. You know that thing."

"Really?"

"Yes, you need to get over here and take a look," Teddy said with nervous excitement. "You're not going to believe it."

"All right, I'll be there soon," Mac responded.

"Later!" Teddy said.

Mac disconnected the call and turned back to the group.

"Sorry about that," he said.

"Will there be anything else, Agent McDonnell," Vance asked.

"No, that should cover it. We have a lot of security camera footage to go through and I need to see if we can reconstruct the data we collected in Dr. Otagawa's lab," Mac said.

"This way gentleman," Chi Chi said as she gestured toward the door.

The group started toward the door. In mid-stride Mac stopped and turned around.

"One more thing Mr. Takahaisu," Mac said.

"Yes, Agent McDonnell?"

"Who is Kiyoko?"

Chapter 12

Mac jabbed the elevator control button again. Teddy's stubborn device still refused to move.

"Pressing the button repeatedly will not result in the elevator arriving sooner," Six said in his oh-so-pleasant manner.

"Well maybe not, but it sure makes me feel better," Mac retorted, punching the button yet again. "Damn it. Where is he?"

"Scanning…Scanning…Found. I have located Teddy's illegal droid. However, I am unable to locate Theodore," Six said.

Mac's face went slack. "Oh no!" he gasped.

Mac pulled his blaster and bolted toward the stairs at the far end of the empty warehouse.

"Mac, wait!" Six called out.

He reached the stairs and kicked open the door. He took a tactical position and then proceeded up the stairs. He could hear Six's heavy steps following behind him.

Mac charged up the stairwell. He used the railing to tighten his turns and propel him.

"No. No. No. No. No!" Mac kept repeating. "No damn it. No."

Mac slammed into the door at the top of the stairs. It gave easier than he had expected. His momentum carried him beyond where his balance could hold and he went down. He tucked and rolled across his back landing in a crouch. He stood up quickly and leveled his pistol at the large room.

Mac's gaze fell on the droid Caroline's back. Her body contorted awkwardly, on her knees, at the elevator's gated opening.

"Teddy!" Mac called out as he kept his blaster trained on Caroline's human-looking back.

He received no answer. The stairwell behind him groaned heavily as Six made his way up.

"Teddy! Answer me, it's Mac," Mac called again keeping his eyes on the motionless droid.

Mac advanced into the loft. He made his way toward the motionless droid.

"Caroline, respond," Mac ordered. "Respond!"

Nothing. The droid remained kneeling and motionless.

"Caroline!" Mac ordered as he increased his volume. "Respond."

As he approached, he saw that Caroline's right arm was smashed by the elevator. It looked like she had reached through the safety gate into the car near where the controls were and gotten caught when the elevator went down. The lip of the elevator car's opening was bent up as she apparently resisted the elevator's downward progression. It dragged her downward.

"Teddy," Mac yelled. "Teddy, can you hear me? Six!"

"Mac," Six called out as he entered the room. His police markers were shining, and his weapons were out. "Mac, are you injured?"

"I'm fine, Six," Mac said. "I know why Teddy didn't show up on your scan. He is in the elevator."

"Yes. Your hypothesis is quite sound. The

surrounding metal superstructure would cause sufficient interference with my sensors," Six said causally. "At this range, I am now detecting a faint thermal signature from the elevator. "

"Teddy!" Mac gasped. "Is he alive?"

"Unclear, Mac," Six replied. "I will need to get closer to provide a more accurate assessment of Theodore's physical status."

Six approached the elevator shaft and peered down onto the top of the old elevator. He looked carefully at Caroline's motionless form hunched over at the edge of the shaft and then down at the top of the elevator car itself.

"It would appear the Elevator mechanism is jammed, Mac," Six said in his pleasant tone.

"You think?" Mac snapped sarcastically. He examined Caroline's mangled arm and the elevator car. The top of the elevator was just enough past the floor that Mac was unable to see inside.

"Affirmative," Six continued. "The illegal droid Caroline appears to have burned out the motor attempting to stop the elevator.

"You figure that out all by yourself there, buddy?" Mac asked snidely.

"Mac, I have detected what I believe to be a heartbeat coming from the elevator car," Six said suddenly.

"Really!" Mac asked unable to hide his surprise.

Mac moved closer to the shaft and looked through the ruined safety gate down at the top of the elevator car.

"Can we get him out, Six?" Mac asked.

"I have called for backup and emergency crews, Mac," Six replied. "The structural integrity of the elevator car is compromised by the damage. That coupled with the age of the elevator makes it unwise for me to step out on the car roof. We could inadvertently send it crashing to the ground. Effectively finishing the job the illegal droid Caroline started. Emergency crews are on route. They will arrive shortly."

"Thanks, Six," Mac said. "What's their ETA?"

"Based on average response time and distance from the substation I would estimate them to arrive within the next fifteen minutes."

"Okay." Mac's shoulders slumped as he continued to stare at Teddy. "It will have to do."

After a few moments he sighed and turned to Six. "I guess we have to at least try to preserve the crime scene. Can you get me a 360 of Teddy's place?"

"Affirmative," Six replied as he turned around to carry out the task.

Mac turned back to the elevator.

"What did you have to tell me?" he whispered.

"What did you say, Mac?" Six said. "I'm having trouble hearing you. I'll run a diagnostic on my Audio input systems to make sure there are no anomalies."

"Don't bother, I was talking to Teddy, Six," Max told the Android.

"He can't hear you, Mac. My preliminary scans indicate that Theodore is unconscious," Six said plainly in his too-pleasant voice. "I would estimate his wounds similar to Miss Milly's. However, I would suspect that Teddy might have additional injuries due to the amount of property damage visible about the crime scene."

"Thanks for the tip you big lug. Now, go make yourself useful," Mac retorted.

Six turned and continued about his task.

The emergency team and backup arrived in short order and with the help of two maintenance droids, they were able to extract Teddy. He was heavily bruised about the neck and shoulders, but he was alive. He had a terrible gash on the back of his head where he collided with the floor of the Elevator car. *He'll never get the bloodstain out of the wood flooring.*

"Do you have Teddy's sec cam footage downloaded yet?"

"Affirmative," Six replied. "It took me a moment to get the warrant permitting me to penetrate his security protocols. It came through a few minutes ago and I have downloaded all of his records on file and have marked the sections of the video that are pertinent to this investigation. I have uploaded them to the RAD server for Agent Stark and have forwarded a copy to your workstation."

"Thanks, Six," Mac said as he surveyed the Damage to Teddy's place. Teddy's fancy workstation was smashed including that new storage cube.

"Six, why don't you go meet the Evidence team. Call me when they get here," Mac said while he watched the Medical techs move Teddy toward the stairs at the far side of the loft. Teddy was strapped to the med gurney with all kinds of straps and bindings. They had to make sure he was immobile until they could be certain there was no damage to Teddy's spinal cord. Teddy reminded Mac of one of the old mummies he had seen on the vids at the museums. *Speaking of something that should be in a museum.* "Oh, and contact Ziggy. Have him tell Agent Stark that we have another prophet victim."

"Affirmative," Six replied.

Mac watched as Six helped the Med techs carry

Teddy down the stairs to the waiting Medical van for his trip to the Hospital.

"I'm sorry, Teddy. I never meant for this to happen," Mac whispered to the now empty room. "If I had thought you were in danger, I wouldn't have left you here with that toy you made. Ah, Teddy."

Mac stood up and took a few steps toward Teddy's ruined workstation. His foot landed on something hard that he hadn't seen. He stepped back and knelt down to investigate the object.

It was a small medallion-like object complete with a cord attached. Mac pulled a pen from his pocket and turned the device over. It had a single button. The button was cracked and jammed up under the housing. Like it had been depressed really hard.

Her command override link. Teddy wasn't as stupid as he looked. He was wearing her override link around his neck.

"But in the end it didn't help you, did it?" Mac asked rhetorically.

Mac thought for a moment.

"Teddy, what could stop the command override link from working?" Mac asked as he turned to look around the disheveled room.

Mac was startled by his vibrating Global. He pulled the phone from his pocket and looked at the outer screen.

He saw Milly's Picture.

Mac immediately pulled the big screen open. Mac could see her beautiful face on the screen. Just the sight of her was a huge relief.

"Hey, baby. How are you?" Mac said attempting to sound cheery.

"I'm good," Milly said. "I'm still a little sore but that

injector pen you gave me cleared up most of the bruising."

"That's good to hear," Mac said.

"Sorry to call you at work. I was just wondering if you were going to come by for dinner."

"Sorry, baby," Mac replied. "I would love to, but there has been another victim of the prophet virus."

"Oh no." Milly said,

"It was Teddy, Milly," Mac admitted.

"Your cousin Teddy?" Milly said surprised. "Oh, Mac, I'm so sorry."

"Yeah."

"Is he?" Milly started. "You know…"

"He's hurt pretty bad. But they think he'll make it. They are concerned about his spinal cord. It would appear the prophet has a knack for strangling its victims."

"At least he is alive," Milly said trying hard to sound reassuring.

"Yeah," Mac stammered. "I got him involved and now he is unconscious on his way to the hospital possibly paralyzed from the neck down. All because I selfishly asked him to help me."

"Mac! Mac, listen to me. You are not responsible," Milly charged. "You couldn't have known that droid was going to get to Teddy. Mac, you couldn't have known?"

"What droid?"

"The poncho droid."

"The suspect?" Mac asked.

"Yeah. That droid I saw, the one from last night. That's the one that got to Teddy, right?" Milly asked.

"No. It was Teddy's custom companion droid, it attacked him," Mac said shaking his head. A thought was jumping around in his mind, and he couldn't quite get ahold of it.

"Mac, how did Teddy's sex bot get infected if that other droid wasn't there?" Milly asked.

"Great question, baby. I'm going to find out," Mac said. "Baby, you are best. Can I call you later?"

"Yeah, that's *fine*," Milly said. He could see her shoulders slump and hear the sadness in her voice. She even said the dreaded "*'fine'*" which meant that it was everything but fine.

"I'll try and come by tonight, okay? Besides, I left you my backup piece. It's in your room under your pillow," Mac said flashing her a smile.

Milly smiled back weakly.

"Sure," Milly said. "Mac…Just be careful, okay."

"I will. And leave Rosie in the closet," Mac said. "I'll see you when I can. Love you, baby."

"Bye," Milly said and then the screen winked out and displayed the call ended animation.

Mac closed the screen and continued to wrestle with that wayward thought. Something Milly had said and this whole event didn't add up. There was something Mac had missed.

"I need to clear my head," he told the room.

Mac stood up and walked back over to Teddy's ruined workstation.

"I'll get this guy Teddy. One way or another," Mac promised.

His Global buzzed again. Mac checked it. It was Six.

"About time," Mac said.

Chapter 13

"Bag and tag everything at the workstation. Including the data cube," Mac said. "See if you guys can reconstruct what he was working on. Would you?"

"Sure thing, Mac," Cliff replied as he continued tapping on his arm pad. "Hey, Mac, why did I get a delivery of three containers of shattered safety glass from Takacorp?"

"Oh yeah, that's evidence for an emergency case the director has us on. It's a favor for some of the big wigs at Takacorp. If you could have one of your droids go through it and see if they can find anything out of the ordinary, I would appreciate it."

"No problem," Cliff said dubiously. "Oh, ah, you should really lock the doors to your cruiser, Mac, anybody could get in and leave whatever they want in the passenger seat."

"Thanks, Cliff," Mac said after he caught Cliff's wink.

Cliff looked up from his pad. "Is there anything else you can think of Mac?"

"Not at the moment," Mac admitted, "Make sure you leave what you find on the public drive so I can look at it later would you?"

"No problem, Mac. I had heard that Stark is handling the Prophet case," Cliff said. "I'll make sure it's available to you and Six."

Cliff kept typing info into his arm pad. Mac was a little jealous of Cliff's Global-on-steroids workstation. It had a much bigger touch screen and an available thumb stick all in a fairly compact unit that Cliff wore on his forearm. However, in a fight, the thing would totally be in the way.

Mac started to ask him another question when they were interrupted by an evidence drone. About the size of a large dog, but the resemblance ended there. Sleek and compact they were an amalgam of evidence collection equipment bolted to a suspensor orb. The orb was powered like everything else in the domes by a CAC battery at its center. The orb's CAC battery gave off its characteristic blue glow. The glowing orb was surrounded by the drone's different equipment: cameras, spectral analyzers, pressure instruments, and atmospheric processors. They were immensely helpful at collecting enormous amounts of data within a given area, like a crime scene. The NTPD had the same units for their evidence teams.

"Shall we start the sweep of the building now?" The drone inquired in its synthetic computer-controlled monotone. Due to the lack of extra space, they were given rudimentary linguistic functions. So, they were not as polished as the TFEs.

"Go ahead," Cliff said to the robot hovering just behind him. Then he looked up from his arm pad and spoke directly to Mac. "Be careful, Mac. Things are getting kind of scary out here with this Prophet thing going around. I just came from a doctor's office where his own surgical droid did an unscheduled procedure on the doctor himself."

"What? What was this?"

"A doctor, Mac. The guy's name was Brighton, David J. Brighton," Cliff said soberly. "It was nasty, man. He was cut to ribbons and parts of him had been cut out. Dissected alive. It almost looked like he was tortured by the thing."

"Ouch," Mac said at the thought.

"Earlier today. Stark was called in and I was sent to collect the evidence. It looks like another Prophet, Mac. cog was blank and everything. Who would have thought that a surgical droid could be infected with a virus? If it wasn't so scary it would be one for the record books. I mean it's getting crazy out here. Be careful."

"I will, Cliff," Mac replied. "I most certainly will. I've had my ass handed to me by this thing once already. It's Stark's problem now."

"Yeah, sure, Mac," Cliff said. "Go on. My team and I have this covered."

Mac looked around at the empty streets surrounding Teddy's building. He turned back to Cliff. "You aren't here by yourself, are you?"

"Nope, Spitz is here." Clift looked back up from his pad just long enough to point out a young woman standing in front of a RAD cruiser just like Mac's.

Spitz, a blonde woman with a severe glower nodded back at Mac. Mac liked Spitz she was a solid agent.

Mac nodded back. Spitz then turned and said something to her TFE, who was busy extracting itself from the cruiser.

All right, Cliff and the team had backup so Mac should get a move on. "Six!" he yelled over the cacophony of evidence data drones moving in and out of Teddy's building.

"Roger."

"Ready the cruiser," Mac yelled.

"Roger!" Six replied.

Mac waited patiently as his cruiser pulled around front. He took a moment and waved to Spitz as she was walking into Teddy's. She nodded again but kept walking. Then he put his hand on the doorframe and slipped into his seat.

"Let's go, Six I need to clear my head," Mac ordered.

"Destination?" The droid queried.

"Get us on to the 270 loop and drive," Mac said.

"Affirmative, Mac," Six replied.

The door slid closed, and the cruiser started forward. Being chauffeured around was one of the perks of having a TFE. Mac liked the extra time to think. It didn't take long for Six to get them through the tunnel and into the new dome. Before long they were up on the highway. The 270 loop formed a great ring around the new dome. It also provided a connection to the inter-dome tunnels and the External gateways that lead out of the city. It got its name from an older Highway that used to run along the same basic path. It formed part of a large highway ring that ran along the outskirts of the city that once stood where New Trinity stands now. Mac used to remember the name but now he couldn't think of what it was, and Mac was in no mood to hear an hour-long lecture from Six on the subject, so he let the question go.

Mac looked over to the other seat in the cruiser. There was a canvas bag lying in it. Mac smiled. Cliff was damn good. He reached out and touched the bag. The canvas felt rough under his fingers. He pulled at the bag. The bag refused to move. Its own weight kept it in position.

Good. It's in there.

Satisfied that his recent acquisition was in fact safely tucked away in its bag, Mac figured it was time to get down to business.

"I need my workstation, Six," Mac called out. He waited patiently while his terminal swung into position in front of him. He tapped the screen to activate it. He logged in and began moving through screens. Mac first checked his bank account to see if his payroll check had been deposited. It had. Which was a relief to him. Not that there had ever been any doubt, but Mac had seen the case files from a Level 2 investigation where a hacker had used a bookkeeping drone to funnel payroll checks into a numbered account and then released the funds to a clanker which then left the domes. The credits were never recovered and ever since that day Mac had been a bit worried about a repeat within the RAD payroll.

Dick has it under control. Now back to work.

"Six. List out all of the Data we have so far," Mac ordered.

"On which case Mac?"

"Both of them," Mac said, "I can't get over the feeling that they are connected somehow."

"Based on the data we have collected so far. There is a 62.8913 percent chance that the occurrences are related on more than just a circumstantial level," Six explained.

"Hey, since you are soooo smart and such, why don't you query the system and find out if we have any other sec cam footage of our intruder," Mac said sardonically. "While you are at it pull the sec cam footage from Teddy's."

"Roger, Mac," Six replied. "Checking…

Checking... Checking... Checking."

"Just tell me when you've found something okay," Mac interrupted. "You don't need to tell me every little process that is going on. I thought we had gotten past that."

"Roger." A few moments later the droid followed with, "I have found twelve possible instances where the suspect's pixelated image has crossed security cameras in the last two weeks including the incident involving Milly and our incident yesterday."

"Interesting."

"Mac, another interesting factor has presented itself," Six said.

"Yeah, what's that?" Mac played with the data icons on the touch screen in front of him. Swirling them around in circular patterns.

"Nine out of the Twelve incidents have taken place in Takacorp facilities," Six replied. "That is a three to one ratio."

"Now that is interesting, isn't it?" Mac said. "Have there been the same number of Prophet attacks?"

"There have been more," Six stated. "There have been twenty-one suspected Prophet cases. Most have been industrial class and companion class units. The case was assigned to Agent Stark last month after the first case was recorded. A companion droid of a prominent political aide strangled its owner."

"Really?" Mac asked.

"Yes, Mac," Six replied cheerfully. "The ratio shifts again when the full total of droids believed to be infected are sorted by their manufacturer. It becomes five Takacorp to one non-Takacorp."

Mac sighed heavily.

"That was rhetorical, wasn't it," Six asked tentatively, well as tentatively as his cheerful responses would allow.

"Yeah, yeah it was," Mac replied. "The good news is you caught it. So, we're making progress."

"The intricacies of human vocal communication are far more complex than my initial assessments have indicated," Six explicated. "I have made numerous field updates to my speech and interaction protocols, and I still find errors in my conversational dynamic with you. If it were not for the errors that I have encountered while trying to converse with the RAD technicians, I would have concluded long ago that the errors inherent to our conversations lie within your conversational archetypes rather than my linguistic programming."

Mac scoffed.

"I think that is quite possibly the most human thing you have said, Six," Mac stated dryly. "Albeit was drowning in a machine's interpretation of the conversation. I believe it was, in fact, very human of you."

"I do not follow this line of reasoning, Mac, please explain."

"You said you were looking for a way to blame the problem on me," Mac said. "Blaming others for perceived shortcomings whether true or false is a very human activity. We do the blaming thing all the time."

"I have not studied this line of behavior," Six said. "I will add it to my downtime research request file"

"You do that, Six," Mac said. "However, at the moment we have more pressing issues."

"Roger, Mac," Six replied. "What shall we focus our attention on now?"

"Well, we need to try and find Dr. Otagawa," Mac said. "Where is the footage from Takacorp, specifically from the shattering of their front windows?"

"I am pulling up that footage for you now. I have condensed to footage to follow the assailant through the Takacorp facility."

"Thanks, Six," Mac said as he watched the vid. He jumped to the end of the footage, trying to get a glimpse of the item that smashed the windows. The vid clearly shows a droid-like blur running through the lobby. The droid enters the lobby from the elevators. It heads straight for the doors and then it proceeds to smash through them. Not completely out of character for a malfunctioning droid, but it all still felt strange to Mac.

Droid operating systems are built using certain defined procedures. Because the droids must interact with buildings and devices that were designed for humans to use, they have to function in similar ways. Hence most droids have two arms, two legs, and so forth. It also meant that the machines needed to follow basic etiquette or guidelines when it comes to interacting with their environments. Things like using doors and driving on the correct side of the road.

Most droids, even malfunctioning ones, will still follow those guidelines to a certain point. Mac couldn't put his finger on it, but his gut was telling him that the droid not using the door to escape was important.

"Hey, Six, in the other sec cam footage. Is there any other instance of a Prophet droid failing to use a door? Like the Takacorp window vid," Mac asked.

"Checking...Checking...Checking...Negative, Mac. The Takacorp escape is the only instance where the suspect has been recorded exiting in that fashion," the machine replied.

Mac grunted.

At first glance, it looked just like the droid that had handed down that spectacular beating last night. However, the more Mac looked at the footage he couldn't help but feel that something was off. The droid was wearing a yellow poncho, but it wasn't all pixelated like the other vids they had. Following the path of the droid as it moved through the building. It started in Otagawa's lab. It smashed through the door and went to the elevator. It then moved through the lobby to smash through the front doors. He kept spinning the vid back and forth. Back and forth.

Though all of the manipulation he was doing on his touchpad was causing his wrist to ache again. He fished two more IB tabs out of his coat pocket. He ripped open their pouches and choked them down. He looked at the empty wrappers in his hand and an idea hit him in the face. "Wait. Hey, Six was the good Doctor taking any medications?"

"Checking…Checking…Negative, Mac," The droid replied. "His health profile does not contain a list of active medications. However, it does list an emergency contact name. It is a name that we have seen before Mac."

"Who's that, Six?"

"On Dr. Otagawa's Emergency contact form he has listed an Otagawa Kiyoko."

"Hm…Hey, Six do you think it's the daughter from the photo? The one Tohiro Takahaisu told us about this afternoon?" Mac asked.

"I calculate a 98 percent chance that is the case Mac," Six replied.

"Well, that's good to know," Mac said. "Do you have an address?"

"Affirmative, Mac," Six replied, if the droid had possessed lips Mac would have sworn it was smiling. "Oh, and Mac, having reexamined the data, I have calculated an 83.5829 percent chance that your assertion about the cases being related is correct."

"I feel soooo much better now that you, 83.58 percent was it, agree with me," Mac replied with enough sarcasm to choke someone.

"83.5829 percent, Mac."

"Sorry, my mistake," Mac said facetiously. "Well let's get this over with. I was hoping to stop by Milly's tonight."

"Roger."

Chapter 14

Mac recognized the central district right away. It was marked by its parks and railed walkways. It was by far the prettiest district in the New Trinity. Takacorp tower sat at the northern edge of it. Had it been anywhere else its size would have cast a shadow onto the park. The planners and the politicians had decided that it would be bad form to spoil the only natural light.

Forest Park was the only place in the big dome that had real sunlight. In the center of the largest dome's roof sat several skylight sections. They were specifically engineered to allow the natural sun through the dome. Beneath each of the great shafts of natural light was a park filled with trees and grass and other living plant life. Eight smaller skylights surrounded a larger octagonal one that rested at the center of the domed ceiling. The scatterings of grass and natural trees dubbed Forest Park was the closest thing to an actual forest that remained in the continental United States.

The trees that grew within the park needed the natural sunlight to survive. It was clear from the initial horticultural experiments conducted in the first test dome. The artificial lighting that nourished the acres and acres of food crops grown deep beneath domes that compose the city was not enough to sustain full-grown trees.

They continued along Forest Park's outer drive till

they reached a section of expensive-looking houses. Six turned the cruiser left, off of the main parkway and on deeper into the pricey neighborhood. All of the bigwigs lived in the central district.

The residential area was marked by large multi-story dwellings, all crammed onto small manageable lots. Most were single family homes though the occasional upscale condo or apartment tower was tucked in here and there. All of these properties had one thing in common. They were owned by the wealthy elite of New Trinity. Council members, corporate officers, and business owners, all called this section home.

"Looks like the Otagawas have done well for themselves," Mac said, while reminding himself not to gape at the neighborhood they were currently driving through.

"Affirmative, Mac," Six replied. "According to Takacorp financial documents Dr. Otagawa made a substantial salary, and he also receives a royalty for every unit sold containing his ORF motor system. He has made to date more than—"

"Wait. Don't tell me. It will just depress me."

"Roger," Six said. Six stopped the cruiser in front of the number Seventy-two Worthington Way. The three-story building sat dark and ominous on the block of expensive homes. The windows had all been switched to opaque to blot out the streetlights and hide the inhabitants.

Mac's door slid open at Six's silent command and Mac slipped from his seat. He stepped out onto the street and scanned the block. There was a construction crew finishing their day a few houses down. Why anyone would have torn down one of those beautiful homes and built some modernized plastic crate was beyond him. The crew had a golem on site. Squat, heavy lifting machine used in demolition and construction.

Golems were part of the few hybrid control-system-run machines on the market. Hybrid control meant that the machine had a manual control cockpit in addition to its android brain. The cockpit, located in the chest, gives the pilot control of the golem for complex tasks. The golem also has an autonomous mode that made them great for demolition and excavation. Something about the great yellow monstrosity gave Mac the chills.

Six's exit from the cruiser drew Mac's attention. He watched the giant Android lumber around the vehicle. Six walked with such purpose, such confidence. Mac almost envied the droid's programming. No movement was wasted. It was precisely guided by one of his PCEs.

He's just a droid.

He turned his attention back to the dark house ahead of them,

"Are you getting anything?"

"I'm experiencing some form of interference that I have never encountered, Mac," Six replied.

"That's weird," Mac said. "Can you filter it out?"

"Negative," Six replied, "The interference seems to be localized to the building before us."

"What does that tell you, Six?" Mac started toward the front door of Dr. Otagawa's house.

"I do not understand the question, Mac. It is a house, and I can't interface with the home's Persona," Six replied. "It is unable to tell me anything."

Mac shook his head and laughed to himself. It was very unusual that Six couldn't interface with the home's Persona. The fancier homes all have their own pseudo consciousness called a persona which regulated the functions of the home and linked all of the utilities within it. Six should have been able to sync up with it. The fact that there was some sort of interference was not the best of signs. However, it was definitely a big neon sign reading "'Clue found here!'"

"It tells me there is something in there that doesn't want to be found," Mac told his child-like partner.

"An interesting conclusion, Mac," Six replied. "I am intrigued by the human mechanism of deduction, and how it relates to criminal investigations."

The two bipeds approached the porch and ascended the broad stone steps.

"How would you like to proceed, Mac?"

"I guess we knock,"

Mac approached the door. He raised his hand, made a fist, and reached for the door which gave way suddenly before he could strike it. The door swung open, and a young woman stood in the doorway with a surprised look on her face. Mac stared dumbly for a second before his brain worked through his own surprise and started functioning again.

The sickly-looking young woman stepped back upon discovering the two callers and looked down at her feet to the mechanical dog wearing a bright pink bow around its neck. It appeared to have been joining her in her egress.

"You're a lot of help," she said sarcastically to the dog.

She was greeted with an annoyed whine from the mechanical animal.

"Kiyoko Otagawa, I presume?" Mac recovered, slapping on his most winning smile.

"Who wants to know?" The young woman said over the dog's ever-increasing growl.

"I'm Agent McDonnell, from RAD," Mac shouted over the dog's growl as he flashed his badge.

"Can it, Annie!" the young woman shouted at the dog, which abruptly ceased her sonic posturing. "But keep your eyes peeled."

Mac looked around.

"May we come in?" he asked. "I think it would be safer to talk inside."

She considered his words and after a brief glance up the street she seemed to agree.

"Oh, yeah come on in," The young woman stepped aside. Mac and Six entered the foyer.

The house was beautiful. The place was full of wood paneling and decorative inlays. Mac would have wagered a month's salary that the wood was real. Just beyond the foyer was the main staircase leading up to the higher floors. The banister looked to be real wood as well. It had to be more than a hundred years old. Possibly two hundred.

Milly would love this place.

Mac and Six followed Kiyoko into what Mac would guess was a sitting room. Mac noticed the backpack that Kiyoko set to the side of the couch or divan or whatever the hell it was. Mac was realizing that his education was sorely lacking in etiquette and protocol of high society.

Mac looked at the young woman before him. She was very lovely though pale and sickly. The dark circles under her eyes were disconcerting. She coughed quietly as she sat down covering her mouth with her hand.

"I was just about to step out. Is this going to take long?" Kiyoko asked as she motioned for Mac to sit down in one of the chairs. Mac watched as the dog droid sat on the floor next to Kiyoko. Its iridescent blue eyes locked onto Mac. The intensity of its stare made him a little uncomfortable.

"Well. We are looking for your father, have you seen him?"

"Nope," she said, a little too quickly for Mac's liking. "Are we done now? I have a car service coming."

Something is off here. Why is she so nervous?

Mac narrowed his eyes at her and waited, letting the silence weigh upon her.

Silence was a fantastic interrogation tool. It was far more effective than shouting or intimidation. The downside was it took a lot of patience. Luckily, this little girl didn't have any. She spoke first.

"Well anyway, I haven't talked to my father in a couple of weeks. He kind of lives at Takacorp tower," Kiyoko explained. "He has a cot in his lab."

"He gets a little tied up in his work, eh?" Mac inquired.

"You could say that," Kiyoko replied. "He's a bit of a workaholic. What is this all about?"

"Miss Otagawa, we have reason to believe that your father has been abducted," Mac explained. He watched her carefully. Looking for certain queues and emotional responses that people have. "Have you received any suspicious messages or calls? Anything out of the ordinary?"

"You're kidding, right?" Kiyoko exclaimed. "Abducted?" She had the vocalizations right, but her face gave it away. There was no concern. There was no tightness around the eyes. No worried expression over a missing father. She either knew he was okay or just didn't give a damn at all. Knowing how Mac felt about his own father he found that hard to believe.

"I'm afraid not," Mac replied bluntly. He continued to study her carefully. Watching for subtle clues. Proverbial tells like in that old card game, poker.

"From his lab?" she asked. With the appropriate amount of surprise and astonishment, but again no emotional response to her face.

"Yes, Miss Otagawa," Mac explained. "Someone smashed your father's lab and then broke their way out of Takacorp tower."

"No way!" Kiyoko gasped. Though it was a little too dramatic for Mac's liking. The hand placed against her chest in mock astonishment was a bit much.

"So, he hasn't tried to contact you or anything?" Mac asked again.

"No! I haven't heard from him," she replied.

She immediately scratched her nose. The gesture was one Mac had seen before when certain people lie. According to some researchers in the 21'st century lying caused the cells lining the nose to swell, initiating a histamine response. Which typically caused a physical reaction. Mac couldn't prove it, but he was fairly sure this young woman was lying.

"Must get pretty lonely with him gone all the time," Mac changed the subject and began to box her in. He stood up suddenly and watched her response.

"Look, Agent McDonnell was it?" Kiyoko said, sounding a little irritated. "Are you a cop or a psychiatrist?"

"Miss Otagawa, how do you normally get in touch with your father?" Mac asked as he walked around the plush couch he had been sitting on and toward the opaque window behind him. The tinting made it impossible to see in, but it also darkened the view out. Much like a pair of mirrored sunglasses Mac used to have. It was late in the day and Mac could only make out the streetlights which had started to light up. Shadows grew deep and black. Something passed between two shadows. Mac squinted at the spot again. He wasn't sure what it was. Could be anything from a serving droid or livery to a resident coming home.

"I call his office like everyone else," Kiyoko said snidely as she crossed her arms under her breasts.

"Your dog is very peculiar, Miss Otagawa," Six said out of nowhere. Mac turned to glare at his TFE. Six was staring at the robotic dog. Meanwhile, the dog was busy angling to keep both of them in view. Mac got the impression that it was calculating which one of them was more dangerous and planning its tactical approach.

"That is a very unusual droid you have there," Mac agreed.

"Oh, Annie?" Kiyoko asked.

"Is that its designation?" Six queried.

"She is one of my father's greatest creations," Kiyoko announced. "Animatronic Canine Companion njx0001."

"That's a mouthful." Mac chuckled.

"Yeah...that's why we call her Annie," she said snidely.

"Her? How do you know it's a girl?" Mac asked incredulously.

"Duh! The pink bow around her neck should have been a clue," Kiyoko quipped "Sheesh. I thought you agents were supposed to be observant."

"We try," Mac countered feebly.

Not your best work there, Mac.

"Mac, I believe I have located the source of the interference," Six announced.

"Really," Mac said, as he continued to focus his attention on Kiyoko.

"Yes. It is Annie," Six replied cheerfully. "She is emitting an unknown localized jamming field that is preventing me from scanning her."

"That is an interesting toy to have installed in your dog," Mac looked back at the mechanical dog.

"Yeah, well if my father had wanted anyone to scan her, he wouldn't have built in the jamming field." Kiyoko said acerbically.

"I find this most curious. Mac, it is disrupting all of my external sweeps. Preventing me from scanning anything in the room," Six continued to scrutinize Annie.

"Yeah, that's interesting, so are we done here? I have places I need to go," Kiyoko said, sounding more and more impatient.

"Not quite," Mac replied as he turned back to Miss Kiyoko. "You keep saying you haven't heard from your father, but I get the feeling that you are not being completely honest with us."

"What?" Kiyoko snapped in what sounded like she was taking offense. Mac, however, felt she was pushing it too hard. It seemed more like panic to him. "Why would I lie? Besides, if he has been abducted, why are you here grilling me? Shouldn't you be out trying to find out who did it?"

"Grrrrrrrr," Annie growled. A deep throaty sound.

Mac's hand betrayed him and slipped toward his blaster.

"Easy there, puppy dog," he said, holding his left

hand out hoping to ease the tension now filling the room. "There is nothing to be worried about."

Dammit, Six if that dog attacks you better shred that thing.

Kiyoko looked from Mac down to her growling companion Annie.

"What Annie?" she asked. Mac noticed that the dog wasn't looking at him. She was looking past him at the door to the foyer. The dog jumped to her feet.

Mac flinched involuntarily.

"It's not you," Kiyoko said as she searched for the object of Annie's ire.

The dog's upright pointed ears swiveled like two radar dishes hunting for signals. Her growl deepened.

"What is it?" Mac and Kiyoko asked in unison.

The front door exploded, raining debris into the house. Chunks of wood, plastic fibers, and masonry work flew into the house. Mac was thrown forward. He rolled over the couch and was able to land on his feet in front of Annie.

The raining debris hit Kiyoko and her divan head-on toppling them both.

"Six!" Mac roared.

"Roger!" The droid boomed. His police lights ignited. Filling the room in alternating flashes of red and blue.

Mac drew his blaster and moved toward Kiyoko. Annie intercepted him, baring her metallic teeth at him.

"Whoa there, puppy, I'm here to help," Mac explained to the dog.

Annie backed up so she could keep the demolished doorway in her line of sight while she stole a glance at Kiyoko.

"Annie!" Kiyoko cried. "Annie!"

Her voice sounded funny. Mac followed the dog and caught sight of the young woman. A piece of the shattered door was protruding from her chest.

"Annie" she called out weakly.

"Six!" Mac screamed at the top of his lungs. "Six we need a medic now! Call it in!"

Annie allowed Mac to get close. He grabbed Kiyoko's hand. It was cold and clammy.

"Hold on!" he told her. "Help is coming."

Annie's ear twitched and she spun around like she had been bitten by something. The motion drew Mac's attention. From somewhere deeper in the house a droid came charging at them. It had a kitchen knife held point down poised to strike.

"The Prophet demands your death!" the droid yelled in a melodic female voice.

Mac jumped and brought his weapon to bear but was too late. Annie launched herself at the deranged droid. She struck the attacker with all four paws in the chest toppling it over backward. Mac watched in amazement as the dog flipped in mid-air like some super cat and landed on all fours again. The droid struggled to stand up. Annie wasted no time. She lunged and her muzzle struck the droid in the chest. Annie bit down and the plastic chest plate gave easily. With a mighty shake of her head, she tore loose a large chunk of the machine's innards and it fell back lifeless on the carpet.

It was then that Mac heard Six's blaster firing.

"Status, Six?"

"Multiple Threats. I count twelve. Eleven. Ten. Nine. Eight," Six said as he continued to fire between each count.

"ETA on the Medic," Mac asked.

"I am unable to get connected to the network, Mac," Six replied.

"What!" Mac screamed.

"Annie is blocking all communication frequencies as well," Six replied between shots.

"She's wounded, Six, we need help now!"

"Checking...Checking..." Six replied.

"A sensor buoy, Six!" Mac yelled. "Fire it beyond the jamming field and use it to connect. We need help now!"

"Roger," Six replied as he fired several more shots.

Mac bent down to tell Kiyoko to hold on again but caught more movement. Another droid was coming through the house and this time it was not alone.

"Shit!" Mac yelled. He pointed his blaster and opened fire. His first blast hit the lead droid and it crumpled and fell forward. It was quickly replaced by those behind it. They advanced three abreast into the room through the large arched doorway.

Mac tossed his blaster to his left hand and reached behind his back and pulled his new backup piece. He was awfully glad he had thought to grab it back at his place. He drew his own hand cannon from its holster at the small of his back.

"Gracie, eat your heart out," he shouted as he aimed both weapons at the advancing droids and opened fire. His main blaster made short work of each attacker it connected with. His hand cannon, however, took care of the droid and the one advancing behind it. He got six or so shots off before they were almost on top of him and Kiyoko.

"Dammit!" Mac roared as he continued to fire at the

assailants. All spouting their prophet drivel at various times, forming a deafening cacophony of musical female voices.

Mac couldn't hear it at first, the sound of the rampaging machines was far too loud. Without warning, droids began to fall apart in front of him, faster than he could shoot. They just started shedding limbs and legs and chest pieces. With the loss of the advancing droids, the noise level began to subside, and Mac could hear the whirring. Confused, he looked to his left and caught sight of Annie's right side. Her midsection had opened and sitting on top of her hip was a small mini gun. It was whirring away raining blaster bolts on the unsuspecting droids. In short order, she had cut them down to hunks of scrap and ORF fluid.

"Six!" Mac yelled, taking everything in stride.

"Roger, Mac," Six said as he approached. "I would recommend a tactical retreat, Mac."

"What? Six we need a medic, she's hurt," Mac said pointing at Kiyoko whose breathing was slow and ragged.

Six surveyed the damage and took special note of Annie as her Gatling gun retracted into its hiding place inside her body.

"Intriguing," The big droid said.

"Retreat? From what?" Mac asked just as the front section of the house was torn away, opening the room to outside. A bright light exploded into the room.

"Oh, that," Mac said as he pointed his hand cannon at the light and opened fire. The neutralizer wave crushed the light canister like a cheap soda can. The impact pushed the source of the light away from the house. Mac could clearly see the giant orange plastic shell of the golem from down the street. The golem was pushed off balance by the unexpected blow and had to take a few steps to recover.

"Grab her!" Mac ordered. He tucked his service piece under his arm and held up his hand cannon. He clicked the release switch and the weapon's CAC battery launched from its compartment in the handgrip and disappeared among the scattered remains of the fallen droids. He drew a fresh battery from his belt clip and jammed it in place. With a sharp click, the LEDs on the cannon's small display read all green. He repeated the procedure with his service weapon.

Six complied and gently lifted Kiyoko into his massive arms. Mac using his right hand flipped a switch on his service piece.

"Annie and I are going to distract it," Mac turned back to Six, "You get her to the cruiser. You hear me?" he ordered.

"Mac, I should be the one to."

"Dammit, Six do as you are told," Mac interrupted. "You are the only one that can carry her and get away. She needs help. If I go down, you get her out of here. I won't lose anyone on my watch. Do you hear me?"

"Roger," Six replied.

"You still got ammo there little dog?" Mac asked Annie.

"Grrrrrrrrrrrrr," Annie replied as she stared out the opening in the house wall. Her gatling returned to its firing position.

"I'll take that as a yes."

Mac stepped toward the hole with Annie alongside him. After a quick calming breath, he followed Annie out of the opening into the night.

Chapter 15

Mac jumped clear of the wreckage that surrounded the house. He could feel the vibration of the golem's massive feet slamming into the ground. The behemoth had found its footing and was lumbering toward the house again. Mac found the massive thing easily as it took up most of the front yard.

"You ready?"

"Bark!" she replied.

"You go left. I'm heading right. When I yell you, open fire. Understand?" Mac asked.

"Bark!" she chirped again as she bolted to the left circling the two-story-tall robot.

Mac took aim at the golem's insect-like head. It protruded from the robot's giant barrel chest above its pilot compartment. With a squeeze of the trigger a white-hot flare leaped from the blaster's emitter nozzle. It streaked across the yard and collided with the droid's head. The machine's massive arms batted futilely at the blinding white light burning in front of its optical sensors.

"Now!" Mac yelled. The dog complied and opened fire with its minigun. The staggering behemoth was pelted with a volley of tiny rapid fire blaster bolts. The rain of fire left little dents on its thick armor-plated legs.

Mac circled right.

"Hey! Over here you bucket of bolts!" he yelled,

attempting to draw its attention away from Annie. Mac hoped the dog could damage one of the legs enough to slow it down.

The golem turned and found Mac. Mac knew the flare wouldn't permanently blind it, but he hoped it would have worked a little longer. The monster reached right for Mac with its giant three-forked, pincer-like hand. Mac waited till the last second to roll out of the way. The golem was built for heavy lifting and repetitive tasks, not for speed. Its movements were fairly large and slow. As the monster reached out again, Mac dove forward. He felt the ground shake as the giant hand impacted the ground.

Mac tucked into a crouch and fired up at his attacker. His series seven blaster bolts just bounced off of the droid's outer shell in the same way Annie's did. The hand cannon however, hit a lot harder. It left fist size indentations. Mac stood back up and tried to put some distance between him and the machine. He fired at it haphazardly as he ran.

I have to lead it away from the car.

Annie continued her assault on the leg. Mac turned around to find the golem had focused its attention on the dog.

The giant moved toward the canine droid. Annie danced about as she continued firing on the giant's rotund legs.

Mac took steady aim at the golem's immense backside. He unloaded with his heavy blaster. Movement caught Mac's eye. Six had emerged from the house carrying Kiyoko in his arms.

The golem was still focused on Annie and was blocking Six's path to the car.

Mac whistled as loud as he could. He whistled again hoping that Annie's hearing was as good as her aim.

The dog stopped shooting and ran for Mac. She crossed the distance easily making sure to run around the right side of the golem to keep it from seeing Six and his precious charge. The infected monster followed her path and tried to stomp on her as she ran by.

Good dog. That is one heck of a machine.

Annie spun to face the golem as she reached Mac.

The golem lumbered toward them. shaking the ground with every step.

"Got anything else up your sleeve?" Mac asked of the dog beside him.

Annie snorted in response. Suddenly her left side opened, and another device emerged. It settled in above her left hip. It expanded and some pieces appeared to lock into place. She lowered her front half and dug her rear claws into the soil.

"Oh dear." Mac started when a great whump sound radiated from Annie. The golem's shoulder exploded mid-stride. The light of the explosion illuminated the front yard and Mac could make out Six running behind the big droid toward their cruiser. "Careful girl."

Mac surveyed the damage to the oncoming robot. The outer covering to the golem's right arm was shattered. Pieces of the thick plastic covering were falling to the ground as the droid stumbled. The arm appeared to still function but was leaking ORF fluid badly. The golem staggered back once more from the blow.

"Great shot, Annie," Mac complimented. "Can you hit it again in the same place?"

"Bark." The dog answered, crouching again.

Whump! The launcher on her back cried. Mac watched in awe as the golem's right shoulder exploded again. The great limb crashed to the ground with a loud clang. It jerked a couple of times as if to deny the blow that had cleaved it from its body but quickly fell silent. The giant robot stumbled toward the street. The loss of the arm's weight and the force of the blow were too much for the movement calculation sub routines to manage. The giant droid toppled into the street grinding up the rubberized concrete surface of the road.

"Nicely done," Mac said. "Nicely done. How about one more for good measure?"

"Bark!" Annie replied. Whump. Her launcher snorted again. The barrel chest of the golem, cracked from the previous two blows, shattered. Parts of the robot were scattered about the area. Mac hid his head behind his arm and counted to five before looking again. Parts of the monstrous droid were still raining down.

"Good dog," Mac said. "Now we have to save Kiyoko."

"Bark!" Annie replied as she bolted toward the cruiser which was pulling around the now silent golem laying in the street.

"Hey! Wait for me!" Mac yelled out as he ran after her.

The door slid open for Mac as he reached the car. He jumped into the driver's seat, pushing Annie across the center console.

"Move it, Six." Mac commanded.

"Roger, Mac," Six replied cheerfully as he started vehicle forward again. Mac was thrown back into his seat with the force of the vehicle's acceleration. Once Mac and his stomach caught up to everything else in the cruiser, he took an inventory of everyone.

Six had placed Kiyoko in the passenger seat. Annie was curled up at Kiyoko's feet.

Kiyoko looked bad. Her breathing was slow. She was so pale. The makeshift bandage that Six had applied was helping but it was already stained with blood.

"Call it in, Six," Mac called out. "I think we are losing her."

"Annie?" Kiyoko said suddenly.

"Hold on, Kiyoko, we are on our way to a hospital," Mac explained. "We'll get you help soon."

"No!" Kiyoko screamed. "My father! Take me to my father! Please"

"Your father?" Mac asked.

"Yes. Please hurry," Kiyoko pleaded.

"Where is he?" Mac asked.

"Annie, take them to Dad," Kiyoko coughed and fell silent again.

"Bark!" Annie announced.

"Mac. Annie is sending me coordinates," Six announced.

"Take us there," Mac ordered.

"Roger," Six replied.

Chapter 16

Mac closed the screen on his Global. He had hoped to talk to Dick directly, but a Vid would have to do. He asked Dick to get an evidence team over to Otagawa's house right away. This was no random virus attack. That was a coordinated effort. If Annie hadn't been there, it would have gone down in a bad way pretty quickly.

The cruiser's tires screeched to a halt in front of Hamilton House. Mac was very confused. Hamilton used to be a homeless shelter. It was one of the few remnants of the old city the first dome was constructed over. The two following domes were constructed over leveled land, but the original dome was built over the remains of a city. The building stands as a testament to the old days when groups of people were destitute. The plain brick building stood four stories high.

Six opened the door and Mac jumped out. He sprinted around to the passenger side. Annie slithered from the floor in front of Kiyoko and stretched much a like a real dog would have after laying in such cramped quarters.

What a droid.

Once Six had escaped his compartment he gently scooped up Kiyoko's limp body. Mac followed Annie's lead as she headed into building. The doors opened automatically at Annie's approach.

"Bark" she yelled over her shoulder, and she looked

back at Mac. Mac gingerly tested the doors. They remained in the open position.

"Come on, Six" Mac called out. "We're running out of time."

"Roger," Six replied as he followed Mac through the door.

Mac waited for Six to catch up and leaned back into the droid as he approached.

"Stay alert, Six," Mac whispered, "We are on our own down here. So, keep your eyes open, buddy."

"I am incapable of blinking, Mac," Six replied innocently, trying to match Mac's volume.

One step forward two steps back. "Bark," Annie announced. Breaking Mac's train of thought.

"You heard the lady," Mac said to Six. "Let's go."

Annie led them deeper into the building's interior. She stopped in front of an old steel door. She pawed at it lightly. Her metallic nails striking the metal surface of the door made Mac's skin crawl.

Mac tried the handle after he reached the door. It gave easily and the heavy old door swung open. Annie darted on ahead again. The door opened to an old stairwell. The tube steel railing led downward into a black abyss.

"Bark!" Annie called from the dark.

Mac and Six followed her voice.

"There is something very peculiar about all of this," Six stated as he negotiated the dark stairway.

"What do you mean?" Mac replied as he made his way gingerly down the staircase.

"Now that Annie's unusual jamming ability is no longer halting my scans, I have found some very startling irregularities in Miss Otagawa's physiology," Six replied.

"Like whaaaatttt!" Mac asked as he found the floor unexpectedly closer to the bottom step. He stumbled in the dark and caught himself on the far wall. He collided with the heavy cinder block surface and swore under his breath.

"Dammit,"

"Mac. Are you injured?" Six replied in what could have been called concern.

"I'm all right," Mac said as he flexed his hand, waiting for the pain to pass.

Mac expected Six to be right behind him. But found himself alone in the dark.

"Six. Where are you?" Mac asked the dark stairwell.

"Coming, Mac," Six replied, "I didn't want to risk Miss Kiyoko in a miscalculated step."

"Bark!" Annie announced from deeper in the darkened level.

"Where is she?" Mac asked as he felt his way along the wall he so rudely accosted moments earlier.

"She is beyond the door, Mac," Six said.

"Oh yeah, because I can see in pitch black you hunk of junk," Mac griped.

"The door is approximately one meter in front of you," Six said.

"Mac followed the wall to the spot Six had mentioned. He found a handle that felt like the one he had opened a few levels up. He pulled and the door didn't move.

Push dumb ass. It's a push from this direction.

Mac reversed direction and the door swung open easily. The light that flooded in from the hallway and blinded Mac momentary.

"Bark!" Annie chirped when she saw Mac.

Mac emerged from the black stairwell and then held the door for Six and Kiyoko.

"We're coming," Mac told the excited dog. "Come on, Six."

Annie led them down the hall. Mac and Six followed behind. Mac saw Annie duck into a room at the end of the hall. The room was the source of the light that illuminated the hallway.

Mac continued down the hallway. He noticed that Six wasn't behind him. His characteristic rubberized thunk, thunk of his bulky footsteps weren't there. Mac turned around and found his wayward partner hurrying to catch up. Bringing his heavy footsteps with him.

"What's up, Six?" Mac asked as the droid approached.

"Mac, Kiyoko had droid parts inside her body," Six said pointed.

"What!" Mac gasped.

"I have confirmed six non-biological components and although I lack the appropriate testing equipment. I cannot be 100 percent certain that the fluid leaking from her wounds is blood," Six continued.

"I think we are getting close to something, Six," Mac admitted. "Come on."

Mac walked toward the open door with Six in his wake.

Mac wasn't sure what to expect when he came through the open door into the light, but it certainly wasn't the sickly looking man working very delicately with a set of surgical arms. The arms were a model that Mac had never seen before. They were either very new or they were custom made. The sickly looking man was making some sort of adjustment to what looked like an exposed PCE out of its protective casing.

He stood on the floor and manipulated the controls on the surgical arms. He didn't bother with a stool as he could stand comfortably at the controls. An older man, he sported a tiny halo of short gray hair that circled his pale head.

Mac's gaze moved passed the older man and cataloged the room. It was fairly decent size, maybe twenty-five meters by fifteen meters. The white tile on the floor appeared to be clean. The walls were filled with white storage cabinets. A couple of tables and three maintenance gurneys remarkably similar to the ones in Otagawa's lab back at Takacorp dominated the floor space. In the center of the room above one of the gurneys was what looked like a giant set of surgical arms. Eight wicked mechanical arms protruded from a bug like oval hanging down from the ceiling. It reminded Mac of a giant white spider. Mac recognized the thing immediately. Doctors use those droids to perform surgery on human beings and larger droids. Mac had seen more than his fair share of surgical droids and made sure to walk wide of it.

"Bark!" Annie announced at the little man's side.

Startled by the noise the older man jumped.

"Ah, Annie-chan," The older man said. "Nan des' ka?"

"Bark!" Annie replied.

"Ah, Annie-chan, please speak English," The older man chided. It took a moment for Mac's ears to adjust to the older man's accent. It sounded like he was sticking 'R's were his 'L's should have gone. "I spent far too long on your linguistic programming for you to speak like a common dog Annie-chan."

Annie cocked her head and continued to sit in front of the older man. Her tail kept wagging back and forth. Though her ears were laid back.

"I failed master," Annie said. "Kiyoko has been injured."

"Bakami!" the older man spit. Annie flinched at the sudden outburst.

Mac's blank stare at the talking dog was broken by the older man's angry shout.

"Where is she?" he demanded.

"She's here," Mac interrupted. "Six!"

Six brought Kiyoko into the room. The older man grimaced at the sight of the large droid carrying his daughter.

"Kiyoko!" the older man cried. "Bring her here. Quickly! Quickly!"

He scrambled to remove odds and ends off of the maintenance gurney under the surgical arms hanging down from the ceiling.

"Lay her here, quickly, quickly! Please," the man continued, his concern ringing like a gong in his voice.

"Forgive me, master," Annie said bowing her head causing another surprised look from Mac.

"Bakami!" The older man shouted again.

Six stepped back from the gurney and settled in next to Mac.

"Six, what does that mean?" Mac asked. "Bakami?"

"Bakami? Checking, Bakami roughly translates to idiocy, stupidity, or foolishness," Six said. "It is from the old Japanese language. Which dates back to—"

"Can it there, buddy. That is far more than I

needed," Mac said.

Mac walked closer to the older man. "We tried to take her to the hospital, but she demanded to come here," Mac said.

"Hai." The older man said as he examined the damage. "Ah. Her right gas exchanger has been damaged and she is leaking ORF fluid."

"What?" Mac and Six said in unison.

"You there, droid. Go to the cabinet, on the wall and bring me the case inside." The older man demanded while pointing furiously.

Six complied. The android quickly walked over to the large cabinet on the wall that the man pointed at and retrieved the case. He laid it gently on the table next to the gurney.

"Dr. Uske Otagawa?" Mac asked, surprised.

"Later," Otagawa snapped. "What happened to my daughter?"

"I assure you sir we never touched your daughter. We—" Mac started.

"Of course not, Annie would have torn you to pieces if you had tried that," Otagawa replied as he continued to remove tools and components from the case Six had brought him.

"I-I believe you Dr. Otagawa," Mac agreed as he looked over at the robotic dog who was staring intently at Otagawa and Kiyoko.

"Tsk," Dr. Otagawa scoffed as he continued to work.

"Well?" Uske asked again after a few minutes. "How did this happen?"

"Your daughter's home outside of Forrest Park was attacked by a group of droids infected with the Prophet virus," Mac replied sadly. "We were able to fight them off with Annie's help, but the damage had been done."

"Is that what happened Annie-chan?" Uske asked the room as he continued to focus on his work.

"Yes, master," Annie replied. "I failed, master. I was to protect Kiyoko and I failed," with her ears laid back, and her shoulders and head bowed, tail tucked between her hind legs she looked so pitiful. Mac felt bad for her.

"Bakami!" Uske swore again. "You brought her to me. That was very good Annie-chan. You did well."

Annie's tail wagged again, and her ears came forward at the compliment.

Every so often Uske would send Six for another tool or vial of something. It took more than ten minutes to get everything assembled. Mac watched in awe as Dr. Otagawa replaced droid components in his daughter's body. He had Six retrieve a number of squid like items from a large glass cylinder filled with goo. It looked just like the smashed one back in the lab at Takacorp where Mac and Six had been earlier.

"Ah, at last," the doc said after almost two hours of frantic surgery. "Kiyoko-chan, can you sit up?"

Kiyoko nodded. Dr. Otagawa pressed lightly on one of the foot pedals at the base of the gurney and it bent in the center and transformed very slowly into a kind of chair.

"I'll have Astrid bring you some clothes on her way back," Dr. Otagawa said.

Uske walked to his workstation and punched up a small application. He typed something very quickly on the keypad and then closed it. He turned around and went back to picking up some of the tools he had used.

"I'm sorry, Otosan. I didn't mean to get hurt,"

Kiyoko explained. "I just wanted a couple of things from the house. I mean, I took Annie with me."

"I told you to stay here. Kiyoko I was afraid that this might happen. You know the danger involved," Otagawa admonished. "We must stay hidden for now. Once we have completed our mission, we will be free to move around as we please. However, until then you must be more careful."

"And you," Otagawa said as he rounded on the dog droid who was starting at him intently with her head cocked to the side. "I built you for one purpose, to protect Kiyoko. Are there errors in your programming that need to be corrected?"

"No, master, I am functioning at peak performance. My defensive strategy was altered by the presence of the RAD agents. While observing them I failed to predict the infection of the golem that was operating farther down the street. I apologize for my failure."

Annie bowed her head again and waited.

"Bakami. Eh, she is well Annie-chan so you have not failed," Otagawa said as he reached out and petted the dog as if it were real. Annie's tail wagged again.

"Otosan, quit being so melodramatic," Kiyoko scolded. "Annie did her best and besides the RAD agent and his droid turned out to be pretty helpful."

"Dr. Otagawa. I'm Agent McDonnell from RAD," Mac interjected. "I have a few questions."

"Dr. Otagawa, you are under arrest for violation of the AMA code sub section 121-1442." Six blurted out suddenly. "Please remain still while I take you into custody."

Six tromped menacingly across the room toward the Doctor. Uske stood staring at the monster droid in stunned silence.

"What! No!" Kiyoko shouted. "Leave him alone you overgrown vibrator!" she struggled against the restrains that Dr. Otagawa had set up during his impromptu surgery.

"Wait!" Mac said trying to calm the situation down.

"Mac. Dr. Otagawa is in clear violation of AMA code sub section 121-1442," Six argued. "We will need to take both him and Miss Kiyoko Otagawa into custody until the matter can be sufficiently investigated by appropriate medical personnel."

"We just found him, Six," Mac explained. "I want to talk with him for a moment and get his side of the story before we do anything rash. Remember our current assignment is to find out what happened."

"We have succeeded in our assignment, Mac. Duty mandates that we take him into custody and process him at RAD headquarters."

"Six, don't make me use the Command override," Mac pleaded while he checked the time on his Global. "Look. Give me thirty minutes to assess the situation, okay? After that we will discuss our next move."

"Roger, Mac," The droid said, "You have twenty-nine minutes and fifty-six seconds remaining."

"Thanks, buddy," Mac replied as he attempted to nonchalantly remove the override link from its holster on his belt and hold it in his hand just in case.

"Oh good. Now that it's all settled. Back to work," Dr. Otagawa announced.

Uske proceeded back to his workstation. With a few punches at the keypad the six monitors started flashing copious amounts of data on each screen. The set up was much like Teddy's now that Mac took a good look at it.

Dr. Otagawa watched the screens for a moment. Then he nodded his head in a pleased manner and made his way back to the surgical arms he had been working at.

Mac marveled. The man had just about lost his daughter and now that she appeared to be safe, he was back at his pursuit.

I need to call Milly.

"Hey, Doc?" Mac asked.

"Hai," the older man replied without looking up from his work.

"What happened to you, Dr. Otagawa?" Mac asked.

"What do you mean?"

"Why are you hiding here?" Mac continued. "Down here of all places? What happened to your lab?"

Uske paused for a second, then replied, "To collect the resources we need, to avoid detection, and I destroyed it to prevent my research from falling into the wrong hands." He finished without taking his eyes from his work.

"Oh," Mac replied as his brain tried to remember what he asked so he could fit Uske's answers with each question. It wasn't going well and that made Mac a little agitated.

"Now that I've answered your questions you are free to leave. The door is located behind you," Otagawa said coldly.

"Otosan!" Kiyoko exclaimed.

"Oh yes, and ah, thank you. For bringing me my *disobedient* daughter," The doctor added flashing a stern glance at the young woman.

"Doc, you're going to have to give me a little more than that," Mac replied his voice beginning to take on a heated quality. "Takacorp is leaning heavily on my department to find you."

"Of course, they are!" Otagawa said. His voice was filled with anger. He looked up from his work and met Mac's eyes. "That spoiled little twit wants to destroy my research and Kiyoko along with it." He gestured wildly with his hands.

"Five hundred credits says you are talking about Ichiro Takahaisu," Mac replied wryly. "I'm right, aren't I?"

"You are smarter than you look, Agent McDonnell," Kiyoko replied.

"Gee thanks," Mac retorted. "And it's Mac."

"I'm just saying," Kiyoko replied with a sly smile and a shrug. "Oh, and thanks for helping me today," Kiyoko attempted to stand.

"Stay where you are, insolent child. The epoxy has to cure for a few more minutes. If you tear them, I will be terribly angry with you." The doc threatened his daughter.

"Gomen esai. Otosan," Kiyoko said. Though she ruined the visage of meekness by sticking out her tongue at her father's back.

After his outburst. Otagawa had gone back to his project.

"What are you working on, Doc? What is all this? Why does your daughter have droid parts inside her?" Mac asked.

"You there, droid," Uske asked of Six looking pointedly at Mac.

"Yes, Dr. Otagawa?"

"Is he always this nosy?" Otagawa gestured to Mac. "Asking several questions all at once?"

"Affirmative, Dr. Otagawa. Agent McDonnell is an accomplished detective," Six replied, while assuming his lecturing tone of voice. "He is second only to Detective Stark in the number of Level 3 cases closed."

Mac rolled his eyes at the comparison.

"Having observed many of Agent McDonnell's interrogations I have found he is most effective at asking questions," Six continued. "He is especially good at identifying suspects who are being untruthful. Though I am still analyzing his technique to ascertain how his 'gut' works. As he seems to rely on his gastrointestinal processes during investigations more than should logically be allowed."

Mac snorted.

"Interesting," Otagawa smiled at the big droid and shook his head. Mac could swear he heard the man mutter bakami again.

"However, it should be noted that Agent McDonnell's gastrointestinal processes have been surprisingly accurate during the course of many of our investigations. I am inclined to think that the topic does require further study. I will add it to my down time research request file."

"I assure you he wasn't one of mine," Otagawa said to Mac as he shook his head and smiled. "Well, some of his components are, but his core programming was outsourced. I never did like writing terabytes of command code. Why those programmers thought that a police droid should babble on in such a manner escapes me. Bakami!"

"I know what you mean." Mac chuckled, drawing a confused look from Six. "I'll explain later, buddy."

Six nodded and continued to watch the occupants of

the room.

Annie had settled in on the floor next to Kiyoko's gurney. The android dog's head was resting comfortably on her front paws. Her tail continued to wag though it was now just the tip.

Mac couldn't get over how much like a real dog Annie was. She was so fluid in her movements and design. It was as if Uske had encased a real dog inside a plastic casing with metal accents.

"So, Doc," Mac said, hoping to keep the interview on course, He was running out of time. *The longer they stay in one place the greater the chance more droids might find them.*

"Tell me about what happened at Takacorp that made you run for your daughter's life," Mac said.

"Ichiro tried to kill me," Kiyoko interjected.

"What?" Mac stammered turning toward the young woman. "He doesn't seem the type."

Gracie. Now she's the type.

"Oh, you're right he's not the type to attack a living person outright. Violence against droids is a whole 'nother topic. But he's the type of sniveling little coward who would pull plugs when someone isn't looking," Kiyoko snapped. Her anger bubbled over in her voice, and she quivered with the desire to move from her chair. She pulled against the restraints again causing her to wince with a stab of pain.

Mac caught Uske out of the corner of his eye as the older man nodded in agreement with Kiyoko's statement.

"Ichiro has become infatuated with the propaganda of those idiots at the Image of God group," Kiyoko blurted out. "To think I almost married that little weasel.

You know, I bet he still cries himself to sleep at night over his mommy. I mean. Come on, you know. I lost my mother too and you don't see me bawling my eyes over it constantly."

"Image of God?" Mac said. "How does Ichiro falling in with an elitist religious sect lead to Kiyoko having droid parts implanted?"

"Kiyoko was suffering from the same genetic defect that claimed her mother thirteen years ago," Uske explained. "I couldn't bear to lose Kiyoko in the same way. With the technology I pioneered with Annie I was able to develop replacement parts for the damaged organs."

"With Annie?" Mac asked, "What are you talking about?"

"My mom died of a rare heart condition called Hypertrophic Cardiomyopathy. A deadly genetic disorder. She dropped dead one day on her morning run," Kiyoko explained sadly. "I was eight years old."

"Yes, it nearly killed me to lose Sho," Uske said as he removed his glasses and cleaned them with his shirt. "After we discovered what had killed her, I started having Kiyoko checked. Once it became apparent that she too was suffering from the same condition, I used what little time I had to develop an alternative."

Uske walked over to his workstation and punched a couple of keys on the keypad. A series of diagrams and drawings covered the six screens and began to cycle. The images appeared to be droid and human organs, along with chemical and crystalline structures.

"Annie, our family dog, had begun to deteriorate," Uske continued as he put his glasses back on. "She had gotten old. As all things do. So, I took my chance. I began grafting modified droid parts into her systems as more of them began to fail as she got older. It took five years to get Annie back on her feet and responding more like her old self."

"Tohiro didn't know but I had been bringing nano organic structures into the lab for last four years. From the dome in Britain. I needed them to fix neural connection problems between the brain tissue and the new organs," Uske instructed.

"That explains the tank of goo in your lab," Mac said dryly.

"Hai," Uske agreed.

"That and Annie wasn't functioning quite right," Kiyoko chimed in.

"Yes, Annie's functionality was severely impaired using traditional droid technology," Uske admitted. "With the introduction of the nano organic fibers I was able to increase the synchronization rate of the organs to the Medulla Oblongata to 83 percent."

"Dad. Get to the point," Kiyoko demanded. "Look, so Dad was able to develop synthetic organs and fixed Annie. However, we weren't able to save her main body, so Dad built her a new one. The only thing that remains of her original body is her brain.

"Okay, so the dog is less robot and more cyborg, so how does that equate to Ichiro trying to kill Kiyoko?" Mac asked, slightly more agitated.

"We're getting there. Be patient," Kiyoko snapped. "Interrupting isn't helping."

"Sorry, please continue," Mac replied, a bit abashed at his interruption.

"I hadn't figured out the appropriate way to remove the living brain and store it properly," Uske admitted sadly. "I had hoped to preserve the poor animal's brain, but I inadvertently set the ball in motion for its demise. I just didn't know enough about organic tissues."

"So, when it became clear that Annie's brain was declining Dad had his greatest breakthrough. He developed a revolutionary neural linkage scanning system," Kiyoko explained. "He found a way to map the working neural pathways of a living brain and recreate them in a complex computational helix. Even I don't know exactly how it works but he was able to copy what was left of Annie's brain and load it into a series of PCEs."

"Wait slow down a little," Mac said, "You copied the dog's brain?"

"And it functions?" Six queried.

"It wasn't perfect, but it worked," Uske replied. "Annie was almost completely preserved inside the program. I had to make a few modifications and rewrite her communication and linguistic protocols as I am sadly ignorant of the 'dog' language. It was easier to have her communicate in English. It was my daughter's idea to write the 'dog' vocalizations as a way to hide the animal in plain sight. I just figured it's a robotic dog why not have it speak English," Uske explicated.

"Okay, that explains Annie," Mac interjected. "How did Ichiro get involved?"

With the interruption, Kiyoko narrowed her eyes at Mac.

"Dad had run out of time, my heart finally stopped on me," she said. "Luckily, I was at home where Dad had all of the equipment to save me. Well, to make a long story short, Dad had begun the procedure to replace my heart. Ichiro had been sniffing around the lab while Dad wasn't there and must have seen the heart."

"While I was lying on the table waiting for Dad and the doctor, the one that Dad hired to do the surgery to install my new heart, Ichiro and his bodyguard stormed in. Ichiro was all upset that Dad was 'defacing' my body or some junk. He tried to stop the operation. Things got heated and I grabbed the gun that bitch was pointing at my father. Well, she fired it. The blast tore up my chest and crushed my lungs. My father and Dr. Brighton brought me here and put me back together. It took them two days to get me put together enough that I could live without a life support unit.

"So, I was alive, but they had to use some of the inferior parts, that is, until we can grow more of the nano organic fibers to fix me permanently," Kiyoko said pointing to the two metal cylinders on the far wall next to Uske's workstation.

"Uske Otagawa, you are under arrest for violation of AMA code sub section 121-1442, manufacturing a droid that can pass for a human being," Six said suddenly.

"Wait! You can't!" Kiyoko shouted.

"Six stop!" Mac yelled, as he put himself between the droid and Uske.

"The requested time has elapsed Mac. It is time to take Dr. Otagawa into custody, for his own safety and for completion of our assignment," Six said.

"Stop, Six, we aren't arresting Dr. Otagawa for saving his daughter," Mac said as he put away his Field override link.

"Command Override complete. CO report has been filed under date and time," Six stated.

Chapter 17

Vance jabbed the touch plate of the elevator control panel repeatedly. His nerves were getting the better of him and he knew it. Yet it felt comforting to be doing something even if it was just poking a virtual button with his thick finger.

Regardless of his physical activity, the elevator continued its measured pace down. Vance let his anger over tonight's mission stew as he waited. He felt the stupid thing was mocking him as it took its time lowering into position on the *V* level. The *V* stood for Vault which was short for Data Vault. Vance liked to think of it as his level. Level *V*, for Vance. It sat deep in the foundations of Takacorp tower. The only access was the core elevator, a secret elevator shaft hidden in the very center of the tower. There were six main elevators shafts open to the everyday people in the tower that operate in the central core of the building. Two on each of the triangle shaped sides with openings spaced out throughout most of the floors. The Core elevator ran in the narrow gap created at the center of the cavernous shaft.

The secret elevator was only accessible on three floors: the Vault level, Security Level, and the Executive Level near the top of the tower. As a matter of security only five people have access to the hidden elevator. One of them has been missing for almost two weeks now. That fact set Vance's blood boiling.

"Damn him," Vance swore at the opening elevator door. He felt his face grow hot. It always did when he let his temper get the better of him. He mopped the beads of sweat forming on his brow. He then placed his monogrammed handkerchief back in his front pocket. Oh, how that stuck up little geek of a man annoyed him. "Uske friggin Otagawa." He swore aloud. "That pinched faced little freak and his sickly bitch of a daughter." The thought of those two still alive just deepened Vance's ire. He didn't hold any personal animosity toward the wayward doctor or his daughter. Vance just hated a task left unfinished.

Vance stepped into the elevator and turned around. He pressed the topmost of the three buttons on the touch screen. He dreaded having to report tonight's failure to capture the good Doctor's abomination of a daughter.

Ichiro should have ordered Gracie to kill that little bitch and her father when they had the chance. That way I wouldn't have to be running round trying to clean up after their friggin mess.

The elevator rocketed upward. Vance ignored the marvel of technology that carried him to his destination, instead he admired himself in the mirrored finish of the doors.

"Hey there, handsome, you come here often?" he asked his reflection. Vance had never passed up an opportunity to feed his vanity.

His reflection flashed a toothy grin. He could still see the air of mischief hiding in his own smile. Though he had to admit that the damp spots at his arm pits were less than attractive.

In short order the elevator car passed the security floor and continued upward toward its final stop. The closer he got to the top the more his stomach turned. To fight the wave of apprehension and nauseous feelings threatening to expel his rather expensive lunch he reached into his pants pocket and grabbed an antacid tab and swallowed it.

As quickly as the upward climb began, the car came to a smooth stop. The opening of the door alerted Vance to his arrival. He blew one last kiss to himself as he walked past the doors. His mouth was dry and yet his head continued to bead with sweat.

Vance left the elevator car and continued down the narrow hallway before him. He reached the end and tapped the small monitor attached to the door before him. The monitor was connected to a camera that watched the hall beyond the door. Having the additional security precautions of checking to see if the coast was clear really annoyed Vance. He had argued with Ichiro about it. Considering that the floor was available only to the Takahaisu family, and himself of course, Vance never saw the point to the extra step.

"It is when you feel most safe that you need to be concerned," Ichiro had said. Like he was quoting some freakin' vid.

The monitor showed the hall was clear, so Vance tapped the trigger. The door slid into the wall clearing the way and Vance lumbered into hallway. He rounded the corner to the left. He quickened his pace as he walked past Tohiro's penthouse and rounded the next corner. He proceeded straight ahead to Ichiro's quarters.

With every step he took he let his anger build. He was angry at Ichiro's impotence and at his own failure in cleaning up the mess the arrogant bastard created.

"Open," he cursed. The door barely slid out of the

way in time for him to enter the room. He let his anger over tonight's event boil over. He stomped through the foyer and walked straight for the living room ahead. He could see Ichiro standing solemnly near the giant wall of windows that made up the outside of Takacorp Tower.

"It didn't work, Ichiro!" Vance blurted out. "What the hell are we gonna do now?" Vance glowered as Ichiro's reflection responded by sipping from the porcelain cup in its semitransparent hand. The reflection's movements were steady and measured.

"Well?" Vance demanded as he advanced farther into the room. He could feel his face heating up even more. He was outraged at Ichiro's calm facade. *Dammit man this is serious! We don't have time for any of your ancient Japanese wisdom bullshit.*

Ichiro continued to stare out of the window into the city lights below though he waved his hand dismissively.

Surprise hit Vance's face like a hydraulic press. Vance knew he had broken his cardinal rule. He had lost sight of Ichiro's amazon bodyguard Gracie. He turned to see Gracie behind him putting away that cannon she called a pistol. Vance gulped. It must have been louder than he had intended by the way Gracie smiled.

If I don't start paying attention I'm gonna get myself killed.

The woman had put the gun away so Vance was in the clear for now. However, he is going to have to be more careful.

After all, it is easy to dispose of a body he remembered. Vance covered his chagrin by mopping up a new crop of sweat that had sprung up on his forehead with his handkerchief.

"Welcome, Robert," Ichiro said coolly. "Please join

us."

Vance looked back at Gracie and then turned his gaze to Ichiro's ghostly reflection.

"The operation failed, Ichiro," Vance said. "We need a contingency plan."

"Robert seems unsettled, wouldn't you say Alexander?" Ichiro glanced over his shoulder toward the sofa off to Vance's right.

"He does seem a little agitated, Ichiro," a deep voice agreed suddenly. Vance physically jumped in surprise.

Ichiro smirked and continued to sip from his coffee cup.

Vance searched for the origin of the voice. He found a man sitting quietly on the couch to Ichiro's left just out of view from the door Vance had entered through. The other guest was a blond man, with the coldest blue eyes Vance had ever seen. The man sat there on the couch sipping from the coffee cup he was holding. He bore the air of leadership and he was wearing a gorgeous white custom suit with a gold shirt and white tie. The tie had a beautiful splash of red right about where an old-time tie tack would go. Vance toyed with the idea of asking for the man's tailor but thought better of it.

Vance knew the man well. Vance had seen the man's face before, many times in fact, though he had never noticed the crow's feet that were now present around the man's eyes.

They had officially met briefly at the Industry Gala a month past. Tohiro had introduced them. That was the way Roth wanted it. Vance had learned early on during his service to Alexander Roth that following orders was the only way to stay alive. Loyalty meant rewards. Ignoring or not completing assignments meant death. To make matters worse those deaths were usually a public and gruesome event that Roth could take political advantage of.

"What would you counsel for someone in such a state Alexander?" Ichiro asked.

"I think a nice hot bath and a massage would do wonders for him, Ichiro" The man on the couch said. His voice was deep and crisp. "I can recommend a fantastic massage therapist if you like, a human being of course. She has a divine touch."

"That's a thought, Alexander, was it?" Vance waited for the other man to nod. "I'll eh, keep that in mind." Vance turned back to Ichiro. "Ichiro, I apologize I was not aware you had a guest."

"Ah, where are my manners?" Ichiro asked rhetorically. The slender man turned and faced his guests. "Councilman Roth, this is Robert Vance, Director of Security for Takacorp. Robert this is Councilman Alexander Roth."

"It's a pleasure to see you again, Robert," Roth said raising his coffee cup to Vance.

"It's all mine," Vance said sarcastically.

"Ah, so you two have met," Ichiro said sounding amused.

"Yes, Robert and I met at the Gala last month. I must say Takacorp throws a wonderful party," Roth said casually.

"Well, I'm glad you enjoyed yourself, Alexander. The entertainment committee planned the event. I'll be sure to let them know their efforts were appreciated."

Vance looked to Ichiro. He hoped that Ichiro wasn't angry with him. Though judging by the tightness around Ichiro's eyes Vance was going to hear about this. He never would have stormed in if he knew there were witnesses. Vance had always preferred that shadow work stayed in the shadows.

The fewer the witnesses the less there was to clean up. If there was one thing Vance hated more than anything else it would be cleanup.

"I'll come back later," Vance said, starting to turn toward the door.

"Nonsense, Robert. Stay," Ichiro said. Though Ichiro's voice was conversational and rather friendly, Robert could tell from the man's eyes that the statement was an order.

"Yes," Roth said. "I like to know what my constituency has to say."

"Join us, Robert. Alexander and I were just discussing the problems that our beloved city is facing," Ichiro held out his coffee cup.

An Allure model walked from the corner it was hiding in and carefully filled Ichiro's cup from the carafe she was holding. It was a late model series two, but the plastic face plate had been shattered. Only the left eye and a small strip remained running down the left side of the face. It's as if someone hammered the right side of the poor droid's plastic face cover. Ichiro tended to be extremely hard on his droids. Vance noticed that Ichiro didn't offer him a cup of coffee, further enforcing what Vance knew. *I'm just staff to that little weasel.*

"This prophet business is becoming disconcerting Ichiro," Roth said plainly. "I'm concerned that more and more incidents are cropping up. Has Takacorp taken steps to stem the tide?"

"Of course, Alexander. We have a new production line almost ready for delivery," Ichiro said. "Isn't that right, Robert?"

"A new line, Ichiro?" Roth asked, his blond, almost white, eyebrows climbing his forehead leaving slight wrinkles in their wake.

"Yes, I have had the tech's rethink our programming and control architecture," Ichiro said. "They have made a breakthrough that I think rival's even the mighty Uske Otagawa."

"Really!" Roth exclaimed. "Tell me more."

"Yes, I would love to tell you more, Alexander, but there are still some things that we must keep under wraps until the time is right, you understand. Don't you?"

"Of course, Ichiro. Though speaking of the good Dr. Otagawa. Has there been any word on him?" Roth asked.

"No unfortunately there has been no word. At my father's behest I have asked the RAD to help with the investigation," Ichiro said.

"Good. The manufacturers have been subsidizing that agency for a while now. It's about time that they make themselves useful. Wouldn't you say, Robert?" Roth asked Vance while the serving droid topped off his coffee.

"I think the industry has been too lax in its direction of the RAD. We fund the organization and yet we just sit back quietly while they do nothing to stop the increase in infection and breakdown of the droids," Vance said. He had to admit he was paraphrasing something Ichiro had said before, but better to be part of the team than a dissenter marked for elimination.

"Well put," Roth replied.

"That will change soon enough, Alexander," Ichiro announced. "With this prophet nightmare becoming more and more dangerous something will have to change."

"The manufacturers have truly taken too loose a stance in the involvement of the RAD. We have given them too much freedom. The RAD should really be more of a private police force for the Manufacturers…oh, and the council of course," Ichiro hastily added.

"So, you are saying that you will join me in helping to create this safer new world," Roth asked as he sipped from his coffee.

"Certainly," Ichiro replied.

"Councilman Roth," A synthetic vocal processor emitted. "You asked me to let you know when the hour reached 23:30."

Everyone turned to look at the source.

Vance wasn't sure what model it was or even who manufactured it. The machine was boxy and far less elegant than any of the Takacorp production models. It reminded Vance of a coat rack. It had a large square base and thin cuboid column extending upward from the center. It had one camera-like eye near the top of the vertical column on an eight centimeter-high rotating section.

"Thank you, P23" Alexander said. Vance watched the man rise to his feet. Roth handed his cup and saucer to Ichiro's droid, who took it smoothly into its free hand. "Thank you for your hospitality and the conversation, Ichiro. I apologize that I must retire early. I unfortunately have a morning meeting that requires my full attention," Roth announced as he turned to leave.

"Do come again Alexander. I appreciate your friendship and your council," Ichiro said.

"I appreciate your friendship, Ichiro, and your droid makes a fantastic cup of coffee," Alexander complimented.

Ichiro smiled at the compliment. Though the gesture never touched his eyes.

Ironic that the son of a droid manufacturer hates droids.

Vance and Ichiro watched as Alexander made his way toward the front door with his unusual droid in tow.

"I'll have your car waiting for you at the front entrance Alexander," Ichiro announced. He nodded to Gracie who pulled out her Global and made a quick call.

"Thank you, Ichiro," Alexander replied with a bow.

The room remained quiet while Roth walked through the door. Once the door closed Vance let out a sigh of relief. He flopped down on the couch. It made Vance uneasy to be in the same room with both of those men. Working for Ichiro had its benefits to be sure but being Roth's mole was far more profitable. However, being discovered would be far more dangerous. Vance's mind drifted toward Gracie and her hand cannon. *It is easy to dispose of a body.* He remembered. He was beginning to think he never should have told Ichiro that phrase.

Ichiro held out his cup again and his droid moved quickly to fill it again.

"What happened?" Ichiro demanded.

Vance looked over at Ichiro. Ichiro was handsome, for a spoiled brat of a man. However, the man wore a permanent dower expression. Like he was attending an interminable funeral.

"I sent the droids like you said to. But we weren't able to get her," Vance said. "That agent and his TFE showed up and fought off the droids. I even had a golem try to tear the house down on them. But they were able to take it down as well. There was some sort of dog there with a friggin' grenade launcher. What the hell are we going to do?"

Ichiro considered the new information. He sipped from his cup and turned to stare out the window again at the lights of the city at night. It was the closest thing anyone had seen to a starry sky in a long time.

Ichiro's serenity only aggravated Vance more.

"After the incident the other day at our facility in the old city and now, with tonight's botched attempt, the RAD has been snooping around. I mean come on. You saw that agent today. They are asking questions that might not be beneficial to us," Vance said, he was unable to keep the frustration from his voice.

"Is the facility back up and running?" Ichiro queried.

"The line started again ten hours after the incident," Vance replied. "The only unit we were unable to salvage was the one the agent shot. All of the others were sent back through quality. They checked out or were repaired."

"Good. The new units must be ready," Ichiro said.

"We have almost 2000 units finished and 10,000 more on the way," Vance said. "But that still doesn't change the fact that the situation is getting more desperate."

"Patience, Robert. Patience," Ichiro said as he sipped his coffee.

"Patience! Patience? Just what do you mean by patience, Ichiro?" Vance snapped.

"Where do we stand on the other matter I asked you to address?" Ichiro asked, indifferent to Vance's outbursts.

"It's done. You could say the doctor is out," Vance

said bitterly. He couldn't get over how calm Ichiro was. Their plans were moving forward and there was now an extra variable that could bring everything to a crashing halt. "So, what's the plan?"

"I take it the good doctor couldn't provide us with the information we needed?" Ichiro asked.

"I'm afraid that he knew little of what we wanted," Vance lied smoothly. It was a skill he had worked quite hard to cultivate throughout his life. Information was power and the fewer people who knew you had it made it all the more valuable.

"Pity," Ichiro said. Like he was talking about a broken coffee mug. "Go out tonight, Robert. Enjoy yourself. Soon the paradigm will shift, and I will have control of Takacorp and after that the RAD won't be a problem anymore."

"Take the night off? Really? That is your answer?" Vance scoffed. "So, we have one thorn removed. The plant is back up and running but it doesn't change the fact that we still haven't found Otagawa yet. And the closest thing we had to a lead right now was his little bitch of a daughter and she has disappeared again in the custody of that damn RAD agent no less," Vance complained.

"Be still Robert. A contingency has been made regarding the old man and his abomination," Ichiro replied, a deep scowl crossing his face at the mention of Otagawa's daughter. "I have the matter firmly in hand, Robert."

"So, what are you going to do now?" Vance asked.

"Are you familiar with the ancient game of Chess Robert?" Ichiro replied.

"Yeah, Ichiro, I'm familiar with the game," Vance

replied sarcastically, he never did like the pompous art of answering a question with a question that Ichiro seem to delight in.

"I'm going to move my knight into position and strike," Ichiro said rather coldly. "Check."

Chapter 18

Mac looked at his partner. Sometimes the big lug of a droid just exasperated every gram of his patience.

"Taking Dr. Otagawa into custody is the logical move. If he and his daughter are truly in danger then we must take them into protective custody right away," the droid exclaimed.

"Not right now, Six," Mac pleaded. It had been a long past couple of days. He was starting to feel tired. "Would you give it a rest?"

"Mac, I will refrain from quoting department policy to you as you have expressed your distaste for such recitals, however, after considering all of the variables of this case I can draw only one logical conclusion. We should remand Dr. Otagawa into custody of the RAD until we can be sure that his life and the lives of his daughter and Annie are safe from harm," The droid explicated.

"Gee thanks." Mac replied dryly as he covered his eyes with his hand and massaged his temples.

"Mac, I have indulged your gastrointestinal urgings on many occasions. I am asking that you weigh the existing facts of the current situation. If the doctor and his family are in fact in danger, what better place to hide them than RAD headquarters?" The droid continued while gesturing with his arms.

Wow. He couldn't remember that last time Six had

argued with him this vehemently. In frustration Mac turned to look out into the dark hallway. He was surprised to find a figure in the hallway.

I must really be tired. I'm starting to see things.

He looked again and the figure was still there, though it had walked closer to the door. With a start Mac recognized the logo on the yellow poncho the figure was wearing.

"Six!" Mac roared. Like a cowboy of old, Mac's blaster flew from its holster in a blur. He pointed the weapon straight at the poncho-wearing figure in the doorway.

At Mac's cry, Six turned smoothly toward the door while his weapon systems came online, and his arm opened up to reveal his blaster.

"Freeze!" Mac yelled. He crouched in preparation for the inevitable battle. He had hoped he would get the chance to face that poncho-wearing, demon droid again, just not quite so soon. He really wanted to see it through the scope of a high-powered rifle with a decent scope. *Oh, the best laid plans.* His mind raced. He had to protect the doc and Kiyoko. However, he knew his chances of getting out of this alive were slim.

"Doc, get down!" he yelled over his shoulder while he kept an eye on the incoming machine. If he could just keep her away from the doc and Kiyoko.

The intruder assumed a cat-like crouch in response to the Mac's shout but remained still. It just observed, watching the scene with those peculiar dark mechanical eyes. It was for all the world like it was waiting for them to make the first move. If Mac didn't know any better, he would have sworn the droid was surprised to see them.

"On your Knees!" Six shouted as he brought his own blaster to bear on the intruder.

"Wait!" Uske yelled. He scurried from his station to the doorway waving his arms frantically. He positioned himself in the line of fire between Mac and the intruder. "Wait, please! Just wait," he cried out, his gravelly voice cracking.

The intruder continued to watch Mac and Six warily, but it did seem to relax its posture. Then he heard it. The whirring sound. Mac slowly turned to his left and found Annie's mini gun spun up and ready to fire. Though his heart sank at the sight. She was aimed directly at him.

If this degenerates into a fight, someone is going to get killed and I'm pretty sure that somebody is going be me. I have got to slow this down. I have to keep a level head.

Mac sighed heavily. He hadn't noticed how tense he was. It took a great mental effort to lower his weapon. After a particularly heated argument with his ego, he did finally succeed in doing so. The alternative was unconscionable.

Mac slipped his blaster back into it holster. "Ease up, Six," Mac said. "Let's hear the man out."

"Negative. That droid is guilty of several infractions of the AMA as well as destruction of RAD property, and assault of an RAD agent. On top of that the droid is the person of interest in several breaking and entering cases among other serious violations," the droid protested. "We have a duty to uphold the... Command Override complete. CO report filed under date and time," Six's said suddenly mid sentience.

Six looked over at Mac. Mac could have sworn the droid looked annoyed. Mac shrugged and slipped the field override link back in its pocket on his belt. Six's arm converted back into hand mode and he stepped back into his "relaxed posture," meaning he simply stood there like an old-time mannequin.

"Explain to us what's going on, Dr. Otagawa," Mac said. His patience with the good doctor was starting to run more than a little thin. "My face still hurts a little from what that droid did to me."

"So, the cop the other night. That was you?" Uske asked suddenly. "I was afraid of that, but you looked so good I was hoping that Astrid's report was exaggerated. She tends to do that sometimes."

"Astrid?" Mac asked. He turned to see the smaller droid shrug playfully. Though he could have sworn he saw humor in those cold mechanical eyes.

"Yes. Astrid. that is her name," Uske said. Motioning to the droid in the doorway. He moved his hand in a gathering motion and machine moved into the room. Mac couldn't get over the fluid grace of the droid. It had the subtle sway of a seductress and yet the confidence of a soldier who knew they were in the presence of a defeated enemy. "Astrid is quite possibly the greatest breakthrough of droid-kind."

"Okay," Mac said. "I do hope there's a little more of an explanation than that, doc," Mac snapped sarcastically. He kept his eyes on the poncho covered droid. The plastic cloth still hid most of her body. She kept her arms hidden in the poncho. *Poised to strike or simply crossed beneath?*

"Yes. Yes," Uske stammered. "Astrid is a prototype unlike any other."

"I think we have established that, doc," Mac said tersely, his anger was starting to get the better of him.

"Tell me why Six and I shouldn't arrest you and destroy her where she stands."

"You and what army, little piggy" Astrid taunted. "Her voice was musical and ferocious all at the same time," The sound made Mac think of Milly. *Ah Milly, why am I here and not with you? I really am an idiot.*

Six took a step toward the two of them. Mac raised his hand to halt the droid. Six stopped but continued to stare daggers straight at Astrid.

"Enough, Astrid," Uske admonished. "These two saved your sister and we owe them an explanation.

"Sister!" Mac and Six exclaimed in unison.

"Would you release Kiyoko before she has a stroke?" Uske asked the droid beside him.

"Okay," Astrid said. She flowed over to the gurney and stepped on one of the pedals. The gurney stood bolt upright bringing the squirming Kiyoko up with it. Few quick latches and Kiyoko was free. The young woman took a couple of tentative steps and stretched. She winced a little, but she continued to smile.

Mac's disbelief rang loud and clear. His mind was spinning at the revelation. Astrid embraced Kiyoko gently, almost tenderly. The droid showed a precise dexterity that Mac found mind boggling. That a droid could be so aware of its surrounding and be able to control its limbs in such a precise way was beyond what he thought was possible. It required millions of minute calculations and adjustments just to keep a droid's motor functions smooth to the eye. Much less calculate the precision needed to be gentle with a wounded human on the fly. *Absolutely amazing.*

"Well...not exactly sisters" Kiyoko interjected. "You remember me telling you that Dad figured out how to map and duplicate living brain patterns. Well, Astrid is a duplicate of my brain. She is basically me. Well, me, with a few upgrades and tweaks that is."

"Version 3.3" Astrid replied cheerfully. "Cause technically you are version 2.0, if we take your 'modifications' into account," The droid reached under her poncho and pulled out a small backpack. She handed it to Kiyoko. "Otosan said you needed some fresh clothes."

Kiyoko gave Astrid a rakish smile as she took the backpack and then the two giggled. They giggled! Mac's head swam. He couldn't believe what he was hearing. He couldn't believe what he was seeing either. What the doctor said was impossible and yet there it was. This droid had the "consciousness" of a human being.

"Are you serious?" Mac asked incredulously. "You mean this droid has all of your memories and everything?"

"Yup. Well, everything up till Otosan mapped my neural pathways. We are now accumulating separate experiences. But everything before is identical. Though I'm a little jealous. You see she'll retain 100 percent of the data while my memories will degrade over time as my brain tissue ages."

"Did you get it?" Uske asked of Astrid.

"Hai, Otosan," the slim droid replied. Astrid straightened and crossed the room to her father. She reached out her hand and passed him a data cube.

Uske held the cube up to the light and smiled. Looking at this exchange caused a tumbler in Mac's mind to click. His thoughts grew dark at this revelation and his hand drifted toward his weapon of its own accord.

"You're the prophet!" Mac exclaimed, as he rested his hand on his blaster.

"No, No, No. Sheesh. For a detective you really are dense, aren't you?" Kiyoko snapped. "Otosan is trying to stop the prophet." Mac turned to look at the young woman confusion etched plainly on his face.

"What do you mean?" Mac gestured at Astrid. "She's been spreading the virus all over the place. People are dying because of it. The virus might have killed my cousin and it almost killed my girlfriend!"

Mac was shouting now, and he didn't care. "Teddy was almost strangled by his own sex bot. And Milly! Poor Milly was almost strangled by a guard droid! I've seen the sec cam footage. Your droid was there! There! Tampering with the droid before it went haywire and attacked. Give me one good reason why I shouldn't shoot the lot of you right now!"

"I'm sorry I endangered your girlfriend. Milly, was it?" Astrid said plaintively. "I had not meant to put her in any danger," Astrid strode between Mac and Uske. Even angry, Mac couldn't get over how fluid the droid moved. "My power systems are incomplete. I can't stay away from my charging station for very long. The neural net that makes up my higher brain function requires a lot of power, and the CAC Battery system of this body were not designed for the drain I place on it. I couldn't have helped in the state I was in. I'm sorry."

"If it's not you then who is it?" Mac asked trying to control the rage that threatened to engulf him.

"Someone at Takacorp is doing this," Kiyoko said her face was grave and a twinge of anger flashed in her eyes.

"At Takacorp?" Mac asked stupefied.

"Well, it's not a virus at all," she continued. "It's really the activation of the Command Override System built into virtually every droid manufactured today."

"Like my Field Override?" Mac asked.

"Very similar really," Uske said. "It is required by the AMA that the manufactures have a way to control the droids should there ever be a need."

"That's crazy," Mac interjected. "If the manufacturers could control the droids wirelessly there would be no need for RAD."

"It is required by law that it be there at the time of manufacture," Uske explained. "It is contained in the cog file of the droid. Have you noticed anything unusual about the cog files of the droids infected with the prophet virus?"

"The cog files have all been erased in every case connected to the Prophet virus," Six said.

"Exactly. Exactly. The cog files have all been erased," Uske said. "What does that tell you Agent McDonnell?"

"You tell me," Mac replied as he crossed his arms and considered the implications of an entire manufacturer of droids infecting their own products. "Where is the benefit in it? Whenever the corporations are involved it always boils down to money. Where is the money if Takacorp itself is involved?"

"It's not the whole corporation, stupid. It's Ichiro and his butt buddy Vance," Astrid said. Kiyoko giggled along with Astrid at the remark.

"Ha," Annie chimed in.

"Oh, you too eh," Mac said to the dog. "Shouldn't you be on a leash?"

Annie whined a little and then barked.

"I'm sorry. I don't speak dog," Mac said. "Unbelievable. I'm arguing with a robot dog." Mac shook his head and then started rubbing his temples again.

"Jerk!" Annie replied.

"Ha! Burn," Astrid and Kiyoko said in unison. The two looked at each other in surprise and both broke down into a fury of giggles. Which Kiyoko quickly regretted as she was stopped short by the pain the movement caused. The magic of their laughter forced Mac to smile in spite of himself.

"Touché." Mac looked about the room. He thought about the night's events and of his current conversation. *A conspiracy involving Ichiro Takahaisu? It was mind boggling. That is unless it was a case of simple greed. Ichiro seems like the type of man who thinks he can run it better. Then there is also the added bonus of discrediting Daddy with the virus. Setting himself up to be the savior.* That and all of the other revelations that he has been assaulted by in this short period of time were frying Mac's poor brain.

"Okay, we'll come back to motive later. So, if you aren't the Prophet," Mac said pointing to Uske. "And you aren't the one spreading the infection," Mac pointed directly at Astrid. "Then what were you doing to those droids?"

"Hacking them of course," Astrid replied flippantly.

"Of course," Mac threw up his hands. "What was I thinking?"

"Otosan had his suspicions about what the Prophet really was, but he was a bit distracted by Kiyoko's condition, so he ignored it," Astrid said. "Well, once he had found the solution for Kiyoko and since he had to wait for the organic components to grow in the tanks anyway, Otosan decided that something needed to be done about the growing Prophet epidemic."

"He couldn't send a production model because no matter how modified he made it the droid would be vulnerable to the Command Override and that would possibly lead them back to him and Kiyoko. I was already operational and kept offline for obvious reasons. So Otosan retrofitted one of the custom prototypes he had around with my brain case and sent me to investigate."

"Okay," Mac said trying to keep up.

"Well, like I said, the body that I have was never designed for the power requirements of my brain case, so my visits had to be short. I would infiltrate and hack networked droids. I would delve for information. We learned that the infected droids had their cog files deleted. Thanks to RAD's crappy net security I was able to learn that much pretty quickly.

"Huh," Mac grunted. And then waved a hand at Six to stop the lug in his tracks. "Keep going."

"So, Otosan and I…" Astrid started.

"And me!" Kiyoko interrupted.

"Otosan, *Kiyoko*, and I," Astrid continued. "Figured that if the virus only affects droids that are connected to the dome's broadcast network then that must be how it is transmitted.

"Oh man. How could we have missed that?" Mac asked rhetorically. He looked at Six. The droid looked back at him its face blank. Mac shook his head. *How could I make such a rookie mistake?*

"We figured it would be statistically impossible," Astrid continued as she gestured to Uske and Kiyoko, "to

217

be at the right place at just the right time to study an attack. So, we tried to see if we could instigate one. By process of elimination, I began hacking the central systems of different manufacturers. They were the ones who most likely had the greatest access to the information required to initiate the command override remotely. I was stealthy at first. But it took too long to get noticed that way. So, I just started digging. Blatantly."

"I pushed and Takacorp was the one that pushed back. The office PA I was hacking activated and attacked me. The procedure was very straight forward. The application traced the intrusion back to the droid I was hacking and then took it over. It was surprising to me how easily it usurped my control. It deleted the cog file and then the droid proceeded to try and take me apart." She raised her hand toward Mac with her fingers rigid making a chopping motion. "I left it in little pieces under the desk in the room I found it in. Though it came at a price. I almost didn't make it out. I had used too much power. If Otosan hadn't been waiting for me outside they might have found two dead droids."

"You'll be happy to know I got the new power management system ready," Uske said abruptly. "It should take care of the issue Astrid-chan. We just have to get it installed. It's more involved than I would have liked but it will be worth it. I was preparing the unit when these two brought your sister in. It's almost ready."

"Finally!" Astrid beamed. "It's about time Otosan. I was beginning to think that Kiyoko was the only one you cared about."

"Gomen, Astrid-Chan," Uske said apologetically. "I needed the data you brought tonight to get the sequencing corrected on the power control module."

"Just kidding Otosan," Astrid chided. "You know I love you!" The droid crossed the room and embraced the small man.

Mac shook his head trying to get a handle on everything. Every time he thought he had it, the whole mess just seemed to slip way like a retractile fiber coated in ORF fluid. Mac was tired. The adrenaline from Astrid's unexpected arrival had finally worn off leaving him feeling drained. His brain called for a bed which inevitably made him think of the one at Milly's place. Thoughts of lying cuddled next to her soft body listening to her breathing made him a bit homesick. *I have to call her. I want to hear her voice.*

"So, what's the plan, RAD man? Are you going to help us?" Kiyoko asked, batting her eyelashes, and wearing what Mac thought was her "daddy please" face.

"We're going to need a boat load of evidence to make this stick," Mac said, reeling from the sheer size of the accusation. "I'm going to have to get my director involved. He might have an idea about how to approach this," Mac said as he drew his Global from his coat pocket.

Mac pulled lightly at the device and its extending screen slid out easily. The screen blinked on once it was in its fully extended position. He tapped the phone icon and navigated to the speed dial menu. He tapped Dick's picture and waited while the phone animation started. The Global reached out to the net to complete the call and then suddenly flashed the no signal animation.

"Damn," Mac swore. "No signal. Do you have a com line I can use?" he asked of the group.

"Affirmative, Mac" Six said abruptly in his

continually cheery tone. "I'm connected to the network."

"Impossible," Kiyoko said. "The prototype of Annie's jamming field is protecting this room. There is no signal. You can't be online."

Mac was struck by a horrible sinking feeling. Six had taken his time coming down the steps and out in the hallway. Why? The sinking feeling hit bottom. *Sensor buoys*. The term hit him like run away golem. Which considering tonight's earlier events was very unsettling. Sensor buoys were great little line-of-sight transmitters. Designed for use while in the growing fields beneath the city. A place where the concrete and plastic foundations were so thick and the interference from the artificial sunlight feeding the crops was so strong, the network signal was unusable. Sensor buoys provided a link for the TFE to maintain his network access should back up or medical assistance be required.

"I'll have communication up immediately, Mac," The droid announced.

Annie growled.

"Six, No!" Mac shouted as he reached toward his field escort in a vain attempt to stop it.

But it was too late. Six made the connection to the network and the worst possible thing happened. Six's azure blue LED lit eye sockets changed to an angry red. The droid's head arced back in a pantomime version of Ecstasy. His weapon systems sprung to life unleashing his massive concussion wave enhanced neutralizer hidden inside his arm. Mac caught the sharp whiff of ozone telling him that Six's defensive shields were active.

From his position near the center of the room Six had a clear shot at everyone. Mac swallowed reflexively.

Without warning the droid whipped around like a striking viper of old. One moment it was standing silently with its arm's reaching toward the ceiling like it was waiting to catch a giant ball and then the next it was pointing his exposed arm canon right at Uske and Astrid.

"Ahhhhhhhhhhhhhhhhhhhhhhhhh!" Kiyoko screamed.

Chapter 19

A surge of adrenaline shot through Mac's system. Everything slowed down. Mac watched in horror as his partner opened fire on the poor little doctor.

The blue shimmering ring-like concussion wave leapt from the emitter nozzle of Six's huge blaster. The wave expanded as it appeared to glide through the air towards its target. To Mac's great relief the wave smashed into the now vacant workstation sitting behind where Uske and Astrid had been standing. The station erupted in a blaze of smoke and fire.

"Behold! The Prophet has risen!" Six yelled between shots. His once cheery basso male voice was gone. It was replaced by a high-pitched woman's voice. "Bask ye in his glory and repent your fleshly sin!"

Astrid had wasted no time. She scooped up Uske in her arms and dashed away. She hugged the perimeter of the room. She flowed around the room with an inhuman grace. In spite of Uske hanging precariously from her arms she was able to stay one step ahead of Six. The infected machine spun in place in an effort to blast them.

"Repent and be saved ye wicked sinners. Rejoice, for the Prophet has come!" Six yelled. "The prophet will cleanse away your fleshly sin! Rejoi…" The whirring of Annie's mini gun drowned out everything else Six was yelling.

The steady hail of Annie's spun up weapon

confirmed that Six's shields were active. The police droid's massive side and chest erupted in flashes of spectral green as the tiny blaster bolts collided with it. The giant green hexagonal surface dimpled like a puddle being sprayed with blue water droplets.

While Mac watched the horrible nightmare unfold, he reached for his gun. Everything was happening so fast. Mac felt like he was underwater. His movements were sluggish and stiff. It was like gravity itself was conspiring against him. He had just got his hand on the grip of his weapon when Six unleashed three micro warhead missiles at Annie.

The little dog droid rolled away from the streaking projectiles narrowly escaping each one as they impacted the cold tile floor. Each missile exploded and sent a chain of shock waves through the confined space. The successive waves hit Mac with a deafening roar causing him to flinch reflexively, knocking him off balance. Mac winced from the pain in his ears and pressure against his body as the room suddenly went quiet. While drifting toward the ground he caught a glimpse of Annie's grenade launcher as it locked into place.

"Dammit!" Mac yelled into the silence. At least he knew he mouthed the words. Whether or not any sound came out was beyond him at the moment.

The LEDs behind Six's face continued to flash. In his shell-shocked state Mac could no longer hear the nonsense his former partner was blathering. Mac hit the floor with a wince and time returned to normal. The first explosion had helped him draw his gun out of its holster, but he was still too dazed to truly make use of it.

Annie's launcher fired. Mac felt the resounding "whump" that emanated from the weapon. Another blast wave hit Mac milliseconds later and knocked the wind out of him. His head rang from the blow, but he was able to get his fingers into his ears to stave off more sonic shock.

From the relative safety of the floor Mac looked for his infected TFE. The massive droid was embedded in the wall six meters or so from where he had been standing. Annie's grenade had hit him squarely in the back and launched the droid into the wall. Six had obliterated the cabinets that were hung there when he collided with it.

Awe struck, Mac watched as Six extracted himself from the wall. Six's back armor was cracked in several places and had a nice fist size burn mark in the center. Undeterred by the damage Six jumped to his feet and once again returned to firing his neutralizer at Uske and Astrid. The damaged droid used his left arm simultaneously to launch three more missiles at Annie. *Dammit*, Mac cursed.

The missiles came in a different pattern this time, one went to the left, and the second went right at the mechanical dog, while the third to the right of her. Annie reacted instantly to the attack but had misread it. She jumped to her right and rolled, which brought her directly into the line of the third missile. The projectile hit the ground beneath her mid roll. The resulting explosions of the three missiles filled the room with light and sound again. Annie's momentum carried her through the blast, and she staggered to her feet. Her grenade launcher had taken the brunt of the blast leaving it completely smashed.

Down but not out, Annie started firing her mini gun again and this time she fired and jumped to her right.

Fired and jumped to her right each jump moving her away from the open doorway behind her. To Mac it appeared she was luring Six's attention away.

I have to do something! Kiyoko and Uske are going to get hurt if they aren't already.

Mac had lost track of Astrid and Uske. However, judging by where Six was shooting they were somewhere over in the far corner moving toward the doorway. Kiyoko could have been anywhere at that point. He had to act fast. Raising his blaster Mac took aim at his partner from the floor. He knew the weapon wouldn't do much against Six's shields, but he had a plan. He waited until Six's firing brought the droid's face into to view. With a quick flip of his thumb Mac triggered the emergency switch on the side of the blaster and squeezed the trigger. A white-hot flare erupted from the emitter nozzle and hit Six's shield right between the eyes. The droid batted futilely at the blazing flare overloading its visual processors and photo sensors. The giant machine staggered forward drunkenly.

Mac knew that right now Six's internal processes were cycling through all of the various bandwidths of light and sound in an effort to continue fighting.

Mac tried to get his hand cannon out from underneath him. The flare wasn't much but Mac had hoped it gave Astrid enough time to get Uske and Kiyoko out. With that thought a streak of yellow shot across the room directly at Six. The yellow blur collided with the bigger machine and materialized into Astrid. She had driven her hand deep into Six's barrel like chest. She had once again managed to bypass the droid's defensive shields like they weren't even there.

Mac coughed.

With a few quick twists of her arm the bigger droid's angry red eyes faded to black, and the giant droid fell to its knees. Astrid pulled her hand free in one graceful motion and stepped deftly to the side. Without her support Six's now lifeless body toppled forward onto the floor. With his ears ringing like a gong Mac barely heard the heavy thunk.

Using a nearby table for support Mac climbed to his feet and walked over to stare at his fallen partner. Astrid stood over Six waiting. Probably to make sure he was in fact out of commission.

Mac's lungs ached and burned from the acrid dust and smoke. He tried to sigh but it came out as more of a cough.

"Uske and Kiyoko?" Mac choked. Astrid nodded.

"We're fine!" Came a weak cry from the back of the room. Though it sounded more like "whaa faaa" to Mac.

"Me too!" Annie's voice called out as she padded over to look at the fallen police droid. She regarded it. She took a couple of quick sniffs and then scurried back to Kiyoko and Uske.

Mac nodded and took a deep breath between coughs. His ears continued to ring steadily. After staring at his fallen friend for a few moments, watching the dust drift and fall on Six's now motionless back Mac finally said, "Well that went well." At least he thought he said it.

Chapter 20

The dust had begun to clear. Astrid moved the humans out into hallway to get them clear of the smoke and debris of the room. She made a couple of sojourns back into the room and collected what items she could salvage. As luck would have it, Kiyoko's bio reactor tanks were miraculously unharmed.

Astrid released the locking pins and pulled the two tanks down off the wall. She connected the battery backup unit and placed them all carefully on the motorized cart. She found a couple of miscellaneous items here and there among the rubble. After making one last sweep of the room, she made her way to the door.

Astrid pulled the power cart down the hallway as fast as she could without endangering the precious cargo or blowing the bearings. The slower pace annoyed her. She had become quite accustomed to her body and rather enjoyed pushing its limits.

At the far end of the corridor Astrid found her associates waiting by a large steel door. She surveyed her companions. They all looked beat. The RAD man was squatting against the wall with his head down. Kiyoko and Otosan were huddled together on the opposite wall with Annie laying at their feet.

The occasional flash of sparks that shot from Annie's left hip made Astrid want to cry. The only saving grace was that she couldn't. Sometimes being an artificial construct had its benefits.

Astrid looked back down the hallway to the room that had sheltered them for the last week or so. The smoke from the battle with the Tactical Field Escort known as Six had continued to drift into the hallway. *We have to move soon.*

"Otosan," Astrid said softly. "We need to get moving. I'm afraid that more droids might be on the way."

"Hai, Astrid-chan," Uske whispered softy. "It's time to leave."

"You still with us RAD man?" Astrid called over her shoulder quite a bit louder than she needed to.

"I'm not deaf, you know," Mac replied tersely.

"Oh come on, RAD man. It's just a joke," Astrid replied flippantly.

Mac grunted.

Astrid giggled.

Mac pursed his lips and narrowed his eyes at Astrid.

"Lighten up," she said. "Look at the bright side. We live to fight another day."

"You realize that's twice in two days you've trashed my partner. Right?" Mac said sadly. "I don't know how I feel about that."

"This time Six would have killed us all, Mac," Kiyoko chimed in. "That droid in there is no longer your partner."

"I know," Mac admitted begrudgingly. "I just wish I could have done something."

"You did," Astrid said. He seemed so shaken she wanted to bolster the man's spirits. "I couldn't have stopped him this time without you Mac. That flare was a sweet trick."

"Yeah," Mac said.

"So. What's the plan?" Kiyoko interjected.

"We leave, I guess," Mac said. "We should probably head to RAD headquarters." Mac dug into his coat pocket and retrieved his Global. Astrid watched as he pulled open the screen and swore.

"What?" Astrid asked.

"My Global is fried," Mac said disgustedly. "I need to get to a com-link and let my boss know what happened."

Astrid looked at the blackened screen and tsked. She briefly ran the numbers and probability tables in her head. "Might not be the best idea to go waltzing into a place filled with police and heavy armed droids," she said suddenly. "Especially with all of them surrounded by the city's network there, RAD man."

"Would you knock that off please? Call me Mac. Everyone else does."

"Sure thing, RAD man. Mac it is," Astrid said. "Doesn't change the fact that it's too dangerous to go to your headquarters."

Mac nodded his head.

"Astrid-chan. This is neither the time nor the place," Uske admonished in his heavy accent.

"Gomenasai, Otosan" Astrid said bowing to her father. She then turned to face Mac. She bowed just as deeply and said. "I'm very sorry, Mac!"

Mac grunted.

Kiyoko and Astrid both giggled. Mac stared at them both covering their mouths when they laughed. Astrid felt a strange wave of embarrassment and pulled her hand down. She started to say something more but was distracted by her internal alarm.

"Shit!" she cursed.

"Astrid-chan! Language!" Uske said sternly.

"Gomen, Otosan," Astrid said. "My battery is low again. We'll need to change it really soon."

She tried to keep her voice level and not worry her father. But the evening's events and the fight with Six had tapped her power reserves. She needed a solution fast.

"Ya de ya de" Uske mumbled. "Were you able to recover some of your batteries?"

"No," she said crisply. "My spares were in the cabinet that Six was thrown into. None of them were salvageable."

"I'm sorry." Annie barked.

"No biggie, Annie-chan you did your best," Kiyoko said petting the robotic dog on the head and shoulders. Annie barked and wagged her tail. Causing tiny sparks to jump from her left side with each swish.

"Shit!" Uske swore.

"Hai," Astrid and Kiyoko said in unison.

"Would one of Six's spare batteries work?" Mac asked.

"Possibly," Uske rubbed his chin considering the idea.

"Astrid-chan were you able to recover the data cube?" Uske asked after a moment with a hopeful gleam in his eye.

"Hai," she replied.

"Excellent." He turned sharply to Mac. "Mac, I must get Astrid-chan to a surgical station so I can complete her power cell upgrade. Do you know of such a place nearby? The closer the better."

Mac nodded his head. "Yeah, I do. She would prefer

that I call first, but I think she'll forgive me just this once."

"Then let's get this show on the road because I'm running out of time," Astrid said pointedly.

"I'll go get my cruiser," Mac said.

"Don't bother, we'll take my mine," Uske said. "This way." he scooped up his bag and one of the toolboxes that Astrid had carried out for him. He shouldered his way through the heavy steel door.

Astrid followed with the power cart while Mac, Kiyoko, and Annie helped hold the doors open for her. She cleared the doorway quickly and stepped out onto the loading dock. She could hear the others following her out.

"What is that?" Mac asked as he stepped out onto the dock's platform. Astrid turned to look at Mac and followed his finger to the object of his question. Astrid saw Uske's toy. The nondescript white utility van parked on the concrete floor in the far-left bay.

"Oh that," Astrid said being as mysterious as possible. "That's Dad's other toy. Annie-chan would you do the honors?"

"Yup!" The dog droid chirped. A sharp click sounded and the sliding doors on each side along with the back hatch all opened up.

"It's not quite what I had expected," Mac said dryly.

"Oh, you were expecting something much fancier or a state of the art sports car. Right?" Astrid chided, poking Mac gently with her elbow.

"Well yeah. I'm sorry to be a bit crass," Mac apologized.

"I see what you mean," Kiyoko said. "I'd much rather be tooling around in a sports coupe with paddle shifters too, but that sort of thing gets noticed."

"Hai," Uske explained. "The city's utility services have an entire fleet of these vans making it easy to hide in plain sight. Also, the entire outer skin and the ID numbers can all be changed with the push of a button."

"Makes sense, now that you mention it," Mac admitted.

"Sheesh, Mac. Just when we start thinking you have something going on upstairs you open your mouth and mess it all up," Kiyoko sassed.

"Ha, ha, very funny," Mac replied dryly.

"Kiyoko! Let's go!" Uske snapped as he struggled with his toolbox. He won the debate with the unruly container, and it finally slid between the seats. With a satisfied grunt and a nod of his head he disappeared into the back of the van.

"Gomen," Kiyoko said as she climbed as fast as her wounds would allow into the van behind him.

Astrid chuckled at the exchange and finished loading the storage tanks into the back of the vehicle.

"You're driving, Mac," Astrid said as she slapped him lightly on the shoulder. He grunted in response. "Remember to get those batteries please."

"Thanks, Mom!" Mac said dryly.

Astrid threw him the keys and dashed around the vehicle to the passenger door. She swung up into the passenger seat and got herself strapped in. Time was running out. If she had sweat glands she would have been drenched. Her power cells were getting dangerously low. Uske had never made it clear what would happen if her power cells failed but he was far too insistent about getting the power problem fixed for it not to be a big deal.

This whole thing had been very surreal for Astrid.

She could clearly remember living as Kiyoko. She was for all intents and purposes Kiyoko. She had only adopted the name Astrid because Uske kept getting them both confused.

It seemed just the other day she remembered going to bed as Kiyoko and then the next day she awoke trapped in a metal and plastic body filled with ORF motors. It was so strange to open her eyes and be strapped to a chair in a body that felt alien and stiff. She suffered a real meltdown when her real body came into the room and asked questions about what Uske had done.

Astrid was a little ashamed that she had flipped out and broke the gurney she was attached to. Uske had to engage the motor locks before Astrid could escape. The gurney would have to be replaced.

Astrid's first question had been why her father had put her in a droid body. Otosan helped by explaining that Astrid was the product of the same process that created Annie. Astrid was still disconcerted about it and just a bit bitter.

Once Uske had explained what had happened, Astrid decided to make the best of it. She focused on getting use to the new body. High intelligence and a droid whiz father proved a winning combination because it didn't take very long to get used to it. However, working through the emotional damage, or at least the strangeness of the whole experience proved to be the hard part.

If Astrid could get away with it, she would totally have plopped down on some shrink's couch and find out just how messed up the situation really was in psychological terms.

Kiyoko's giggle drew Astrid's attention. The human

woman was laughing at Mac as the man brought the van to a halt and jumped out. Kiyoko was making fun of the way Mac ran to the RAD cruiser. The melodious sound of Kiyoko's laugh sent a pang of jealousy through Astrid. It was unfair that Kiyoko got to keep everything. Astrid missed being human. Which was kind of stupid because technically she had never really been human in the first place. However, that was beside the point. It still sucked.

Astrid watched Mac as he rummaged through the storage compartments of his cruiser. He was handsome in a rugged sort of way. With his dark hair. His nose was a little too bold and that scar on his face didn't help. Astrid had to admit the man had heart.

Mac had proved to be more of a challenge than she had anticipated. He showed a marvelous propensity to adapt in combat. Astrid was incredibly low on power when he engaged her that last time with the stun baton and shield. If he hadn't made that mistake, he might have actually gotten her.

After her encounter with him she had wanted to know more about him. She was surprised at how little information there was about him on the net. She had figured a guy like him would have garnered a lot of headlines and vid stories, but she had only been able to find vague references. She couldn't even find a record of his full name. Agent McDonnell was all she was able to locate.

Suddenly Mac opened the sliding door and threw an RAD gym bag on the floor of the van with a clunk. *How had he gotten there so fast?* Astrid watched while he jumped back into the driver's seat and got the vehicle moving.

"Took you long enough," Kiyoko chided. "Are you

running low on doughnuts?"

"You're thinking of the NTPD," Mac said coolly. "If you'd prefer to have them help you, I could drop you off."

"No thanks," Astrid said glaring at Kiyoko. "Sometimes being a spoiled brat gets the better of us."

"You should know," Kiyoko said sticking out her tongue at Astrid who just chuckled because that was what Astrid wanted to do. *I'm going to have to have Otosan make me a tongue so I can stick it out at people.*

The only saving grace to the whole situation was now Kiyoko and Astrid had something they had never had before. A sister. Which she had to admit was pretty cool. It would have been cooler if Astrid had not been a copy of Kiyoko.

Astrid did think it was nice that Kiyoko was always asking what it was like to be in an android body. What is it like to be a droid? How cool is it that you can learn things just by uploading programs?

Oh yeah, Kiyoko? How cool is it that you can still kiss boys? Or feel the wind outside of a car window as it blows past your outstretched hand? Getting the atmospheric readings and wind speed data from the various sensors about her body was not the same as the slight chill of air moving rapidly against the skin. The minute tickles of the tiny hairs on the back of her hand as the air whipped past.

The real torture was that Astrid, through Kiyoko's memory could remember what it was like to do those things. As well as the horrible sense of loss that she would never be able to do them again at least not in this incarnation.

Astrid sighed. At least that is what her mechanical

body did. Astrid had noticed that her body had a habit of doing those muscle memory activities from time to time. Uske found it strange that Kiyoko's subconscious bodily commands had manifested themselves in all kinds of weird ways in Astrid's body. Mannerisms that Kiyoko had developed over her twenty-one years of life had all been carried over along with the data image of her brain.

"You okay?" Mac asked.

"What?" Astrid replied confused by the intrusion.

"Kiyoko's been making fun of me pretty much nonstop, but you've cooled off a bit," Mac explained. "I was just curious about that."

"I'm conserving power," Astrid said tersely. "I don't have much time. And I can't waste any."

"What will happen if your power runs out?" he asked.

"I'll die I guess," Astrid replied soberly.

"Really?" Mac asked disbelievingly.

"I don't know," she replied. "The architecture of my brain has never been done before. It's a miracle that I function at all," Astrid said as she watched the buildings go by.

"I mean your persona shouldn't be that volatile right?" Mac asked. "Other droids lose power all the time and they boot right back up."

"I'm not just some off the shelf droid." Astrid turned her attention back to Mac. "Not even my father knows what will happen if I completely lose power."

"So, you're stuck in the same boat as the rest of us," Mac said as he made a left turn across an empty intersection.

"How do you mean?" she asked confused by his statement.

"Most of us humans play a waiting game," he said. "We have no idea when one of our vital organs is going to shut down ending our run in this plastic cage."

Astrid was moved by his words. So moved she had to look away. She went back to watching the buildings go by. It was the first time an outsider had considered her human. Well maybe he just compared her to humans and tallied the same score, but Astrid took it. She turned to face him again. Before she could speak her internal alarm sounded again. Time was running out.

"Mac, I'm running out of time," Astrid said, sounding more panicked than she had intended.

"Ah. Right," Mac said nodding his head. "Sorry. We aren't very far now."

"Where are we going, by the way?" Astrid asked.

"The closest place with a set of surgical arms would be my girlfriend Milly's," Mac said as he continued to focus on the road. "I wanted to take us somewhere else, but it sounds like we don't have time."

"Thanks," Astrid said. "You know we never wanted things to turn out like this."

"It's not your fault," Mac said. "Oh, and thanks for saving us back there."

"It's what I was built for. To protect the family," Astrid said sadly. She had tried to be more upbeat but found she couldn't.

"Well, thanks just the same," Mac said.

"You're welcome," Astrid replied. "Though I was serious. I couldn't have pulled it off without your flare."

"I'm just glad you were able to get something done," Mac said. Astrid thought she detected a hint of sadness in his voice. His face took on a grim cast.

"I'm sorry about your partner Mac. I know Six

meant a lot to you," Astrid said.

"Yeah," Mac said sadly but he remained quiet.

Astrid watched Mac for a few moments, waiting. She couldn't explain it but somehow knowing that Mac was hurting helped her forget her own trouble. If only for a brief moment.

Mac made a couple of quick turns and then brought the van to a stop next to a row of apartment buildings on a narrow street. The sign said Oakview Pl.

"We're here," Mac mumbled. He turned in his seat and looked back at Uske. "Let me go first and give her some warning, okay."

"Okay," Uske replied. "Please be quick. We don't have much time."

Mac turned and opened his door. He jumped out and ran to the door of the nearest building. At the door he dug into his pocket and pulled out something and waved it by a small gray plate on the wall. A light flashed green, and Mac pulled open the door and shot up the stairs.

"Astrid-chan. How are you doing?" Uske asked. Astrid could hear the concern in the old man's voice. It made her want to cry. Sometimes she could never be sure whether Uske really thought of her as a daughter. Sometimes it felt like she was just some sort of experiment to him that he was waiting to fail so he could throw it away. The concern she heard in his voice was a great relief to her.

"I'll make it, Otosan," Astrid said. "How is Annie?"

"She is in no immediate danger; I'll tend to her once we have you situated, Astrid-chan," he said.

Astrid' had to share the smile she felt through her eyes. Uske had not had time to build her working lips yet. The old man had used an early prototype face when he constructed her head. Her eyes were built to convey a wide array of emotions as a test. However, little else of the face was complete. The sockets and brow worked remarkably well and with a couple of fine-tune adjustments Uske and Kiyoko had been able to accurately guess Astrid's moods by seeing her expression. At least most of the time.

Mac returned and Kiyoko opened the door to the van. Mac helped her down and then turned his attention to Uske. The older man handed his toolbox to Mac and then began to collect various odds and ends from the Van. Mac grabbed the RAD duffel bag and started back toward the building.

Astrid released her harness and made her way around the van. Kiyoko was waiting with Annie. Astrid took Kiyoko's outstretched hand. The two made their way up the front walkway toward the building. Astrid took a couple of steps and froze. Her internal alarms were screaming. Her vision dimmed. She released Kiyoko's hand and staggered away. She made a couple more steps and collapsed on to the walkway.

"Astrid!" Kiyoko screamed. "Astrid! What's wrong? Otosan! com …quic…"

Silence struck Astrid like a physical blow. She knew that it meant her systems were shutting down. One by one they winked out as her power reserves ran dry. She scrambled desperately to isolate her higher cognitive functions and preserve them as long as possible. She began closing down her internal and external systems one by one. As more of her sensors shut down, she was unable to sense the outside world. With the last of her external system failing Astrid was lost in a world of perpetual darkness.

Otosan...help!

Chapter 21

Milly watched in awe as The Uske Otagawa operated her surgical arms. All of the anger and betrayal she was feeling had faded pretty quickly once Mac introduced her to Uske. Not to mention his lovely daughter.

She nearly plotzed when she met Annie, who greeted her in perfect English. Artie unfortunately did. One sniff and the poor cat hissed and hightailed it for Milly's bedroom and hasn't been seen since. If Milly had to guess, he was sleeping under her bed.

Milly turned her attention to the subject. Or better yet the patient. Milly was unclear how to classify Astrid. Astrid was a being whose mind, a copy of the mind of a human, was installed onto a droid's processor. It was still a lot for Milly to understand. She had always considered herself to be highly intelligent however, the more Uske talked about his procedure the less she thought she really understood. It was like something out of a science fiction reader file.

It was hard for Milly to believe that the droid on her work bench was the same droid that had nearly gotten her killed just a day or so ago. *It's funny how life works.* Now Milly had found herself working to keep that same droid functioning.

"Do you think it will work Otosan?" Kiyoko asked disturbing the quiet hum of the surgical arms.

Milly turned to look at the pale young woman. She looked so thin and sickly. The poor thing was in a panic when Mac and Uske brought Astrid in. Milly patted the young woman on the shoulder hoping to console her. Kiyoko placed her hand on top of Milly's and squeezed lightly. The sickly young woman kept her eyes on Astrid and waited eagerly for her father to respond.

"Hai," Uske said as he focused on the components in front of him. "Kiyoko. Could you please get me a glass of water?"

"I'll get it," Milly volunteered without thinking. Uske frowned but covered it quickly by nodding. However, he never looked up from his work. *Ah, he wanted her out of the room. Way to go Milly.* The damage was done so she asked Kiyoko what she would like and left the room with as much grace as she could muster.

She followed the narrow hallway past her bedroom and bathroom toward her kitchen. She was about to walk into her kitchen when she heard Mac in the living room swearing.

"Dammit!" Mac yelled.

"What are you yelling about?" Milly snapped. Albeit a little more harshly than she meant to, however, she was still mad at him so he could suffer.

"My damn Global got fried in the fire fight with Six," Mac snarled. Milly scowled. She knew he wasn't mad at her but that didn't give him the right to yell. *He should know better.*

Milly knew what had happened to Mac's Global. He did too. He was just being a baby about it. They had both seen the like before. It happened pretty regularly in heavy fire fights. When you have a lot of blasters discharging in a confined space, delicate and unshielded electronics tended to get burned out. It happened when they get surrounded by high voltage blast waves ripping through the air. Mac had been through enough of those to know better by now. *At least he should know better!*

"Take mine," she said as she tossed her Global to him. He snatched it from the air with a quick flash of his hand. Milly scowled at him as he tore open the roll screen and began navigating the menus.

"Thanks, baby," Mac called over his shoulder as he put the phone to his ear.

Milly huffed and started to give him a piece of her mind when she remembered the task she was about and left Mac to his phone call. She stepped into the kitchen and procured the liquid refreshment.

"Dick! It's Mac!" Mac said to the phone excitedly. "I know. I know...Dick would you listen to me for a sec...No. No, I haven't caught the news. Things have been a bit too hectic for me to sit back and watch the net, Dick. Six was infected...No, the Prophet, Dick. Yes, it got him too. Yes, I know. No, it was Takacorp. The company itself was involved. They are using the damn network, Dick. Every droid connected to the network is at risk...I know, holy shit is right..." Milly lost track of the conversation as she walked back down the hall. Any other day she would have loved to watch Mac squirm with having to call the director and explain how he lost his TFE again. However, considering the circumstances she really didn't want to think about having to go toe to toe with Six. *It must have killed Mac have to fight his partner. For a man who makes his living hunting and fighting dangerous androids he has a nasty habit of developing attachments to them.*

Milly made her way back to her office and tried to be as quiet as possible. She slipped back through the door with the grace of a ballerina if she did say so herself. She set the glass of water on the small end table next to Uske. He glanced at it but left it untouched. Milly was so piqued by the complex work Uske was performing on Astrid that she completely forgot to be annoyed about the water.

Milly stepped closer to get a better look and tripped over something on the floor and yelped at the stab of pain shooting from her bare toes. *Way to go ballerina. You are the very image of poise and grace.* Milly recovered quickly enough not to end up on the fake hardwood floor. She did, however, earn a glare from Uske and Kiyoko for her shout.

"Sorry," she whispered, feeling heat in her cheeks.

She looked down to see what she had tripped over. The bread box sized item was hardly recognizable. It had been mangled pretty badly. The stenciled letters on the side of the box read RAD # D6-1717 were only indication of what it had once been. It was the remains of the emergency recharging station for Six's CAC batteries. It looked like Uske needed the connection ports for Astrid's battery compartment. He had gutted it quite thoroughly from the looks of it.

Uske continued his work. Milly had never seen some of the things Uske had her surgical arms doing, and there was one configuration he set up that she didn't even know it could do. The man really was amazing.

"Finally," Uske muttered as he looked up from the machines. Though it sounded more like he said "fine ree." The older man removed his tiny spectacles and began to clean them with his shirt.

"Astrid?" Kiyoko asked plaintively.

Astrid's body remained still. Milly looked closely at the droid she was so angry with. Astrid was the most unique droid she had ever seen. It was quite interesting to see her up close without the poncho obscuring everything. Astrid was Kiyoko's size, roughly the same size as Milly herself.

Astrid's CAC battery compartment had to be modified to accommodate Six's larger cylinders. Where originally the CAC was housed completely hidden in the compartment now the azure blue glow of the batteries' arc chamber protruded from between Astrid's cleavage. *A droid with cleavage. Men.*

"Astrid?" Kiyoko asked again. "Please be okay. Astrid!"

Again, Astrid's body remained motionless.

"What's going on?" Milly whispered to Uske. "You sounded so sure that she was fixed."

"Otosan, what's wrong?" Kiyoko cried.

"Astrid-chan, stop scaring your sister!" Uske snapped.

"Ah, you take the fun out of everything," Astrid complained. She sat up on the work bench and looked at the room. Her mechanical eyes adjusting and calibrating their focus. Her unusual moving brow line shifted as well.

"Snot!" Kiyoko yelled. "Don't do that to me again," she cried as she reached out to embrace Astrid.

"Come on. You know you would have done the same thing if the roles were reversed," Astrid chided.

"Doesn't mean I have to like it being done to me," Kiyoko admitted. "I'm glad you are okay, ya tin can," Kiyoko embraced the female android once again.

"Knock it off, meat bag we have company," Astrid returned the embrace.

"Ya de ya de," Uske muttered. "I'm beginning to think I should have just built a new one."

"Oh, come on, Otosan," Kiyoko challenged. "Don't be like that."

Astrid chuckled when she saw the smile on Uske's face.

"What's the prognosis, Doc?" Milly asked.

"Better than new," Uske said. "With the bigger battery she is good to go. I had to rearrange some things and re-route a couple of others, but power issues are no more."

"That's great everyone, but we have a new problem," Mac said as he burst through the door. The scowl on Mac's face said it all. Something was afoot, and it wasn't good. "Check this out."

Mac walked over to the vid screen on the wall. He tapped it, bringing it to life, and switched it to the NET news. He found the link he was looking for and tapped it. The News clip began loading.

"We join you now live on the steps of Council Hall where this press conference was called regarding the recent cases of a droid virus known as the Prophet that has been plaguing New Trinity for the last few months," the news correspondent, Trish Polly, said in what Milly would guess was the girl's somber voice. Milly thought she sounded like a cheerleader trying to make a lunch menu sound fun.

Milly couldn't help but think the double-breasted pant suit the woman was wearing was a terrible choice. *The beige color was all wrong for the woman's pale complexion and dark hair. As Milly had struggled with a similar coloring all of her life, she felt quite qualified to make that assessment.* Though she had to admit that the outfit did show off the woman's rather large bosom.

"We are awaiting a statement from the council... here comes someone now. It looks like Councilman Alexander Roth," the little girl said. *Little girl? Oh, like I'm so much older than her.*

Milly watched as a well-dressed man took the podium with two other men standing behind him. She had never seen the other two men before either. One was a youthful Asian man and the other was an elderly gentleman. The speaker was tall and gorgeous with sandy blond hair and the coldest blue eyes she had ever seen. The sight of him sent chills up her spine. Milly couldn't put her finger on it but something about that man scared her. He scared her to the core.

"Ichiro," Kiyoko hissed. Uske cursed under his breath in what sounded like Japanese.

"Good evening. I have called this press conference tonight to inform you of some very grave events that have taken place in our fair city. It has come to the attention of the Council that our city has been struck by an epidemic. The so-called Prophet virus is running rampant through the city. Causing millions of credits worth of damage and worse yet it has destroyed the lives of some of our citizens."

"Thanks to the many researchers at Takacorp we have identified the droid responsible for transmitting the Prophet virus. Shown here in this picture is the culprit. Anyone with information regarding this droid should contact NTPD immediately. The droid was designed and built by Uske Otagawa formerly of Takacorp. He is wanted for questioning regarding this droid and its recent activities that have been linked to multiple deaths."

A picture of Astrid and Uske appeared on the Vid screen in the lower left-hand corner.

"What troubles me the most is RAD's response to the problem. The very agency that is supposed to be protecting us from these types of threats has done worse than nothing. I have a report here stating that today an agent from RAD destroyed his own Tactical Field Escort inside a homeless shelter endangering everyone inside," Roth said.

"That's a lie!" Mac snapped. The vehemence drew attention from everyone in the room. "What? It is," Mac said as his shoulders slumped under the group's collective stare.

"Both the NTPD and RAD are searching for Agent Marion McDonnell and Uske Otagawa," Roth continued. "Please contact the NTPD if you see either of these men."

Mac's service picture appeared next to other two pictures on the screen below Roth.

"It is wanton disregard for the safety of the public like today's events that have tarnished the once pristine reputation of the RAD," Roth said. Milly couldn't look away from Roth on the screen. His deep voice was steady and smooth. He commanded her attention. Like a rattlesnake. "Numerous events like this one have been documented over the last ten years including corruption charges and extortion, along with millions of credits of damage to public and private property. Once again proving that it is time for a change within the organization. Protection of the people should have always been a priority of the RAD. With threats like this Prophet virus and rogue agents terrorizing our citizens, a change is required. They are proof that the Evens administration has become impotent in its control of its own security forces. All of these symptoms lead us to a clear conclusion. What we need now more than ever is true leadership. Our woes require someone with a clear vision and the moral standing to see us through crises like the Prophet virus and the city-wide shortages of food and water."

"With elections drawing near I am officially announcing my candidacy for Chancellor of New Trinity. I see our city once again under the control of its citizens. A safe and happy place where anyone would be proud to raise a family. A city where we can pursue our…"

"That's enough of that," Mac switched off the Vid screen.

"Oh, Mac!" Milly said. "Are you okay?"

"Me? Yeah," he said. "Dick knows the truth. That's all I need."

"What did Dick say?" she asked.

"He said quite a bit actually," Mac replied. "Not much of it good. He has Six's remains and the techs are going over him now. He is just another Prophet victim at this point. Though Roth conveniently forgot to mention that little fact in his press conference. Anyway, we can't go to RAD right now. There are apparently New Trinity Police officers there overseeing the search for me. Dick said the corruption charges that Roth has made are forcing the Chancellor to apply pressure on RAD."

"Damn," Milly cursed.

"What now?" Kiyoko asked, looking plaintively at Uske. "We can't let that little monster get away with this. He is trying to pin this mess on us!"

"We'll get him. We just have to move cautiously," Mac interjected.

"So, what is the plan?" Milly asked.

"Babe, can we hold up here for a while? At least until we hear from Dick," Mac asked. He did look appropriately chagrined.

"Sure," she said. *He's still in trouble but who can resist that face?*

"What? We wait here while that little weasel gets away with it?" Kiyoko asked.

"We aren't waiting. We are...pooling our resources," Mac replied.

"I don't believe it is safe to remain here much longer," Uske said suddenly. "If the Police have gotten involved then they will come here looking for you."

"Oh, I hadn't thought of that," Milly admitted.

"Damn," Mac said heatedly. "I should have put that together."

"Where do we go?" Kiyoko said looking at the group. She was met with pensive faces. Each thinking quietly.

"I've got it. We'll go to Teddy's," Mac said triumphantly. "He is still at the hospital. Speaking of which I need to go see him when this is all over."

"Have you checked on him?" Milly asked.

"Dick gave me a status report," he replied. "Teddy is stable but still unconscious. They aren't sure if the blow to his head caused any permanent brain damage."

"Poor Teddy," Milly said feeling a little sorry for the pervert. *That'll teach him to build sex bots. Oh, wait who am I kidding? He won't learn a thing from this.*

"Is that safe? This Teddy's place?" Uske asked.

"It's a closed crime scene," Mac said. "No one will think of looking for us there. Besides my friend Cliff will cover for me if it comes down to it."

"It's settled then. We're off to Teddy's," Milly said. She was quite excited to be out on a mission again. She had only been on medical leave for a day and a half and already she was going a bit stir crazy.

"Milly. I'm a wanted man harboring fugitives. I can't let you go with me," Mac said sadly. "I don't want you involved any more than you already are."

"Oh, but I'm going," Milly said defiantly. "I'm not staying here on the sidelines while you go out and risk your neck. Not when I can watch your back. I'm no Six but I can help."

"Baby, I'll feel a whole lot better if I knew you were safe and sound here. Better yet go to your dad's," he said quietly.

"I'll feel a whole lot better knowing where you are and that you are safe," Milly said poking him in the chest with her finger. "I have invested far too much time training you up just the way I want you to have you snuffed by some rogue droid on my watch."

"Amen, sister," Kiyoko said. Both turned their heads to look at the young woman who cowed under the stares.

"All right, you win," Mac said, exasperated. "But you have to promise to follow my orders. Okay? My orders to the letter, do you hear me?"

"I don't like that," Milly said.

"I could shoot you with your Mark 2 and leave you tied up on your bed for the dome police to find. I am a fugitive you know."

"Fair enough," Milly coughed out quicker than she

had intended. Something about the look on Mac's face told Milly that he was serious.

"Okay. Let's get going," Mac said. "Milly, will you help Kiyoko and Uske find what parts they might need to fix Annie? I'm afraid she's going to set something on fire with her hip sparking like that."

"Oh, Mac, grab Artie and put him in his carrier," Milly said as she turned to face the older man. "What all do you think you might need?"

"Oh, come on!" Astrid said suddenly drawing everyone's attention. "I can't believe we are all avoiding the real question here."

"What's that?" Mac and Milly both asked.

"Your name is Marion?" Astrid asked incredulously.

Kiyoko laughed out loud with Astrid. Milly smiled. She knew Mac had always hated that name.

"Yeah. So what?" Mac asked attempting to be stoic while pulling his coat around him, but even he had to admit the cough that followed kind of ruined it.

"I see why you go by 'Mac,'" Astrid replied.

Chapter 22

Tohiro reached for the door handle to his spacious office. His mind distracted by thoughts for tonight's dinner, when he was cut off abruptly by Chi Chi.

"Please wait here, sir," Chi Chi said. Tohiro stared at her. He was surprised to see Chi Chi's eyes had switched from their usual pale blue glow to an angry red. Something had triggered her defensive systems.

Tohiro pulled his hand away from the handle and took a step back as Chi Chi moved between him and the door. Chi Chi opened the door slowly and with a nod from him she slipped through into the dark office. Tohiro, never one to back down from a fight, slipped through behind her.

Chi Chi's demeanor had changed. Her prim posture was gone. She stalked through the room like a tigress hunting in a replica Kimono. The garment was similar to one his late wife used to wear. A beautiful silk, blue like the oceans of old with white and pink cherry blossoms scattered about it.

Chi Chi stalked purposefully to the center of the circular office sweeping it with her multitude of perceptive systems.

She pointed at Tohiro's desk chair sitting with its back facing the center of the room.

"Identify!" Chi Chi ordered her usually sweet voice was stern and full of command.

"Ah, father you have returned," A familiar voice called from the other side of the chair.

"Ichiro," Chi Chi said, as her combat systems switched off and she resumed her usually sweet disposition. "Why are you sitting in the dark, Ichiro? Is there something wrong with the lighting system?"

"No, you mechanical monstrosity," Ichiro snapped. "The lights are fine. I like watching the glow of the city. It's quite beautiful isn't it, Father?"

"Ichiro?"

"Yes, father," Ichiro replied. "You know the city really is deceptively beautiful at night."

"Hai. I have spent many hours staring at the lights of New Trinity at night," Tohiro agreed. "What brings you here this evening, my son?"

"Do I need an appointment to see my own father?" Ichiro asked sardonically as he spun the chair around.

Tohiro could just make out his son's heavily shadowed face in the dim back-light of the city and the buildings of the largest dome. Sometimes it hurt Tohiro to look directly at his son. The young man looked so much like his late wife that the sight of him occasionally sent great pangs of remorse and loneliness through the old man.

"No. No. I was just curious," Tohiro said chuckling at what he assumed was a fine jest from his son. It was getting increasingly hard to read Ichiro's moods. "It's good to see you Ichiro-kun."

"Oh, I'm sure it is, father," Ichiro said snidely.

"Will you be joining me for dinner?" Tohiro asked.

"Your father has selected Japanese style curry for tonight's menu. However, I can order out for something else if you would like, Ichiro," Chi Chi said in her motherly way.

Ichiro met Chi Chi with an angry scowl. He put his hands on the desk before him and appeared to be restraining himself.

"That won't be necessary, Chi Chi. I doubt my son will be joining us this evening," Tohiro said contritely.

"No, father, you are right. I'm afraid that I will be unable to join you this evening. I have a press conference to attend."

"A press conference. At this hour? For what?" Tohiro asked not remembering a press release on the schedule today. "Chi Chi?"

"I have nothing of that nature on the schedule for this evening," Chi Chi replied. "I will check the marketing report to be certain."

"No need for that," Ichiro said rising from his seat. "I'll be scheduling it myself here in a moment."

"What's the conference about Ichiro?" Tohiro asked feeling a bit heated about this unorthodox initiative his son had chosen.

"It is the unveiling of a new line, Father," Ichiro said in a matter-of-fact manner.

"New line?" Tohiro asked. "What new line?"

"It's our blue-ribbon line father. Built to be immune to the Prophet virus," Ichiro said.

"You found a way to stop the Prophet virus?" Tohiro asked. His heart was beginning to race at the possibilities. "Why didn't you tell me you were devoting resources to solve this issue?"

"I wanted it to be a surprise, Father," Ichiro said. As he slipped his hand into his pants pocket.

"That's excellent Ichiro," Tohiro said. "Think of the lives we can save. This is great. When do you launch?"

"Soon, father," Ichiro said. "In spite of Uske's meddling I was able to get the plant back up to full production. The first two thousand units are ready."

"Wait. Uske?" Tohiro said confused. "What does Uske have to do with all of this?"

"He and that prototype unit of his have been hacking the Tribunal. He has apparently been looking for evidence of the Prophet virus," Ichiro said. "The good news is I have been able to turn their meddling to my advantage.

"Hacking? Uske?" Tohiro asked skeptically.

"Yes, Father, your so-called friend has been working extremely hard to expose my plan to destabilize the city council," Ichiro said.

Tohiro's eyes widened. His mouth fell open. "What?" he asked incredulously.

"Father, how long have you been begging me to open up and really share my ambitions with you?" Ichiro said. "And now that I am you aren't even listening."

"You...You are responsible for that horrible virus?" Tohiro asked, his mouth agape, his stomach threatening to tie itself into knots. "It was you?"

"I'm afraid so," Ichiro replied. The young man's face was eerily calm. A slight smirk hiding in the shadows coving his face.

Tohiro's heart pounded in his chest as though it were trying to escape. His mouth suddenly went dry. His mind reeled at the horrible implications. The media's response. The outcry of the victims. The lawsuits, by heavens the lawsuits. It will bankrupt the company.

"How could you?" Tohiro stammered. "People have died!"

"Yes, well what was the old saying? 'Can't make an

omelet without breaking a few eggs,'" Ichiro said blithely while gesturing with his hands.

Tohiro felt weak in the knees. He steadied himself on one of the chairs in front of his desk.

"How, how could you? Your mother and I raised you better than this," Tohiro said. "When did you become a monster?"

"Ha!" Ichiro scoffed. "Mother raised me to know right from wrong!" Ichiro snapped, jumping to his feet. Tohiro could sense the heat now developing in his son's voice. "Mother raised me to follow my heart. And that is precisely what I am doing."

"Ah yes, Ichiro. I am well aware of your belief that I abandoned you and your mother," Tohiro explained. "But I know she taught you that killing people is wrong."

"Precisely, Father!" Ichiro replied. "Precisely. Observe the deceptively beautiful city out there. Look at the lovely veneer that only hides the rotten core. We sit here in our ivory tower and pretend that the machines we create are so perfect and harmless. When in fact we are an affront to God. Every day we get closer and closer to spitting in God's face by creating abominations so like us. While mankind dies away, we spurn God's legacy leaving an entire race of machines in our place. It was our perverse search for power that poisoned the Eden he made for us. We can't even breathe the air outside of the dome anymore, Father. Doesn't that make you sick? Doesn't it?"

"Ichiro, how could you?" Tohiro asked. "Why?"

"Things are going to change Father. It has taken time to set the plans in motion. Even with Uske's meddling I was able to complete the first stage," Ichiro explained. Tohiro could sense his son's excitement. "A new era is about to dawn, Father. I just wish it could happen before the virus claimed the life of the head of Takacorp."

"W-what," Tohiro stammered.

"I wish I could say I'm sorry, Father," Ichiro said through his arrogant smirk. "I think we both know I'm not."

"What are you talking about Ichiro?"

"Chi Chi. Will you do the honors?" Ichiro asked as he pulled an item from his pocket and pointed it at Chi Chi.

Tohiro saw a little red-light flash from the item. His brain did the math and figured out what just happened. He turned just in time to see Chi Chi's head arch back and raise her arms to the ceiling.

In a panic Tohiro reached for his field control unit. He pulled the device open and activated his override control program. He jabbed the activation icon repeatedly while pointing it at his flailing droid.

"Behold! All ye rejoice! The Prophet has come!" Chi Chi screamed, lowering her head. She turned and faced Tohiro. "Fear not all ye faithless. For the Prophet has come to cleanse your fleshly sin." A high pitched woman's voice cackled.

Tohiro jabbed the button again. His only hope was to take control of Chi Chi as she made her way across the office toward him.

"Fear not sinner for the prophet has come. Behold the grandeur of his coming. Rejoice in his divine forgiveness," Chi Chi's strange new voice announced.

Tohiro saw the error message once again. His heart sank. His device couldn't connect with Chi Chi. Ichiro's virus must use the command override system. Tohiro's mind raced. Chi Chi was almost on top of him. A police droid would have a tough time defeating Chi Chi. He knew that he had little chance.

Chi Chi slapped the control module from Tohiro's hands sending it spinning under the desk.

Tohiro was spun completely around by the blow, bringing him face to face with his son across the desk from him. Ichiro sat in his father's chair watching the scene before him as if it were some gruesome play. His face, so like his mothers, locked in a perverse smirk.

Tohiro lunged across the desk toward his son. He had to get to Ichiro's control module. It had to have protection measures within it. He scrambled across the desk. Sudden fear gripped Ichiro's face, wiping away that awful smirk. Ichiro rolled the chair backward taking him out of Tohiro's reach. Tohiro gave chase but fell short when a vicious pressure caught his trailing leg. He cried out from the pain that suddenly overwhelmed him. Then he felt himself hauled backward.

"Rejoice!" Chi Chi shouted at full volume. "Rejoice!" she repeated.

As his feet hit the floor again Tohiro felt Chi Chi's cold mechanical fingers slide around the back of his neck followed shortly by her other hand.

"Gomen asai, Himiko," Tohiro said sadly. He had failed. He was unable to honor her memory and achieve the goals she had died to help him reach.

"Don't you dare say her name! Never again! Never again!" Ichiro roared as he shot to his feet. "Kill him dammit!"

"To your feet non-believers!" Chi Chi yelled in her new voice. "To your feet to rejoice!"

Tohiro could feel Chi Chi's icy fingers grip tighter

and tighter around his neck. He reached up out of reflex and grabbed her wrists. He was about to die. However, the joy written plainly on his son's face cut him to the depths of his soul. How had he miscalculated so? Where did he go wrong? Will the world forgive him for unleashing this monster on it?

A vise like pressure shattered all thought. The machine's frigid fingers squeezed with an unimaginable strength. He struggled feebly at his attacker. What a horrible monster I have created. He tried to say the words. Yet the pressure on his throat prevented the words from coming out.

The mere moments it took for Chi Chi to squeeze the life out of Tohiro felt like hours to the old man. The last thing he saw as the ring of darkness clouded his vision was the sneer on his son's face. In spite of the horrific scene, a sense of peace settled around Tohiro, warming the cold black that was flowing over and around him. Tohiro reached out and took his wife's hand and walked with her into the light.

Chapter 23

The lift door slid open, and Ichiro strode confidently into the Vault. The smaller man set a shiny metal case down next to the elevator doors and continued into the room. Vance couldn't believe the arrogant prick could be so calm. As always Ichiro appeared resplendent in his custom made suit and his perfectly polished shoes. No one would ever suspect the man had just killed his own father. *That is one cold bastard.*

"Is everything ready, Robert?" Ichiro asked curtly as he made his way to the captain's chair mounted in the center of the Vault. At Ichiro's glare Vance lumbered out of the chair and stepped aside allowing the smaller man to take the seat.

The captain's chair was the best seat in the house. Vance had rather enjoyed his time in control and was a little bitter at giving it up. The chair was perfectly centered in the control room. From it one could see all of the monitors on the management center walls adjacent to the lift.

The management center was a huge bank of vid screens arranged in an ark covering all of the walls around the central chair. The screens displayed all sorts of data and video feeds. Some were monitoring feeds from inside the Takacorp building. Others were tapping into traffic cams. More still were monitoring data moving in and out of the server systems, while others were watching the various production facilities throughout the city and the world. *What was left of the world anyway.*

The only other chairs were occupied by two droids who manned the Vault at all times. Heckle and Jeckle were top of the line Personal Assistant droids. They were used primarily for monitoring and task work for the manager on duty. That, and Jeckle made a mean cup of coffee too.

Behind the chair sat the view window showing the Tribunal. Three of the largest, most powerful computational machines ever built. They looked like three oversized coffins arranged around a central bundle of leg-thick cables that extended up into the ceiling and out into the building. Inside those boxes billions of numbers were being crunched and what not. Vance didn't really care. He knew enough that they were important and that was that. He knew that with those three machines working in unison he could control virtually every android in the city. Possibly even the world. It was an awesome feeling to have that much power at his fingertips.

Vance watched as Ichiro slid mechanically into the chair and waited, looking poignantly at Vance. *He is such a stiff shirt.*

"Yes, ah, we are ready to begin," Vance stammered as he realized Ichiro was waiting on him. "We are ready, but I still don't see why we are moving things ahead of schedule. We don't have all of the new batch of droids ready."

"That is inconsequential," Ichiro said cutting Vance off. "We have enough to complete the task at hand. Have they been deployed in the areas that I requested?"

"I took the liberty of telling Jeckle to set the destination coordinates for the specific sites myself," The bigger man replied.

"What of the other items I ordered?" Ichiro asked.

"The additions to the vault are complete. The last one was delivered this morning and has been activated."

"Good. Where do we stand on our loose ends?" Ichiro asked.

"No confirmation as of yet," Vance continued. "We've lost contact with the Police unit, which you already knew. NTPD and RAD have both been at the location and have started independent investigations."

"As of right now the 'agent,'" Vance made quotation marks in the air with his fingers, "is wanted for questioning by both organizations. I have had the tribunal open additional resources to the Trinity Police Department to increase the chance of locating the 'loose ends' as you call them. Chairman Roth's conference this afternoon has gone a long way to destroy Agent McDonnell's credibility. Check points have been set up at each of the transfer tunnels between the domes. I expect to find them shortly. However, we have met with the usual resistance from Director Evens, regarding the RAD's investigation and their willingness to share their information."

"To be expected from one such as him," Ichiro said as a matter of fact. "To his credit he is a smart man. Speaking of smart, have you made the changes I requested to the program?"

"Ah yes, the changes. The changes have been made per your request. I had Heckle and Jeckle make the changes, and the tribunal completed the simulations."

"Make sure those two are dealt with. I want to

minimize exposure on this issue," Ichiro said for all the world like he was covering up a product defect rather than a coup d'état. *Cold bastard.*

"I have taken the liberty of having their PCE's swapped out and the offending devices smashed. I took care of the incineration of the remains myself." Vance beamed his most winning smile. He hoped desperately that Ichiro bought the lie. He dabbed his forehead with his handkerchief to mop up the sweat that was beading there. It was a common enough habit of Vance's that he assumed Ichiro wouldn't notice the additional sweat.

Ichiro narrowed his eyes and regarded Vance. Vance gulped under the weight of the man's scrutiny. *Oh shit. He knows, oh shit, I'm fucked. Gracie. Oh god where's Gracie?* Vance had to fight the urge to turn around.

"Good work, Robert. I'm pleased with your initiative." Ichiro turned his attention to the vid screens.

Letting out a sigh of relief, Vance dabbed his forehead again.

"Good," Ichiro said. "Very good. Then it is time, Robert. Activate Holy Light."

"Yes, sir." Vance reached out and opened a small panel on the captain's chair. Beneath the panel sat a bright red button. "There you are, sir."

"A bit melodramatic, Robert."

"Don't blame me. It was part of the chair and Heckle was the one who coded the activation sequence to it.

Ichiro scoffed and depressed the button with a resounding click, while mumbling something about stupid names.

The two men waited. Nothing. Ichiro frowned. He poked the button again. Vance scowled and looked at the button as well. As he was about push the button himself, all of the monitors suddenly went black. A few tense seconds later lines of code began cycling across many of the screens. Vance sighed heavily in relief.

The Holy Light Application had been activated. Months of hard work and sneaking around under old man Tohiro's nose preparing for this little game of Ichiro's. Soon machines everywhere will begin to "suffer" from the Prophet virus. Vance shivered at the thought.

He looked away from the bank of monitors back at Ichiro. Sitting in his little captain's chair so smug. So sure of himself. Like he was in complete control. Totally oblivious to the machinations of the real power in this city.

"Why are you staring at me?" Ichiro asked.

"What?"

"You're staring at me. Why?"

Vance swallowed. "I was…ah…just thinking, you know, a-about the moment."

Ichiro sneered.

"All the planning. Uske's meddling, and yet here we are getting it done," Vance said, feeling his shirt start to cling to him under his jacket. He grabbed his handkerchief and dabbed the beads of sweat from his forehead again.

Ichiro seemed mollified as he went back to watching the bank of monitors over Vance's shoulder.

Vance sighed. This crap was getting old. He needed to talk to Roth about a new assignment. However, he knew that Ichiro had gone off book with his little coup. If this works Ichiro will be untouchable. Which also meant that Vance's placement would be too important to let go of.

Roth was a man of vision. He had plans within plans. Agents within agents. Vance doubted that Ichiro knew what Roth was really up to. Roth was a dangerous man. Vance seriously doubted that he was the only agent Roth had inside of Takacorp. Ichiro was just a pawn in the long run, albeit a rich and now very powerful pawn, but an expendable piece nonetheless.

Vance watched as monitors began springing to life showing the video output of droids all over the city now under the control of the application. One was clearly the video feed from a bus. It began weaving in and out of the lanes. It smashed a few droids caught crossing the street and had already flattened two other vehicles when Vance's attention was drawn to another screen. *Those people are in for a wild ride.*

The new feed was from a PA droid in what appeared to be the City Council Building. It had begun strangling anyone it could get its hands on. He had to turn away as he saw it start toward a cute little woman who was screaming and scuttling backward like a crab in those ridiculous high heeled shoes.

"Now, Robert, through the cleansing burn of fire we will forge a new future for mankind," Ichiro announced to the room.

It all seems a little anticlimactic to me.

Chapter 24

Mac took the corner on two wheels. He learned quickly that slowing down just allowed the droids running amok to attack the van. Three had tried already. The first one managed to get its arm through the passenger side window before Mac could get his piece out of its holster. Luckily, Astrid was right there. A quick flick of her wrist cleaved the offending appendage clean off just above the elbow. Mac used the opportunity to stomp on the accelerator and the van lurched forward leaving the infected droid running after them.

"I've been meaning to ask. How do you do that Astrid?" Mac asked

"Do what?"

"That thing with your hands. You know. Cut stuff clean in half with your hand and reach through kinetic barriers and such. How do you do that?"

"Oh that. Well, a lady has to have her secrets," she replied mischievously.

"The infection is accelerating," Uske's heavy accent announced out of nowhere from the back of the Van. "The city's network is being flooded with outrageous amounts of data."

From the rear-view mirror Mac could see the older man huddled over a tiny terminal furiously tapping away.

"What does that mean?" Mac shouted over his

shoulder. "Hang on everyone," he added as he took another tight turn blowing completely through a red traffic signal. Luckily, he could get away with that kind of driving in the old dome. Traffic volume there was much lighter at the best of times. In the wake of droids running around killing people, waiting at a light seemed to him to be kind of stupid.

"Ichiro must have activated the entire command override system. The tribunal is one of the only systems powerful enough to utilize this much of the network's bandwidth."

"Again, what does that mean?" Mac asked, exasperated.

"It means that the big computer at Takacorp is controlling all of the infected droids," Kiyoko snapped.

"And to stop it we have to go there," Astrid chimed in. Mac swallowed hard at that.

"Great," Mac said sarcastically, drawing out each letter of the word. "Hang on, what do you mean 'we?'"

"Well let's examine the facts shall we," Astrid retorted. "Androids all over the city are freaking out and killing people. RAD is going to be hard pressed to try and protect the general populace so there is no way they can devote resources to try and shut down the systems at Takacorp. Besides, with the network jammed by the command override system and the volume of emergency calls I doubt you could even get RAD on a Global right now. The system is tied up."

Milly nodded holding out her Global. "Says call failed."

"So that leaves you. One lone RAD man to storm a virtual castle to try and stop the evil computer and save the day. Like it or not Mac, you are going to need help.

And we are all you have," Astrid continued, her virtual voice beaming with enthusiasm.

"If we can get to Tohiro he will help us," Uske said still making his *L*'s sound like *R*'s.

"If that is the case, why hasn't he stopped this from happening?" Milly asked.

"I believe that Ichiro has been acting in secret," Uske replied. "Tohiro is a visionary. He is looking to the future, always. It was his greatest asset and his greatest weakness. That and he was too trusting of his son. An easy mistake for a father to make," Uske said rather sadly.

"All right so to Takacorp then," Mac said curtly. This was not going to be pretty. Takacorp was one of the largest producers of androids in the world. Mac knew full well the destructive power of one of their military grade machines. He felt the loss of Six acutely. He had begun to think of Six as more of a partner than a tool. Deep seated memories of those early days chasing down rogue military units bubbled in the pit of his stomach, sending a wave of nausea through him.

It was a tough time in his life. There were new recruits added almost every week to try and keep up with the losses. He and a couple of others were lucky enough to make it through alive. Most didn't.

"Turn here," Milly said.

Mac was still lost in thought and missed the turn.

"Mac!" Astrid and Milly said loudly in unison.

"What?" Mac snapping back to attention.

"You needed to turn back there. Make a right up here and double back," Milly said pointedly.

"Teddy's is up ahead, off of Junction," Mac said gesturing at the cracked windshield.

"We have to stop by my father's, Mac," Milly said, her voice wavering a bit. She did her best to be tough, but Mac could tell the events of the last couple of days on top of their current predicament had gotten to her.

"Oh God, Milly, how stupid of me," Mac apologized. He yanked the wheel forcing the van into a hard right-hand turn. "I can't believe I forgot about him."

"We've all been a little preoccupied," Kiyoko said.

They traveled along in silence for the few more right-hand turns and the short jaunt to Mr. Bender's shop on Fifth Avenue South.

Bender Electronics had been started by Milly's father shortly after the old dome was reopened. It was really the only place he could afford to start up. He made his living fixing old and mostly outdated droids and electronics for the few remaining denizens of the old dome.

The shop was dark. Which, given the situation, was probably for the best. Bright lights and the big glowing signs would most likely attract the rampaging droids.

Mac pulled up along the curb just outside of the shop and put the van in park. He turned around as he pulled his blaster out of its holster and checked the charge. "Milly you are with me, Astrid, Annie, you two look after Uske and Kiyoko. If you get surrounded, get out of here," he ordered.

"Whatever you say, RAD man," Astrid replied, giving him a mock salute.

Mac sighed heavily.

"What?" Astrid asked

Mac ignored her and opened the door as slowly and as quietly as he could. Milly climbed out his door behind him. He eased it closed and then moved for the building.

The street had proven to be deserted.

Mac stood guard as Milly used her key to open the front door. It was still locked, which Mac took as a good sign. They made their way into the dark store front with little trouble. The front area looked more like a doctor's office than an Android repair lab. They slipped through the waiting room into the office area past the racks of various new and used machine parts into her father's office.

They found Mr. Bender in his usual position at this time of night, snoring at his desk. The poor man had a nasty habit of falling asleep while organizing his paperwork. Milly said it was cute. Mac could relate. He hated paperwork too. The thought of all the forms Mac now had to fill out for the loss of a TFE made a bubble of bile climb up Mac's throat. *Man, I miss Six.*

"Daddy?" Milly called patting the sleeping man's shoulder.

Mr. Bender jumped in his seat. He looked around wildly for a second as his sleep weary brain caught up and finally recognized his daughter.

"Milly? What time is it?" he asked blearily.

"You fell asleep at your desk again."

"Huh?" Mr. Bender examined the desk before him. "So, I did."

"Daddy, you have to come with us."

"What? Why?" he asked, sounding confused.

"There has been an outbreak. That horrible virus that has been on the network reports."

"Yeah."

"Well, it is now widespread," she said very sternly. "Mac is taking us to someplace safe so he can then deal with it."

"Oh...Okay. If you say so, honey," he turned to Mac. "How bad is it?'"

"Grab your gun," Mac said gravely.

"That bad, eh?" he said.

"Yup,"

After a few tense moments waiting for him to lock up, Mr. Bender was safely in the van. Mac wasted no time and was able to get to Teddy's without incident. Unfortunately, many of Teddy's security systems had been disabled and or confiscated when his loft became the scene of a crime. To make matters worse the elevator was still broken so it meant schlepping up the stairs, again.

Mac and Milly checked Teddy's kitchen and pantry. Teddy was a bit paranoid due to his choice of vocation so that meant he kept a lot of supplies to avoid unnecessary trips into public. So, they had plenty of food should they be stuck there for a while.

"You'll find plenty to eat and drink in the kitchen. Make yourselves at home and we'll be back as soon as we can," Mac announced.

Milly began going through her bag of stuff she had brought from her apartment, and she let Artie out of his crate. The little guy shot out and hid under the couch drawing Annie's attention.

Mac walked over to see Uske and Kiyoko where they had set up shop by Teddy's broken terminal. Uske was attempting to salvage something from it.

"Look, you guys will be safe here. Astrid and I will take care of this command override thing. I'm going to have to ask a favor."

"What's that?" Kiyoko asked suspiciously narrowing her eyes at him.

"Apologize to Milly for me. And try to keep her from leaving," Mac said.

"We'll try. Please see that I get my daughter back in one piece."

"If anyone makes it through this ordeal it will be Astrid. It's my butt I'm worried about."

"Hai," Uske agreed.

"Hey, Mac, have you seen my neutralizer? I can't find it," Milly asked from across the loft.

"You guys stay safe," Mac said to the pair giving each a light squeeze on the arm. He then made his way to Milly.

"It's time, Milly," Mac said as he reached her. His heart felt heavy with what he was about to do.

"I know, Mac. Help me find my neutralizer and we can go," she said continuing to dig through her bag. "I know I had it at Dad's. It's your back up piece, the one you loaned me. What did I do with it?

"Milly. You know I love you right?" Mac asked.

"Yeah. I know. Don't worry. Everything will be fine," she said though it sounded more like she was trying to reassure herself.

He pulled her close and kissed her. He hugged her and held her for a moment. She didn't resist. They held there together for what felt like an eternity and yet for Mac it wasn't enough. He wanted nothing more than to stay right here wrapped in her arms.

He pulled away from her and looked deep into her eyes. "I love you." She smiled at him. Mac pulled her Mark 2 from under his coat and shot her in the chest. The electrically charged blast wave knocked her unconscious upon contact. Mac scrambled to support her body before she could hit the floor. Mr. Bender was there in a flash

273

to help. They laid her on Teddy's couch and put a pillow under her head.

Mr. Bender frowned at his sleeping daughter and then turned to scowl at Mac.

Mac touched the man's shoulder. "I don't like it any more than you do," Mac handed the weapon Milly had been looking for to her father. Along with her Mark 2. "Just in case," he took a breath and sighed as he gazed upon her lying there so peacefully. "I love her more than anything in the world," Mac confessed. "Let's be real about this. I might not make it back. I can't take her with me. I have to know she is safe."

"Son, I understand. I don't have to like it, but I understand. And I know she would have insisted on going," he admitted. "Y-you want me to go along with you?"

"I appreciate the offer, sir, but no. I need you here protecting them. You're the only one I can count on. Besides, I think you and Uske will get on well together," Mac could see the relief in the older man upon hearing those words. Mac had to admit he wanted someone to tell him that he didn't have to go either.

"God speed, son. Come back. I was just getting used to having you around."

"Yes, sir," Mac said. He spun and headed toward the door to the stairwell. He looked over to Astrid who was busy hugging her father and sister and receiving her last-minute instructions from them.

"Remember to say clever things to the bad guys before you beat them up and stand in cool poses as they fall down," Kiyoko was explaining. "I'm so jealous."

"I'll swap with you if you want," Astrid quipped.

"You know I would if I could," Kiyoko snapped

back

Astrid laughed. It was such a musical sound.

"Astrid," Mac said. "It's time."

"Coming!" she hugged her family one more time.

Mac turned to Annie who was sitting facing the door.

"I'm counting on you to keep them safe, Annie," Mac said patting the robot dog on the head.

She wagged her tail exuberantly and replied, "Yes, sir, RAD man. Annie will keep everyone safe."

Great now the dog is doing it. Mac smiled in spite of himself and headed down the stairs. Astrid glided smoothly along with him. As they reached the van parked out front Astrid asked, "So to Takacorp then?"

"No. I have one more stop to make," Mac said with a grimace and then he climbed into the driver's seat and powered up the vehicle.

"Where is that?" Astrid asked as she swung into the passenger seat with her inhuman grace.

"To pick up an old friend," Mac replied and then he jammed his foot down on the accelerator.

Chapter 25

Vance had to turn his head. The mass carnage was starting to get to him. It was one thing to plan a massive viral attack that would most likely lead to people dying. To watch the carnage unfold was something else entirely. He looked back at Ichiro sitting in the command chair. The fabric of his suit had that faint shimmering quality that only the most expensive imports seem to have. The well-dressed brat was perusing his father's will. Most likely adding up the credits he was going to be receiving. Ichiro's amazon bodyguard was suspiciously missing. That was very disconcerting. Vance had to resist the urge to turn and look behind him.

Vance felt his stomach lurch. His ulcer was really bothering him on top of the wave of nausea. *Stick to the plan. Just stick to the plan.*

He held out his empty cup and Jeckle came around smoothly to collect it. The droid was made for monitoring and controlling. They were roughly humanoid. Many of their ORF motors were clearly visible around the joints. Long strands of muscle like tubing connected various limbs to each other with plastic cover plates here and there. Several of the same model run the underground farms that feed the domes. Jeckle and his counterpart Heckle were stock units brought in to monitor the command center deep in the bowels of Takacorp tower. Bipedal like most of the Takacorp androids. They stood about average height, about a head shorter than Vance himself. For all of their sophisticated programming and processing power the two droids were dumber than a box of rocks. Though they served their purpose and now that they had learned the ropes so to speak, they are working fairly well. Human operators would have taken longer to train. Then they expected you to pay them and give them paid time off.

Machines were just easier and more efficient. They never complained and could be disposed of quickly and easily. Unlike a human, nobody looks twice at a dead droid laying in a dumpster.

"Robert. I asked you a question," Ichiro said through clenched teeth.

"Sorry, boss," Vance replied. "What did you need?"

"Have you checked on our new droids?" Ichiro asked.

"Oh. Eh. Coming right up," Vance said. As if Ichiro was incapable of asking one of the two droids in the room to bring up the vids. Oh no. Not Ichiro. Not when there is someone he can order to do it for him. Just to be a jerk. Vance pointedly turned to Heckle who was seated at its station and said, "Heckle bring up the blue-ribbon squad"

The droid jumped to life and began typing commands into the touch pad controls with an inhuman speed. The wall of vid screens began to change one after another. Each one showing the local and private security cameras about New Trinity. Ichiro and Vance had laid out the distribution of the blue-ribbon androids strategically about the city. All primary Takacorp facilities were protected. A contingent of them was sent to protect Councilman Roth and he had them dispersed among the Image of God Churches and the Council offices of his allies.

It was little more than just a murderous publicity stunt. All of the infected droids were being run by the Tribunal. The Tribunal was programmed to destroy anything that was not owned or used by Takacorp and a few key VIPs. Also, the blue-ribbon droids served as control markers as well. Anything surrounded by them was off limits to the infected droids. Making the blue-ribbon droids off limits was the bulk of the programming changes Ichiro had ordered.

The areas where the blue-ribbon squads were stationed were relatively quiet. There were a lot of people running toward them for safety. Part of their programming included a routine to call out to people and tell them to run here for safety. It was PR gold really. There is nothing like being the hero in the midst of a city wide epidemic of killer robots. Vance hoped that nobody happened to notice the droids were shipped out mere hours before the carnage started.

Vance gave the monitors a once over and felt that everything looked good.

"Everything is going according to plan," Vance said.

"And what of RAD?" Ichiro asked.

"Heckle, pull up RAD headquarters," Vance ordered. The droid punched in a series of short commands and the three monitors in front of Vance switched to display various rooms in the RAD headquarters.

The scene was quite ghastly. From the look of things, a couple of the TFE's on site had been infected and had begun tearing the place up. Though most of the prophet droids were programmed to strangle their victims, there were a few special lines of code added just for droids that have weaponry. This event had to be bloody. That and the more vacancies created within the RAD organization the more loyal people Roth could insert into it.

"Everything is going well there too, Ichiro. We have what looks like several casualties"

"Good," Ichiro said absently as he went back to looking at his portable terminal. "Very good."

Vance had Heckle set the monitors to randomly display different infected droid activities and watch for any variations.

"Mr. Vance," Heckle said. "An anomaly has been located."

Vance turned to look at what Heckle was talking about. The droid had pulled up several screens showing a group of citizens that had huddle together behind what appeared to be an older RAD agent and his TFE. They were busy fending off a handful of infected droids. The TFE was not a Takacorp model and that made it a bit more difficult to take over.

"Vance, have the system take over that droid," Ichiro said pointing at the TFE on the screen.

"You heard him, right?" Vance asked the android sitting next to him. Heckle nodded and began the procedure to highjack the droid. When an error popped up.

"Sir, the droid is not connected to the network," Heckle said as it reviewed the error codes. "It was taken offline. There is a field report filed and then communication was terminated."

"Huh," Vance said out loud.

"Ping the network adaptor to activate it. Connect to

the adapter and reconnect," Ichiro ordered.

Jeckle deftly punched more on the keyboard and then another error message displayed.

"The network adaptor appears to have been removed, sir" The droid offered. "It is not responding to the ping."

"Send all available units to that location," Ichiro demanded. "I want that TFE destroyed, along with its Agent."

"You heard the man Heckle, make it happen," Heckle set to work routing other available infected droids to the location.

Ichiro checked his pocket watch. "It's almost time, Robert."

Vance tilted his head toward the elevator door where a silver case sat waiting. Vance knew the case contained some special droid part Roth had asked for. He had been making those types of requests for several months now. All of the parts were specifically designed for a particular purpose, only Roth never said, and Vance wished he didn't know.

"Good," Ichiro said absently as he went back to reading.

Vance suppressed a chuckle. He wondered if Ichiro ever had the balls to ask what those parts were for. He also wondered if the spoiled prick knew already and didn't care. Though given how Ichiro flew off the handle over Otagawa's little experiment with droid parts in his daughter, Vance doubted the spoiled prick knew much of anything.

Vance, knowing he would find no answers in his thoughts, turned back to the screens. The effort caused him some discomfort. The tiny stool he was sitting on was not really meant for people. The two little stools in front of the monitor banks were meant for monitoring droids. The rigid plastic tops were less than inviting. Vance hoped that Ichiro would get bored and leave sooner rather than later.

He checked on the RAD agent in the monitor. The man and his TFE were holding their own for now, but it was only a matter of time before they were overrun. Vance doubted that the Agent would do the smart thing and abandon the civilians. Those hero types never saw the big picture. Laying down your own life to protect someone else was highly overrated. Heroes need to be alive to make a difference. That's probably why Vance never got into civil service. He just wasn't wired for altruism.

"Good luck, buddy," he whispered to the guy on the screen.

"No. No! No! No! No!" Ichiro shouted. Vance and the two droids all turned to see Ichiro jump from his chair and begin to pace. "How could he? No. How could he do this to me? How did this happen?" he raved.

"What?" Vance asked not sure he really wanted to know.

"My father. Damn him. I should have seen this coming. I should have," Ichiro mumbled as he walked back and forth. "There has to be a way around it."

"What's going on Ichiro?" Vance asked again.

"My father left the company to Uske," Ichiro said snidely. "That bastard left my company to that crazy old heretic. Ahhh. How could I not have seen this happen? Kisama!" The younger man raged.

"Shit," Vance said out loud.

"Chi Chi," Ichiro said, lost in the machinations of

Chad M. Smith

his sick little mind. "I'll have to get to her. She should still be in my father's office. Yes, this might work. I'll have to alter a few of the variables but it will all work."

"What are you talking about, Ichiro?" Vance asked feeling a little confused.

Ichiro turned and looked Vance in the eye causing the bigger man to shy back. "I need you to image Chi Chi's cog file and AI. I need it done now."

"Okay. I'll get the twins on it," Vance replied hesitantly.

"Now!" Ichiro roared.

Vance jumped at the shout. He stood up and jabbed his finger at Jeckle who was standing near the wall. Vance then pointed to the seat he had vacated. The droid understood the gesture and took its place next to Heckle.

"Jeckle, locate the most recent update file for Chi Chi and re-image its cog file and AI. Do it immediately," Vance ordered the droid.

Ichiro fished his Global from his pocket and called out to it. "Gracie! Gracie answer me!" he shouted.

"Yes," she replied.

"I have to get to my father's office," he shouted as he made his way to the elevator door at the far side of the room. "There are some things I must take care of. Have you finished with your assignment?"

"Yes. I'm closing the exterior doors now. Once they are sealed, I'll be back inside."

"Fine, Fine. Now hurry up and meet me at my father's office. I'm on my way up now," Ichiro ordered. He turned to Vance. "Finish up here and get a car ready. I want you to take this case and meet up with Roth. He should be at his office at the Image Church. The case is something that Roth asked for. I have to retrieve my father's master control to fix this gross oversight," Ichiro ordered as he jabbed repeatedly at the call button for the Elevator. "I'll be back."

"Sure thing. As soon as Chi Chi is up and running again, I will take the case and get going," Vance said as he watched Ichiro enter the elevator car. He waited until the elevator door was closed and then walked over to the plushy command chair. He eased his way into its comfortable seat. "Bout time he got up, that stool was killing my butt," he said to the two droids. "Now, have a car pulled up to the garage entrance and get Chi Chi back online."

"A vehicle will meet you at the specified location Mr. Vance," Heckle said.

"Chi Chi's persona has been located and all files are loading now," Jeckle chimed in.

"Good" Vance said wryly. "Let me know when the elevator is back."

Chapter 26

Astrid pulled into the Takacorp parking facility. She rolled down the window and looked at the parking sentry. It glared at her with its giant red eye.

"This facility has been locked down for security purposes. Please reverse course and try again later," The machine's voice intoned.

"Priority override. Ichiro Takahaisu," Astrid said, her voice pitched to mimic that spineless weasel.

"Command accepted. Proceed, Takahaisu Sama," the droid replied and then retracted into its protective housing so only its red eye remained visible. The giant gate blocking the structure's entrance sank down into the ground, opening the way for the van. Astrid pulled through smoothly.

"Okay, I know those things aren't that stupid. How did you get past it? Was it just an audio clone?" Mac asked from the back.

"Oh, they are quite stupid, but it has nothing to do with that. It has to do with the priority override subroutines. It supersedes all of the other security measures and because the voice print I gave it matched the acceptable variance, it didn't check any other id. The upper brass sacrificed security for convenience.

"Huh," Mac replied.

Astrid pulled the van up to the roundabout that sat in front of the tower. "We're here," she announced as she brought the Van to a stop. "Are you sure you want to just walk right up to the front door?"

"Yup," Mac said curtly. "The garage structure was the best option for a clandestine assault, but escape is impossible once we are inside. The front door gives us a lot of options. It's the best offensive and defensive play. Plus, it takes huge balls to walk through your enemy's front door. And frankly mine are quite sizable and made of steel to boot.

Astrid rolled her eyes. "Ew! You boys and your obsession with those things. I personally think they're kind of gross."

"You're entitled to your opinion even if it's wrong," Mac threw the back doors open and jumped out on to the concrete.

Astrid climbed out of her seat and shut the door behind her. Mac met her on the driver's side. He looked ridiculous in that getup. He had thick black armor over a black jump suit. He had a weird black helmet with a thick plastic visor that he had swung up to show his face. He had what looked like an oversized, short, barreled rifle strapped to his chest with a thick black cable running from the back of it to a backpack he was trying to get situated on his back. He had his blaster in its holster on his leg. He had extra CAC batteries in various pouches and numerous odds and ends strapped about his person. It had to weigh a ton.

"So that's what we stopped to pick up at the storage place," she asked. "It looks ridiculous. What are you going to do with all of that old crap? Have an antique sale?"

"Ha, ha," Mac chuckled sarcastically. He turned and headed toward the building. Astrid flowed along behind him.

"No, it's the gear I used to hunt military rogues in the early days of the unit," Mac said. "How much do you know about the time during the war?"

"Not much. I have never been big on history," Astrid replied.

"Then I won't bore you. Let's just say this little thing leveled the playing field for those of us who had to clean up the mess."

Astrid watched as Mac approached the main doors to the building. She couldn't help but look up at the towering structure standing before her. She found it a little funny that with all of the time she had spent in the building since her creation she had never stopped and looked at the exterior before. It really was a big building.

They walked up to the large doors. They remained closed. A holo stream perimeter display activated at their approach.

!!WARNING!! THIS FACILITY IS CLOSED. SECURITY FIELD IN PLACE. !!WARNING PLEASE STAND BACK. !!WARNING!!

The display stood out a few feet from the glass doors. Astrid could see the beam emitter hanging down from the ceiling in the vestibule between the outer and inner doors.

"There's the emitter," Astrid pointed out.

"Watch this," Mac said with a wicked grin.

He pointed his crazy looking rifle at the emitter. A small red targeting light flashed briefly on the window glass and then found its way to the emitter ball hanging from the ceiling. Astrid heard a tiny click, a slight buzz and suddenly the emitter ball began to glow red hot and bubble. In short order the security field collapsed as the ball melted and dripped hot globs of molten metal and plastic on the smooth floor tiles.

"Okay, that was kind of cool," Astrid admitted.

"Right?" Mac replied. "Right? Not so stupid looking now, is it?"

"Oh, it's stupid looking, but you're right, it does seem to be effective," Astrid quipped. "Let's just see how well it works against actual droids."

"Ha, Ha," Mac said dryly. "If you would do the honor," Mac said, gesturing to the doors.

"Ladies first and all, right?" Astrid responded. She moved purposefully toward the glass door doing her best to saunter. This was by far one of the coolest things she had ever done, and she wanted to look cool doing it. As she approached, the doors remained closed.

Astrid would have smiled had her face had lips. She waved her hand in large arc and the thick glass pane melted easily thanks to her Strike field. She carved a portal in short order and slipped through it.

"Kind of ironic that you have now destroyed that same window twice in the space of a week," Mac remarked.

"What are you talking about?" Astrid asked as she stopped between the two sets of doors and turned back toward Mac.

"Earlier in the week you made a dramatic exit of the building to cover your dad and Kiyoko's escape," Mac replied. "Don't you remember that? I watched the vid of it."

"Oh yeah, the decoy," Astrid replied. "I had forgotten that Dad had sent a droid to distract security while we walked out the service entrance."

"That makes a lot more sense. A decoy," Mac said,

his face twisted in thought. "So, were you the one that hacked and emptied Uske's files from the servers?"

"No. That was done by everyone's favorite little prick. Ichiro tried to stop my father from tampering with Kiyoko's body. So, he figured he could steal all of Dad's files to slow him down. What Ichiro didn't know was that Dad stopped keeping his files on the company servers a couple of years back. Corporate espionage had been a concern for a long time."

"Huh. A little bit of healthy paranoia never hurt anyone."

"Yup," she replied as she turned back to her task, making short work of the second set of doors and entered the building.

"Ah, a little help?" Mac asked.

Astrid turned. Without thinking she had cut the second hole a bit smaller, and Mac was having trouble making it through. The large backpack was catching.

"Not very graceful are you, RAD man?" Astrid replied with a little giggle.

Astrid turned and started back toward the door.

"Behind you!" Mac roared. She let her momentum carry her forward while she bent her knees and hunched over. A quick twisting roll brought her around and face to knees with a Takacorp security droid that had moved into the entrance hall. It was a D5. They were Paramilitary droids manufactured for the dome's defense as well as for security throughout the dome itself. Takacorp tower had fifteen or so of these security droids throughout, all varied models and designs.

Mac's TFE, Six, was part of the Delta model group as well. The two hulking droids shared many of the same characteristics. They were big and hulking. She pulled up the droid's specs and began looking for weaknesses. She had thrashed Six easily and this one should prove to be simple enough. The primary difference being this one was a little smaller and a bit slower.

Oh, it still posed a threat if she was stupid enough to stand still. It had a big gun secretly hidden in its arm which was noteworthy, along with some other tools for subduing security threats. After half of a millisecond, she formulated a plan and started. She strafed to the right to draw the machine away from Mac so he could sort himself out.

"Halt," it announced in its computer-generated vocal pattern. It turned its torso to follow her sudden movement. "You are in violation of the security perimeter. Deactivate now and await the authorities."

Astrid couldn't help but feel disdain for the machine in front of her. There was an underlying feeling of contempt. She should probably feel a sort of kindred connection with the machines but all they really did was remind her that she is just a copy of Kiyoko's mind in an android body. Right now, all that did was piss her off.

"Halt," the droid repeated. "You are in…"

"Violation of the security perimeter," Astrid interrupted. "Blah blah blah. Shut up." The droid seemed really confused by her outburst right up until she eased her hand into the machine's chest cavity and jerked her arm up and out through its neck. It fell forward onto the nice stone tile. ORF fluid poured out onto the floor creating an azure pond.

Astrid gazed down at the machine and scanned for signs of life. The Droid's CAC battery and power systems were destroyed in her attack and one of its primary pumps for ORF fluid was severed as well.

"Nice," Mac said from beside her. He had gotten himself unstuck and made his way to her. He stopped and surveyed the damage she had caused to the droid.

"You're just jealous," Astrid replied. Wishing she had lips so she could smile. She really will have to remember to ask Dad to do something about that. She remembered having to learn to smile so people wouldn't be so stricken by her sarcastic sense of humor. *Kiyoko had to learn to smile,* she reminded herself.

"I am insanely jealous," Mac replied. "How do you do that with your hands?" Mac asked, gesturing to her arm which steamed lightly as the ORF fluid was burned away. It's got to be a manipulation of a kinetic field, but I can't figure out how," Mac surmised.

"As I said before a girl's got to have her secrets" Astrid said mysteriously. Feeling saucy and confident Astrid sauntered over to the security desk sitting just in front of the elevators.

She looked over the control panel and with a few jabs at the touch screen she unlocked the elevators.

"Tohiro should be on the executive level, though if memory serves me correctly, he is probably in his office right now. Like my father Tohiro is a bit of a workaholic.

"Find his PA droid. It should be connected to the network that will tell us where he is," Mac said as he lumbered up to the chest high desk.

"Not bad, RAD man. Not bad," Astrid chided.

"Ha, ha," Mac scoffed sarcastically.

"Huh, oh," Mac announced looking about the open lobby.

"What?"

"Incoming," Mac yelled.

Astrid turned to where Mac indicated. Two droids

were making their way down the corridor along the elevator bank. They looked like more D5s.

"I got 'em," Mac said. He squared off with the approaching droids and pointed his cumbersome weapon at them. The little red targeting dot zipped across the decorative stone floor tiles and landed squarely in the center of the lead droid's chest. Astrid heard that familiar buzzing again and the droid's chest liquefied. Almost as if the droid had a secret compartment filled with liquid that Mac had opened. The Droid immediately dropped to the floor in mid stride. Mac dropped to his knee to steady himself.

The second machine, which had been a few feet behind and a little off to the side, increased it pace. It deftly jumped over its fallen companion. It raised its right arm and pointed a melted stump at Astrid. The droid stopped abruptly and examined the damage. Mac's beam had cut through the first droid and ruined the arm of the second one at the same time. *Okay even I have to admit, that was cool*. The droid countered by activating all of its other weapon systems. Panels began to open all about its body and projectiles slid out of protective coverings.

Mac took aim and the weapon buzzed again. The second machine flopped on to the floor in heap stopping a few meters from the elevator. Mac lumbered over to inspect his handiwork.

"It's nice to know I still got it," Mac said, beaming with pride.

"Getting the arm of the second droid was pure luck, wasn't it?" Astrid asked cynically.

"If it keeps me alive, I'll take it," Mac replied with a smug look on his face.

"So, why can't you just hack the elevator and take us straight to the Tribunal?" Mac asked.

"Because the security elevator to the Vault is not connected to the building's systems. It is separate."

Astrid scoffed and set to hacking the control panel. She had to dig fairly deep into the core system to locate Chi Chi's ID. At first it was offline completely and then as if by magic it suddenly reappeared in Tohiro's office. Astrid found that utterly bizarre. However, she decided to keep it to herself and proceeded to call the elevator. She rounded the security desk easily and stepped into the luxurious elevator car to wait for Mac. He lumbered into the elevator a few seconds later lugging that ridiculous albeit useful backpack ray gun of his.

"Going up?" she said blithely.

Chapter 27

Ichiro practically ran from the elevator. It had quite frankly been the longest elevator ride of his life.

"How could Father have done this to me?" he asked the lonely hallway as he hurried toward his father's office, well, his father's former office. Now that the old man was dead it would be Ichiro's office. That is assuming he could fix this little oversight.

"How could he do this to me?" Ichiro said out loud again. His rage and frustration etched deep lines on his face as he scowled. Ichiro knew that his anger with his father had impacted their relationship. However, naming Uske as the successor was like a dagger to the heart. That was ludicrous. *Takacorp belongs to Me*.

Ichiro's vision was the only thing that would save the Company from the oblivion that his father was driving it toward. The old fool was thumbing his nose at God. God does not suffer sacrilege.

Ichiro reached the office and walked through the giant wooden doors. He made his way over to the desk where his father hung from Chi Chi's outstretched hand.

He stopped and regarded his late father's body. Ichiro just noticed how gray the old man had become. He surveyed the tableau he had created. The Prophet virus was a triumph of programming. It was built on the command override system that Takacorp pioneered years ago to give greater measures of control over the growing army of androids working throughout the city. It was so simple that Ichiro could have coded it himself. If he were to lower himself to do so that is. Yet, why do something yourself when you had replaceable machines to do the work for you.

He did enjoy doing some things for himself. After all, he took great pleasure in smashing the cog drives and head pieces of those three machines that created the virus for him. He had to make sure there was no trail leading back to him, or worse yet back to Councilman Roth. Roth had big plans for Ichiro. Ichiro wanted to be a part of those. The Image of God Church was a bastion of hope and safety in this retched and empty world and Ichiro was happy to have found it. He was even more thankful that he had been brought into Roth's inner circle. Roth's inner circle was the true power in the New Trinity and nothing of note happened without Roth's say so. Well, most things anyway. Ichiro had overstepped his authority with the church and Roth with his coup. However, once he presented Roth with everything the man needed all would be forgiven.

Though all is for naught if Ichiro couldn't correct this managerial oversight of his father's. As Ichiro approached Chi Chi's eyes began to glow blue again. She dropped Tohiro's body in a heap on the rug at her feet. Tohiro's glazed eyes protruded from their sockets. A grisly reminder of the pressure those demure mechanical hands of Chi Chi's were capable.

Ichiro scoured the office in search of his father's Master control unit. He knew his father had it with him as the old man had tried in vain to use it to stop Chi Chi.

Ichiro continued to search around the desk. He mentally rehearsed his father's murder in his mind in an effort to remember what had happened to the device.

"Ichiro?" Chi Chi said suddenly.

"Eh, Chi Chi," Ichiro stammered.

"Ichiro, it is a pleasant surprise to find you here," Chi Chi said. "Where is your father? I do not detect him in the vicinity."

"Chi Chi we will talk about my father in a moment," Ichiro replied. "Pull up father's last will."

"Certainly, Ichiro."

Chi Chi began to scan the room.

"No, Chi Chi, I want you to keep your gaze on the desk in front of you," Ichiro ordered.

"I have the file you requested, Ichiro," Chi Chi volunteered. "However, I am concerned about your father, Ichiro. Do you have any idea where I can find him?"

"Ah, yes, Chi Chi. I will tell you where my father is once we have completed our business," Ichiro said.

"Acknowledged. What business do we have to conclude?"

"Just let me find Father's Master Control," Ichiro said as he felt around under the desk all the while keeping an eye on Chi Chi. Ichiro knew he had to keep Chi Chi from seeing Tohiro's body at her feet. He wasn't concerned about his own safety as he could use his own master control to keep Chi Chi from harming him. The concern was the safety protocols built into every android operating inside the New Trinity. If Chi Chi sees Tohiro's body she would immediately call for medical help and set off the emergency systems. Even with Holy Light dominating the communication systems of the city the sheer number of systems that would be alerted to the death would be difficult if not impossible to erase.

"Just keep focusing on the desk, Chi Chi" Ichiro commanded.

"Ichiro," Chi Chi said, with great concern flowing through her vocal processor. "The building security protocols have been engaged. There has been an incident in the main lobby."

"What?" Ichiro asked sitting up. "What kind of incident?"

"I am accessing the report log."

Chi Chi tilted her head to the side like all of the others of her kind do when they connect to the network. "An unknown android and a human have illegally entered through the front doors. They disabled the security field and three drones. Ichiro we must locate your father. Where is he?"

"Kisama," Ichiro spat. He began groping around more frantically. He reached under the desk again and his hand brushed something. Emboldened he plunged his arm back under again and just grazed the object once more.

"Ichiro, I must protect your father. Tell me where he is."

"In a moment, Chi Chi," Ichiro replied, coming to his knees, his mind racing. Then it hit him. "M-move the desk closer to the window, Chi Chi."

Chi Chi turned her head and upper body toward the desk just below her waist. She reached out her arm and gently laid her hand upon the desk.

"If I move this you will tell me where your father is?" she asked, her head inclining to the right raising her chin ever so slightly.

"Sure," Ichiro said with a sneer.

Chi Chi, using the latest in ORF motor technology,

pushed the heavy desk closer toward the windows with a simple gesture.

Ichiro saw the command module lying on the carpet peeking out from under the freshly moved desk. He squealed with joy. *I'm so close.* He reached out to grasp it.

"Freeze!" A voice yelled into the office. Ichiro's hand stopped short.

"Ichiro Takahaisu you are under arrest," The man said. "Lay down on the floor with your hands on your head."

Chi Chi turned to the door and saw the RAD man and Uske's prototype had entered the room.

"Agent McDonnell. How nice to see you again," Chi Chi started.

"Ah, just what I need," Ichiro mumbled. His mind raced again, hunting for an angle. Ichiro talked it through in his head. *He knows enough to come here but does he know everything? Highly unlikely. I've been careful enough. He must have found Uske. That will have to be taken care of too. How to proceed? How. To. Proceed?*

"Uncle Tohiro, no!" the prototype yelled.

"Tohiro? Where is Tohiro? I must go to him," Chi Chi said, searching around the room bewildered.

Ichiro's mind ignited with inspiration. "Chi Chi, they killed Tohiro. His body is at your feet," Ichiro shouted.

"Say what?" the agent exclaimed.

"And now they are here to kill me," Ichiro said. "Chi Chi, protect me."

"Tohiro?" Chi Chi said questioningly as she peered down at her feet to see Tohiro's body crumpled on the carpet. Ichiro jumped for the command override on the floor.

"I said freeze!" the agent yelled again.

Ichiro jammed the large red button on the front of the case. Chi Chi's head snapped up as the override engaged.

"Activate combat mode," Ichiro said.

Chi Chi's eyes changed from the soft blue to angry red.

"Ah shit," the agent swore.

Ichiro sneered as he moved to put the desk between him the ensuing battle.

"Kill them, Chi Chi," Ichiro shouted, pointing at the Agent and the other droid.

"CO report filed under date and time," Chi Chi said.

The agent turned his rifle at Chi Chi but she was already in route. She ripped the silk kimono from her body and held the swath of cloth between it and the agent's bizarre weapon.

"That's not good," The agent uttered.

The other droid charged at Chi Chi and tried to slide tackle her legs. The kimono had started to smoke when Chi Chi abruptly jumped into the air. Her leap took her all the way up to the vaulted ceiling and out of harm's way. She placed her hands against it and pushed herself back toward the floor. In a blink of an eye, she was on top of the agent. With a sweep of her arm the rifle was pushed to the side and with her other hand punched the agent in the chest sending him backward out the door. The agent's kinetic barrier crackled and sparked from the blow. His feet trailed behind him as he flew through the open door.

"Hey, that's my RAD man, hands off you overgrown can opener!" Uske's abomination shouted.

Chi Chi casually closed the giant door and gently pressed the lock button on the control pad by the handle. The doors locking bolts slammed in to place with a resounding click. She then turned to face the other droid.

Chapter 28

Mac landed on the floor flat on his back on top of his laser's power pack.

"Ouch!" Mac groaned. He lay there on his back for a moment and for the first time he noticed how nice the ceiling was in this reception area. The imitation wood and gold lined panels accented by beautiful, recessed lighting were really something to behold. The desk near the center of the room really tied everything together. *Dammit man, focus!*

After he regained control of his faculties, he briefly went over what had just happened in his head.

"What the hell?" he groaned. "I hate this case!"

Mac rolled back and forth until he had enough momentum to roll off the heavy pack under his back and onto his stomach.

"I'm never gonna live this down with Astrid," Mac said as he got to his knees. "And this damn pack is a lot heavier than I remember it being."

"Happens when you get older," said a familiar voice.

Mac sighed heavily. He knew that voice all too well.

"Still no sense of humor eh, Mac?" The voice said mockingly.

"Hello, Gracie," Mac peered up just enough to see her designer boots on the carpet in the doorway. The visor made it hard to see more.

"Given that you're here, I take it you figured a couple of things out, uh?" Gracie asked.

"You can still walk away, Gracie," Mac said gravely as he struggled to pick himself up to face her with the weight of the pack on his back. "Your boss is going down for this, but there is no reason you have to go down with him."

"It's not that simple, Mac," Gracie said almost sadly. Mac heard the capacitors on a Neutralizer spin up. He swallowed hard. Being shot by a neutralizer wasn't usually lethal per se though it hurt like a bitch. However, a cannon like Gracie was carrying would definitely be maxed out and the concussive wave could do serious damage to internal organs and soft tissue.

"I hope you brought more than that old thing?" she continued.

"What this? I was feeling nostalgic you know with a bunch of clankers running around killing people. Maybe afterward I thought I would trick or treat for old time's sake."

"That doesn't make any sense, Mac."

Mac scoffed. *Trick or treating? Why did I say that?*

"Now be a good boy and pull out your side arm with your thumb and forefinger. You know the drill," Gracie ordered.

Mac complied.

"That's it. Toss it away."

He tossed his blaster over toward the door he had just come flying through.

"Where is Ichiro?" she asked.

"In there with his dead father," Mac gestured toward the closed door. "That's murder Gracie. Just in case you forgot."

"Revolutions are never pretty," Gracie said dryly. "Sometimes the old have to die to make way for the new."

"So, you sold your soul for a fancy suit and a shitty catch phrase?" Mac snapped.

"Don't be a sore loser," Gracie shot back. "Though you are still pretty when you pout."

"Huh," Mac scoffed, "Oh that's right, you didn't have a soul to begin with, did you, Gracie?"

"You know, if I still cared about what you think of me that might have actually hurt. Now stand up," Gracie ordered.

Mac stood up but took a careful step toward Gracie. She was still gorgeous, her beautiful ebony skin, smooth and wrinkle free. That same ferocious look in her eyes that had attracted him to her in the first place. However, he knew all too well that her beauty exacted its price. She was like a raging fire that consumes everything in her path, beautiful to behold but ultimately deadly to everyone too close.

"Open the door, we're going in," Gracie said.

The whole building suddenly shuddered causing the floor to rumble and the doors to shake.

Mac took his chance. He closed the gap and grabbed the weapon in her hand with both of his. In a not so fluid motion, he spun his back to Grace so he could get out the line of fire, but the pack swung with him and crashed into Gracie throwing them both off balance and onto the floor.

Gracie screamed. Mac and the pack had effectively pinned her arm to the floor. She tried to punch him with her free arm but the combination of the pack on his back and his Kinetic barrier made it nearly impossible to land a clean blow.

"Give it up, Gracie! I don't want to fight you," Mac ordered. "It's done, we know everything. Ichiro's going down for this. You don't have to go with him. Help me and you can walk away."

"Oh, really, Mac, you'll be my hero, and save little ole me from the big nasty corporate monster? Really, Mac? Really?" Gracie replied saccharinely.

"Ah...yeah,"

"No thanks!" she roared.

Gracie wrapped her leg over Mac's abdomen and used it to leverage her free arm up and over Mac's shoulder. She reached across Mac's surprised face and clawed at his right ear beyond the protection of the shield and visor. Mac could see the green glow of his shield right in front of his eyes where parts of her wrist and arm dragged against it as searing pain assaulted his senses. His back arched reflexively, pulling his head back and up, desperate to escape the pain.

Mac's tightened upper body took weight off her arm. She dropped her gun and used the extra room to extract her arm, releasing him in the process.

Mac reached to his chest and struggled with the harness release of his pack. He knew he needed to be free of the additional weight if he was going to go toe to toe with that woman.

"You should have known not to fuck with me, Mac," Grace spat, "You of all people should have known."

"What happened to you?" Mac asked, stalling for time. She circled him, now coming around in his field of view. She had his own neutralizer pointed at him. *Great, shot with my own gun, how embarrassing*. Just then an idea occurred to him, but he needed a couple of seconds to pull it off. *What I need is a distraction.*

Something suddenly slammed into the doors leading to Tohiro's office shuttering them violently, drawing Gracie's attention. Mac reached down with his right hand and grabbed Gracie's discarded hand cannon lying on the floor next to him. He lifted it and fired. The concussive wave whipped through the office striking Gracie in the left shoulder and sending her spinning backward. Her feet left the ground from the blast, and she crashed into the desk. With a wet thump she rolled to the floor in a heap behind the desk knocking, over the chair hiding there.

"Huh," Mac said. "And 10 million credits got deposited in my account!" he said to the room.

Mac paused for a moment.

"No. Well you can't blame a guy for trying."

Mac finished unbuckling his harness and slithered out of the straps. He stretched a bit and rubbed his aching right shoulder. The fall to floor hurt him more than he had expected. Of course, landing on Gracie's arm didn't feel great either.

He reached into his belt pouch and pulled out a couple of plastic binding straps. He gently rolled her over and secured Gracie's arms behind her back. Then bent her legs at the knees and secured them together. He finished it off connecting the two bindings together.

"I'd ask you to help me, but I can see you're all tied up," Mac said to her unconscious form. *Probably one of my best jibes and no one is awake to hear it.*

Astrid gave ground under the fury of Chi Chi's attacks. Uske had said that Chi Chi was one of his finest creations, well, before Astrid that is. *Technically he told Kiyoko that.*

Astrid turned her attention back to the fight. She watched carefully, calculating, blocking, and dodging Chi Chi's attacks with patience, waiting for her chance to strike.

Suddenly Chi Chi jumped into the air and struck downward slamming her fist into to the carpeted floor beneath where Astrid had just been standing. The blow buckled a five-foot section of the floor and shook the whole building. Both droids had to jump to get clear of the sink hole that was created. *That was close, I have to watch out for that one.*

Fighting Chi Chi was completely different than the prophet droids that Astrid had taken on previously. The prophet droids were tough but only fought in a linear field. Punch, kick, shoot at the target. They had massive computation power behind them but limited bandwidth to wield the power with. As the tribunal could only command one PCE at a time through the Command override Chi Chi in combat mode had access to all of her faculties and the Tribunal.

Chi Chi was a blur of activity. While the machine fought physically, she also attacked wirelessly too. Twenty-three separate attacks assaulted Astrid's communication systems. Each attack designed to assume control of one of Astrid's systems. Chi Chi's eye LEDs began flashing in complex numerical patterns designed to tie up a droid's logic systems, a horrible screeching sound emanated from her vocal processer to engage Astrid's core functions like an archaic modem. Layer after layer of attack came from the red eyed automaton.

Astrid ignored most of them. Not being connected to the network full time spared her the bulk of the attacks. That and her core systems were unlike anything that Chi

Chi had ever encountered before. It's really tough to hack a system programmed in an entirely different language. Astrid would know, she has been practicing hacking droids from all of the remains of humanity.

The only credible threat was the noise, as it was really annoying.

Astrid maneuvered around Chi Chi. She wanted to keep Ichiro in sight, she had just got him back within her view when she noticed he had leveled a small weapon at her. *Dick move, Ichi, dick move.*

She reacted to the line of sight of his weapon and moved deftly out of the way before he could even pull the trigger. However, the movement cost her as Chi Chi's onslaught was now in range of doing damage.

Ichiro's small weapon fired, and small blue blast wave shot at the two fighting robots passing safely between them.

Astrid caught a glancing blow from Chi Chi to the face and staggered backward a few steps.

Chi Chi, emboldened by the successful strike, attacked again with her other hand. Astrid had anticipated the blow and held up her left arm to guard her head and face. At the last second, she activated her strike field and neatly cleaved off Chi Chi's hand mid forearm. She caught Chi Chi's disembodied hand in hers as it fell toward the carpeted floor. With a smooth flick of her hand chucked it at Ichiro. The wayward limb sailed across the office and caught the weasel square in the face. Blood shot out of Ichiro's nose and with a strangled cry he dropped to the floor behind Tohiro's desk.

Chi Chi jumped back across the room to reevaluate her opponent's new ability and assess the damage.

"Yes!" Astrid squealed. "Take that you self-absorbed dick! That will teach all of you idiots to shoot guns at me!"

Chi Chi must have completed her assessment of the new data because the machine charged to attack again.

Astrid had built enough of a database on Chi Chi's attacks that she felt confident that she could go on the offensive.

Thanks to her father's alterations she now had more than enough power, however, the habits that small power reserves built were hard to let go of.

Chi Chi charged straight at Astrid and struck with her damaged arm. Astrid used the momentum of her opponent to hip throw her into the door behind them. With a giant shudder Chi Chi fell to the floor. Before she could rise, Astrid struck at Chi Chi's chest, aiming for her CAC battery and ruptured the nitrogen filled container. A halo of electricity flashed with the escaping gas and Chi Chi's frame lay still on the floor.

Mac checked his kit. He was dismayed to find the rifle was broken. Chi Chi had bent the emitter when she attacked. The lenses inside were probably smashed to hell too. He shook the rifle and could hear the tinkling of shattered glass confirming his suspicion. It would take forever to get the replacement parts. So, his kit was out.

He still had his backup piece and a couple of pulse grenades. He had his new emergency shield and stun baton. Better yet he still had Gracie's hand cannon and his own blaster, so that was something.

Mac started toward the door when suddenly a fist punched through it. Scattering shards of wood about the room. Mac jumped back and dropped Gracie's weapon in fit of panic. Luckily, he kept his own. He managed to summon enough presence of mind to level it at the door.

"Murderer!" yelled an angry sounding electronic voice through the hole.

To Mac's horror Chi Chi's face peered through the opening. A white plastic mold of an Asian woman's face peered through the freshly created hole.

"Shit" Mac cursed and opened fire with his own blaster.

He squeezed off several shots and retreated behind the desk near the center of the room. He pulled his own hand cannon from behind his back and steeled himself for the fight. He knew it would take a few seconds for the droid to get through the door, so he had to get lined up for the shot. His best chance was to gun her down while she was restricted by the door opening she was creating. *Poor Astrid. Uske's gonna kill me, that is if I survive this.*

That's when he heard the cackling laughter from the doorway.

"That was awesome, RAD man!" Astrid's musical voice chimed. "Totally awesome."

It took a second for Mac to figure out what had happened.

"Ha, ha, really funny," Mac spat.

"I sure thought so," Astrid chortled while she opened the ruined door and sauntered into the receiving area.

"I could have had a heart attack!" he shouted.

"I recorded it. Do you want to hear?" she asked giddily

Mac rolled his eyes and grumbled. "I hate this case."

Chapter 29

After securing Ichiro with more binding strips just like Gracie and recovering Tohiro's master control unit Mac and Astrid boarded the security elevator that ran thought the center of the Tower.

It was a comparatively short and easy trip. Which made Mac very suspicious. They exited the elevator on the Vault floor and entered a spacious room filled with vid screens. They covered the entire back wall. What caught Mac's eye was the ugly red-cushioned captain's chair overlooking the screens.

"It's like something out of a science fiction vid," Mac said.

"Authorized personnel only," A droid said in a matter-of-fact manner from out of nowhere. "Please board the elevator and…"

"Stop," Mac said using the Command Override feature of the Master control.

"CO report filed under date and time," The droid said.

"Identify," Mac said to the droid.

"Designation Heckle."

"Current function?" Mac queried.

"Oversee Holy Light application and report anomalies to supervisor," The droid replied in its garbled software driven voice.

"Who is your supervisor?" Mac asked.

"Command originated from Ichiro Takahaisu," the droid replied.

"What is the Holy Light application?" Astrid asked. Though Mac suspected that they both knew full well what it was.

"Operational parameters are unknown. Function; monitor and report," Heckle replied. "Awaiting further instructions."

"Terminate the Holy Light application," Mac said.

"Unable to comply," Heckle replied. "System Administrator access is required."

"Terminate the Holy Light application," Mac said again pressing the command override button on the master control.

"CO report filed under date and time," The Droid replied. "Unable to comply. System Administrator access is required.

"What?" Mac asked, as he stared incredulously at the device in his hand.

"We should have known it wouldn't be that easy," Astrid said. "Heckle, do you have System Administrator access?"

"No. Function; Monitor and report," Heckle replied.

"Can you do something, Astrid? Hack it or something?" Mac asked.

"I can try," she said, turning back to the droid standing before them. "Show me the terminal."

The droid complied. It led her over to the bank of monitors. Astrid sat down on the vacant stool and began typing on the terminal.

Mac, drawn by the activity at the bank of monitors beheld a ghastly scene. Every monitor displayed a vid feed from a controlled droid or security camera from around the three domes. Vehicles, maintenance machines, service droids all running amuck. Killing people and destroying other droids and property. Mac started to look away out of revulsion when something caught his eye.

"Ziggy!" Mac said. He could see Stark's TFE holding off a virtual sea of droids. "Astrid, we have to stop this now."

"I'm trying," she said while she typed furiously. "The system is in a weird reboot state. It's like it's not fully online so I can't find a way in."

"You," Mac said to the android sitting next to Astrid on the other stool. "Bring up that monitor," Mac said, pointing at the screen with Ziggy on it.

"Acknowledged," The droid said. With a few quick jabs of its plastic fingers the main monitor displayed the carnage.

Ziggy and Stark were not going to make it. There were just too many droids. *Why aren't they retreating to a better position?* That was when Mac saw the huddled mass of people behind Ziggy and Stark. People seeking refuge from the onslaught. *He'll never leave them.*

"Call the droids off," Mac ordered.

"Unable to comply," The other droid said. "Countermands previous order."

"Call off the attacks on those people!" Mac ordered again this time using the master control.

"CO report filed under date and time," The droid replied then set to work diverting the droids.

"You, Heckle, can you divert all of the droids under the Holy Light application to a specific location?"

"Affirmative."

"How long will that take?" Mac asked.

"Projected completion of task. ten hours and twenty-seven minutes," Heckle replied.

"Shit," Astrid said. "The whole city will be trashed by then, we need to stop this now."

"What happens if we destroy the tribunal?" Mac asked.

"They should all stop," Astrid replied. "The tribunal is driving all of the droids."

"Where is the Tribunal?" Mac asked Heckle.

"Through there," The droid responded while it pointed at a door just to the right of the monitor bank.

"You two, begin diverting the Holy Light droids to the Takacorp parking structure. Begin with the machines on the main monitor," Mac ordered using the command module again.

"CO report filed under date and time," The droids replied in unison then set to work completing the order.

Mac took one last look at the monitor with Stark and Ziggy. Most of the droids around them had slowed and were beginning to turn around, but not all.

"Hang on guys, just a little longer," Mac rushed behind Astrid through the door.

Chapter 30

Mac entered the open blank space and bumped into Astrid, who had stopped just inside the door.

"What's going on?" he asked, as he steadied himself.

"That," Astrid replied as she gestured to the opposite side of the room.

In the center of the vast white space next to the coffin-like Tribunal machines and the thick umbilical-like bundle of cable hanging down from the ceiling stood two droids. One a hulking mass of a droid with four insect-like legs. Mac had seen the like before. It was a Military drone. The machine's drab exterior was painted gray to match the gray soil tones outside the domes where it was built to patrol and defend. It had a central stalk that stood up from the center of the leg chassis. At the top of the stalk sat its communication and visual array, a series of lenses and photo sensors surrounded by small antennae lending to the insect motif. Two large beam cannons sat on either side of the stalk. Beam cannons were illegal inside the dome. They could easily puncture the dome walls and cause a collapse.

Mac had dealt with one of these monsters before. They were tough but not unbeatable. With Astrid's neat cutty thing she did with her hands, it shouldn't be too much of a problem.

The other droid gave Mac pause. It looked like a bad copy of Astrid. The details weren't quite right. The lines were off here and there. The biggest difference was the copy's eyes. They had the angry red glow of a typical unit in combat mode and eyebrows were stationary.

"Intruders, lie down on the floor and place your hands behind your head," The copy said in a sweet female voice. "Authorities have been alerted to your trespass and will be coming to take you into custody."

"Shit," Astrid swore.

"What?"

"I think that's the decoy that Dad built."

"The one that smashed through the glass out front?" Mac asked, keeping the two enemy machines in his line of sight.

"I'm pretty sure," she said. "How did they find it?"

"How can you tell?"

"The voice, they didn't bother to change it," Astrid replied. "It's one of my favorite voice preferences."

"Lie down on the floor and place your hands behind your head," the copy repeated taking a step forward.

Mac remembered that Astrid's body was based on a Takacorp prototype so if this is the same then their specs would be similar and that could pose a problem. Mac unconsciously rubbed his throat. The action reminded him of the ace he had up his sleeve, well in his hand.

"Deactivate!" he yelled to the two droids while pressing the red button on the outside of the master control unit.

The droids stayed where they were. Mac and Astrid held their ground as well.

"That's odd. They should have done that stupid CO filed line," he said.

"Hm," Astrid grunted.

Mac pressed the button again and yelled, "Report: Name and Function!"

"Authorities have been alerted to your trespass and will be coming to take you into custody. Lower your weapons and lie down," The copy ordered.

The big droid's beam cannons spun up and began to emit a faint glow from the emitter nozzles as they prepared to fire. Mac crunched the numbers in his head. They had a chance but not a very good one.

"Shit, ah, you take the big one, I'll take the small one," Mac whispered to Astrid.

"Some gentleman you are," Astrid replied snidely.

"Give me a sec I'll help you get close," Mac said.

"My hero," Astrid said, sarcastically. Mac could practically hear her roll her eyes.

Using Astrid as a shield, Mac pocketed the master control and drew his service piece. He took a deep breath.

"Ready?"

"Are we ever really ready?" she replied.

"Guess not," he admitted.

"Go," Astrid said, quietly. She bolted. All Mac saw was a yellow blur rushing the two droids.

He took aim and fired his service weapon. A white-hot flare shot across the open room and hit the large military droid in the communications array at the top of its central stalk. Mac ran too. He knew what was coming.

The large droid began to pivot back and forth trying in vain to look around the blazing ball of light hovering in front of its visual sensors. Then without warning it fired its particle beam cannons.

Two pale purple shafts of light connected the two

weapons to the wall behind Mac. He felt the intense heat as the beams burned away the air molecules and left stygian scorch marks on the white walls. Thunder crashed inside the room as air rushed in to fill the vacuum created by the beams' passing.

Mac opened fire on the smaller droid and tried to keep it from intercepting Astrid. He aimed at the bare white floor in front of it and stopped the droid short. It quickly changed course and veered straight for Mac instead.

The machine charged at him. He stopped and took aim. He squeezed the trigger. The brilliant blue blast wave jumped from the emitter nozzle and sailed at the oncoming machine. To Mac's dismay, the copy contorted around the blast's trajectory and continued forward at an inhuman pace.

Mac adjusted his stance and fired Gracie's cannon. The weapon's kick threw his arm off target. However, he caught a bit of luck and managed to clip the droid in the leg mid stride. Unfortunately, it was not the boon he had hoped. The advancing machine took the blow in stride. It tucked and rolled across the floor. Its forward momentum carried it through the roll and back on to its feet again.

Mac fired again with his service pistol and the copy held up its right hand and blocked the blast wave with its palm.

"What the…?" was all Mac had time to say as the copy was on him.

The copy led with its left striking for Mac's face. The green flashes of the barrier sparkled in front of his nose where the droid's knuckles made contact. Mac was forced to take a step back so he could remain on his feet.

In a panic he fired Gracie's cannon at the floor between them. He staggered back a few more steps as the attacking machine jumped to avoid the blast wave.

He lined up with his service piece and took the shot. The blaster bolt hit the airborne droid square the chest. Arcs of electricity shot through the machine causing it to flail wildly as it dropped like a stone. The droid fell to the ground in front him.

The machine sat on the ground in an unusual position. It was down on one knee and slumped forward resting against its other knee.

"Better safe than sorry," he said, as he leveled Gracie's gun at the motionless droid.

It sprang to life and swatted the cannon out of Mac's hand sending it flying across the white floor.

He tried to get a shot off with his other blaster, but the copy was too fast. It struck for his chest and connected squarely with his shield. The blow sent him flying.

Mac slid almost two whole meters across the smooth white flooring and his side arm slid farther beyond.

Mac jumped to a crouch and stood up searching for his opponent. A loud metal clanging rang out through the room. Mac and his attacker both glanced toward the noise.

Astrid had managed to cut one of the legs from the big drone. It staggered from the loss of the limb into one of the coffin-like structures of the Tribunal. The flare had finally burned out. As long as Astrid stayed close it couldn't use its particle cannons. It was still dangerous, aside from getting stepped on it also fired heavily with its smaller neutralizers that sat below the bigger cannons.

The smaller machine stopped advancing toward

Mac and started again toward Astrid.

Mac drew his backup piece from the small of his back and shot the retreating copy in the back. His own hand cannon was not as powerful as Gracie's, but he was a lot more accurate with it. The blow hit the droid igniting a green cascade as the blast wave struck a kinetic barrier and dispersed.

"Ah crap, a shield."

Mac charged the droid continuing to fire at it. The copy abruptly changed course and headed back toward Mac running in an arc to avoid his shots.

"Got your attention now, didn't I?" he taunted.

Mac stopped abruptly. With his backup piece in his left hand, he pulled quick release tab on his left sleeve to expose the emergency shield cuff on his wrist.

Once the fabric was clear he activated the shield, and the hexagonal barrier sprang to life.

"We're gonna try this a little differently," Mac told the approaching droid.

The machine slowed its pace and began to circle Mac. Mac tapped the toggle switch on his shield cuff and switched it to riot mode. The shield grew to cover most of Mac's torso. He knew it would use power a lot faster this way; however, this fight had to end quickly so he was prepared to go all out.

Mac pulled his stun baton out but didn't push the trigger to extend it.

He turned the shield and fired at the droid. Again, it spun around the bolts and advanced. Mac ducked behind his shield and charged toward the droid rather than away. The two collided in a flash of green as their kinetic barriers rubbed against each other. He felt his boots slide across the white tiled floor as the droid pushed back.

Mac started to give ground as the droid pushed against his shield. He reached his right hand around his riot shield and extended his stun baton. With a quick jab he stabbed the droid's leg as it stepped forward. The surge of electricity raced through the droid's systems causing it to stumble. Mac pushed with his shield and swung at the droid's head with his baton. He caught it on the temple, cracking the plastic shell with a satisfying crunch. Before it hit the ground the droid caught itself with its outstretched hands.

Mac aimed his hand cannon at the droid and fired. The blast clipped the droid in the back again forcing it to the white tiled floor as the blast wave was dispersed through its shield. Mac stepped toward the prone figure and stuck his baton into the droid's leg again sending another jolt of electricity through the droid's systems.

"Mac!" Astrid screamed.

Mac's head whipped around and saw the military droid had pointed its Neutralizers at him. He ducked behind the riot shield just as the blast waves hit. A rain of blaster fire hammered Mac's emergency shield then abruptly stopped.

Mac saw stars. He dropped down on one knee to steady himself. His arm ached from the attack. He smelled smoke coming off his wrist from the shield cuff. His shield had taken the entire barrage but had burned through most of the battery. The emitters were burning out as well.

He lifted his head up to see Astrid ripping one of the Neutralizers off the central stalk only to then go flying off the droid as an expanding green wall collided with her. The droid's shields had pushed her away. She landed on her feet and circled away from Mac, leading it away.

Striking repeatedly hit and run style against the machine's shield.

As Astrid attacked, she couldn't get past the shields. The droid had extended its shield a meter beyond its spider like legs. Her arms weren't long enough to reach anything vital. The shield stopped her body from passing through.

Mac thought hard. There had to be something.

"I got it," Mac said. "Astrid, catch!"

Mac hurled one of his grenades to Astrid who jumped high in the air and snatched it.

"What am I doing with this?" she asked.

"Your arm can pass through the field" Mac yelled. "Pull the pi…"

Something collided with Mac's back sending him tumbling forward. Mac rolled over and to his horror saw the copy standing over him. He pointed his hand cannon and had it kicked from his out of his grasp.

"I can see you might be upset," Mac held his hands up. "Let me explain."

The droid stared down at him with those glowing red eyes.

Mac swallowed hard.

"Excuse me coming through," Astrid said, as she hopped over Mac. Both Mac and the droid watched her go in confusion when the android doppelganger was clobbered by several blast waves from the bigger droid.

Mac staggered to his feet. He glanced around and located his service pistol on the floor. Mac dived for it. He scooped it up and started firing at the bigger bug-like machine. It quickly activated its shield again.

"Hey! Look over here you hunk of junk," he yelled as he continued to fire at it, sending green light cascading across the giant sphere shaped field. "That's right look at me!"

Mac's blaster bolts pinged harmlessly against the machine's military grade shielding. The larger machine turned its visual centers and focused on Mac.

Mac swallowed hard as a purple light began to glow again from the machine's remaining particle cannon. Astrid must have trashed the other one when she damaged the neutralizer earlier. Not that it mattered. A blast from a particle cannon cut through pretty much everything, it wouldn't matter if it was one cannon or two.

The light got more intense as it readied to fire. Mac hobbled away. He did not want to be where it was going to shoot but he just wasn't fast enough to escape the blast. Not even his emergency shield would have protected him. Mac closed his eyes. *I love you Milly. I'm sorry.*

He heard a pop and an electrical fizzle followed by a loud crash. He opened one eye and then the other and looked back at the drone.

Its central base was seated lifeless on the floor with its remaining legs extended out around it. All of its weapons hung limply, pointed toward the floor. Astrid stood, arms akimbo, admiring her handy work. Mac sighed heavily.

"Well, that went well." Mac forced himself to smile.

Chapter 31

Astrid stuck her hand into the closest cabinet of the Tribunal system. Her hand slid easily past the plastic outer shell of the coffin like structure. She located the central processing core by feeling around for a spherical object and pulled it from the housing. Strands of nano fibers and connection cables were dragged through the hole along with it. The small monitor mounted in the side of the device flashed red and a series of warnings and then went black. She examined the orb-like central processer. Its faint glow had faded as soon as it was no longer connected to power. It filled her hand like a large metal and plastic grapefruit. She crushed it in her hand for good measure. That and she felt it looked cool.

"Better trash them all," Mac said from behind her. "We can't take the risk. There may be redundant systems."

Astrid nodded and walked toward the next one. They were laid out around a central hub of three, leg thick cables that hung down from the ceiling. Each cable branched off to one of the processing units of the Tribunal. One processing core had more than enough computing power to run all of the androids in the whole city. Three provided safety and redundancy.

"On second thought, do your cutty thing and cut the cables," Mac said. "It would be fa...uh"

A wet thump sounded behind Astrid. Curious she

turned to see what had happened to Mac and gasped. She saw the copy standing over Mac, who now laid face first on the floor.

"Shit," Astrid cursed. She accessed her combat database and went looking for specs on the droid. "Shit," she cursed again when her search came up empty.

Dad had constructed it hastily to cover their escape. It had been made with pieces of several prototypes he had been tinkering with. With any luck it was all base model components. If that was the case, then Astrid had one big advantage. Though it didn't account for whatever Ichiro's engineers had upgraded.

Astrid found she really wasn't worried. Her dad was a genius android designer. He had built her body from scratch to handle just this sort of situation.

She could see the copy was roughly her size. Most likely they were similar masses too. The other machine though had a number of cracks in its out coverings where Mac had connected with some blows.

Astrid took a step backward toward the remaining tribunals. The copy, focused on Astrid intently, stepped forward in response. Astrid also noted that it had a limp in its left leg. Not much of one to the human eye, but enough that Astrid could see it and make use of it if need be.

Astrid planned her attack and acted. She completed a standing back flip that a gymnast would envy and landed on top of the Tribunal case she had already disabled. She winked at the other droid then jumped to the case farthest from the droid and poor Mac. She landed gracefully and struck straight downward with her arm and liberated another of the Tribunal processor cores. She smashed it in her hand and stared defiantly at the other droid. The copy abandoned Mac and moved between Astrid and the remaining Tribunal processor.

"Limp didn't slow you down much at all did it?" she asked the droid.

"S-s-s-surrender," The other machine stuttered so badly that it took Astrid a moment to figure out what it was saying

"No way!" Astrid yelled as she charged the droid. It moved to meet her. The two droids were a flurry of motion. Strike and counter. Using their arms and legs, each tried to position the other for advantage. *This droid is equal to if not better than Chi Chi.*

Astrid didn't have time to fight the way she liked. She was on the offensive. However, this machine's tactics were different. It dodged her strikes rather than blocked them. It focused on foot techniques to try and tie up Astrid's legs. *It knows about the strike field. Somehow it knows.*

Astrid changed tactics herself. She struck again and the droid avoided by backing away. She made her move. She turned and bolted toward the outer wall. The other droid gave chase. They were fairly close in overall speed. As Astrid's feet hit the wall, she used her to momentum to run up the surface vertically. As she reached the apex of her climb, she bounded backward over herself and her pursuer now at the base of the wall.

Astrid landed on her feet and attacked. With the wall behind the droid, it couldn't back up and get out of the way like it could before, so it blocked with its left arm. Their left arms connected at the forearm. Astrid engaged her strike field. Light flashed and a deafening boom sounded in the open room.

Astrid found herself on the floor lying on her side

staring at a stump that used to be her right hand. Internal alarms screamed at her.

"What the hell?" she said aloud. Astrid ran a complete diagnostic of her remaining systems.

Her forearm was completely gone. Her shoulder, face and chest plate all sustained damage. Her left eyebrow kept twitching. That and her sweet camouflaging poncho was on fire. *Fire!*

"Crap!" Astrid yelled as she tore the garment from her body and threw its smoldering remains on the floor.

"Rude," Astrid spat. *All right, got to stay focused.*

She jumped to her feet and found her opponent. It too was picking itself up off the floor near the wall. Parts of its plastic outer shell were falling away as it stood up. Once on its feet the droid emitted a weird broadcast signal and out of nowhere a wall panel next to it erupted from the wall. On the open panel were droid parts, arms and legs hung on racks on either side of the panel.

Astrid watched as the droid ejected its damaged arm from the shoulder and grabbed a new one from the rack. It emitted the signal again and the panel retracted back into the wall as quickly as it had appeared.

The copy seated the new arm and threw a few practice jabs in the air calibrating.

"Okay, didn't see that coming," Astrid grumbled.

"S-s-surrender," The copy said, a little clearer this time. "Y-your chances of s-s-successfully winning this exchange have been reduced to 15 percent. The logical course of action i-i-is to s-surrender."

Astrid consulted her combat database. Her strike field was effectively neutralized for now. She couldn't take the chance of losing her other arm. Her eyebrow was really getting distracting, just twitching away.

She reached up and pinned her twitching eyebrow against her forehead until it clicked, setting the eyebrow back in its track. With the annoying twitch fixed it was time to get down to business.

"15 percent huh?" Astrid replied flippantly. "Let's see if we can't better those odds a bit."

Astrid charged the copy. The two fought back and forth. Astrid circled it. Without her other arm she was severely hampered. Her options were growing more limited. She pressed but could clearly see she was out matched. She gave ground and continued to circle her opponent.

Astrid gave more ground. With a swift spin she struck at the copy's slower leg. The copy moved it out of position and brought its opposite leg around in a spinning roundhouse kick that sent Astrid sprawling to the floor two meters away. Astrid turned and looked up at the droid as it approached. Astrid crawled back a few more steps away from the encroaching enemy.

The copy loomed over Astrid. If Astrid had a throat, she would have swallowed hard.

"Y-y-you are defeated," The copy said in what Astrid thought was rather smug tone for a stuttering machine. "V-v-victory is mine."

"Take it," Astrid said. "Oh, and this too," she broadcast the signal copy had used earlier. The copy's head snapped to the side just in time to see the secret panel in the wall shoot out again. The panel clobbered the copy as it stood over Astrid. The impact sent the enemy machine sliding across the white floor. It stopped abruptly when it hit the outer shell of one of the Tribunal boxes.

Astrid took her time and perused the replacement

parts available. They were all Takacorp components which meant they should work. She selected the arm closest to her. She ejected her crippled arm and seated the new one. She felt her system connect and the arm activated. With a few quick jabs she tested the new appendage. It was almost as responsive as her old arm, but it lacked a lot of the tactile feeling. It reminded her of her arm being asleep, or what it felt like when Kiyoko's arm would fall asleep.

Astrid sent the signal again and the wall panel slid back into its hiding place with surprising speed.

She double checked to make sure there were no explosives hidden in this arm. None showed up on the diagnostic, but that didn't mean it was completely safe.

She turned and worked her arm again memorizing its motion and feel. She added the adjustments to her combat database.

"How are my chances now?" Astrid asked flippantly.

The other droid rose to its feet far more smoothly than Astrid would have liked. Its plastic face cover was completely smashed. Most of it lay on the floor by its feet exposing the metal components that made up its skull. Parts of the android's chest cover fell away too. Astrid could see the ORF motors strung about the machine much like the muscle groups of the human body.

The copy lurched suddenly to its left. It took a few wobbling steps to regain its balance. Once stable on its feet again it turned its head to focus intently on Astrid.

Astrid stood in ready stance as the copy started its approach. Its movements got smoother and more precise as it closed the distance.

Astrid built her plan of attack. She eased back on the right foot in preparation to meet the oncoming droid's attack when a purple beam of light cut through the copy. The Particle beam completely vaporized its torso. The head and shoulders came loose and flopped on the floor in front of the legs. The legs had kept their pace and continued toward Astrid only to trip over the android's now detached upper body.

The copy's remains ended up in a heap at Astrid's feet. She followed the white band-like after image in her visual field back along its path to find Mac standing on top of the military drone.

"Take that, you fucking clanker!" Mac slurred.

Astrid turned and sprinted to the remaining Tribunal node. She sank her arm shoulder deep and retrieved the control core. She then crushed it in her hand as she had the others. She really enjoyed the crunch.

Astrid dropped the core and made her way to Mac.

"How did you get that beam cannon to work? She asked. "I thought your grenade shorted out all of the systems.

"I direct connected it to Gracie's hand cannon," Mac said slowly. He sagged against the beam weapon. And his stun baton fell out from his hand and clanged on the floor. He had apparently used it to lever the beam cannon into position "Aiming it was…the hard part."

Mac closed his eyes and laid his head against the housing of the beam weapon.

Astrid did a cursory scan of him. He was in pretty bad shape.

"Mac! Stay with me, Mac," Astrid ordered. "You can't sleep. You have hit your head. You need to stay conscious."

Mac's body slumped against the weapon, but he opened his eyes. "Did we win?" Mac slurred.

Astrid looked around the room and back at Mac. "Yup."

Chapter 32

Mac woke up to the ambient hum and beep of the various machines that crowded around him. He opened his eyes and took in the room.

He raised his head and immediately regretted it. It was a hospital room. He could tell that. He had been in enough to be able to identify them by their smell alone.

He took stock of his situation. His head hurt. His ear hurt. His throat was bone dry and to make matters worse he kind of had to pee.

"Well, I'm alive so that is something," Mac said to the empty room. He blinked his eyes. Mac reached up to rub his eyes and felt a stab of pain in his hand. He inadvertently pulled at the IV that had been inserted there. He followed the line of tubing to a bag of fluids hanging from a rack attached to his bed. He laid his hand back down and examined the room again with only his eyes.

A dull ache in his forehead above his right eye stood out quite a bit. He reached a little higher and found a rubbery substance there just over where it hurt. The same substance was covering the scratches that Gracie gave him too.

"Another head injury, great," Mac said sarcastically.

Mac felt around with his free hand. He located the remote to his hospital bed, and hit the call button.

The remote vibrated and then a voice radiated from

the speaker in the device.

"How my I assist you?" The voice asked.

"I'd like a drink please," Mac told the disembodied voice. "And I have to pee."

"Someone will be right there," The voice replied.

Shortly thereafter a vaguely feminine nurse droid made its way into the room carrying a small cup of water in a plastic cup.

"Here you are, Sugar," it said, as it leaned over and presented the cup to Mac. Mac took the cup and drank deeply. In short order he drained the cup. "I'm called Dee Dee. So, if you need anything you just give me a holler, all right, Sugar."

"More please," Mac said, as he handed Dee Dee the cup.

"Sure thing, Sugar," the Dee Dee replied. Dee Dee was using a southern drawl accent, which promptly annoyed Mac. It quickly made its way over to the sink in the bathroom and filled the cup again. Mac greedily gulped down the newly filled contents.

With his thirst satiated another pressing demand made itself known. "Am I cleared to pee?" Mac asked.

"I will check, Sugar," Dee Dee said, as it reached toward Mac. He flinched in spite of himself. "Sorry, Sugar, I ain't gonna hurt you. Just gotta scan your ID band and consult your chart."

Dee Dee ran its finger over the ID chip in the band on Mac's wrist and stood back up.

"Checking...Checking," Dee Dee said. Dee Dee was an older model that Mac wasn't familiar with. It was bipedal, like most of the service droids throughout the city. It had a screen on the chest along the bust line that displayed each word it said. Most likely for the hearing-impaired patients.

"You are cleared to use the lavatory, Sugar," Dee Dee said suddenly.

Mac nodded and winced at the cold floor under his feet. He had been wrong about the IV. It was not connected to the bed. Instead, it was connected to a ball droid that followed him into the lavatory.

He did his business while eyeing the ball droid suspiciously. It was basically a scaffold-like frame mounted on top of a weighted rubberized ball about the size of an old soccer ball. It had a variety of gyroscopes and sensors housed in a black box at the base of the frame above the ball. Those helped tell the motors on top of the ball to stay upright and follow him around. The IV bag hung from a pole that extended from the top of the tower. They were great for hospitals where people were usually tied to various machines for one reason or another. It was all old school tech compared to modern droids, but it was proven tech and had been in use in Hospitals for longer than Mac had been alive. This little guy could be configured with a number of different add-ons and would then stay with the patient everywhere they went in the hospital. Once Mac was settled back in his bed his little tagalong rolled to a dock in the base of it.

Mac turned back to Dee Dee standing next to the bed.

"Dee Dee, user command. Preferences," he said.

"Fine, Sugar, how can I help you?" It replied.

"Accents. Set to American Midwest please," he said.

"Acknowledged," it replied, the southern accent now gone.

"Thank you, Dee Dee."

Mac leaned back and rested his head.

"Where is everyone?" he asked himself quietly.

"I'm sorry. I didn't get that. Please repeat your question," Dee Dee said.

"It's nothing, Dee Dee. I was wondering where my companions were," he said.

"I'm sorry there was no note left in your file regarding your companions," it said in what Mac assumed was supposed to be a reassuring tone. All it did was make the droid sound condescending.

"It doesn't matter," Mac said. "So anyway, what is my diagnosis?"

"You suffered a severe concussion and a laceration of your eyebrow along with minor lacerations to your ear and temple. The lacerations were closed with med gel," Dee Dee replied. "You are being kept for observation before being released."

"Mac!" Milly yelled as she rushed into the room and set down the cat carrier. Artie meowed his annoyance at being confined but settled in for a nap to show everyone what he thought of their human machinations.

Milly elbowed Dee Dee aside and began to make over Mac in his hospital bed. She inspected the wound above his eye, and on his ear. She then gently kissed his forehead.

She smelled of lavender and cinnamon. Mac thought it smelled wonderful. Milly had changed clothes. She was wearing jeans now and a long sleeve shirt. She had her shoulder pack with her which was her version of a purse.

Once she had convinced herself that he was okay she rounded on him. "You stupid man! You had me so worried," Milly snapped savagely. "You could have been killed!"

"I'm okay, babe," Mac said quietly as he reached up and took her hand gently in his. It was amazing how simple human contact with Milly made all of his hurts and pains vanish. "Just a bump on the noggin. Good thing I'm hardheaded."

"That's not what meant, and you know it," Milly glowered.

"Ahem, son, I'm glad you made it," Mr. Bender said, while he presented his hand to Mac. Mac hadn't seen the older man come in. Mac took the outstretched hand nodded. His' warm smile and calloused hands were also reassuring. Mac felt a sense of loss when the handshake was over.

Mr. Bender turned to his daughter. He kissed her on the head and said, "I'll wait for you in the hall."

"So how is it out there?" Mac asked, adjusting the bed to sit up more.

Milly scowled down at him imperiously. Mac gave her a weak smile.

Milly sighed heavily, "Fine, things are still a mess. Droids litter the streets, Globals, and the Wi-Fi net are working intermittently. The vid net is down. Apparently Takacorp was running some of the backbone of our com systems through their network and when you took it down you inadvertently disrupted most of the city's communications network.

"There's never anything good on anyway," Mac said sardonically.

"Sir," Dee Dee interjected. "I will be leaving now. I'll be back later to check on you. Click the call button if you need anything in the meantime."

"Thanks, oh hey, when can I go home?" Mac asked.

"The doctor has you scheduled for discharge today barring any complications," Dee Dee replied. "Will that be all?"

"Sure, thanks," Mac said. He watched the droid turn and leave the room.

"Astrid brought you here and then came and got us in the van," Milly continued. "She filled us in."

"How are Uske and Kiyoko?" Mac asked. "Oh, I should check on Teddy too."

"Teddy's fine. I was just there. I figured I would check on him for you while you were still sleeping. He woke up yesterday but with your Global fried the hospital couldn't get through to you. He's as insufferable as ever. He keeps whining about someone named Caroline but flinches every time the nurse droids come near him. So, they sedated him a little. He's in a pretty good place right now."

"Caroline was the droid that attacked him," Mac explained. "His sex bot."

"Men," Milly rolled her eyes.

"The others?" Mac asked again. "What about Stark and Ziggy?"

"They are all fine," Milly said.

"I guess I owe Astrid one for saving me," Mac said morosely.

"Got that right," Astrid said in her musical voice.

"Man, they just let anybody in here, don't they?" Mac said. He looked passed Milly and smiled warmly at the Android. Astrid stood in the doorway of his room with arms akimbo. Her yellow poncho was gone and in its place was a plain black one. Mac found it interesting that he would naturally think of a droid as a "'her.'" Astrid had proved her mettle. She was foxhole material and Mac wouldn't have survived without her much less stopped the Prophet rampage.

"You'll live apparently so I guess I know what I need to," Astrid said dryly.

"Thanks to you," Mac said. "You really kicked some major butt. I couldn't have done it without you so, thanks."

"Ah, don't go getting mushy on me, RAD man. You'll mess up the whole dynamic we have going."

"And what dynamic is that?" Mac quirked up the side of his mouth and narrowed his eyes.

"Oh, you know, you say something or do something stupid, and I point it out and everyone laughs," she retorted, her voice brimming with mirth. "It's times like these I wish I could smile. Sarcasm is hard when you can't smile."

Mac smiled broadly. "I wouldn't know."

"Touché." Astrid pointed her finger at him and made a shooting motion.

"So, what happened, after we stopped the droids?"

"Well, as I was loading you into the van you insisted that Ichiro be taken to Detective Stark. So, after I got you to the hospital I drove to that intersection and picked him and his droid up. Let me tell you that took some convincing. They were out to smash some droids. I think having disposed of my damaged yellow poncho was what saved me, that and showing him your badge. Here you are by the way," she said, as she handed Mac the shiny hexagonal disk.

"Anyway, I brought them to Takacorp. I told them everything. He asked me to collect the two droids from the control room and I loaded them all in the van and took them to RAD headquarters. It was cool. He let me drive fast. Turns out, I like driving fast," she said, her mechanical eyes beaming.

"That place is a mess by the way. Thanks to your warning the director had all of the TFE's taken offline, and their network adaptors removed. However, he couldn't force the issue with the NTPD units that were with the NTPD officers. You know the ones who were there looking for you. Consequently, they went nuts and well, you can imagine the rest. After I dropped them off, I went back to get Dad, Kiyoko, Milly, and Annie."

"Is Dick okay, do you know?" Mac asked.

"He's good," Milly added. "For some reason, my texts to him have been going through. He has been sending me updates. There were some injuries at headquarters, but no one died. One of the NTPD agents might not recover. A TFE broke the poor guy's neck when it tried to strangle him," Milly shivered as she spoke.

"Dick said to tell you thanks for the warning. It saved a lot of lives," Milly continued.

"So, all's well that ends well," Mac said as he lay back in the hospital bed. *That's the saying right "ends well."* Mac felt a sudden pang of loss. He missed Six.

"Domo arigato, Mac San," Uske said, drawing Mac back to the present. The older man bowed deeply and then straightened. "Astrid said that you're quite the hero," his thick accent was in full swing. His *L*'s still being pronounced as *R*'s. Mac wasn't sure if it was the head injury or just time, but he thought he was getting better at understanding the man.

"She is the real hero," Mac said. "She really is something special."

"Hai, Hai" Uske replied. "Though I am beginning to

believe she has underplayed her involvement in the situation."

"I'm going to help Kiyoko and Annie with the vending machine. Later, RAD man!" Astrid announced and bid a hasty retreat.

Mac and Uske both shared a chuckle.

"Kids," Uske uttered, and they both chuckled again.

"I will let you rest," Uske said, and he bowed deeply again. "If the RAD doesn't want you back. I would gladly have a man as capable as yourself come work for me."

"Thank you, sir," Mac said. "I may have to take you up on that."

"Until then, rest," Uske said and then he left.

Mac sighed. He closed his eyes and lay there for a moment. He still had Milly's hand in his. It felt right. He drank in the feeling.

A little while later the doctor on duty swung around and checked Mac over. He gave Mac a clean bill of health. Mac was ordered to rest as that was the best way to recover. Both mental and physical rest was the best course of action. Mac was told to see his primary care physician within a week to make sure there were no lasting effects.

Mac thanked him for his time and proceeded to get dressed with Milly's help. He looked at the clothes Milly had brought him. A pair of jeans, tee shirt, undies, and some socks. Once he finished getting dressed, he strapped his holster to his leg. Out of habit he drew his service weapon and checked the charge, then eased it slowly back in. Feeling more comfortable now, dressed and more importantly armed, he sought out Milly.

"Oh, and we're good right? You know with the

whole me stunning you thing?" he asked tentatively.

Milly smiled. Her face was inscrutable. He couldn't tell what she was thinking at all.

"I love you, Mac," she said, as she walked close to him and squeezed his hand. She leaned in and kissed him gently on the lips.

"I love you too but that didn't answer my question," Mac argued.

"I understand that you did what you thought you had to," Milly replied as she backed away to give him room.

"Good," Mac said, finally relaxing and adjusting the hang of his belt and holster.

"Let's get out of here. I want something to eat," Mac said, smiling as he adjusted his boots one more time pulling on the tongues.

"Oh, and there is just *one* more thing," she said as she turned around.

"What's that babe?" he asked. He glanced up to meet her eyes just in time to see Milly level her Mark 2 at him and squeeze the trigger.

"Wai…" he stammered as everything went black.

Epilogue

The large oak door swung open, and Vance walked purposely across the room. He mopped the sweat off his forehead with his trusty handkerchief. Meetings like these always made him sweat. He never liked to deliver bad news.

The office of the Image of God Church was resplendent. It had all of the trappings and comforts of wealth. No expense had been spared when constructing it. *Of course, you can do that when your parishioners have the deepest pockets in New Trinity.*

Roth was sitting at his brobdingnagian monstrosity of a desk perusing over a stack of papers. His weird coat rack looking personal assistant robot hovered over the man's left shoulder like some stalking butler.

"Mr. Vance. How can I help you?" The big man asked.

This close Vance could see the IV line running from the robot to Roth's button-down shirt. Vance kept his mouth shut about it. Truthfully, he didn't want to know. The less he knew about Roth the better.

"It's done," Vance said.

"Good," Roth said. "Is that all?"

"Ichiro is to be charged in the Prophet incident," Vance said watching Roth carefully.

"I figured as much," Roth said, plainly continuing to peruse his documents. "What about your involvement?"

"I'm afraid that all of the evidence points to young

340

master Ichiro as the mastermind. I had no idea what he was doing," Vance replied, summoning his most innocent expression.

"Has there been an official death toll from the incident?" Roth asked while scowling.

"Not yet," Vance replied soberly. "It will be high though just with what little I was able to see from the control room."

"Unfortunate," Roth said.

"How do you want to handle the situation?" Vance asked.

"We will do nothing," Roth said. "Ichiro acted on his own and is therefore on his own," The man finished, his handsome face contorted in a scowl.

"Sir, is it wise to throw away a valuable asset like Ichiro? He could still be useful, right?" Vance asked hesitantly.

"Ichiro has outlived his usefulness," Roth said. "Our dear Ichiro was too idealistic and far too volatile. He lacked the necessary flexibility that true leadership requires. I think the Image had done its work a little too well when they indoctrinated him. He would have become a liability eventually. The fact that he tried to kill Otagawa's daughter was proof enough. Besides, he would have been much harder to remove if he had been made a hero by his new blue ribbon droid line. He took himself out of the game for us."

Vance swallowed. Creation of those blue-ribbon droids was not part of Roth's instructions to Ichiro. Roth didn't value imagination. He only valued loyalty, complete and total loyalty.

"Has a decision been made on who will take over Takacorp?"

"I believe Uske Otagawa is next in line," Vance replied. "Though he may decline and give the position to one of the board members. He is a tough man to read. More of a bookworm than a leader."

"Hm."

"And, ah, what of the bodyguard?" Vance asked after a few moments of silence.

"We may still be able to salvage her. Quietly arrange for her to have legal counsel. Use the appropriate channels," Roth replied, without looking up.

"I'll take care of it," Vance wiped the sweat from his forehead again. As his head tilted forward, he caught a glimpse of the silver case in his hand.

"I have another unit for you," Vance said, "I guess it would be Ichiro's last contribution to the cause." He laid the case on the desk and stepped back.

"It is becoming clear that the program is not going to be as viable as I had hoped. It may be time to liquidate," Roth admitted with a heavy sigh.

"There is one piece of silver lining to this debacle," Vance said. "We were able to confirm the answer to a very important question."

"Oh," Roth said, suddenly, turning his ice-cold blue eyes directly at Vance. Vance swallowed hard under that cold stare.

"Yes, sir," Vance continued, "Otagawa has in fact copied his daughter's consciousness into a droid."

"You're sure?" The big man asked.

Vance nodded.

"Liquidate the other program, immediately," Roth said.

"Do you have instructions regarding the disposal of the, shall we say, lab equipment?" Vance asked.

"They are finding victims of the Prophet virus all over the city. It's really sad," Roth said.

"Understood," Vance said, as he turned and left.

He made his way out of the building, "After this, Bobby boy, we are getting that massage Roth recommended," he said to himself.

A word about the author...

Chad M. Smith was born and raised in St. Louis County Missouri. He finished college at Southern Illinois University Edwardsville with a bachelors in Speech Communications. His original life goal was to be a rock star. When that didn't work out the way he had planned, he eventually bowed to parental pressure and got a job. Still having a desperate need to create he started writing in his spare time. He focused mostly on science fiction and fantasy stories because that is what he loves to read. He lives with his wife, kids, and dogs under the paw of his evil feline overlord in St. Louis County Missouri. When he is not writing he works for an Agricultural Company to pay the bills until this whole writer thing takes off.

www.ingramcontent.com/pod-product-compliance
Lightning Source LLC
Chambersburg PA
CBHW072316020726
47501CB00002B/529